Amazon reviews of the first edition of Volume 1:

Truly bizarre, utterly unique

I've never read a novel quite like this before. The author takes you on an exciting adventure full of unforgettable and vivid imagery. Solidly written with each character's personality shining through. If you find physics fascinating you will not be disappointed by the author's keen intellect and clear understanding of this most challenging (for me anyway) scientific subject. This is not a novel I will forget anytime soon, I would highly recommend it.
Andrewly

Very imaginative tale

Anybody interested in a very imaginative and engrossing sci fi story needs to check this one out. I have been reading sci fi for decades and this story has elements that surprise me which is very unusual considering the number of novels and stories I have over the years.
ric freeman

A fascinating book

An amazing book - I literally could not put it down... and I was reading it in Acrobat! Not the easiest format but it didn't matter, I wanted to know what happened next each time I had to leave it. I have a huge interest in The Hadron Collider so it was a foregone conclusion that I would enjoy this book and I wasn't disappointed. A great story - one that I can not wait to read the next episode of - with very complex characters and even more complex relationships. The author manages to combine his obvious extensive knowledge of the subject with an incredible imagination. I loved it!
Vicki

Wyken Seagrave

Wyken Seagrave is an author, scientist, software engineer, teacher, lecturer, inventor, science communicator, publisher and entrepreneur. The history of the universe (sometimes called "Big History") is his lifelong obsession. He is the author of the History of the Universe website at http://historyoftheuniverse.com/ and several books about the subject.

Other Works by Wyken Seagrave

Illustrated Cosmic Monopole - Time Crystal Volume One
  http://cosmicmonopole.co.uk
History of the Universe
  www.historyoftheuniverse.com
B4A - Rapid Android App Development using BASIC:
  http://basic4android.info
Time Crystal website
  www.timecrystal.co.uk
Wyken's diary
  www.wykenseagrave.co.uk
Wyken's page on Amazon
  http://amzn.to/1M7oBNF
Wyken's page on Goodreads
  http://bit.ly/1JVKuNm
Wyken's page on Shelfari
  http://bit.ly/1JVKGMJ
Cosmic Monopole Web Page
  http://cosmicmonopole.co.uk
Subscribe to Wyken's newsletter
  http://bit.ly/1r2KbXq

The Time Tunnel

2nd Edition

Time Crystal Volume Two

Wyken Seagrave

Penny Press Ltd, 176 Greendale Road
Coventry CV5 8AY, United Kingdom
sales@pennypress.co.uk
www.timecrystal.co.uk

British Library Cataloguing in Publication Data:
A catalogue record for this book is available from the British Library.

ISBN 978-1871281347 (eBook)
ISBN 978-1871281354 (paperback)

Table of Contents

List of Illustrations

Episode 26 George's Revival

Where's the bitch gone?

One moment the Irish girl had been flying straight down towards the floor of the ATLAS cavern surrounded by a huge time bubble, and the next thing George knew she had disappeared, leaving him hurtling towards a little white spot in the concrete, astonished and dismayed at letting her get away. At the last moment his fat fists turned his crystal, he swerved to one side and the only damage he suffered from his collision with the concrete was a narrow strip shredded out of his grey CERN firefighter's overall.

He pressed the crystal's front and stopped. *Bitch! First she helps Karolyi escape and now she gets clean away, damn her hide! Did she just vanish or did I dream it?*

He could still remember seeing the soles of her feet and her legs leading up into her short black mini-skirt. He had even seen the flash of her red pants as he followed her head-first flying down beside the big brown wheel. He remembered her mop of ginger hair flapping over the collar of her green blouse, remembered seeing glimpses of the enormous crystal she was clutching between her outstretched hands, and then, suddenly, she just seemed to shrink and vanish.

Unable to believe the memory of his own eyes, and convinced she must still be here somewhere, he spent an uncomfortable five minutes angrily scouring the lower part of the huge cavern, peering between cables and behind cabinets, searching beneath the curving flanks of the enormous barrel-shaped ATLAS detector, but she was nowhere to be found. However, there were compensations.

He found the first crystal sticking into the door of a blue metal electronics cabinet. His heart leaped. *A victory for the Service at last!* He had two missions now: to find the girl and to find more crystals. Eagerly he broadened his search and found another stuck in the balcony framework against one wall and yet another embedded in one of the foam sprayers in the ceiling. Within ten minutes, George had explored most of the eastern end of the cavern and collected six crystal fragments, but he had still not found the girl. Her disappearance worried and annoyed him. He went back to the spot where she vanished for one last look, hoping for some clue about what had happened, feeling calmer and thinking more clearly than before.

I'm sure she didn't just vanish. She shrunk, shrunk down like Sam and Michael did when the black hole hit them. He pressed his crystal and changed his position so that he was looking down exactly as he had been when she vanished. Then he looked at the little triangular pyramid he was using to fly with.

Her crystal was much bigger than this. That would explain why she had such a huge time bubble too. And her stone was a different shape, round, almost like a ball, not triangular like this one.

All the crystals George had seen so far were little tetrahedral pyramids. He looked down again at the floor, trying to remember exactly where she had vanished, hoping it might give him a clue as to where she had gone. There was a white spot in the concrete just below him. *I saw that before, just after she vanished!* He flew down and examined it closely. It was a clean, fresh little dent chipped out of the dirty concrete floor. He rubbed the tip of his finger over it. *Nothing special about it, but I'm sure this was where she vanished. So what made her shrink? Could it have been that big crystal she was carrying? Could that have absorbed her somehow? Was there some sort of black hole inside it?*

George's mind went numb. *I'm just a firefighter, not a scientist. I don't understand about black holes. I'll have to ask somebody. Professor Romani would be best. Okay, admit it Gábor, the bitch has gone, you've lost her. Get on with your work. I've got to give these crystals to Romani. He's the Director General of this place so it's up to him to decide what to do. There's a hell of a lot of decisions to be made. So where is he? Last time I saw him he was with the Irish Ambassador woman, running along one of the balconies on the south wall heading back to the USA15 cavern. I'll go and find him, after I just do one more thing.*

George pressed the bottom of his crystal, left the cavern floor and flew straight up, the red and green rings travelling down through his bubble. He reached the massive beam pipe shield that spanned the space between the cavern wall and the ATLAS detector. He flew round it until he found the stretcher. *Robert Moore's got to be here somewhere.*

He caught sight of the orange stretcher cover first, and stopped. *The last time I saw that, it was being winched up with Marianne Schneider inside. Robert was hanging beside her.*

He flew towards it and a pair of legs came into view, clad in firefighter's overalls. George began to feel nauseous, his head swimming, his heart pounding, but he had to confront this. He flew on, his bubble drifting slowly up to enclose the other firefighter's hips, his chest, his head and George was staring straight into the agonised death mask of Robert Moore.

George wasn't in Switzerland any more. He was driving his fire engine slowly behind a cortege of fourteen black-plumed horses hauling seven black hearses along a Budapest street. He was watching the bankers remove their hats and bow their heads as the procession passed. He was crossing the river, wishing he could drive off the Lanchid Bridge into the Danube's welcoming grey waters. He was listening to the clatter of hooves on medieval cobbles. He was lifting one of the seven yellow firefighter's helmets from one of the seven coffins. He was carrying it into Saint Matthias Church, its vibrant colours licking up the walls like flames. He was kneeling on the floor, tears falling onto his clenched fists, his shoulders shaking as the Cardinal Archbishop's droning voice echoed around the church. 'They have not died in vain. Their memory will live forever.'

That was precisely the problem. It was those seven ghosts which had driven George out of Hungary into Switzerland, and now there was an eighth to haunt his dreams. *Poor little Robert Moore.* Like a drowning man, George forced his mind up to the surface and back to the present. He stared into Robert's eyes, desperate to find something there which would ease the pain. In Budapest he had never seen the faces of the men he had sent to their deaths, only the bones and ashes which he had helped to collect from the burned out bank. Now he was eager to confront the truth, to find some meaning, some hope, some forgiveness in Robert Moore's face. All he saw was pain, confusion, fear and hopelessness. It sank deep into his soul, wrapping itself around the misery that already lived there, and George's heart died a little more as his burden of guilt grew heavier.

'Was it my fault, Robert?' he said aloud. 'Was I supposed to know there was a bloody black hole lurking inside ATLAS, just waiting to come out? What was I supposed to do? Why didn't Francesco Romani warn me it could be dangerous for you? He's the Director General. He's supposed to know about things like that, not me. I'm just a humble firefighter. I've got to find Ludo and recover your body as soon as possible. You must be laid to rest with the respect every firefighter deserves. But first I've got to find Romani and show him the consequences of his splendid scientific experiment. He needs to see what he's done to the world. Then we'll see how clever he really is.'

George glanced at the two white ropes attached to the stretcher's harness, one straight, one gently curved, then turned and flew rapidly along the curved one. *This must be the rope I was using to control the descent of the stretcher before the disaster.* He was right. The rope led to one of the balconies which lined the cavern walls. He followed the balcony until he reached a door and paused, his hard eyes searching for more crystals. He had to force himself to go through the doorway. *Now's not the time for that,* he told himself. *I've got enough for now.*

He flew down the low white tunnel and emerged into the centre of the USA15 cavern where two corridors intersected. He passed a red cabinet holding breathing apparatus and turned left, following the central corridor to the far end of the cavern.

Crystals are now a primary tool of the Fire and Rescue Service, as fundamental as a respirator or a helmet. That bastard Alex Karolyi has got pockets full of the stuff. I'll find you, Count Karolyi, don't you worry. And you just watch out when I do.

'Ah, here is the fireman. At last,' Francesco Romani said as George flew into the Safe Room in the USA15 cavern. He was sitting on the stairs with the Irish woman a few steps below him, leaning against his legs, almost in a state of collapse. George had already met Ambassador Brigit O'Brien when he first came down into the caverns. Her vermilion trouser-suit was smeared in concrete dust, her mass of blonde curls hung around her face like a dead ferret, yet she still looked as sultry as a Csabai sausage.

'Is it safe to go now?' Francesco said, then he squinted as his eyes ran over the green, black and red bubble as if he was staring into a bright light. Neither he nor Brigit was completely inside it.

George took two of the crystals out of his pocket. 'Hold these please,' he said. They looked at him for a moment in puzzled silence then took the crystals. George checked that both their bodies were fully inside their two bubbles.

'What's this?' Brigit said, looking at him.

Francesco put his glasses on and examined his crystal closely, then looked at George with a deep frown. 'What's going on, Fireman? Has the black hole evaporated?'

'Yes, Professor,' George said, seething inside. *See this label on my uniform? That's my name.* 'The black hole's gone,' he said, 'but these crystals came out of it. It seems that time has stopped.'

The Director General's mouth fell open then snapped shut, his jowls wobbling like an angry bulldog's.

George would have laughed if his heart had not been so heavy. 'I know that seems impossible but we've proved it. When a watch is left outside the bubble it stops. Also your blood seems to stop. My colleague Robert Moore was killed, and the only reason was because his head was outside Marianne's bubble but his heart was inside, so I advise you both very strongly not to let any parts of your body outside your bubbles.'

Francesco seemed to be taking it all in, staring at him with unblinking eyes, but the Irish Ambassador kept shaking her head and glancing from George to the crystal and from Francesco to the bubble then back to George, obviously not really listening.

'Another reason we think that time has stopped is that there isn't any gravity. Alex Karolyi and I went on a trip to the top of the atmosphere and only got down because we learned how to fly—'

'Stop!' Francesco shouted. 'This is all totally preposterous. I insist that you go over everything that happened in the cavern since the Ambassador and I left, Fireman.'

George's temper flared but he kept it under control.

He's still the boss, I guess. Would be more respectful if he used my name, though. It's written here on my chest clear enough.

Nevertheless George dutifully related everything in detail. It took a long time and he was still eager to go and find Ludo, but Francesco kept asking questions. When George reached the part where Michael Zhang and Sam Fitzpatrick were hit by the black hole, Brigit too began to pay attention.

'You mean it absorbed them?' she said then started to float away from the stairs as she turned and said 'What's going to happen now, Francesco?'

Francesco turned to her with a big confident smile. 'I don't really think things are so bad, Brigit. This story about time stopping, it is impossible. The laws of relativity mean that—'

'Relativity be damned,' Brigit shouted, hanging onto the banister to stop herself drifting away. 'You can see it for yourself. Look at me! I'm floating! My hair's sticking out like a bush and you don't think it's serious? I feel sick.'

'It's the weightlessness,' George said. 'You'll get used to it very soon.'

'I don't want to get used to it,' she screamed. 'I don't want this to be happening at all. Oh, I'm sorry George. It's not your fault. Can we get up to the surface now, please?'

'Yes, Madame Ambassador, but please let me show you how to use your crystal to fly first.'

'Really? To fly? Okay, and for God's sake call me Brigit.'

George showed them how to fly using their crystals, then led them back into the ATLAS cavern. At first he was going to avoid passing Robert Moore, but he decided he wanted Francesco Romani to see the body, to know what price the Fire and Rescue Service had paid, so he followed the rope back into the middle of the cavern and confronted them with the evidence.

'This is what happens if you let any part of your body outside the bubble,' he told them. 'Marianne says his head was outside the bubble while his heart was inside.'

Francesco made some mournful noises as they hovered near the corpse and Brigit looked embarrassed but George didn't feel that either of them really cared very much. Instead they seemed much more interested in the empty stretcher where the pregnant woman had been. Brigit began asking urgent questions about Marianne Schneider. George wasn't surprised. *It's natural for them to be more concerned about her than about Robert. Firefighters are expected to risk their lives in the course of their work. Visitors' guides aren't.*

He explained how she had been hit by a fragment of crystal which had made her lose the baby. 'At one point she seems to have been the only person left alive on Earth. Luckily she managed to get herself out of the stretcher and pulled herself up the rope to the balcony where she met Alex Karolyi and your daughter, Brigit.'

'Catriona? Where is she now?'

George hesitated. 'I took Marianne over to the Medical Centre, then came back to try to find more crystal. She and Alex Karolyi were in here—'

'Count Karolyi?' she said.

George shrugged. 'If he is a Count. I must admit I doubt it. He showed his true colours as soon as he saw me. He and your daughter flew away, both of them taking crystals with them. Your daughter had a massive one. Last time I saw her she was down near the floor of the cavern. She seemed to shrink and vanish, the same way that Sam and Michael did. I've searched for her but I can't find her anywhere, so I've no idea what's happened to her.'

'Have you looked for Count Karolyi?' Francesco said.

'Yes. I followed him up the shaft into SX but couldn't find him. He could be anywhere. He's almost certainly flown away somewhere, taking a pocket full of crystals with him.'

'I can't believe he would steal crystals if he knew how valuable they were,' Brigit said.

'No? Well I know Karolyi a bit better than you, Brigit. We're both Hungarian, and I'd say that's exactly what he would do. He's just out for what he can get. He once bragged to me how much he was earning by writing computer programs for CERN.'

'Certainly anything found in this cavern belongs to CERN,' Francesco said. 'Have you searched the whole place?'

'Not yet, Professor. That's another job I need to do. In fact the first thing I would like to do is...I'd like to recover Robert Moore's body and take him back to the Fire Station, if that's okay with you, Professor Romani.'

'Of course, of course,' Francesco said distractedly. 'Let's go now, can we?'

George led them up the winch rope and through the wide shaft which led to the surface. When they reached the SX1 building, George warned them against losing contact with the ground and tied them together using a short rope which he collected from the fire engine.

'The Ambassador and I will go to the Medical Centre to see Marianne,' Francesco said. 'Tell me, fireman, how many spare crystals have you got?'

George took out his four spare fragments.

'I will need all those,' Francesco said reaching out for them.

George's big fist closed over them and he was gratified to see a look of alarm flash in Francesco's eyes. 'I was hoping that I could revive Firefighter Narkosa,' George said quietly, 'the other member of my team, so we can escort Robert Moore's body back to the Fire Station and pay our respects.'

'Oh,' Francesco looked surprised, then nodded. 'Yes, of course. That is no problem, George.' *Well at least he's managed to read my name now.* George's fist opened and Francesco took three of the crystals.

'Report to me in the Medical Centre when you've done that,' Francesco said.

George saluted and flew back down the shaft. He found two more fragments of crystal embedded in the balcony and wall while he was searching for Ludovico. He finally found him on a balcony on the northern wall, running towards the stairwell in an adjoining cavern.

'So is some sort of hour glass, no?' Ludovico Narkosa joked after George had revived him and given him a piece of crystal accompanied by the usual warnings. He seemed to take it all in his stride, as if it was all part of the job. George felt proud of his crew, remembering that Sofie too had coped well. He showed him how to fly and explained the other known facts about crystal. Only when he broke the news about Robert did Ludovico show any emotion, but he turned his face away and soon took control of himself.

There's no room for emotion in this job, George thought as he led the Italian across the Big Wheel to the beam pipe shield. *Discipline is an essential aspect of being a firefighter. And yet there's no way to escape from emotion either. It's a paradox. You can't risk your life to save others without a deep and profound love of your fellow human beings, yet you cannot afford to let it affect you as you do the job and face your fear of fire. I guess that's why so many firefighters like Ludo put on an outward show of bravado and cynicism. Only afterwards, in the secret silence of the night, can we afford to let the emotion out, alone, unseen, without affecting our brother firefighters. A fire crew is a family of brothers, but each one lives in an emotional bubble.*

They flew up to Robert's body and floated beside him in respectful silence. Ludovico looked at the stretcher, at the ropes, at the harness, at anything except Robert Moore's face. But George couldn't take his eyes off it. Quietly he told Ludo about Marianne's theory on why Robert had died. *He has to know. He has to understand how dangerous crystal can be if he isn't going to misuse it.* When Ludovico finally looked at Robert's face George knew he had learned the lesson. He was seeing him now not just as a dead colleague but as a training aid.

'He died to teach us not to make the same mistake,' George said. 'Come on, Ludo old chap. Let's get him back to the station.'

They unclipped Robert from the harness and flew him slowly upwards, one holding each arm and George holding his helmet as he tried to chase out of his ears the ringing of horses hooves and clattering of iron-rimmed hearse wheels across cobble stones.

The Chief should never have put him in my crew this morning. George remembered Laron Parfait's little moustache twitching as he said: 'I've explained why Foxtrot Four Seven has to be part of your crew, but I'll go through it again if you can't remember what I said over breakfast.'

Foxtrot Four Seven my arse!

Episode 27 Sports Centre

As soon as Catriona let go, Alex surged upwards, hurtling through the shaft with the air hurricaning past his face and the red and green rings flowing rapidly around the curving wall of his bubble. He was expecting George to grab his feet any moment but emerged into the SX1 building safely and accelerated away upwards.

It's dangerous but I'll have to take that chance, Alex thought as memories of the last time he had made this exact same journey flashed through his mind. *It's less dangerous than being caught by György anyways.*

He began counting the seconds as he rocketed away from the ground. *Budapest one. Budapest two. Budapest three. Budapest four.*

Then he heard Catriona call 'Sam! Please Sam! Please please answer me darling.' There was no mistaking the urgency in her voice.

So it's not just Sam who can talk through crystals, Alex thought. *Sounds like she needs help.*

'I can hear you, Kata,' he called. 'It's Alex.'

She did not reply.

Where's she gone? She said she saw Sam in one of her crystals. Can I see her in this?

He pressed the front of the crystal he was flying with, checked that the bubble's rings had broken up into a random pattern so he knew he had stopped moving, then looked at the gem. Inside it, all he could see were the same six small triangles he had seen when he looked into the crystal in the ATLAS cavern. He turned it but saw the same in each face.

He moved the little pyramid close to his mouth and shouted 'Can you hear me, Kata? What's happening?' Then he held it to his ear and listened. She didn't answer.

There's got to be some damn way of seeing what's going on!

Angrily he drew the crystal as close to his eye as he could and squinted into it, blinded by the inner blue glow, and began moving it round, trying to see something, anything.

Now the inner faces looked blurred and he could see the pattern of the bubble, refracted through the crystal's sides. He cupped his hands around it to obscure the pattern and saw something blue floating in the middle of the crystal, a shade darker than the rest. As he moved the crystal to get a better view, it disappeared. Mystified, he moved it back until he was looking straight down into the middle of one face and there it was again, a thick sloping line of blue with a brown blur at each end. But the crystal was so close to his eye, he could not bring the image into focus. And when he moved the crystal a few centimetres away to get a better view, the objects disappeared from sight.

What the hell was that?

He moved it closer once more, his frustration becoming unbearable, and the objects reappeared. The darker blue thing looked like a blue cylinder sloping across the crystal and the brown things seemed like round discs.

Could that be what I think it is?

To make the blue cylinder look horizontal, he tilted his head and, to his surprise, the image changed completely. This time it was clearer. He could still see the two brown discs and now he was sure they were ATLAS's two Big Wheels. Beyond them he could see the cavern ceiling and, very small and indistinct, to his astonishment he saw a man floating in the shaft that led up to the surface.

The man seemed to be looking closely at something he was holding in his two hands. It was so weird it made his skin crawl. The man's shirt looked white, indeed the whole scene lacked colour but there was something disturbingly familiar about the man's posture. Alex moved one arm and his suspicions were confirmed as the man's arm moved. He could hardly believe it. *That's me!*

Then a grey object appeared and moved across the top of the cavern ceiling, apparently searching for something. Even though the image was very small and blurred there was no mistaking that shape. *It's Gábor György! He's looking for me.*

He rotated the crystal again and now he saw Catriona, her blurred face looking straight at him, clearly in distress, and heard her calling 'For God's sake Sam!'

Behind her, Alex could still see George. He had left the ceiling now and was flying down the brown disc of the Big Wheel straight towards her.

If she doesn't move soon he's going to catch her!

'Press the top Kata!' Alex shouted into the crystal. He saw her fingers close around the crystal she was holding and the Big Wheel began to stream past as she moved down. *Good girl, Kata,* he thought. *I wish I could see where she's going.*

Remembering how the view had kaleidoscoped when he tilted his head, he rotated his crystal, but still looking straight down into the middle of the same face, and was delighted to see the little white dip in the concrete floor rapidly approaching. *It's like controlling a remote camera.* The dip was off to one side. *She's going to miss it!*

Alex was almost certain this was the entrance to the tunnel. There was just one lingering doubt in his mind. *Maybe that dent was made by one of the crystals not the black hole. That's a chance she'll have to take.*

'Point it to the left,' he called. The little dip in the concrete moved until it was dead ahead. 'That's it Kata. Fly into it!'

She headed straight towards the tiny white mark in the floor and he held his breath.

Even if the tunnel really does start there, will she actually be able to fly into it or will she be killed? Alex felt a tiny twinge of guilt as he watched the dip hurtle towards him.

The kid's got guts, I'll give her that, he thought as he realised that his attitude towards her had changed. When he first met her, there had been almost nothing about Catriona that Alex had liked. She was too young, too plain, to naïve, too stupid. She was infatuated with him, of course, but he was used to sycophantic females drooling over him. But since they had gone down into the cavern and she had tried to seduce him, he had felt a grudging respect for the plucky little Irish girl whom he was now sending to a possible horrible death.

To his relief he saw the little depression balloon out and what seemed to be a large rocky canyon suddenly open out around her. Alex felt elated.

So I was right, that dip IS the entrance to the tunnel! Now she was flying into a sort of funnel. *Is Gábor following her? Should I go and help her?*

Alex rotated his crystal again and saw her arms and body stretched out almost behind her as she flew, with the round entrance to the concrete funnel slipping away behind her feet. From here it looked like the upper ridge of a crater on the moon, vast and rugged. Looking through it he could still see the ATLAS cavern and there, flying down towards him, was George Gabor. The firefighter was heading straight towards her, but at the last moment he swerved and vanished behind the curving rim of the opening.

'Well done Kata!' Alex shouted and he meant it. *Not sure I would have had the guts to do what she just did,* he thought as he said 'György isn't following you anymore. I'll wait till he's gone then I'll come after you. Wait there.'

Alex was beginning to grow uneasy, floating in his bubble without sight of the ground. Memories of his earlier trip into the upper atmosphere began to haunt him. There were ill-defined bands of red rotating slowly around the bubble and he had the suspicion that he might be turning. *That could be dangerous. The Earth might not be where I think it is. Want to get back down to the ground as soon as possible.*

He rotated the fist holding the crystal and pressed one face. Rings began to slip sideways through the bubble and the crystal pulled him to the side. Hoping he was flying horizontally now, he counted for five seconds before turning the crystal again, heading in what he hoped was the direction of the ground, and started counting again.

Budapest one. Budapest two. Budapest three. Budapest four. Should have reached the ground by now. Budapest five. Budapest six. Budapest seven. Budapest eight. Budapest nine. Budapest ten…

He began to get worried. He was flying slower so he would have a safe landing, but even so it was taking a long time to get back down to the ground. *Must have misjudged the angles. It had been hard to turn through exactly 90 degrees. Could I be still flying horizontally? Or even upwards? Now listen, Karolyi, you found the Earth before and you can do it again!*

But after sixty seconds he was getting seriously worried. He had counted seventy-three seconds and was considering starting a circular search when, to his enormous relief, a field of short winter wheat rushed up into the bubble. He skimmed over the stalks and stopped.

Thank God for that. Now what to do? Don't want to go too far from Kata. I'll hang around for an hour or so and give György time to leave. Maybe hide in the woods somewhere. The nearest one I know is just over the French border behind, the St Genis golf course. I'll have to find the Route de Meyrin first.

He flew low across the field, still heading in the same direction, when some bushes and a green sheet of metal loomed into the bubble. *Looks like a wall.* He flew up, trying to remember a green metal building in CERN, until he reached the roof. That was green metal too, with a plastic strip to let the light in. *Where's this place? Most of CERN's built from glass and concrete, not this green stuff.*

The roof curved down to meet another one curving the other way. He followed the valley between them until he reached a path, a tall wire mesh fence, then a green surface and a red surface, a string net.

Tennis courts? Of course! The Meyrin Sports Centre!

He turned and flew towards where he thought the main road would be. When he passed over water he stopped, hovering above the open-air swimming pool. *We lay here many times last summer, me and Marianne, her head on my lap, me drinking vodka and coke and thinking about the night to come.* The memory of it and the sight of the water made him suddenly feel very thirsty.

I haven't had any kind of drink for hours. And there won't be anything to drink in the woods. There's a cafe here. I've got to drink something before I go.

He flew back and found the steps leading up to the low white clubhouse.

György'll never look for me in here.

On the terrace he struggled to get through the door. It wouldn't open until it was all inside his bubble. He went into the restaurant and flew across the room to the bar, keeping near the ceiling to avoid the coffee drinkers seated at little pine tables. Behind the bar, rows of spirit bottles glinted against the mirrored back wall. Alex flew towards them, his tongue burning with desire, and selected a bottle of Courvoisier, but when he opened it and turned it over the liquid didn't pour out. *No gravity!* Angrily he shook the bottle. A stream of brandy glooped out from the open neck, rounded itself into an oval ball and wobbled across his bubble. He flew after it, hungrily sucking in a mouthful before it hit the bar and exploded in a shower of droplets which rained over a pink plant in a pot. *Shit! I need a straw.*

He carried the bottle along the bar. A woman standing on the other side was pouring coffee from a jug into a cup. He hurried past and luckily she didn't notice him floating horizontally above the barstools. After some searching, he eventually found a box of straws on a shelf at the other end of the counter and pushed one into the brandy. The liquid burned down his throat and crashed into his stomach like a traffic accident. *God that feels so good!* He sucked harder and his heart began to race. The thought flashed momentarily through his brain: *This is stupid. I need water*, but his mouth didn't seem to be listening to what his brain was saying and his lips and tongue just kept sucking.

As the alcohol went down, his spirits rose. *I'm going to have a party for the whole world. Cheers world!* He blew a strawful of brandy at another plant standing on the bar. *Congratulations, Earth! You've survived being hit by a black hole you lucky little planet! Okay, you have the small problem of being frozen in time, but that's no big deal. We got crystal for yah, baby! Happy Birthday!*

The brandy stopped coming up the straw. He put his finger over the bottle's neck and shook it so the liquid swooshed round to the top then continued to drink.

'Here's to you, Mr Cosmic Monopole,' he shouted. 'I knew YOU were going to be freaking trouble as soon as I saw that Mercator track.'

Alex threw the empty brandy bottle away and went back along the bar to get some more. The woman was still pouring coffee. Her head lifted as he drifted past. She was middle aged and reminded him vaguely of his mother. He felt like stopping and chatting, telling her what had happened. It would be a relief to have a laugh with somebody about it all, but the expression on her face began to grow alarmed as her eyes ran along the length of his floating body.

'Bonjour Madame,' he said. Even he could hear the slur in his voice as he tried to get his Hungarian tongue round the French words. 'I'll have black coffee and three croissants please.' He felt hungry now as well as thirsty. He almost giggled at the absurdity of the situation, calmly ordering breakfast when the world was in a state of disaster.

The coffee stopped running out of the jug in the woman's hand. She watched it as it formed itself into a round steaming blob and began to float out of the jug. She started screaming.

'Shit!' Alex said, and flew on, the imagined taste of croissant in his mouth. There weren't any on the counter.

Must be out the back, he decided, *but she's standing in front of the doorway. I won't be able to get past her. Never know how she might react. Could be dangerous with a flask of hot coffee in her hand.*

He tried to pull a vodka bottle off the shelf at the end of the bar, missed his aim and send bottles flying all over his bubble. *Shit, I'm drunk! I've got to eat. Can't help Kata in this state.*

He put a vodka bottle in his pocket and flew round all the tables in the restaurant searching for food. Most were set for lunch. A few people in sports clothes were sitting near the door, but none had any food. He managed to steal a mouthful of cold coffee from one table, then flew out of the restaurant towards the front door, looking for a way to the kitchen.

The only door he could find led to a toilet. *Oh good. I could use that,* he thought and slipped inside. His amber urine mixed with the water in the bowl and began to splash up the sides towards him. He had to duck to stop one spinning globule hitting him. He tried to flush the rest away but nothing happened. *Needs gravity. Pipes frozen.* More golden drops were heading up towards him.

He flew out into the foyer, through the front door and round to the back of the building, searching for a way into the kitchen. A delivery man was standing unloading boxes from a trolley and carrying them through the doorway.

Shit! Can't get in this way. Where else can I find food and drink? Dare not go into CERN with Gábor on the warpath. What about the BP garage? It's right next door, and they've got a shop!

'György isn't following you anymore. I'll wait till he's gone then I'll come after you. Wait there.'

That was what he said, wasn't it? Catriona hovered and waited, glancing back the way she had come, hoping every moment to see Alex flying down after her but terrified that George would come in first.

Above her there was a huge pale grey circular ridge. *That must be the hole in the concrete floor,* she thought. *When I flew into it, it looked tiny, but now it's vast, like the rim of a volcano or something.*

She was so anxious about which man would fly down after her that it never occurred to her to wonder why it was so large. The ridge was spanned by an impenetrable wall of blackness. She could see nothing of the ATLAS cavern.

Finally she began searching for Alex in her crystal, staring into each face in turn, calling his name, but she saw nothing, heard nothing, her anxiety increasing with every failure. She felt terribly lonely.

Surely he won't let me down, will he? But he didn't fetch the doctor to help Marianne even though he loves her, so I suppose he might not bother with me even though he promised.

After searching the crystal for what seemed like hours, she began to look around, trying to decide what to do. She was in a sort of large funnel, its circular walls fissured by cracks and crevices, like weathered limestone cliffs, glowing pale blue in the light from her crystal. Below her, the funnel seemed to grow narrower and in the distance, far below, she could see another light, small and bright blue.

Should I go down there, or stop here? Sam and Michael need my help. Sam said he was at the bottom of the tunnel. That must be it down there, where that blue light is. It's not too far. I've got one crystal to give him. I can't just stay here waiting for Alex for ever. I might as well fly down and see if I can find Sam and give him this and see what he wants me to do next. Better than staying here and getting caught by George Gabor.

She pressed her crystal, turned to face the distant blue light and began to fly towards it, her eyes fixed on it, trying to make out what was creating it. At first she assumed it was another crystal. *Must be quite a big one.* She did not notice the change in the funnel around her, although she was aware it was gradually getting darker. But after a while she stopped and looked back to check whether Alex or George were following her, and she noticed that the funnel wall had almost completely faded away. She could just see it, glowing dimly blue.

What's happened to it? There was only one explanation she could think of. *The walls must be getting further apart down here! It's not getting narrower like I thought, it's getting wider!*

Puzzled by this, she flew on towards the light. It was getting bigger. *If it's a crystal, it must be huge.* Although it glowed with the same blue colour, it didn't look anything like her crystal. Instead, it looked like a large, flat surface. *It must be the light at the end of the tunnel!* Catriona's heart began leaping, soaring. *When I get there I'll meet Sam and give him this crystal. I wonder if Michael will be able to restart time with just this one? Oh I do hope so. Or maybe he's already collected some, and that's where the light's coming from?*

She was getting closer to the blue surface. Her eyes scanned it avidly but she could not see Sam or Michael. *I'm near the bottom of the tunnel now, so where are they?*

The blue light glowed so brightly that it lit the tunnel's craggy walls, throwing every crack and crevice into sharp relief. The shiny blue light started abruptly where the craggy surface ended.

The closer she came to it, the bigger it seemed. It was not the same brightness all over. A glowing band curved in smoothly from one side towards the middle where it terminated in a small round bend. At first, she could not understand what she was looking at. Then, with a sinking heart, it dawned on her. *It's not flat. It's a sort of big round blue hole. That has to be the tunnel. The real tunnel! It must be. I haven't even reached the tunnel yet!*

Episode 28 Tunnel & Theft

I'm still in the concrete floor! I must be tiny! Now, finally, Catriona thought about what had happened when she had flown into the little dip in the cavern floor, how it had ballooned out around her, distorting and bulging as if she had been looking through a strong lens. *I've shrunk, like Sam and Michael did when the black hole hit them!*

She looked at the blue curving surface ahead of her. *That's the real tunnel. No wonder I can't find Sam. He isn't here. He must be down there. I don't have any choice. I've got to go down and find him. Oh Sam, how much further?*

As she flew towards it, she examined its shimmering blue surface. It seemed to be getting bigger every moment. Now it was obvious that it was snaking away into the distance like the digestive tract of some giant blue worm waiting to swallow her, getting smaller until it finally disappeared around a bend. She couldn't see Sam in there either, although the tunnel was so vast she might easily have missed him. But then another thought struck her.

Is the tunnel really getting bigger, or am I still getting smaller? And if I'm getting smaller then what's going to happen to me if I keep shrinking like this when I go down there? I'm going to disappear altogether. If I shrink away to nothing I'm not going to be any good to Sam at all.

Once more she stopped flying and peered desperately into one of the sides of the big round blue crystal she held in her trembling fingers. She could see blue triangles and diamonds of light glinting inside it, but she could not see Sam's comforting face. 'Where are you, Sam?' she called, and when she saw and heard nothing she turned the crystal and repeated the search in the next face, again and again until she couldn't remember which faces she had checked and her voice was a pathetic croak.

She tried to remember what he had said, imagining him as he had been when he talked to her through this crystal, tiny and blurry and without his glasses, his long sparse strands of hair no longer plastered across the dome of his head to hide his bald patch but now hanging stupidly down the side of his face.

"I want you to give all the fragments to George Gabor and tell him to bring them down the tunnel."

Yes, that's what he said, she thought. *I'm sorry Sam. I've failed. It's just me. Little Catty, with just one crystal.* She began to cry. Huge sobs of self-pity overwhelmed her, but then stopped suddenly as she realised a profound and obvious truth which had been staring her in the face for the past six years but which she had never seen before. *Sam loves me! He didn't want me to come down here. He said it could be dangerous. He didn't want me to do anything that would harm me. And at least I've found the tunnel. I never even thought I'd get this far. I can't stop now. I haven't got all the crystals, but at least I've got this one. Maybe that'll be enough.*

And with this thought she began to feel calmer and stronger. It was astonishing to think how Sam had come into her life just when she needed him and helped her to overcome the grief of losing her father and then grow through the horrible confusion of puberty.

Well he needs my help now. And he survived shrinking so I must be able to survive it too. I'll have to go down there to help Sam. Nothing else matters.

She turned the crystal to point herself at the middle of the blue tunnel and gently pressed its back face. The huge round glowing opening didn't seem to move. She pressed harder and felt the wind rushing through her hair but the mouth of the tunnel hardly changed. *I must still be miles away from it. It's absolutely vast! I'm like an astronaut approaching an unknown planet, only this is an unknown tunnel.*

She pressed harder, building up speed so she was flying even faster than when she entered the dip in the floor of the ATLAS cavern. The wind whipped her ginger hair into her eyes and flapped her green blouse viciously against her body with a noise like a machine. Slowly the ragged circular entrance passed behind her. Finally she was completely inside the blue tunnel, blinking, in the brightness of its smooth round wall flooded with pale blue light. *I'm really in the tunnel now!*

She was awe-struck by its vastness. Looking around, still searching for Sam, she noticed that the tunnel wall seemed less blue when she looked straight into it. Ahead it looked bluer and brighter, especially where it disappeared round the bend, but the wall around her was almost transparent and she could see two larger patterns outside the tunnel which seemed to travel with her as she flew. At first, all she could make out were two flickering regions. On her right, the flickering was very strong so it hurt her eyes to look at it. It went from being dark grey, almost black, to pale blue. The region on her left flickered much more gently, and the overall colour gradually changed from green to blue-grey then back to green.

Ahead of her, through the right side of the tunnel wall, she saw a broad curved band of white light. She slowed down, trying to get a better view of everything outside the tunnel, wondering if maybe Sam was out there somewhere. As she slowed, so the flickering around her also slowed. The curving arc became a moving line of light, still flickering but moving back and forth within the band.

The flickering was very slow now, painful to watch, and the line of light became a moving dot, flying slower and slower around the right side of the tunnel until it came to rest, a little ball of stationary blue light, and the flickering ceased.

She looked out through the tunnel wall, which was almost completely transparent, just tinting everything beyond it with a faint blue haze. It took her a few moments to understand what she was looking at because everything was tilted over. When she worked it, out she was amazed and shocked.

The area to her right was the sky and the ground was on her left. It made her feel dizzy to see them like this. She felt as if she was going to fall over, so she used her crystal to tilt herself over to the right until the sky was above her and the ground was below. Now she could see that she was floating above a wintry landscape, with a sweeping snow-covered hillside spread out far below her.

Between the ground and the sky were two mountain ranges, one on each side of her. Clouds formed like smoke on the peaks of one range and drifted towards her in long slow trails. They passed just above her head and broke up as they moved towards the second range of mountains. The dizzy feeling persisted when she realised how high she must be, with only a blue tunnel to hold her up, but then a thought struck her which lifted her spirits.

I can see for miles. The bubble's disappeared! Hurrah! I don't remember seeing it since I flew into the dip in the concrete floor. And...Oh my God! The clouds... They're moving! They're really moving. Time is working again! Oh thank you, God!

And with this realisation she suddenly felt liberated, full of fresh hope. She turned her crystal to survey the whole horizon and saw a long thin curving lake.

It's the same shape as the lake we saw from the aeroplane when Sam and I flew in to Geneva a few days ago.

The thought of that flight from Dublin, of coming here on a trip which she had wanted but had turned out so disastrously, was so painful that she could hardly bear it.

I wish we'd stopped at home. No, stop it, Catriona! she told herself. *This crystal is all part of the mystery of daddy's death. You need to go down this tunnel and ask Michael how he died. You need to take this crystal down so Michael can restart time. I just hope this one will be enough. That is my life's mission now. Nothing else matters. I've got to get on with it and find Michael and Sam.*

She peered down at the icy landscape. *I wonder if they're down there somewhere? Oh I do hope so.*

The whole hillside was covered in snow. She wondered momentarily where this snow had come from, but it was just another one of the mysteries confronting her and she dismissed the question. She was so high that she could not make out any details, certainly nothing as small as a person. From up here she could see Geneva cathedral standing on top of the hill at the near end of the lake, and the little houses clustered around it, their roofs covered in snow, but she could not see the airport on the hillside below her. Nor could she see the tower-blocks Sam had driven past this morning, nor the sprawling industrial estate which was CERN. As she looked straight down, all she could see was an undulating blanket of ice, cut by a long thin dark line which ran across the whiteness from the mountains to the city.

Eagerly she flew on along the tunnel, pressing the back of her crystal as hard as she could, keen to get round the next bend, hoping that it would lead her down to the ground. It was only slightly worrying to see both sky and land darken, to see them begin to flicker again, light, dark, light, dark, faster and faster, to see the dot of light begin to move overhead and form first a line and then a broad white band across the sky once more. She had just entered a straight stretch when, without warning, the tunnel itself disappeared. The white band of light vanished. The landscape stopped flickering. She was floating high up in the cold wintry air, hanging without support in a blue-grey sky. She could see the snow-covered hillside below her more vividly now, the tops of trees poking up through the whiteness and casting shadows on the dark line, which she realised was a track.

Then an icy wind began rushing past her, biting through her thin clothes and roaring in her ears. Looking down she saw the landscape lurch up towards her, getting clearer and opening out. *Gravity's working again! I'm falling!* She screamed in terror, a wordless scream that came from deep inside her, not from her stomach but dredged up from her soul. *I'm going to hit the ground.* She knew it would only take a few seconds, a minute at the most.

She looked down, hoping to see Sam standing waiting to catch her but with a dizzying sense of shock saw there was nothing beneath her but a tiny horse and cart on the brown track and two tiny human figures beside it. *Even if one of them's Sam there's no way he can catch me at this speed. I'm going to die!*

'Very good,' the Entroilian said in a voice soft as silk. 'You know what to do with it.'

I know that voice, Sam thought, and looked round, trying to find the Entroilian who was speaking. At first, all he could see were the huge white jaws and head of the ant-like Argolath which had stolen the Cosmic Egg from Cjingha's laboratory. It was hanging head-down in the vertical shaft beneath the Sedtia University, the Egg (containing Sam) dangling from its jaws, its pincer-like feet clinging tenaciously to the rough-hewn wall.

It had stopped just above a side-tunnel and suddenly an Entroilian's head emerged and loomed down at Sam. Its hairy face was black but its eyes were completely white. Squinting into the tunnel, Sam could just make out the Entroilian's painfully thin bee-shaped body, the segments of its abdomen alternately black and white. Sam had only ever seen one Entroilian like this.

It's Commander Bogmon!

'Do it,' Bogmon went on in a tone hard as steel, 'or all the Argolath slaves in the mine will die. Take this.' He pushed something towards the thief. 'It will protect you if anyone stops you.'

Why is the Commander of the Entroilian Central Office of Intelligence helping this Argolath to steal the Cosmic Egg? Sam wondered in bewildered astonishment. *He knows the Queen thinks it is of supreme importance. He was there when she said it.*

Sam was still trying to solve this puzzle as the Argolath thief turned and ran head-first down the tunnel, his white body glowing in the dark, still carrying the Egg in his ant-like jaws. Sam cowered in his hiding place within the Egg's outer blue crystal shell, frightened lest he slip between the gaps and fall into the pink surface of the Egg far below him. Sam was still terrified of that pink ocean, where he had almost drowned when he and Michael Zhang came out of the Universe, after the black hole had absorbed them.

The Argolath ran on down the shaft and the crumbling wall soon firmed to solid granite, feldspars sparkling with the occasional glowing violet amethyst and red blushing garnet beneath the Argolath's pincered feet.

It finally emerged into a much broader horizontal tunnel, illuminated by smoking oil lamps. Wagons loaded with rocks rumbled past along metal rails, hauled by large cockroach-like animals with small Argolaths riding on their backs. *This must be the mine*, Sam thought.

He could see other Argolaths in side tunnels, hacking at the rock with picks, supervised by armed Entroilians. One of them challenged the Argolath thief in a language Sam did not understand, looking curiously at the Cosmic Egg in its jaws. The Argolath held out a piece of paper which the guard read and, reluctantly it seemed to Sam, pushed a signal's lever. A wagon stopped and Sam's Argolath jumped on board the cockroach. The signal changed, the cockroach scuttled forward and hurried through a maze of tunnels which sometimes broadened out into workshops, foundries, forges and storerooms. Sometimes they pulled into a siding to allow the passage of long trains of wagons, drawn by a dozen cockroaches, hauling metal rails and spears, coils of rope, wooden girders or crowds of Argolaths.

Eventually Sam's Argolath spoke to the driver and the wagon stopped. He jumped down and took a side passage where an Entroilian stood guard. Behind him was the entrance to a shaft leading vertically up into the darkness. The Argolath showed the paper to the guard, who slowly read it in the smoking lamplight, then pulled on a rope hanging beside the shaft. A bell tinkled somewhere high overhead. Something began clattering down and eventually a wooden platform appeared. The Argolath stepped onto it, the guard rang twice and the platform began to rise slowly upwards. Even before it reached the top, Sam could smell cool, clean, fresh air replacing the smoky dampness of the mine.

After a long ascent, the platform finally creaked to a halt and the Argolath hurried out along a short unlit tunnel and emerged into a small rough-hewn cave where two red and black Entroilian soldiers were looking out of the cave mouth. When they heard the Argolath they called him over and he stood beside them.

'I can't see him, Captain Sundwor,' one of the Entroilian guards said, looking down from the mouth of the cave.

Peering out from his hiding place in the Egg's shell, Sam felt dizzy as he looked down the sheer drop beyond the cave mouth, wondering who they were waiting for. He could see Sedtia spread out far below.

It was late evening and the Entroilian city lay in almost total darkness, lit only by the warm glow reflected from the glorious pink clouds overhead. The late evening sky splashed rosy speckles across the distant ocean, throwing into sharp relief the magnificent bulk of the huge pyramidal Temple near the shore and the white maggot-like Royal Palace lying at the Temple's foot, guarded by the two gigantic Entroilian statues. Sam was struck again by how similar these creatures were to bees; their almost transparent wings, their hairy heads bearing long antennae, their bulging rear segments.

And yet, he thought, *in many ways they're nothing like bees. For one thing, they're huge. And they're as intelligent as people. The claws on their front legs are like hands and their bodies have different colours, depending on their role in society.*

'He's so fat it will take him all night to fly up here,' Captain Sundwor said. 'Keep watching.' He turned away from the cave mouth and glowered down at the Argolath. It was much smaller than the soldier and, under his gaze, it retreated until its rear segment bumped to a halt against the cave's granite wall. Sam could see its skin glowing white in the deep shadow, could see its two massive jaws curving down towards him, one on each side of the Cosmic Egg, gripping it tightly between them.

The Entroilian's head came closer and peered at the Egg. Sam could see his long antennae quivering with excitement. 'That's it, isn't it?' he hissed.

The Argolath didn't answer; his jaws didn't even move.

The Entroilian brought one of its massive multi-faceted eyes close and Sam instinctively ducked, even though he knew the creature could not see him. Compared to the guard the whole Universe was just a small round ball made of pink jelly and Sam was a mere speck of dust on its shell.

'That's the Cosmic Egg, isn't it?' Sundwor said and he moved closer still. 'The one everyone's talking about? The one that's produced the Son of Beeing?'

Sam could hear the greed trembling in his voice. *I don't trust him*, he thought. *Perhaps I should tell him that it's not the Son of Beeing.* Sam knew that, if he shouted, the Entroilian would be able to hear him, his voice amplified by the network of crystal pipes which constituted the Cosmic Egg's shell. *No, I'd better not say anything. If they know I'm here they might decide to take me out and do things to me. I don't think I'd like that.*

Impatient with the Argolath's silence, the Entroilian drew a short dagger from a scabbard and held it at the white ant's narrow neck. 'Give it to me!' he hissed.

At that moment, the Entroilian at the cave mouth stepped back whispering 'Not now Sundwor! He's here.' Sam heard a buzzing and clanking as something flew up towards the cave entrance. The guard moved back and a huge Entroilian landed heavily on the cave floor.

It lay there, wheezing for a minute before it recovered its breath enough to gasp 'Show me that Cosmic Egg, my clever little thief!' The fat Entroilian spoke in a high-pitched voice which Sam instantly recognised.

It's the other one at the meeting—what was his name? Gallrage! Marshall Gallrage! But "my clever little thief"? What's going on?

The Argolath's jaws lifted the Universe so Gallrage could examine it more closely. Looking out Sam could see the crinkled skin of his face puffed out with the fat that lay beneath.

'It's too dark,' Gallrage squeaked angrily. 'Strike a light!'

The Argolath struck a light with his arm-like front feet and a small flame flickered beside the Universe.

'Wonderful,' Gallrage said, eyeing the Universe closely before looking at its carrier. 'Put it down. Carefully now.' The Universe was lowered to the cave floor. 'Good. Now, can you write?'

'Write?' the Argolath said, speaking Entroilian in his heavy accent. 'Yes, I can write.'

'Good! Here, take this.' The Marshall produced paper and a pen from a pouch at his waist. 'Write this down in Argolathian.'

'No! I've brought that thing for you. I've kept my side of the bargain, now it's time for you to keep yours.'

'Fetch the other rebels,' Gallrage piped. The two guards went into the tunnel and Sam heard a whirring and clank of something mechanical.

'Don't worry,' Gallrage said. 'Your comrades will go free provided you write me a little note. That's not much to ask, is it?'

'What kind of note?'

'Here.' Gallrage handed him the pen and paper. Sam noticed the paper was brown, the same as the structures in Entroilia, and the pen looked like an animal's sting. 'I'll dictate. To Councillor Moshendiar.'

'Stop!' the Argolath said. 'If I write what you want, I want that Cosmic Egg. That's it, isn't it, the one that everyone's talking about? I'll write you that note but you'll have to let me take it to King Flenkt.'

Gallrage began to laugh. The two Entroilian guards laughed as well. 'My dear foolish slave. There is no way on Ent that you can have that Egg! It is the most precious object in the whole of Entroilia. Now either you write this note or you die and I get another Argolath to write it. Well, what's it to be?'

The Argolath hesitated then laid the paper on the cave floor beside the Universe and began to write.

'Sensible fellow.' Gallrage cleared his throat and spoke slowly. 'To Councillor Moshendiar.'

Sam watched as the Argolath wrote it down in symbols that splattered across the page like shredded leaves.

'If you want the Cosmic Egg,' Gallrage dictated, 'go alone and unarmed to the top of Mount Karla at midnight tomorrow.' He waited until the pen had stopped scratching the paper, then he took the note as the guards came back with a dozen Argolaths.

'You are all free to go and be sure you tell your King that the Son of Beeing has emerged from this Cosmic Egg and when he leads our army against you we will defeat the Argolath Kingdom once and for all.'

The Argolaths began to move towards the cave entrance.

'No!' Gallrage said, pointing at the one who had written the note. 'Not you. You know too much.'

It howled and made a dash for the cave mouth but Gallrage, with surprising agility, drew his sword and chopped the creature in half, holding the paper high so that the spurting pale green blood would not soil it. Even before the little white legs had stopped twitching, he lifted the Universe and handed it to one of the Entroilian guards. 'Keep this safe. Don't let it out of your sight. Lock all the slaves up tomorrow night and bring all your guards here. I want to greet our visitor in style.'

He folded the note into his pouch and flew away down the mountain.

'Okay,' Sundwor said to the other Argolaths. 'You can go.' The rebels scampered to the cave entrance, climbed the wall and went out the top, heading up the mountain.

Captain Sundwor picked up the Universe. 'I've got it! You saw that didn't you? He gave it to me!' He started giggling as the two soldiers flew to the shaft at the back of the cave and rang a bell. Sam heard the lift whirring and clanking up towards them.

'What are you going to do with it, Cap'n?' the other guard said as they waited for the lift to collect them.

'Do with it? Why, I'm going to—'

'—give it to me!' an Argolathian voice said, and Sam saw a pair of white jaws grip the Universe, saw the two guards falling into the shaft, felt the Universe lurch as it was carried back to the cave mouth, out onto the dark mountainside and upwards towards the summit.

The rebels squeaked excitedly in Argolathian until the one carrying the Universe, who seemed to be the leader, spoke sharply to them. The rest of the way to the top of the mountain was run in silence, their white bodies glowing pink in the light from the sunset sky. Sam lay on the floor of his crystal cave, trying to make sense of the events he had just witnessed.

Gallrage and his buddy Bogmon are traitors, that's clear. Bogmon helped an Argolath steal the Universe and Gallrage made him write a ransom note in Argolathian and then killed him. Why does Gallrage want Moshendiar to come up here tomorrow night? What are they going to do? Kill him too? I wouldn't be surprised. It's obvious they hate him. And now Gallrage has let these Argolaths steal the Universe. He's not only a traitor, he's totally incompetent. Now what will happen to me?

When they reached the top of the mountain they ran without a pause past a smoking vent and down into the darkness on the other side. The sky here was full of stars, but the land below was in the shadow of the mountains and it was very hard for Sam to see anything. Eventually the leader stopped and put the Universe down on a rock. All the Argolaths gathered round, chattering excitedly, and Sam took this opportunity to stand inside his crystal cell and search each wall, anxiously hoping for a sign of Catriona.

Episode 29 Romani Takes Control

'I cannot see any sign of a join,' the doctor said as he stared at the crystal. He sounded astonished, which was exactly how Sofie felt. A moment ago, she and Danny had been watching the doctor playing with the two small triangular blue pyramids as they huddled in two little bubbles. Now there was just one crystal floating before them, and the bubble had disappeared.

It was astonishing to be able to see everything around her, the little kitchen area, the desks covered in paper, the floating chairs tilted at odd angles, the broad flat ceiling. After being crammed into a tiny bubble for the past few hours, it was a great relief to be able to see so many things all at the same time, mundane as they were.

'But doctor,' she said, her voice subdued with awe. 'Where's the bubble gone?'

The doctor looked around and frowned. 'I'm afraid it's still there, Sofie.'

She hooked her foot under the desk below her and rotated herself until she saw part of a large bubble just beyond the Medical Centre reception desk, curving down from ceiling to floor. Her spirits fell when she saw it. Although hidden behind the walls, she could feel the rest of the bubble surrounding her like an invisible prison.

She kicked the desk again and turned her back on the glistening, alien surface, but through the windows she saw another part of it, lurking outside the building.

'At least it's a lot bigger than before,' the doctor said, encouragingly.

Sofie breathed in deeply and sighed. 'Yes, Doctor. I hated that claustrophobic little bubble.'

Hardly bigger than herself, a single bubble reminded her too vividly of the hours she had spent trying to help Marianne to give birth. This bubble was much bigger.

But as well as relief, she also felt a sense of unease. An image of Marianne flashed through her mind, just down the corridor, supposedly outside a bubble, frozen in time to keep her protected from any infection she might have picked up during the birth. She glanced at Danny, wondering if he too was thinking about his wife. The invisible bag seemed to have dropped back over his head, his face completely expressionless, his mind apparently in a different world.

Dr Plaisent plucked the large crystal out of the air where it had been floating between them, saying 'I wonder if we can still use this to fly?'

Gently he pressed a finger of his other hand into one face. Immediately the crystal moved sideways, pulling him along with it. Through the windows, Sofie saw the bubble begin to move, its pattern changing, and then more of the bubble moved through the wall into the room. He pressed the crystal again and stopped.

'So is Marianne still outside the bubble?' Sofie said. When she mentioned his wife's name, Danny Schneider seemed to awaken from sleep. He looked around, apparently seeing the big bubble for the first time. Sofie too looked at the red and green areas swirling between black patches, the feeling of imprisonment returned. 'Do you think this bubble might be big enough to revive her? Shouldn't we go and check she is all right?'

'I'm sure she is,' the doctor said. 'This bubble is not big enough to reach her.'

Danny pushed himself against the counter, floated across to the doctor, and held out his hand. The doctor gave him the crystal. Danny first pressed it to stop himself moving further and then brought it close to his eye.

Sofie felt relieved that he was finally taking an interest in something. *Marianne will need his support. He was no help to anyone the way he was.*

'The two fragments have completely fused together,' he said, squinting against the blue-green light which shone out from inside the crystal. 'I can't even see the join.'

'No,' the doctor said. 'It is as it they have become a single stone. It is truly very curious.'

'And the bubble's a lot bigger too,' Danny said, looking around. 'How big is it? Four metres, would you say?'

'What, from the crystal?' the doctor said. 'Yes, something like that. Why?'

'The bubble from a single crystal was about three metres in diameter,' Danny muttered as if talking to himself. 'This bubble is about eight metres, roughly three times as much. So the volume must have increased about twenty-seven times.'

'Really?' Sofie said. She couldn't quite believe it, although it certainly felt a lot bigger.

'So I wonder what would happen if we fused some more?' Danny muttered, looking at the crystal again.

'But we haven't got any more,' the doctor said.

'George will be back soon,' Sofie said. 'Perhaps he's found some in the ATLAS cavern.'

'Shall we take a bet on it?' the doctor said. 'Look, I'll bet you a thousand francs—'

'Ah, here they are,' a man's voice said. Sofie turned to see a fat man flying into the bubble from the direction of the Medical Centre door, a crystal in his outstretched hands. Sofie immediately recognised Professor Romani's nose. She had often marvelled at it when she saw the Director General's photograph in the "CERN Courier[3]". It was the most elegant piece of human flesh she had ever seen, its luxuriously sculptured tip arising proudly from those flared nostrils and leading straight to that high bridge. It always seemed to Sofie a wasted work of art, for the rest of his face, not to mention his body, held no appeal whatsoever, and today he was truly in a sorry state.

His smart blue Italian suit and dyed black hair were smeared with concrete dust and the thick layer of fat which normally hung from his jaws now floated when he moved and wobbled when he spoke, giving his face a grotesque cloud-like appearance which was disturbing and slightly sickening to behold.

Romani immediately took charge. 'Does everyone here know each other? I am Francesco Romani, the Director General of CERN.'

'Is Marianne here as well?' said the woman who flew in behind him. Sofie didn't know her but was intrigued to find out who she was. Her thick mane of blonde curls wafted around as her head turned, scanning the room. Her heavy breasts bobbed about in the neckline of her low-cut vermillion trouser-suit which was also smeared in concrete dust. She had lost both her shoes but, incongruously, she still clutched a large yellow handbag. Her dark eye make-up was smeared down her cheeks as if she had been crying, but it bore signs of a recent attempt to repair it.

The doctor explained that Marianne had been left outside a bubble in the treatment room at the end of the corridor. Francesco became very excited when the doctor showed him the large crystal. He wanted to know exactly what he had done to

---

[3] Printed copies of the CERN Courier, the International Journal of High-Energy Physics, are distributed free to CERN staff every month, and is also available online. See bibliography (12).

make it, and looked at the fused crystal very carefully, then said 'That's extremely interesting. And you are?'

'Dr Plaisent. Jean-Pierre Plaisent. I work at H.U.G.[4]'

'Pleased to meet you, doctor,' Francesco said. 'Thank you for coming to help us. May I introduce,' he turned his head towards the woman in red, 'Her Excellency Brigit O'Brien, Irish Ambassador to the United Nations in Geneva, who was unfortunate enough to be on a visit to CERN when this accident happened. I—'

'Accident, Francesco?' the ambassador snapped. 'Disaster I'd call it. Didn't any of you scientists ever think about what you were doing before you built this, this what do you call it, ATLAS machine thing?'

There was silence in the room as Francesco frowned at her, two deep creases puckering the fat between his eyebrows. 'Of course we did, Madame Ambassador. We thought about the possible dangers of the LHC and its detectors very carefully, and we concluded that under normal circumstances there should be absolutely no danger[5]. But the incident which happened this morning, when ATLAS captured a cosmic monopole, was entirely unexpected. Nobody could ever have predicted such a thing. Scientists had never before even seen a monopole, although many had searched for one. It was a purely theoretical particle until today. Scientists can only calculate the risks of possible events. This event, if anyone had ever considered it, would have been regarded as so unlikely as to have been impossible.'

'But it obviously was not impossible!' Brigit retorted. 'It's happened, and the result is that you created a black hole which

---

[4] Hôpitaux Universitaires de Genève, the largest hospital in Geneva.

[5] For examples of reports on the possible dangers from CERN experiments see bibliography entries (7) and (8).

not only absorbed my husband and one of my nation's best scientists, but it caused time to stop! So far, Professor Romani, you have expressed no regret at all about this.'

'Regret?' Francesco's fat face was quivering with suppressed rage, a purple glow spreading upwards from his neck like a dawn sky. 'I regret nothing, Madame Ambassador! I am extremely proud of what we achieved here. We constructed the largest and most complex piece of scientific equipment in history. We co-ordinated a world-wide team of the best physicists and engineers to develop, construct and operate it. We discovered—'

'You discovered that time can stop,' Brigit interrupted him, 'and that almost everyone in the world can be killed, yes, I know. Hello Danny,' she said, pressing the crystal she held and turning away from Francesco. 'George told us about the baby. I'm very sorry. How's Marianne now?'

'The doctor has left her without a crystal, Madame Ambassador,' he said in a monotone.

'We considered it safest to leave her outside a bubble,' the doctor said.

Brigit nodded and held out her hand to him, her blonde curls billowing. 'Hello Doctor Plaisent. I'm Brigit,' she said. 'Very pleased to meet you.'

'So how many crystals do we have altogether?' Francesco said, sounding impatient, his colour gradually returning to normal. 'Can you all please show me what you have?'

'We only have that one,' the doctor said, pointing to the large crystal floating before him.

'Oh dear,' Francesco said. 'Can we see everyone's crystals please?' He stared meaningfully at Brigit.

She placed her crystal alongside the large one. 'And where's yours?' she said.

Francesco's eyes narrowed, then he took three crystals from his pocket and added the one he was flying with. 'So we have five small crystals here,' he said, arranging them in a little circle. 'And this big one.' He took the large fragment the doctor had made and put it in the middle. 'The fireman has two more,' he went on, 'and apparently Count Karolyi has many more but he's run away.'

'I still can't believe that,' Brigit said. 'Alex seemed such a nice young man. Why would he want to run off with crystal?'

'Because, Madame Ambassador,' Danny said, his voice as tight as a firefighter's knot, 'he is a completely selfish bastard, if you'll pardon the expression. I've known Karolyi for a couple of years and his behaviour doesn't surprise me at all.'

'I think that is not an insuperable problem,' Francesco said. 'We have not yet made a complete search of the ATLAS cavern.'

'My team leader, George Gabor, is doing a search,' Sofie said, feeling somewhat indignant that she had not been spoken to so far. 'I'm Sofie Dialektaki, by the way.'

Francesco nodded. 'We have already met him, young lady. It was he who gave us these crystals, and I think we might well find more when we have time to do a proper search. The key question now is this: is Marianne well enough to be moved? What do you think, doctor?'

Jean-Pierre looked at him, considering. 'Where were you planning on taking her?' he asked.

'To one of the Hostels,' Francesco said. 'They're only a few hundred metres away from here.'

'And the benefit of this move would be what, exactly?'

'We all need a rest and there are many rooms in the Hostels. Also they are close to the main Cafeteria where there is plenty of food. I think the Cafeteria will be the best place for us to make our base. And there are some small laboratories nearby.'

'I'm sorry, Professor,' Jean-Pierre said, 'but I do not think there would be any benefit to my patient in being moved to a hostel.

She is currently in a state of suspended animation and Mr Schneider and I agree this is the most appropriate way to manage her case. I would prefer to leave her here. She would be less likely to be accidentally revived by others passing by with crystals. I will come with you if you decide to move to a different location and return here regularly to check her state. Do you agree?' he said, turning to Danny.

Danny nodded. 'Totally.'

'Very good, doctor,' Francesco said. 'Leave her here by all means but I think it's very important to get these people comfortable and also to start experiments on crystal as soon as we can.'

'Oh my God!' Brigit said but Francesco didn't seem to notice.

'I want to check for radiation and investigate crystal's properties.' He took a small piece of crystal out of the circle and looked at it closely. 'This material is incredible, don't you think Danny?'

Danny nodded. 'It certainly is, Professor Romani.'

'In fact,' Francesco went on with an excited gleam in his eye, 'this whole situation is an incredible opportunity for us to explore completely new areas of science. I am certain many new discoveries will be made, my friends. Discoveries that could potentially lead to benefits for the whole of humanity.'

'I can't believe what I'm hearing here,' Brigit said. 'Discoveries? For God's sake, Francesco, how many more "discoveries" like this can humanity take? Don't you think science has done enough damage for one day?' Sofie saw Francesco give her a cold look. Brigit stared defiantly back at him as she said. 'Surely the main issue now is how we are going to survive on a daily basis?' She turned to Sofie. 'What do you think, Sofie?'

Everyone turned to look at her. Hitherto, Sofie would have dreaded being the centre of attention like this, but now, after what she had been through today, it seemed perfectly right that

Brigit should ask for her opinion. 'What do I think?' she said. 'I think our first priority must be to look after Marianne. She's been through a terrible ordeal. But at present she's frozen, so she should be okay. I think we should leave her here. After that, well I suppose I agree with you, your Excellency. Our next priority should be to survive.'

Brigit gave her a nod and an indulgent smile. Sofie began to take a dislike to her. She had never met the Ambassador before, but she seemed a bit too full of her own importance.

'But I agree with Professor Romani too,' Sofie went on. 'We're definitely going to need the food and water in the Cafeteria. There's none here in the Medical Centre. I think we should leave Marianne here and the rest of us should move over there. As far as I can see, our main problem is going to be toilets. I think we should dig latrines.'

'Latrines?' Francesco said. 'I don't think they will work. There's no gravity. What will happen when—' He paused, waving his hands and looking embarrassed. 'We have to think like spacemen. Does anyone know how they go to the toilet in space?'

'I believe astronauts have special toilets,' Jean-Pierre said.

'That's right,' Brigit said. 'I made a programme about it once for Irish T.V. They have sort of vacuum cleaners. It's a bit gruesome actually.'

'It sounds like we have an expert here,' Francesco said, shooting a secret wicked smile at Sofie. 'That is very good.'

'But I agree with you, Francesco,' Brigit added. 'A hole in the ground just won't work.'

'Then it sounds like we have a problem,' Sofie said. 'I think we must get that sorted out, and all the other basic needs of life like washing and sleeping, before we start worrying about science.'

'But science offers us the only hope of survival,' Francesco said. 'We have already discovered that fragments of crystal will fuse together and create a bigger ball.'

'You mean a bigger bubble,' Sofie said. 'That's what Marianne called it.'

'I calculate' Danny said, 'that the bubble from the big crystal is almost twenty-seven times larger than the originals.'

Francesco nodded. 'Excellent! Just imagine how big it might be if we can fuse all our fragments together. We might make a very big bubble so that hundreds of people are revived. We do not know what is possible. And another important point, perhaps even more important, is that we don't know whether these crystals are dangerous or not. They might be radioactive, for example. And of course, if they are, we have a serious problem. But on the other hand, there might be ways to shield us from the radiation while still using the crystal to fly. But we've got to know the answers to these basic questions and only science can tell us.'

'I must say I agree with you Professor Romani,' Danny said.

'Yes, we definitely need to know if it's radioactive,' Jean-Pierre said. 'I never thought of that. Look, why don't we try to do both? There are five of us. If the Ambassador will help me sort out the toilet problem and—'

'No way! 'Brigit said. 'Sorry but I'm not a toilet expert and I'm not digging a hole in the ground.'

'I'll help you, Dr Plaisent,' Sofie said.

'Very good,' Francesco said. 'Danny you want to help me with the research? And perhaps you wouldn't mind investigating the food and bottled water situation in the Cafeteria, Madame Ambassador? How does that sound to everyone?'

They all nodded their agreement.

'I'm happy to help in any way I can except for toilet work,' Brigit said, 'but you'll have to show me where the Cafeteria is.'

'We're going there now,' Francesco said.

'I'll go and tell Marianne what is happening before we leave,' Jean-Pierre said. 'Danny, would you like to see her too?'

Danny frowned, as if he couldn't remember who Marianne was, then nodded once.

'You will each need a piece of this crystal,' Francesco said. They each took one of the small fragments. Francesco also took the large one saying 'I need this for the experiment. Now, I think we need to meet again in about, say two hours, and decide our next step.' He looked at his watch. 'Say in the Cafeteria at three o'clock? Can we all check our watches tell the same time? It's eleven fifty-five now. That will be CERN time from now on.'

'Oh, mine's different,' Jean-Pierre said.

'It depends how long you were frozen,' Danny said.

'That's right,' Francesco said. 'Please all set your watches to eleven fifty-five.'

Everyone began to reset their watches but Sofie said: 'I'm sorry. My watch is the same as George Gabor's. He and I will need to use the same time. Would you mind if everyone used the same time as us?' Francesco frowned, thought about it, shrugged and nodded. 'Why not?' he said.

'So I make it eighteen hours six,' Sofie said.

'So is it six minutes past six in the evening?' Brigit said as she set her watch. 'It doesn't feel like it.'

'It does to me,' Sofie said.

'I suggest we all meet again in three hours,' Francesco said. 'Say at nine o'clock in the Cafeteria, so we can catch up and decide how to proceed.'

Everyone agreed and they flew towards the exit.

Episode 30 Hôpital de la Peste

Fear and the freezing wind paralysed Catriona as she fell head-first out of a grey sky towards the snow-covered hillside.

She was high, about as high as the peaks of the distant mountains, and an icy wind was blasting into her face and whistling past her body as she plunged downwards. A million thoughts were rushing through her overheated mind. But a moment later her panic vanished and she seemed to be watching this disaster happening to somebody else, as if she wasn't in her own body any more but floating beside it, looking at herself, watching with interest but without fear. She seemed to be falling much more slowly. A sudden and profound peace of mind descended upon her, as she accepted the inevitability of her own death. But this was mixed with a feeling of enormous sadness and disappointment.

I'm never going to see Sam again. I'm never going to tell him how grateful I am to him for everything he's done for me. I won't be able to give him this crystal either. I wonder where he is. Will he find it when I'm gone? Will Michael restart time?

She looked down again, hoping against hope to see him. The ground was hurtling up towards her so fast it took her breath away. The horse and cart still stood beside the muddy track which cut through the pure-white snow. They grew larger with every passing moment so that now she could see the two figures quite clearly, a little girl kneeling beside an adult who was lying in the snow. She could even hear the child crying. There was nobody else in sight.

Sam isn't there! I've failed! It's all been a waste of time. I'm going to die for nothing.

A moment later, she lost sight of them as a strong cross-wind blew her over a crest in the undulating ground. Now she was hurtling towards a row of ice-covered trees. She studied them with calm curiosity, glad of something to take her mind off the tragedy. They looked like Christmas decorations on a cake, thick icicles hanging from every branch and even growing upwards into a cascading white rind.

I wonder which one of those trees will kill me? They must be pretty hard with all that ice frozen onto their branches. I do hope it's quick.

'Turn the crystal you bloody fool!'

It was not so much the urgency of Sam's voice which shocked her into action as his bad language. *I've never heard Sam swear before.* Her eyes flicked to the crystal which she still clutched forgotten in her frozen hands. She forced her rigid, almost frozen fingers into a fist, slipped the crystal in and pushed against the exposed face. The crystal yanked her to one side and she swooped past the wall of trees like a bird, clipping one frozen branch. A shower of ice fragments sprayed out around her.

I can still fly!

She pressed first the top and then the bottom of the crystal, slowing to a halt and hanging in the air like a balloon, exulted still to be alive.

'Oh Sam thank you, thank you!' she called. 'Where are you? I can't see you.'

There was no answer and a moment later she felt herself begin to fall.

Gravity's pulling me down.

She pressed the bottom of the crystal and slowed her descent. The icy wind felt like a million razors slicing through her thin clothes and cutting into her flesh as it blew her sideways towards the row of trees. *If I get caught in them I'll be frozen to death.*

She let herself descend rapidly almost to the ground and by tilting her crystal into the wind and pressing it with exactly the right force she managed to hover almost stationary in the lee of a snow bank. She stared again into the crystal.

'Where are you Sam?' she called again but heard only the howling of the wind or it might have been the sound of the child crying. 'Sam?' she called. 'Can you hear me?'

Awkwardly she rotated the crystal, looking into each face in turn, searching for him while keeping herself above the snow and out of the wind. It was not easy. Finally, to her enormous relief, she found Sam's face. He looked really worried. 'Where are you, Catty?'

'Where are you, Sam?'

She heard Sam sigh. 'I told you. I'm at the bottom of the tunnel.' He sounded terribly tired. 'Where are you?'

'I'm at the bottom of the tunnel too but I can't see you. I'm really cold, Sam. It's all snowy here and freezing. Where can I find you?'

'That's not the bottom of the tunnel, Kitten. Wait a minute. They're going to move the—'

His face suddenly slipped down and vanished as if he had fallen over.

'Sam? Sam! Can you hear me?'

There was no answer. Catriona's heart sank. *Not at the bottom? Will I have to go back into that tunnel?* She looked up, preparing herself in case Sam told her to go back, but she couldn't see it. There was a whole wide grey sky reaching over her but no sign of the tunnel entrance. Her desperate eyes swept the sky in disbelief. *It isn't there! Where's it gone? How can I take this crystal down to Sam if I can't find the tunnel? Alex was right. The tunnel entrance was tiny, just a little dip in the cavern floor. If it's the same size here then I'll never find it up there in all that sky. I might be trapped here on my own for ever.*

Fear began to grow inside her. She tried to calm herself, talking gently the way that Sam used to talk when she got one of her panic attacks before an exam.

Now let's just think about this Kitten. You know you're still near Geneva. You saw the mountains and the lake while you were up in the tunnel so CERN's got to be down here somewhere. All you've got to do is find it! Then you can go down the shaft to the cavern and back into the tunnel that way.

Now hope replaced fear. She pressed the bottom of the crystal and rose rapidly into the air, searching for the big brown wooden dome which had dominated the CERN site. The landscape broadened beneath her feet and she examined each of the thick banks of snow, trying to work out which of them was hiding that dome. *It's incredible how much snow there is,* she thought. *It must have fallen really fast this morning while we were down underground. Do they normally get this much snow in April?*

She was staring so hard at the white surface, that speckled patterns began running across her vision, making it hard to distinguish any features at all. All she could see now were the muddy track, the horse and cart, the tops of trees poking up into the grey sky and, in the distance, the lake with the city wrapped around one end of it, dominated by the cathedral on the hill.

I must be roughly in the right place, so where's CERN gone? She looked again at the child kneeling beside the man on the snow. *I'll have to ask those people if they know where it is. Hope they speak English!*

She suddenly realised that, if they saw her flying, they might get frightened and run away. She let herself descend so she was hidden by a ridge, flew low until she reached it then dropped into the snow up to her knees and put the crystal in her pocket. She began to walk and immediately lost her shoes but struggled on without them. The cart was further away than it had looked. Already chilled to the bone by the wind she now began to shiver uncontrollably. She kept wanting to fly but dared not risk alarming the people.

Finally, her teeth chattering, she emerged onto the track twenty metres from the cart. The child, a girl of about five, was now lying across the body of the man who seemed to have fallen off the driver's seat of the cart.

Oh God! This is all I need, Catriona thought. 'Hello,' she called as she struggled down the frozen, rutted track.

The girl stopped crying and looked up.

'Everything all right?' Catriona said and immediately felt stupid. *Of course it isn't.*

The girl stood and staggered toward her. Catriona was struck by her odd clothes and pageboy haircut. She wore a brown pleated skirt and a baggy jumper of the same dull colour but neither hat nor gloves. She said something that sounded like French, grasped Catriona's hand with burning hot fingers and pulled her towards the man, still talking and crying.

Catriona followed her, amazed at how hot her hands were. Once again she wished that her school had taught her first aid as she looked at the man lying face down in the snow.

The horse had pulled the cart so one front wheel was jammed against his legs. He wasn't moving and the wind had partly covered one side of him in a little snow drift. He had obviously been lying there for some time. He wore a long, elaborately embroidered cloak over a thick padded jacket that reached down to his thighs. Instead of trousers, he wore what looked like women's tights.

Catriona knelt down, not sure what to do. He smelt horrible. She leaned over and tried to see his face but it was pressed into the snow. She brushed it away to let him breathe and to her horror saw a large red lump with black spots on his cheek. Her hand recoiled in alarm. His nose and mouth were encrusted in ice.

The little girl began violently coughing. In a panic, Catriona reached out and pulled the man's shoulder, trying to lift his face out of the snow, hoping against hope that he was still alive and could tell her where CERN was. He felt very cold. His whole arm lifted, as rigid as a tree branch, his hand sticking out, the palm covered in red blotches, the ends of the fingers and nails black. She let go his shoulder and stared in horror at the hand. Some fingers had a white coating all over the end, as if they were going mouldy. The girl's coughing was becoming worse every second.

Catriona stared at the man, still unsure what to do, then looked at his chest. *He isn't breathing. He must be dead.* She stood up and turned to the girl who suddenly stopped coughing and vomited onto the snow which became streaked with blood.

Oh my God! She's ill too! What should I do? I don't want to get involved with this but I can't just leave her here. She needs help. Got to get her to hospital.

Catriona looked at the cart. The horse looked cold, miserable and exhausted.

I can't drive that. Never driven a horse and cart before. No good messing with that. Only one thing to do.

She took the crystal out of her pocket, lifted the girl between her arms and began to fly along the track down the hillside towards Geneva. She couldn't see the city, only the little stream which cut across the track at the bottom of the snow-covered valley. A village dominated the ridge on the far side. She could see a big stone barn at the side of the road. She was sure that was where Sam had nearly crashed into the tram.

She hesitated, hovering with the girl heavy in her arms. *I don't really want to fly past people. Can I go round the outside? Maybe this stream will join the river that runs out of the lake at Geneva. What did Sam call it yesterday? The Rhine? Or was it the Rhone?*

Doesn't matter. If I can find that and follow it I should get to Geneva without meeting many people.

She turned right and followed the stream through a little wood, eventually flying over a little stone bridge where the stream opened out into a sort of marina full of boats covered in ice. *Must be getting near the river.* She swerved to the bank and stopped. The boats didn't have tall masts. They weren't like the expensive yachts she had seen moored on Lake Geneva. These boats were wooden, like old-fashioned canal barges. She flew past them and reached the broad river. It too was covered in snow. It looked like a highway curving across the countryside. *The whole river looks frozen! How could that happen in just one morning?*

She was still trembling with cold and the child was still burning in her arms so, with a feeling of confusion, she turned left and flew low along the broad white river, around gently meandering curves, keeping beneath the trees on one bank. There was no sign of the city. *Am I going the wrong way?* Finally she came to a fork where two rivers flowed together. *Left or right?* The one on the right was narrower. She gambled and took the broad left-hand one.

Round another bend she saw some wooden buildings standing on stilts in the river near the left bank, ice thick on their roofs. *I'll have to ask someone where the hospital is.* She hovered above the snowy bank but couldn't see anyone to ask. A short way ahead two frozen rows of wooden stakes stuck out of the ice-covered river, stretching from bank to bank. Beyond them were more houses on stilts. *Where is this? It's nothing like Geneva. I've obviously come the wrong way.*

The little girl groaned, her body hot and limp, her clothes wringing with sweat despite the freezing wind. Catriona's arms were aching with the effort of holding her. She lifted her higher and as the girl's head fell onto Catriona's shoulder she noticed for the first time that she too had a nasty red swelling dotted with black blotches, just like her father's, although hers was on the back of her neck.

She needs urgent attention, Catriona thought with panic starting to well up inside her. *Too late to go back to Geneva now. This looks like a big town. There must be a hospital here somewhere.*

There were high stone walls rising above a moat on both banks of the river, each topped by several small stone towers and a parapet. *That must be the city wall.*

That must be the city wall[6]

She flew up the wall on her left. There was a paved roadway running along behind the parapet. On the far side of the road were wooden houses. The snow was harder here, compacted by many feet.

Catriona put the crystal in her pocket and looked around for help. An old woman in a long dark cloak was walking along the road. Catriona called her and she stopped and turned.

---

[6] Drawing by Claude Chastillon from bibliography entry (15) copyright Chancellerie d'Etat, Genève. The chapel of the Hôpital de la Peste can be seen bottom right.

'Do you speak English?' Catriona said, her cold bare feet slipping beneath the child's weight as she hurried across the snow towards the old woman who stared at her blankly.

Catriona swallowed and dredged her mind for some French. 'Ou est le,' she paused. *What's the French for hospital? Why didn't they teach us useful words in school instead of how to conjugate stupid verbs?* She tried her usual trick: take an English word and make it sound French. 'Ou est le ospital?' She amazed herself. *That almost sounds right!*

The girl began to sneeze.

'Mon dieu!' the old woman said. 'C'est la peste!' She clamped a handkerchief over her nose and hobbled rapidly away, screaming at the top of her voice 'C'est la peste! C'est la peste!'

Catriona ran after her. 'Le ospital,' she shouted. 'Ou est le ospital?'

The old woman stopped and turned. 'Vous cherchez l'Hôpital de la Peste?' She pointed over the city wall and across the river at a little chapel surrounded by a high wall just outside the city on the far bank. 'Voilà! Ça c'est l'Hôpital. Allez-y ! Tout de suite!' She spat on the road then hobbled off.

Catriona looked across at the building. *It looks more like a church than a hospital, but the old woman definitely said the word so I suppose it must be. I could fly over the river but I think it might be better to walk and not attract too much attention.*

There was a bridge not far away flanked by wooden buildings on stilts. It led to an island in the middle of the river dominated by a tall stone tower and another bridge ran from there to the opposite bank. She walked quickly along the road and onto the bridge. It was busy, obviously a major thoroughfare. The buildings on either side were shops. As she crossed the river Catriona was overcome with a sense of confused foreboding.

Something's very strange about this town. All the buildings are old. Most are made of wood. Can't remember seeing this place when I was up in the tunnel. It's much nicer than Geneva, but where is it? It looks sort-of medieval. Must be a great tourist attraction. Why didn't Mother mention it to us?

She could see no cars or buses, no trams, not even a bicycle. The only vehicles she saw were horses and carts. The people were strange too. They all looked as if they were going to a fancy dress party. The men wore big baggy shorts bulging out like babies' napkins, their legs sticking out into long leather boots. Most had heavy beards which hung down over their thick padded waistcoats which they wore under velvet cloaks. Most of the women had long full skirts and cloaks that almost hid their figures. It was all very strange. Then it dawned on her.

This must be some sort of Easter celebration! Easter's next Sunday. This might be the Swiss form of Mardi Gras! No, that can't be right. I'm sure that happens well before Easter. Still, I think most people in Geneva are Protestants aren't they? They might do things differently here. Perhaps holding Mardi Gras on the wrong day is their way of protesting!

These thoughts ran round her head as she reached the far side of the river and followed the road along the top of the city wall to a gateway. She crossed a wooden bridge over the moat and went through some fields to the walled chapel. It was a very long way round. By the time she got there, she was exhausted from carrying the child. The sign above the dark wooden door said:

Hôpital et Chapelle de la Peste

She rang the bell. A wooden shutter slid open in the door and a pair of eyes peered out. When the eyes saw the child the shutter closed, a key turned in a lock and the heavy door swung open to reveal a man in a full-length hooded brown cloak. His nose and mouth were covered with a long leather mask that tapered to a point like a gigantic beak. A strong smell of perfume mixed with vinegar hung about him. Velvet bags dangled from a cord round his waist. Catriona almost burst out laughing, he looked so ridiculous. *Even the doctors take part in this carnival*, she thought.

He stepped forward and lifted the girl's head. When he saw the lump on her neck he moved aside and beckoned Catriona with a leather-gloved hand. 'Entrez, vite!' he said, his voice muffled by the leather mask.

Catriona carried her in, the front door slammed behind them and the man locked it then pushed her into a small wooden building and closed the door.

It was dark inside. The only light came from some tiny windows near the roof and a fire in the stone wall at the far end of the room. Somebody was sitting in a high-backed wooden chair beside the fire. The smoke that was drifting around made Catriona's eyes sting and the child coughed violently. The sitting person also wore a mask and brown cloak but from the long hair protruding from the hood Catriona guessed it was a woman.

'Do you speak English?' Catriona gasped through the smoke as the woman stood and took the child off her. After glancing at the child's neck she said something in French and the man went out.

Suppose she didn't understand me, Catriona thought, moving towards the fire trying to get warm. She watched as the woman laid the girl on a rough wooden table and began to take her clothes off, throwing them into a big iron pot hanging over the fire. Catriona was shocked to see more large swellings at the top of her legs, red with black marks like the ones on her neck, and even more shocked when the last of her clothes came off and she saw that the child was in fact a little boy.

The man in brown came back with another man in a mask, this one wearing a grey cloak. He stood near the door and watched the man in brown walk down to Catriona and pull at her blouse, saying 'Enlevez vos vêtements! Vite!' The buttons of her blouse burst open.

Catriona didn't understand what he said but she knew very well what he meant. She backed away and found herself in an alcove beside the fire. The woman picked a dirty knife off the floor and said something to him. He left Catriona, held the boy's feet down on the table and the woman began making cuts in his leg near one of the lumps.

'Don't do that,' Catriona shouted, 'it isn't clean!' But the woman ignored her. The boy screamed as a thick black liquid oozed out onto the table and a foul stench filled the room, mingling with the smell of smoke and vinegar and perfume. Catriona felt like vomiting. She just wanted to get away, to fly out of this mad place.

I've done my duty. I brought the girl I mean the boy to the hospital. Now I can go and find CERN.

She took the crystal out of her pocket, intending to fly up to the window, but stopped when she heard Alex's voice.

'Kata! Where the hell are you?' His voice was coming out of the crystal.

She brought it close to her eye, hardly noticing as the man in brown stepped forward, peering at her closely. She could see Alex's gorgeous face and in the background was a shop. 'I've come down the tunnel Alex, but it's vanished now and I'm stuck. You've got to come down and help me!'

The man in brown began gesturing at the crystal with a gloved hand, talking to the woman in rapid French.

'What do you mean Kata, vanished?' Alex said, then the man made a sudden grab for the crystal and Catriona only just managed to snatch it away.

He held out his hand and said 'Donnez-le moi!'

She clutched it close to her chest but he pushed her violently backwards against the wall and the crystal was knocked out of her grip. It went spinning through the air towards the fire. She bent, trying to catch it, terrified it would be burned and she would be trapped here forever, but she was too slow, the heat seared her hand and she pulled back. It fell into the fire and disappeared into the pile of logs and ash.

Episode 31 King Flenkt

Just as Sam said 'That's not the bottom of the tunnel Kitten,' the leader of the Argolaths had picked up the Universe in its huge white jaws. 'Wait a minute,' Sam shouted into the crystal wall of his cell, 'They're going to move the—' But before he could finish, the Argolaths had begun to run down the steeply sloping mountain and Sam fell over. He lost sight of Catriona as he slithered across the floor, desperately hoping to avoid the gap where one crystal was missing. Luckily his trousers got caught in the pool of Entroilian honey which Michael had regurgitated into the cell, so he was pretty sure he would not fall out, but it was impossible now to position his head and see what Catriona was doing.

What was it she said? He wondered as he jammed his arm into the honey pool.

"I'm at the bottom of the tunnel. It's all snowy here and freezing."

Well she obviously isn't at the bottom. It's not snowy and freezing here! So where the hell is she? And if she does manage to come all the way down the tunnel, where will she come out? Will it really be there? He looked down at the little pink Universe. He was too far away and too short sighted to see the hole which Michael Zhang had made, but Sam had always assumed that somehow Catriona would pop out of that hole too. He knew the hole went all the way down to its centre, all the way back to the creation of the Universe, and he guessed that the tunnel must start there and go up to the ATLAS cavern.

But if she comes out of that hole and starts floating in that pink jelly stuff how will she survive? I know what it's like and I don't think she's going to last very long. But if the Universe was in Cjingha's lab when Catriona arrived then the Professor could send her probe down and collect her! Yes, that would save her. Somehow I've got to get this Universe back over this mountain to the Entroilian University. How the hell can I do that? These Argolaths seem to think they've captured some sort of prize. They're definitely not going to turn round and take it back. This is not good, not good at all.

Still, there is one good thing. At least Catty's found the tunnel! Wonder how much crystal she's bringing down? Cjingha said she would need it all to fix this crystal network and restart time. I wonder if George Gabor's with her? I couldn't see him. Just Catty, falling through the air.

The Argolaths jolted and slithered down the mountain towards a plain which lay at the eastern foot of the range. Overhead an explosion of stars was splattered in glorious profusion across the deep blue sky. On the plain below little lights were moving slowly back and forth. Finally the ground levelled out and the ants picked up speed as they raced across the plain following an invisible path which, from the way the leader's white antennae kept searching the ground, Sam guessed was marked by some sort of scent. The heads of tall flowers passed above them, silhouetted against the stars. As they traversed the plain, they entered a forest and the flowers were replaced by trees. Now he realised that the moving lights were the glowing bodies of thousands of white ants, running through the branches, up and down the trunks of trees and across the forest floor, carrying in their jaws segments of cut leaves.

When the party of escaped slaves arrived they began to call to these Argolaths in their own language. The workers dropped their leaves and began shouting and jumping in an extraordinary fashion. Soon the path was lined by dozens of them all cheering and reaching up trying to touch the Universe. Leaves began raining down from the trees, thrown by the ants in ticker-tape fashion. It was obvious that the Universe was seen as a great prize.

I suppose that's good. At least they won't throw it away as so much junk, and me with it.

The leading Argolath reached a large hole in the ground and without hesitation he ran over the edge and began to descend headfirst down a vertical shaft, a long precession of other Argolaths following him. They soon emerged into a well-lit horizontal tunnel. The tracks of a railway line ran down one side. The tunnel was lit by electric lamps and every few minutes trains rumbled past, their sophisticated engines powered by overhead electric cables, their huge trucks laden with different kinds of ore. *It's a mine,* Sam thought, *but very different from the Entroilian one. Those tunnels were lit by oil lamps, not electricity. In fact I don't think I saw electricity anywhere in the Entroilian city. Certainly not in the university. Not even in the Royal Palace!*

He was still wondering why when one of the electric trains stopped and the party of Argolaths climbed into an empty wagon. The train proceeded on its journey and every Argolath miner they passed stopped work to call and cheer as the leader of the escaped slaves held the Universe aloft. The train travelled underground for miles and Sam had plenty of time to think about the contrast in the two technologies.

Before I came here I thought Entroilian civilization was quite advanced, he mused. *They had a palace and a temple and a university, and the Queen even wanted to dig a tunnel under the mountains and defeat these Argolaths, yet they didn't have a single electric light bulb. I wonder why not? Entroilians aren't poor. On Earth you get some nations without much technology, but that's because they can't afford it. And even in the poorest nations you get cars and telephones, just not many of them. The Queen needs Argolaths to dig the tunnel for her. Why doesn't she just tell the university to open a department of mining? And how does she expect to conquer them if her culture is so far behind her enemy's? On Earth, technology would quickly spread from one nation to another. Maybe it's because they're not just different nations but different species. Perhaps they just see each other as rivals. And we think we've got problems on Earth with racism! Species-ism must be far worse!*

After a journey lasting perhaps half an hour, the train stopped, they disembarked and entered a lift, also lit by electricity, and Sam's ears popped as they were whisked down to a far deeper level.

They emerged into a huge cavern, lit by soft artificial lights shining down from a gently domed roof. Sam had thought the ATLAS cavern was big, but it was nothing compared to this. Its size was stunning. The roof was so high that little clouds gathered beneath it. Beneath them a huge Argolath city was laid out across the wide floor. Sam almost felt he was out in the open air. He couldn't work out if this cavity was natural or had been dug by the Argolaths, but he suspected the latter.

The escaped miners boarded a sort of open-topped trolley bus, held the Universe precariously over the front and drove through streets thronged with cheering Argolaths. Sam saw electric cars driving along wide roads, boats and barges purring along a canal, wide streets lined by houses and shops. This city had all the trappings of an advanced civilisation, making Sam realise how crude Entroilia had been by comparison. In the city's centre stood a large black pyramid which Sam guessed must be a temple. Nearby stood a structure in the shape of an egg, guarded by five huge Argolath statues. It closely resembled Queen Karolinda's Palace and Sam was sure it must be the Palace of the Argolath's queen.

The crowd was densest around the Palace entrance. The bus stopped outside the gate and the group marched up to the huge door, walking on four of their legs and waving their hand-like front claws at the crowd. The doors swung open and the Argolaths marched in, their heads held high.

At the end of a large hall stood a huge living Argolath. Like all the others, it resembled an ant but, in contrast to their small white bodies, this one's head and body were yellow, its little eyes were green, its long legs, mouth parts and antennae were pale brown.

From its size, manner and imperious stance, Sam guessed that this must be the Queen. As the leader approached, she said something then brought her face close and peered at the Universe, which was not much bigger than one of her eyes. It struck Sam that she was somewhat smaller and much less attractive than Queen Karolinda. Her whole body was much thinner and sleeker, more like a torpedo in contrast to Karolinda's, which was like a deep ocean liner.

The Queen made a short speech in Argolathian to the little group of escapees. They all bowed, the one who had carried the Universe bowing lowest. A servant stepped forward and handed him a large bag, giving smaller ones to all the others. Then the Queen lifted the Universe out of his jaws and held it up. The ragged group of freed slaves walked backwards out of the hall, bowing and waving and cheering. The Queen nodded and waved her antennae at them, holding the Universe high above her head and calling in a cheerful way.

When they had gone she carried the Universe across the huge main hall to a much smaller side-chamber. Tall banks of equipment with little twinkling lights lined every wall. Argolaths were sitting around a large central table staring into what looked to Sam like computer screens. When she entered, they stood and bowed. One Argolath took the Universe and carefully carried it to a cabinet where he pressed a button. A glass door opened and a metal drawer slid out. He placed the Universe into a dip in the centre of the draw and pressed the button again. The draw carried the Universe into the cabinet and the door closed behind it.

Inside the dark compartment, Sam could indistinctly see an arsenal of shiny gadgets and utensils ranged around him. Then a hundred tiny beams of light were switched on and began rapidly scanning the Universe, both the pink surface and the crystal network. Sam crouched in a corner of his crystal cave hoping to make himself unobtrusive, but when one of the lights shone upon him it paused, flickering back and forth over him, and more lights came to focus on him so that soon he was illuminated in a brilliant floodlight, but this lasted for less than a minute and the lights moved on.

He was still wondering about the implications of this when a voice spoke behind him in Entroilian. 'Welcome Samfitzpatrick!'

He spun round and saw, floating inside his crystal cell, a glowing image of the Argolath Queen not much bigger than Sam himself.

How did she get down here? How does she know my name? How can I understand her?

'I believe you speak Entroilian?'

'Yes, Your Majesty,' Sam said, thinking *So she speaks Entroilian and that's how I can understand her.*

'Ah, so you know who I am?' the Argolath said.

'I think so, Majesty. I assume you are the Queen of the Argolaths.'

'The Queen?' The Argolath said and began to make a noise which might have signified either anger or amusement. Sam was not sure which. As he watched her, mystified and a little anxious, he realised that this was not a real creature. *It's just a projection, a virtual image of some sort. These creatures certainly are very advanced.*

The Argolath gradually recovered her composure. 'No, Samfitzpatrick, I am not the queen. May I introduce myself? I am King Flenkt.'

'I'm so sorry,' Sam said, acutely embarrassed. 'I can't tell the difference between, between—'

'Between males and females,' King Flenkt said benignly. 'Never mind. Why should you? Well,' he went on, looking closely at Sam. 'I assume you are another Emergent. You will please excuse the enthusiasm of the crowds outside. Yours is the first Cosmic Egg we have ever seen in Argolathia and since it appears to be very special I think my subjects are right to be excited. Tell me, is it true that it has produced the Second Beeing?'

Sam thought fast. *Should I tell him the truth? The Universe is in his hands now. What does he expect from this prize he has stolen? Why is everyone here so excited about it? Obviously they're expecting something out of it. Well they won't get anything in its present state. He's going to have to fix it and restart time if he wants to use it in some way, and that's what I want too.*

But should I let him use it? Could he harm it? Would it be better to leave it frozen and try to get it back to Cjingha? But how could I do that? I'm just a tiny speck in their world. No, I'm here now, and I'm going to have to work with him. He's got better technology than the Entroilians had anyway, so maybe he stands more chance of fixing the Universe. If Catriona does manage to bring the crystal fragments down the tunnel, it's him or his people who will have to join them together to fix the network. He's going to need to know as much as possible. Does he even know that time has stopped in there? I'd better tell him what little I know. There's no point in lying about anything. He probably already knows the answer to the question anyway. He knows my name, after all. So what is the true answer? Has the Universe produced the Second Beeing?

'Yes, Your Majesty, I think it has,' Sam said. 'A human emerged who has been transformed into an Entroilian and now bears all the marks of the Chosen One.'

'He has large external genitalia?'

'Yes, Majesty.'

'He has King's excrement?'

'I believe so, Majesty.'

'Ha ha! Of course you wouldn't be able to recognise the smell! And he is as bright as the Szemzion on a summer's day?'

'Yes he is indeed very intelligent, Majesty. On Earth he was one of the brightest scientists. After he got here, he gained a lot more knowledge and now knows all the secrets of my Universe.'

'Wonderful.' The king brought his face closer so that Sam could see the little hairs sticking out between the crinkles of his yellow skin. Flenkt seemed to see the anxiety on Sam's face. 'May I say that you appear to have been through a traumatic ordeal. I would like to offer you a chance to rest and recuperate. Please do me the honour of being my guest.'

'Thank you, Your Majesty,' Sam said but he was thinking: *I don't have much choice, do I? I'm your prisoner anyway.*

'Also,' Flenkt went on, 'I would much appreciate it if you could indulge me with a little of your time and tell me something about your race and your home world.' He was floating nearer now and peering at Sam with his tiny bulging bright green eyes. 'I will ask my technicians to remove you from your present rather uncomfortable quarters and transport you to a more hospitable environment. I assure you that they will take very good care of your Cosmic Egg while you are away. I will see you again tomorrow, Samfitzpatrick. In the meantime have a good rest. I will send one of my daughters to look after you. Farewell!'

As the King's image rapidly faded from Sam's sight he thought, *I never had chance to tell him time's stopped. Ah well, too late now.* He stood and started peering into Catriona's crystal. He now knew exactly which one was hers. It was almost on the opposite side of the cave to where one crystal face was missing, the gap Michael Zhang had made when he broke one of the crystal pipes and caused time to stop. As soon as he got his head exactly in line with the centre of her crystal, Sam heard her calling: 'Alex! Can you hear me?' But a moment later something pushed Sam in the back. He fell over and spun round. A small, pod-shaped metal capsule had descended from the darkness, dangling on the end of a long metal stalk, and silently entered his cave through the gap. It came to rest on the floor beside him. A glass dome opened and revealed a very small, cream-coloured Argolath sitting inside, smaller even than Sam, about the size of a large dog.

'I am so sorry!' the Argolath said, speaking perfect Entroilian. 'I hope I didn't hurt you!'

Sam shook his head. He was speechless. It was obviously real, not a hologram. Sam had not seen a living creature this small since he had left the Earth.

'I am Princess Trissitia. Welcome to Argolathia, Samfitzpatrick. Please enter and I will take you to the room I have prepared for you.' One of her front legs patted the empty seat beside her.

Sam couldn't move, couldn't do anything but stare at her in amazement. Her triangular head was covered in short sparse hair. Her eyes were green, like her father's, but large and ovoid in shape. Her skin was an ocean of little ridges that ran in waves from her eyes to the two long antennae that protruded from what looked like nostrils in the middle of her face. Two massive jaws were hinged just below the eyes and hung down either side of her mouth. They too had short fine hairs. Her whole creamy body glistened with a waxy, healthy looking sheen. Her legs were so thin he could hardly believe they could take her weight. Here, at last, was another living creature that seemed as small and vulnerable as himself. He suddenly realised how much he needed a friend.

When Sam didn't move she said 'Is there something wrong, Honoured Sir?'

'I just didn't realise,' Sam spoke slowly, searching for the right words to express how deeply moved he felt, 'I didn't realise that Argolaths could be so, so beautiful.' He hadn't planned to say it. It just came out that way.

Trissitia smiled. Yes, Sam was sure she had smiled, although it wasn't a human smile. Her face didn't bend. It couldn't, it was hard and stiff, but her jaws swung up and covered her mouth, her antennae flipped back to rest against her head and their long flexible tapering ends hid themselves behind her eyes. *Yes, that's a smile.* Sam was sure of it, and suddenly he felt like hugging her.

He clambered to his feet, climbed up into the capsule and sat beside her. Trissitia pressed a button, the glass top closed and the slender metal arm lifted the capsule smoothly out of the gap in the crystal network. They rose rapidly through the cabinet. Sam was fascinated at first by the sophisticated equipment that surrounded him, all of it directed down towards the place he had just come from. Then he looked down.

This was the first time he had ever seen the Universe from the outside, a gorgeous pink ball wrapped up inside a shimmering crystal shell. He could see the thick trunks which supported the crystal network. From a distance it looked like the fruiting head of a little delicate dandelion. It was so utterly fragile that Sam felt alarmed until he thought about the hazardous journey it had taken to get here and remembered King Flenkt's assurance that the technicians would take good care of it.

They were almost at the top of the cabinet before the other thought struck him and he looked at Trissitia with a sudden feeling of panic, shouting 'Stop! Stop! I want to go back!'

'Why, Honoured Sir? What's wrong?'

'Catriona! I won't be able to help Catriona if I leave! Please, Princess, take me back.'

Episode 32 Dra-go-mir

'You're doing fine, Marianne,' the doctor said as he gently tied her onto the bed with a sheet to stop her floating away and injuring herself. 'Francesco Romani's taking us all to the Hostel but we're going to leave you here. Danny and I think that—'

'Danny?' Despite her utter fatigue, Marianne's heart was suddenly pounding with excitement. 'Is he here? Can I see him?'

There was so much to talk about. She wasn't even sure whether Danny knew she had lost the baby. She felt she would burst if she didn't see Danny soon. She had been longing for this moment for hours. Poor little Sofie had done her best but it was Danny she had really wanted to be with her. For the last few months, she had been planning how she could ensure he was there at the birth, certain that it would help to bring them closer together.

Early April was Danny's busiest time of year, getting ATLAS ready for the start-up after the winter shut-down, and she had been relieved that the baby had not arrived early. Before she started going out with him, ATLAS had been Danny's whole life and she knew it was still very important to him. He was the most senior Run Co-ordinator. For the last few weeks he had been working fourteen hour shifts seven days a week and she had hardly seen him except over breakfast. This morning he had looked really tired. Now that ATLAS had been destroyed and his son had died, she was really not sure what mental state she would find him in.

'He's just outside,' Jean-Pierre said. 'I'll send him in.' He flew to the door and she heard him say 'Okay, Mr Schneider, you can go in now. Please don't tire her. She's still very weak.'

As soon as she saw him she knew Danny was going through some sort of breakdown. His eyes were dull and lifeless as if he was half asleep. He did not smile or show any sort of emotion. He didn't even look at her face, just hovered before her, staring unblinkingly at her flat abdomen. That was upsetting enough, but the thing which really worried her was his nose.

There was a secret about Danny which always warned her when he was angry: the tip of his nose would go white. She had seen it a few times and knew that it meant danger. Danny was normally calm but sometimes he would lose his temper, shouting and swearing like a different person. It frightened her when he was in those strange moods. She could see the violence inside him and sometimes she was even afraid he might hit her, although so far he never had. But she was certain he was in one of those moods now, for not just the tip but the whole bottom half of his nose was as white as the sheet which his empty eyes were staring at.

He didn't speak. He didn't need to. The pain which was written in every line of his face instantly made her feel guilty. *If I had not lost the baby then he would not be in such a bad state,* she told herself. *Losing ATLAS was enough pain for him, but I have made it worse by failing to deliver our son alive.* At that moment, in spite of her fear, she felt more tenderness for him than she had ever felt before. It seemed to her that somehow he was the baby and she was his mother. *He needs me, needs me just as I need him.*

'Come here mon chou,' she whispered, reaching over the sheet and pulling him to her. His rigid body moved closer like a piece of driftwood floating in an ocean of misery. Tenderly she stroked his cheek but his jaw muscles clench beneath her fingers and still he spoke not a word.

Desperate for some sign of forgiveness, she wrapped her arms around his neck and squeezed him feebly. At last he responded. She felt his trembling hands move slowly down her body. When he touched her flat abdomen, the flatness where the baby should have been, she found, to her own surprise, that her body did not recoil from his touch as it usually did. What happened next astonished her even more. His shoulders began to quiver.

He's crying! she thought.

This was utterly out of character. Danny hardly ever showed any emotion and certainly not grief. She made soothing noises in his ear, trying to comfort him, stroking his hair, telling him it was going to be okay, hardly able to stop herself from crying, she was so moved by this unexpected demonstration of tenderness.

Why did he never show me this side of himself before? she wondered as she wrapped her arms around him. He did not pull away. The pulses of his grief built to a climax then slowly subsided. She felt they were closer at that moment than they had ever been before.

'I'm so sorry, Marianne,' he stammered at last.

'Sorry? Why are you sorry, mon chou? It wasn't your fault.'

'Wasn't it? I let Romani and Zhang persuade me to leave ATLAS running. Don't you remember? Zhang said that this one experiment alone would be worth the entire cost of ATLAS and Romani agreed. Don't you remember? But he left the final decision to me, so in the end all this is my responsibility. If I hadn't agreed to leave it running, the black hole would never have come out of ATLAS, or at least not at the time it did, and Dragomir might still be alive.'

'Dragomir?' Marianne stopped stroking his hair. 'Who's...' Suddenly she realised who he meant. 'Dra-go-mir?' she said slowly. 'You were going to call him Dragomir?'

Danny nodded. 'After my grandfather.'

In spite of everything, or perhaps because of all the terrible things that had happened, she found this ridiculous name funny, and the more she thought about it the funnier it seemed. *Did he really think I would ever call my baby Dragomir? Yes, I told him to choose the name, but I never dreamed he would choose one like that!*

Once more she wrapped her arms round his neck and hugged him. 'Only you could give such a name to a baby, chou.' She felt like giggling but tried to hold it in. *Danny hasn't got much sense of humour at the best of times and now's not the time for laughter.* But the more she tried, the more it welled up inside her. She wasn't sure if she wanted to laugh or to cry, but whatever it was, the emotion was overwhelming, and finally her shoulders began to shake.

'Don't cry, Marianne,' he said.

That was it. She was off. Her giggle burst out into a laugh. 'Oh Danny, my poor sweet chou.'

He pulled back and stared her full in the face. 'Is it funny?' he sounded appalled. She could see him breathing deeply, obviously trying to stay calm. 'It was grandfather's name. It means precious and peaceful in Bulgarian.'

She could tell it meant a lot to him. 'It's a lovely name,' she said, laughing with her old laugh, tinkling, relaxed now. She was sure that everything was going to be all right. 'Don't worry darling. We'll have another Dragomir soon.'

'No! There was only one Drago, Marianne, and Michael Zhang has killed him.'

The laughter died in her heart. The tone of his voice was deadly serious.

'But Professor Romani said it was okay too. It's their fault, not yours, chou.'

'It's my fault that the black hole came out when it did, but it's Zhang's fault that it was made in the first place. This whole thing is Michael Zhang's fault.' His voice sounded thick. 'He knew that a cosmic monopole had got trapped in the beam pipe. He knew it could turn into a black hole. He must have known it from the beginning. But did he warn us or try to stop it? No! Instead he tricked me into wasting time going down to fix a fault, a fault which did not exist. He knew perfectly well there was no fault with ATLAS but he put on an elaborate charade. And he persuaded me to leave the beams intersecting while we investigated the so-called problem. Why did he do that? I'll tell you why. I've been thinking about it very hard and there's only one possible explanation.'

Marianne didn't even recognise Danny's voice any more. It was dark and full of bitterness, almost of hatred.

'He did it because he wanted to make sure that the monopole would be given time to grow into a black hole.'

Marianne felt an icy finger of fear run down her whole body. 'No, you can't be sure that he meant to—'

'Oh I'm sure Marianne. There can be no doubt. While we were coming down in the lift I actually suggested to him that this might be a black hole. Can you believe it? But that was the only thing I could think of that could cause the huge numbers of missing energy events we were getting in ATLAS. You know what he said? That the most likely explanation was a fault, a fault! With ATLAS! But he had already seen the cosmic monopole's track! Karolyi told us that. Yet he didn't say a word about it. Not one word! In fact he said that any black hole would evaporate by Hawking radiation! So naturally I dismissed the whole idea as impossible. After all, he was the scientist, not me. I'm just an engineer. But he knew what was going to happen, Marianne. You heard him tell us about Wells and Watts' prediction that a stable black hole could form on a cosmic monopole. He was hoping all along that would happen, and he must have been afraid that I would turn off the beams and stop it. That was why he pretended there was a fault. It was delaying tactics. Zhang deliberately engineered that black hole, Marianne. It didn't just happen by accident. And even then, when we knew that the black hole was there, I let him persuade me to keep ATLAS running. That was my biggest mistake.'

'But chou, even if you'd switched ATLAS off sooner you still wouldn't have—'

'If I'd switched the magnets off then the black hole would not have come out of ATLAS. It would have stayed inside. Things would have been totally different. This crystal might never have been created and, even if it was, Drago wouldn't have been hit. He'd still be alive now. I could have saved him, Marianne.'

'I've told you mon petit chou, we'll have another—'

'I have no doubt that Michael Zhang was responsible for this disaster, Marianne, and the direct cause of Dragomir's death.' Danny was getting angrier with every word. 'He ruined ATLAS, he killed my son and he's put the whole world at risk. And why? I'll tell you why. For his own ego, that's why! So that he could be the first to investigate a persistent black hole.' He paused and stared at Marianne. 'D'you know what? It's a good job for him that the black hole did absorb him because if he was still alive now I would kill him. He deserves to die.'

Marianne looked at him, unable to speak. *He's like a stranger. Mon pauvre chou. He's not rational any more.*

She tried to hug him but he pushed her arms under the blanket.

'You must rest now, Marianne. Did the doctor tell you we're going to leave you without a crystal so if you have an infection it won't get any worse?'

She nodded, unable to speak.

'We're all going to the Cafeteria. Professor Romani wants me to help him do some experiments on crystal. I'll come back as soon as I can.' He kissed her briefly and flew out of the room.

'Danny, would it be all right if I go in and...' Sofie said but Danny flew past without even looking at her, his face contorted with some inner pain. She flew into the Emergency Room, full of concern. *Is Marianne all right?* Sofie hadn't seen her since she had helped Jean-Pierre clean her up when they first brought her into the Medical Centre.

There was a look of anguish on Marianne's face which changed to joy when she saw Sofie. She reached out and put her arms round her neck, giving her a feeble hug.

'How are you Marianne?' Sofie tried not to sound worried but Marianne still looked terrible. Her face was pale and there were large dark patches under her eyes. In the light from Sofie's crystal it was hard to tell, but she thought her skin looked slightly yellow.

'I'm all right,' Marianne said shaking her head, but Sofie knew she wasn't. 'What's happened to my baby?'

'He's in the helicopter. It hadn't actually landed when the disaster happened, Marianne. I'm so sorry. The radio message was wrong. It took me ages to find—'

'I'm glad he's dead, Sofie,' Marianne said. She must have seen how shocked Sofie was because she said 'It's the sadness of being a woman, Sofie. If he'd lived he would have been premature. I don't think he would have survived very long. He would have needed intensive care and that's just not available here. I think it's all turned out for the best. In a way he has saved us all, hasn't he? I mean, if the crystal hadn't hit him then none of us would be alive now. I keep thinking about that, Sofie. I keep thinking…I think he gave his life to save us, Sofie. I know that's silly but I can't help it and it makes me feel better about everything.'

Sofie nodded. 'That's…That's a really beautiful idea, Marianne. It must be some comfort for you and Danny. Anyway I just came in to say goodbye. Most of us are going to the Cafeteria and—'

'I'm coming with you,' Marianne said.

Sofie looked at her. 'Are you? The doctor didn't say—'

'Jean-Pierre doesn't know yet. I've only just decided.'

'Are you well enough, Marianne?'

'I will be when the antibiotics get a chance to work. Being here frozen isn't actually helping me to get better.'

'But the doctor thinks—' Sofie said but Marianne cut her short.

'And I want to be with Danny. There's something worrying him. He seems to have had…He's acting very strangely.'

So I wasn't mistaken. Sofie had never met Danny Schneider before but he struck her as odd, preoccupied about something, even slightly unbalanced.

'He said…,' Marianne hesitated. 'He thinks Michael Zhang killed the baby.'

'But that's ridiculous,' Sofie said.

'I know. He said that if Michael was still alive he'd kill him.'

'He's just upset, Marianne. People say strange things when—'

'But he meant it, Sofie. I've never seen him like this before. I want to be with him. He needs me.'

'Okay. Shall I go and tell Jean-Pierre? There might be a problem with crystal. We haven't got any spares. Only, only the big one.' She explained about how two crystals had fused to make a larger one with a bigger bubble. 'I'll ask Professor Romani if you can use that if you like. He and Danny and the Irish Ambassador are going to the Cafeteria and I'm going with Jean-Pierre to do some tests with latrines. It's amazing what firefighters in CERN have to do!'

'I'm going to need some clothes Sofie.'

Sofie nodded, looking at the hospital gown Marianne was wearing. 'Of course. I'll fetch you my spare uniform from the Fire Station. I need to go there anyway to get a shovel.'

'God bless you Sofie. I think I'd be dead now if you hadn't helped me with the baby. Give me a kiss before you go.'

Sofie flew to the Fire Station just up the road from the Medical Centre. She had collected two shovels and was taking her spare uniform out of her locker in the garage when Ludovico Narkosa flew past, carrying a huge flag. 'I borrow this from the visitor car park,' he said and led her into the kitchen at the end of the garage where George Gabor was trying unsuccessfully to make coffee. She told him what everyone was doing and mentioned Francesco's meeting at nine. They all checked their watches then flew to the top of the climbing tower, where George had laid out the body of Robert Moore with as much dignity as possible.

They draped the British flag over him, George said some solemn words, and made sure Sofie understood how and why he had died. Then they flew back down to the kitchen.

'You going do some gardening, Sofie?' Ludovico said looking at her shovels.

'The doctor and I are going to do some experiments on latrines,' she said.

'Experiments?' Ludovico burst out laughing. 'On latrina? What, you want see how far you can both piss? I volunteer to take the measurement when is your turn, Sofie.'

She ignored him, but George gave him a disapproving look.

'Just keep your fantasies to yourself, Ludo, old chap,' he said. 'Let's go and find out what Romani wants us to do next.'

They flew to the Medical Centre and Sofie took the uniform to Marianne. The doctor was trying unsuccessfully to persuade her to stay where she was.

'No, Jean-Pierre,' Marianne insisted. 'I've got to be with Danny. I think he's had some sort of breakdown. He needs me.'

'But I'll keep my eye on him, Marianne,' the doctor said. 'I think the best way you can help is to get better.'

'But I won't get better frozen in time! I want to give the antibiotics a chance to work. And Danny needs me, Jean-Pierre. I'm going with him. Is that my uniform, Sofie? Ugh, grey!'

They helped her dress, then went to find Francesco. They found him out in the car park, talking to George. Sofie explained the situation and asked if Marianne could borrow a crystal.

'But the only spare I have is the large one,' Francesco huffed. 'I need that for the experiments.'

'Don't worry Professor Romani,' the doctor said. 'Once we get to the Hostel I will try to persuade her to stay frozen. If we put her up on the top floor, she will be out of the way of any bubbles. But at the moment she's determined to go with us and I really don't think we can refuse her. It could be very damaging for her health to leave her here against her will.'

Francesco nodded and gave Sofie the double-sized fragment. She took it back to Marianne and taught her to fly, first inside the Medical Centre and then out in the road.

'This is beautiful, Sofie,' Marianne said, a little colour returning to her cheeks. 'It's like when you dream of flying only a million times better. I love it. I don't even mind that horrible bubble anymore.'

A few minutes later Francesco found them and led Marianne and the rest of his party down the Route Einstein towards the Cafeteria, leaving Sofie with the doctor each holding a shovel as they hovered outside the Medical Centre.

'If everyone's going to the Cafeteria,' Jean-Pierre said, 'then that's obviously going to be where we'll have to put the latrines. We'll need two, of course, one for each sex. Are there any open spaces near there?'

'Yes, there's a big grassy area outside, just beyond the terrace, but don't you think perhaps we ought to try it out somewhere else first? I don't want people flying around me while I'm, well, you know, having a go. There are vineyards that way,' Sofie said pointing down the side of the Medical Centre, 'but I don't think they'll be much good.'

'No,' Jean-Pierre agreed. 'Too many sticks and wires. Any flat fields around here?'

'Ummm, well there's a golf course but it's some distance away. The nearest farm fields are over that way.' She pointed across the Route Einstein.

'Okay, let's go there first.'

Episode 33 Garage

Alex flew over the swimming pool, through a gap in the hedge surrounding the Sports Centre, across a car park and was just flying round to the front of the BP garage[7] when his bubble exploded. One moment he was flying along in a normal-sized bubble hardly any bigger than himself. The next he was floating inside what seemed, by comparison, to be a huge open space.

He stopped near the petrol pumps in the forecourt and surveyed the bubble, trying to work out why it had suddenly grown so big. When he stopped the usual thing happened: the regular pattern of moving red and green rings was replaced by the randomly drifting red, green and black blotches. It had the glossy sheen of oil floating on water combined with the dynamic iridescence of a soap bubble. He understood well why Marianne had called it a "bubble".

It seemed vast, reaching all the way to the shop-windows where it traced out a large circle on the glass. There was another circle above him, where the bubble intersected with the white flaking underside of the roof overhanging the petrol pumps. The largest circle was below him, where the grey concrete floor intruded into the bubble.

This was the first time he had been in such a large open space for hours and he felt liberated. In celebration he took the vodka bottle from his pocket, unscrewed the stopper, pushed a straw inside and drank greedily, hovering above a petrol pump. Then he brought the crystal he had been using to fly close to his eye, searching for signs of change.

Can't see anything special about you baby.

---

[7] Since Crystal Day, this shop has closed.

He looked around, searching for an explanation of why the bubble had suddenly grown bigger.

Could it be something to do with the gasoline in these pumps? Some sort of chemical reaction?

He flew away from the shop but the bubble didn't go back to its previous size. With his eyes spinning from too much vodka, his mind overwhelmed by too many questions and his stomach rumbling from too little food, he put aside the mystery of the big bubble, flew past the forecourt to the store and pushed open the door.

Wiper blades, headlamps, fuses and batteries hung from the side wall of the shop. He flew as far as the back wall, searching for water, without meeting anyone. Bottles of oil, antifreeze and screen-cleaning sprays stood on shelves along with a collection of pastel-coloured towels on special offer. He flew deeper into the shop, grateful it wasn't busy, and a tall chiller came into view. Through the glass door he could see shelves full of food and drink. He flew to it and yanked open the door. He reached in and pulled out a portion of Gâteau à la Carotte and another of Gâteau Maison Exotique. They felt cold as he wolfed them up, swilling them down with a bottle of chilled orange juice and another of mineral water, squeezing the plastic so the liquids squirted into his mouth. The spinning of the world before his eyes slowed to a gentle drift.

He found some plastic bags which he filled with bottles of juice and water, bars of chocolate and food from the fridge until he thought he wouldn't be able to carry any more. His hunger satisfied, he began to relax. He polished off the last of the vodka and checked his watch.

Eighteen twenty-four. Wonder what time I came out of ATLAS? Not even an hour ago I guess. Wonder if I can still see Kata in any of these crystals?

He took all the crystals out of his pockets and immediately solved the mystery of the big bubble while discovering another conundrum. He had six crystals, five normal ones each with four faces and one large one with six. He looked at it in some surprise.

Where'd you come from? How come you've got six sides?

It didn't take him too long to work out that two of the smaller crystals must have stuck together while they were jiggling about in his pocket.

Is it you this big bubble's coming from?

He waved the double crystal around and coloured patterns began to flow up the bubble. Its circle of intersection began dancing around on the shop's far wall but stopped when he held the crystal still.

'Well done Karolyi!' he said aloud. 'Solved one mystery at any rate.'

He looked at the crystal again, still puzzled. Like the others it shone with its own inner light, although this was a little brighter than the rest, but what he saw inside it was very different. The complete confusion of images caused by internal reflection within the little tetrahedrons had been replaced, at least in part, by a view of the objects on the crystal's far side, as if light was now travelling straight through. But what really surprised him was that there did not seem to be any mark across the centre where, he was certain, two smaller crystals must have joined together.

Wonder if I can see little Kata, or perhaps even Marianne?

He brought it close to his eye, squinting in the blue light, and began to search in each face. In the first, all he could see was the shop's floor. In the second he could see the refrigerator but as he searched in the third face, looking not straight into it but at an angle, he was almost blinded by some spots of bright blue light.

He blinked then squinted at them trying to work out where these lights were coming from. There were five of them, brilliant and tiny, arranged almost in a circle. He moved the big crystal away and looked at the five little ones floating before him. They too were in a circle, but when seen directly they looked normal, glowing faintly.

So, looking through one crystal makes the others seem brighter.

He found the same effect when looking through one of the smaller crystals. He had to hold it at just the right angle and look in exactly the right place, down near one corner.

Okay, another freaking mystery.

He arranged his crystal collection neatly before him like a celebrity line-up, six blue cherries in a row, each glowing with its own inner light. Still hoping to see Marianne, he picked one at random and held it close to his eye, squinting slightly and peering inside it. He saw the left side of his own face. He turned to the left and what he saw only half surprised him. Another crystal was floating there. He reached out and moved it closer, then checked in the first crystal. Sure enough, his face looked closer.

These things are connected together like little mobile phones but without batteries! So that's how I saw out of Kata's crystal when she was flying towards the floor.

He stared at his little crystal collection.

These blue cherries must be incredibly valuable, even just for that ability alone, let alone the fact that they give you life. Shit, you little babies must be worth a stack of cash! So which crystal did I see Kata in? They all look the same to me.

He took another drink of water and began to look into each crystal in turn, holding it close, slowly moving it, searching for Catriona but hoping to see Marianne's face floating inside. It was while he was looking through the fourth one that he finally saw the Irish girl.

She was standing before a roaring fire with her blouse undone and a man in a brown hooded cloak standing behind her. He looked really weird, with a long beaked mask over his face.

Wow, that looks like one groovy party, Alex thought, holding the crystal closer to get a better look. *The little minx. And her boobs look bigger than I remember. Where is she? Wouldn't mind joining in.* 'Kata!' he called. 'Where the hell are you?'

Her face came towards him. 'I've come down the tunnel Alex, but it's vanished now and I'm stuck. You've got to come down and help me!' The man in brown began waving his hand and shouting.

'What do you mean Kata, vanished?' Alex said, but before she could respond there was a blurred rapid movement, he glimpsed a dimly lit wooden hovel spinning around him, then the flames of a fire leaping up and suddenly a blinding blue light shone out of the crystal in his hand. He yanked it away from his face and clamped one hand over his eye, the spot of blue light still burning in his retina.

The man in brown snatched up a metal rod and began poking about among the logs in the fire. He must have found the crystal because he lunged the poker and something flew up out of the fire in a shower of sparks. It bounced off the bottom of the big iron pan then rolled away, leaving a smoking trail across the straw-scattered floor before disappearing under the table. He threw down the poker and dived after it.

'Where did you get that stone?' a muffled voice said in English behind Catriona. She turned to see the man in grey standing in the shadow by the wall, his long bird-like mask pointing at her.

'Give me my crystal back.' Catriona shouted. She was relieved to find somebody who spoke English but still deeply uneasy about what she was seeing. *Is this really some sort of strange*

Protestant Easter Carnival? she wondered. *I've never heard about it.* 'Let me out!' she shouted at the man in grey. 'You have no right to keep me here. Open the door.'

He shook his head. 'It is the edict of the Council of Two Hundred that anyone who enters this hospital shall not leave until either dead or declared clear of the peste. You will have to be examined by Monsieur le Maître d'Hôpital.' He gestured towards the man in brown who was lying on the floor examining the crystal he held in his leather-gloved hand. It was still glowing blue in the darkened room. She was very relieved to see it didn't seem to have been damaged by the fire. *I'll need that to escape.*

'Take your clothes off child,' the man in grey said. 'Le Maître will need to examine you.'

Catriona looked at him in alarm. 'Is he the doctor?'

'Doctor? No. He and his wife treat all the pestiférés here. Take off your clothes my dear. You will not get out of here until you do. They have to know if you are clear.'

'Clear? Clear of what?'

'Of the peste of course. This is l'Hôpital de la Peste.'

'Pest? What's a pest? I never heard of it.'

'You must have heard of the peste. Everybody has. I know they have it in England too. What do you call it there? Ah yes. The Black Death.' His tone was nonchalant as if he was talking about influenza, but a chill ran through Catriona.

The black death? This is a hospital for the black death? No, no no, it can't be. This is Switzerland. This must be just one of their carnival games.

There was a metallic clang behind her and Catriona spun round. The woman had thrown the knife onto the ground and was hobbling back to her chair. The naked boy on the table had stopped groaning and was lying still.

'Is he all right?' Catriona whispered.

'I'm sorry, no.' the man in grey said. 'He's dead. Was he your brother?'

'No, I don't know him. I only just met him.' She turned to look again at the man in brown. He was sitting on the floor now. He had taken off his mask and was holding the crystal in both hands, staring at it in wonder. Its blue light shone on his grizzled hair, his mean eyes, his hard thin lips. When he saw her watching him, a cunning smile crossed his face.

'My advice to you is to show yourself and get out of here as soon as you can,' the man in grey said. 'I am a friar so you need feel no embarrassment in exposing yourself before me. Things of the flesh mean nothing to Franciscans.'

'You're a Catholic?'

'Yes my child. The pastors of the Reformation are unwilling to minister to the patients in this hospital for some reason, so they kindly allow me to remain here while most others of my faith are banished from the city. I assume you are a Huguenot?'

'No, no I'm a Catholic too, Father,' Catriona said.

'So you must have been driven out of England by Henry Tudor? It is truly terrible what he is doing there to the Mother Church.'

'Henry Tudor? Who's Henry Tudor?'

'He's the King, my child. Surely you must know that.'

'King? Do you mean Henry the Eighth?'

'Yes of course.'

Catriona thought he was joking at first, but as she looked at his mask, at the naked boy dead on the kitchen table, as she remembered the condition of the town she had come through, a horrible truth began to dawn upon her.

'What year is this Father?' she said, half dreading the answer.

'That is a strange question my child. It is the year of our Lord fifteen hundred and thirty-six.'

As if a light had been switched on inside her head, Catriona suddenly understood everything.

1536! This is 1536! I must have gone back in time when I came down that tunnel! Suddenly it all made sense. *And why not? Everything else has gone crazy, so why shouldn't you go back in time? But why would Sam and Michael go back to 1536? No, wait a minute!* Another realization suddenly swept over her and this one made her heart sink. *They're not here, are they? Sam said this wasn't the bottom of the tunnel. I've still got to get back into it and go down even further. Does that mean I'll be going back further in time? Anyway I've got to get out of this mad place as soon as possible. I need my crystal.* She looked at the hospital master. He was standing beside the woman now, showing her the crystal.

'Will he let me out of here if I take my clothes off?' she asked the friar.

'Yes, certainly, as long as your body is free from any signs of the disease.'

Catriona knew she had no choice. She quickly stripped off her clothes, hanging them on the back of the chair beside the fire. The three of them watched her, making sounds of astonishment when they saw her underwear. Finally she stood naked before them, staring at the hospital master defiantly. He handed the crystal to the woman, put his mask back on and made a sign for Catriona to lift her arms, then peered at her armpits and neck. He knelt before her, his mask close to her crotch. Catriona trembled with humiliation and indignation, glad that his ugly face was hidden from view.

Finally he stood and said something to the woman. She gave him the crystal, lifted Catriona's clothes and began to throw them into the pot over the fire.

Catriona screamed and stepped forward trying to stop her but the hospital master grabbed her wrist with his free hand.

She spun round and looked at the friar. 'Can't I go now?'

'No, child. They say you have marks which could be the peste.'

'But that's ridiculous! I've only just got here. I've never seen anyone with the disease before. I can't possibly have it.'

'I'm sorry. They say you might have and will have to stay for a week to see whether it develops. The Maître d'Hôpital will look after your crystal until...'

'He can't. I need it. He must give it back. There's no way he can have it! It's very precious and it isn't mine anyway. I'm just looking after it for somebody. Please, this is crazy. Please tell him to let me go. I haven't got any diseases. He's just saying that so he can keep my crystal. This isn't right.'

'I'm sorry.'

'Oh Father I can't stay here.'

'It is out of my hands, child. There's nothing I can do.'

Catriona stared at him, trying not to cry. 'Can you pray for me?'

Sofie led Jean-Pierre over the pedestrian crossing up the little Route Balmer to the Route de Meyrin. They crossed the main road at the customs post between Switzerland and France and turned right, looking for the lane that ran up past the Sports Centre. They were flying over the BP garage when they entered the top of a large bubble.

'Where's this bubble coming from?' Jean-Pierre said.

'I suppose there must be another big crystal down there, doctor,' Sofie said, thinking *I wonder if it could be the dreaded Karolyi?*

They flew under the overhanging forecourt roof to the front of the shop. Through the large window they could see the back of a man's bright yellow shirt. Floating in the air before him were half a dozen crystals. *So George was right about him!* Sofie thought. 'It's Alex Karolyi!' she said.

'Ah yes,' Jean-Pierre said, 'the notorious crystal thief! I already met him in the helicopter when he kindly lent me his crystal. I'm sure he's not really as bad as George and Danny make out. Looks like he's fused some crystals together. I think he's got a little collection of them. They will be very useful. Let's go and pay him a little visit, shall we?' He pushed open the door and Sofie heard Alex say 'What do you mean Kata, vanished?' then he gave a startled cry of pain and clamped one hand over his eye.

Jean-Pierre flew towards him, saying: 'Who are you talking to Mr Karolyi?' Sofie could not see anyone else in the shop.

Alex spun round. He seemed to be winking at Jean-Pierre. 'Why hello, Doctor!' he said with a warm smile as he casually glanced at his hoard of crystals with one eye and scooped them together.

'Where did you get all those crystals, Mr Karolyi?' Sofie said.

'Ah Sofia!' Alex said, rubbing his cheek with one hand as he shoved the crystals into his trouser pocket with the other. 'How lovely to see you again my dear. I have such fond memories of our last meeting.'

'You stole those crystals didn't you, Karolyi?' she said. 'I think George and Professor Romani would like to see you.'

'Have you managed to join two of them together?' Jean-Pierre said flying towards Alex.

'Yes, doctor. George knows all about them. As a matter of fact I was just about to take them to him. Do you know where he is?'

'I think it would be safer if we took them for you,' Sofie said.

'You don't trust me?' Alex said. 'I'm so hurt, Sofia darling.'

'My name is Sofie and I am definitely not—'

'I don't think Alex is going to steal those crystals Sofie,' Jean-Pierre said. 'He knows this is an emergency. People tend to rally round at times like this and help each other.'

'Most people would, doctor, but you don't know Karolyi's reputation.'

'Well that's a little unkind, my dear,' Alex said as he reached for four bulging plastic bags which floated near him. 'I've a good mind not to tell you about the other crystals now.'

'Other crystals?' Sofie said. 'What other crystals?'

'The ones I just left in the Sports Centre Restaurant.'

'Is that where the Ambassador's daughter is?' Jean-Pierre said.

'Kata? Ah, yes, that's where she is. She was, she was tired so I left her there while I came over here to collect these.' He hooked the carrier-bags over his arms. 'It's water and stuff like that. She was asking for it. So where's Gábor now? I'll just take these crystals over to him.'

Sofie and Jean-Pierre looked at each other. There was a smile in the doctor's eyes that said "I think we can trust him."

Sofie sighed. 'He's gone with Professor Romani and everyone else to the Cafeteria.'

'Oh yes, which one?'

'The Cafeteria in the main building, near the hostels.'

'Okay,' Alex said as he flew towards the door, his carrier-bags dangling from his elbows and wobbling at his sides. 'I'll take this stuff over there right away if you want to go and collect little Kata and the other crystals from the Sports Centre, Sweetie. She must have about a hundred.'

'Marvellous!' said Jean-Pierre. 'All right, we can certainly do that.'

Sofie sighed again. 'I suppose there isn't time to argue. We'll talk about it at the meeting.'

'Meeting? What meeting's that?'

'Francesco Romani's called a meeting in the Cafeteria at nine. Everyone else has gone over there.'

'So Romani's been revived too huh?' Alex flew past them towards the door. 'That's good. Okay, so I'll see you both over there at nine?'

'Wait, Karolyi,' Sofie said. 'You haven't synchronised your...' But he was gone.

Episode 34 First Night

'Catriona?' the little Argolath princess said. 'Is this a friend of yours, Honoured Sir?'

'She's my stepdaughter. She's on a very difficult mission and I have to help her. Please, take me back.'

'Your stepdaughter?' Trissitia sounded mystified. 'Please don't worry, Samfitzpatrick,' she continued, her tone somewhat colder than before. 'The Cosmic Egg and all it contains are perfectly safe.' But even her charming Argolathian accent did little to dispel Sam's profound worries.

How's Catty going to cope on her own? Sam thought as his balding head pressed longingly against the glass cover of the capsule, watching the network of crystal pipes, which for so long had been his home, dwindle away to a faint blue haze surrounding the pink Universe. Resting on the bottom of the huge dark cabinet, surrounded by a vast array of metallic arms and probes all pointing towards it, it looked like a tiny fragile egg waiting to be broken open and dissected, alone and vulnerable.

The last thing I heard her say was 'Alex! Can you hear me?' So has Alex gone down the tunnel too? I wish I knew what was happening down there. Still I suppose it's too late now, he thought as the egg disappeared from his sight. *King Flenkt wants me out of there and that's that.*

Looking around, he saw that the arm which had raised the capsule had now lowered it onto a platform near the top of the cabinet. Standing before him was what looked like a small bee. Sam was astonished.

What's that doing here? I thought Entroilians and Argolaths were enemies!

It was the tiniest Entroilian he had ever seen, not much bigger than the capsule he was sitting in. There were neither guards nor evidence of any restraints to stop it flying away, yet the Entroilian was patiently waiting.

Trissitia pressed a button, the capsule's glass top opened and she hopped out onto the platform. Feeling rather dizzy from the huge gap yawning below him, Sam followed her as she hurried across to the Entroilian. When she approached it, Sam was startled to see its middle section split open to reveal a hollow space inside.

It's not real, he thought. *It must be a machine built in the shape of an Entroilian!*

She climbed in and Sam followed. Two seats faced a joystick and a panel with controls and dials at the front. He took a seat beside her, the body closed over them and he looked out through the transparent head. Trissitia pulled the joystick and with a steady hum the bee lifted gently off the platform and flew out of the cabinet through a small opening into the side-room of the Palace. Banks of equipment surrounded a central table where Argolath technicians were busy at computer screens. Compared to them, the Entroilian-flier was tiny, no bigger than a bee on Earth compared to a cow or a buffalo. They did not seem to notice it as Trissitia flew rapidly out of the room.

She crossed the Palace Hall and flew into a side-tunnel, keeping close to the ceiling to avoid the huge Argolaths which were running about on the floor below.

'I am very honoured that my father has asked me to look after you, Samfitzpatrick,' she said. 'I have prepared everything you will need for a complete rest. You must be very tired.'

Sam did indeed feel completely exhausted. Just to sit in this soft comfortable seat felt like utter luxury after days of lying on hard slippery crystal. He could feel the tension and nervous energy begin to drain out of him, leaving him feeling limp. All he wanted was a hot bath, a good meal and a warm bed.

After passing through several tunnel junctions and a number of automatic doors, they flew into an oval room which seemed small compared to the Palace rooms they had just flown through. The Entroilian-flier landed beside a pool covered with steaming soap bubbles, its body opened and Sam followed Trissitia out to stand and look around in utter amazement.

This is like a luxury hotel apartment! he thought.

Cupboards and mirrors lined the walls. Thick brown carpet covered the floor. The domed ceiling glowed pale cream from concealed lights. At one end stood a table full of food and there was a huge bed at the other. Sam could hardly believe his good fortune and immediately began to feel guilty.

The Universe is frozen in time, he thought. *Catriona is somewhere down the tunnel calling for Alex and here I am about to have a hot bath!*

'Please take off your clothes, Honoured Sir,' Trissitia said, 'and I will bathe you. Then you can eat. Or would you like to mate with me first?'

Sam was stunned and stared at her in silence, hoping that she was joking.

'I can't wait to find out if you are built the same as the Son of Beeing!' She sounded excited and began to pull at Sam's clothes, obviously not sure how to get them off.

He stepped quickly away, tearing his jacket out of her grip, saying 'Er, I think I can manage on my own, thank you Trissitia.'

'Do you not find me attractive, Honoured Sir?' She sounded hurt and her words only made Sam even more uncomfortable.

'Yes, of course I do,' he said, and it was true. She was not only a delightful little creature, sensitive and intelligent, but she was also the only being he had met in this whole crazy world who was about his own size, the only one who seemed to want to care for him, and he felt he could not afford to lose her. *Without her help how am I ever going to get back into the Universe?* 'It's just that I'm very tired,' he said. 'I'd rather just bathe now and sleep. But thanks all the same.'

'Very well, Honoured Sir, then I will bid you a good night's sleep.' He was not sure whether her tone was hurt or not. She went back to the flier, waved, called 'See you tomorrow,' and flew out of the room.

She doesn't seem upset. God, what am I going to do if she asks me again tomorrow? Still, I'll face that when it comes.

He stripped off his clothes and took a long delicious bath. He found some clean clothes in a closet and put them on, then sat and ate some of the food which, although not as delicious as Entroilian honey, certainly made a pleasant change. Most of it had the texture of mango, the colour of avocado and the taste of hazelnut.

He also found a hole in the ground which he used as a toilet, hoping that was what it was intended for, then he climbed into the bed and soon fell into a restless sleep troubled by dreams of ants crawling down tunnels to palaces full of bees flying through blue crystals into holes in broad pink oceans.

'Would you like breakfast, Honoured Guest?'

Even as Sam's dreams slipped away he knew there was something strange about the way Trissitia was talking. It took him a few seconds to realise that she was not speaking Entroilian anymore, and she was certainly not speaking English.

So what language is that? And how come I can understand it?

As he emerged more fully from sleep he realised that her speech was full of the same kind of clicks and pings and little grating vibrations that he had heard when Argolaths spoke to each other, the only difference now was that he could understand every word.

But how?

'Er, good morning, Princess Trissitia,' Sam found that he too could speak this strange language without effort. He knew immediately what had happened. 'I guess I've learned your language just by eating your food last night. Is that right?'

In response she crossed her antennae over her head, a gesture which Sam guessed meant "Yes".

'That's the same way I learned Entroilian,' he went on. 'I really wish it was as easy as this to learn languages at home.'

'Yes, it is very convenient. Here, eat a few more of my words.' She placed a tray of food on a bedside table. 'And you'll learn a lot more this evening. My honoured father the King has asked for the pleasure of your company at dinner. In the meantime, I am entirely at your disposal.' Her antennae folded back behind her eyes and fluttered alluringly. 'Would you like me to come to bed with you now?'

'No! No thank you, that won't be necessary.' He grabbed handfuls of the food and began to cram it into his mouth, wondering whether Argolath males died after mating the same way that Entroilians did.

Trissitia's antennae dropped to hang lifelessly at the sides of her face. 'You don't like me, do you, Honoured Sir? I will ask my father the King to send one of his other daughters to you.' She turned and ran across the floor towards the Entroilian-flier.

'No no, Trissitia, please come back.' Pieces of food sprayed out of his mouth across the bed.

She stopped, turned and looked at him.

'It's just that, well, we do things differently where I come from,' Sam stuttered. 'It is very bad manners to go to bed with the daughter of your host, especially on the first night. Please, don't leave me. You're my only friend here.'

Her antennae immediately picked up. 'Do you really think of me as your friend, Honoured Sir? I am so proud. I am so flattered. Oh thank you.' She ran back to the bed, sat on the edge and began brushing away the crumbs. 'Please finish your breakfast. Try the drink. It's delicious.'

Sam resumed eating, concentrating on the food in an attempt to take his mind off Trissitia, whose antennae had begun to stroke the bald top of his head. The food of breakfast had much the same texture as the night before, soft and chewy, but this time it tasted more like almonds and carrots. It was not unpleasant and certainly a change from Entroilian honey, although the drink which stood on the tray seemed to be honey-flavoured. As soon as he sipped it, he felt a warm feeling of well-being spreading throughout his body.

'When you have finished, Honoured Sir, if it would please you,' Trissitia said, 'I would like to show you my city.' As she spoke, Sam felt one of her antennae run down his neck and slip under the collar of the loose soft clothes he was wearing. 'It would be a great honour for me, Samfitzpatrick. Tell me, Honoured Sir, do you really consider me to be your friend? That makes me so very happy.'

Sam too felt happy. The food and the warmth and the honey drink and the security were in such sharp contrast to the fear and uncertainty he had been feeling since he was absorbed by the black hole. 'Yes please,' he said, 'I do consider you a dear friend and I'd love to see your city. But tell me, Trissitia, what's happening with my Universe?'

'Do you mean the Cosmic Egg? Our scientists are still examining it.' The little soft hairs of her antenna gently massaged his back, rubbing his cares away. 'Don't worry, they are taking great care of it for you. Please, try to relax.'

Only when she said it did Sam realise how tense he was. 'I can't get used to this alien world,' he said. 'No, not world, this whole alien universe. No, that's not right either because it's bigger than the Universe isn't it?' He stopped eating, overwhelmed by sudden confusion. 'My Universe is just a tiny part of this whole place, isn't it? So what is this place? Can you explain it to me? Where are we, Trissitia?' Sam's head was spinning. He was feeling happy and scared at the same time. It was awful to feel at home yet to be utterly lost.

'No, Samfitzpatrick, I cannot explain it to you. I am just a simple little Princess. Please, just relax.' The tip of her antenna moved from his back round to his stomach and gently probed his belly-button. 'Why don't you ask my father? I'm sure he or one of his scientists will be able to tell you everything you want to know. They are very clever people.' As she spoke the feathery antenna slithered softly down his stomach. 'I am just a simple little Princess, your Princess who likes you very, very much.' The antenna reached his groin and wrapped itself lovingly around his private parts. Sam was totally relaxed now, his eyes closed and he felt his body begin to respond to her tender caress. He seemed to be watching a movie of all this happening to somebody else.

'Ah, that's very good, Samfitzpatrick,' Trissitia whispered. 'I think you are ready to mate with me now?'

For a moment, just for a moment, Sam wondered what it would be like to make love to her. *How would it work?* He opened his eyes and saw her head, crinkled as a walnut, bending towards him, her ant-like bulbous body and long spidery legs straddled across the bed and he shuddered and suddenly felt utterly outraged, first at her and then, even more strongly, at himself.

He jumped off the bed, the embarrassment of sexual desire replaced by nauseous self-loathing. *What the hell is happening to me?* 'I'm sorry Princess,' he stammered, 'but I need to bathe and use the toilet now. Can you come back in half an hour please?'

When Trissitia returned to collect him Sam, was inspecting his appearance in one of the mirrors. The suit-like jacket and long trousers which he had found folded beside the bed were as soft and supple as fine leather. Although a rather unbecoming shade of khaki, they were nevertheless well-made and an excellent fit. Unable to find any underwear he had decided to still wear the pyjama-like clothes beneath the suit. The shoes too were exquisitely made from thick layers of the same soft material. The only thing that puzzled him was the long slit cut into one of the jacket sleeves.

Neither of them mentioned the incident over breakfast but she seemed to feel no resentment about his rejection of her proposition. As she flew the Entroilian-flier out of the room, Trissitia explained that all these clothes had been specially made for him while he slept. 'A team of our best Argolathian chemists and artisans have worked tirelessly all night for you, Honoured Sir. The chemists transformed the leaves of the goaglindo plant into material suitable for clothes. Then the artisans used it to make exact copies of those you removed from your most respected body yesterday.'

Oh, Sam thought. *So that explains this slit in the sleeve*! He felt again the horror as he remembered nearly having his arm sliced off when Michael Zhang had shaken the crystal network, trying to escape.

'And this whole section of the palace was designed and constructed just for you in record time,' she said as they returned to the main hall. 'My father regards your visit as a great honour, Samfitzpatrick, and has spent a huge sum of money both in these quarters and in this laboratory.'

They crossed the hall and flew into the side chamber filled with scientific equipment. Sam's eyes scanned the walls trying to identify which cabinet held the Universe, while Trissitia hovered the Entroilian-flier above the large central table. 'The King has brought the best scientists and engineers here from all over Argolathia to examine your Cosmic Egg,' she said proudly.

On the computer terminals below him, Sam saw detailed maps of the crystal network and images of the Universe's surface. One screen showed the hole which Michael Zhang had made in the pink Universe. Sam saw a capsule descending on a long arm towards the hole.

'As you can see,' Trissitia said, 'your Cosmic Egg is perfectly safe and being well looked after.'

But Sam wasn't so sure. 'Can't we fly into the cabinet and see what's inside that capsule they're lowering towards the hole in my Universe, Trissitia?'

'No, Honoured Sir. I am afraid of disturbing the scientists' work and I am sure you would like to see our beautiful city.' She flew out of the laboratory, through the Main Hall and out of the Palace towards the huge black pyramid with flat sloping walls nearby. To Sam's eyes it seemed identical in size and shape to the Entroilian Temple.

So it was no surprise when Trissitia said 'This is the Temple of the Great God Anting,' as she landed near the little doorway. A white-robed Argolath bowed as she and Sam walked in. But although, from the outside, this temple resembled the Entroilian one, inside it was very different. Instead of one huge open space, this temple was a maze of tunnels and little chambers, rather like the mine which Sam had passed through under the mountains but without the railway line. They walked through the tunnels until they came to a small chapel where white-robed priests and acolytes chanted and devotees offered sacrifices to the god Anting.

'Why is your god called the Anting?' Sam whispered, not wanting to disturb the ceremony taking place.

'He is the One who created the Ants. The Beeing created the bees and the Anting created the ants. Isn't it obvious?'

Sam had to admit it was.

She led him into a larger chapel containing a huge golden statue of an ant. They stood before the statue, Trissitia took Sam's hand in her hairy claw and a priest said a few words in a language Sam could not understand. Trissitia repeated the words. Sam looked at the little creature standing beside him and began thinking again about breakfast.

I wonder why I let her touch my private parts like that? I can hardly believe I didn't push her away. I know I was feeling really relaxed and happy. I think it started with that honey drink. Could she have put something into it?

Trissitia turned to Sam. 'Can you just say "Ngola meeroa dabuta rundanema tsona," please, Samfitzpatrick?' she asked, speaking slowly and sweetly.

'Why? What does it mean?'

'Oh nothing, nothing at all. It's just part of this little ceremony, Honoured Sir. It's in our ancient Argobol language. I would deem it a great honour if you would say them.'

So Sam tried and she helped him to repeat the words which the priest said over and over until he got them right. 'Ngola, meeroa, dabuta, rundanema, tsona.' Sam was quite relieved when the little ceremony finished and she led him out of the temple. He was rather surprised as groups of worshippers called and cheered as they past, but he gave it little thought as she took him on a long sight-seeing tour of the great underground city, ending in a popular eating house, where, because he was with the Princess, Sam was treated like royalty as he was served lunch, consisting of half a dozen different tasty thin slices of the same unknown substance he had eaten at supper and breakfast.

'What is this?' Sam asked as he chewed one of the slices. They all had subtly distinctive tastes.

A waiter was bringing another tray of the food to the table and heard Sam's question. 'It's fungus, your Royal Highness,' he said as he placed the tray before Sam. 'Does your Highness like it?'

Sam stared at him, then turned and looked at Trissitia as the cold truth crept into his mind like a thief in the night.

Episode 35 Paul Volpone

Alex flew out of the shop and over the road whistling an improvised jazz riff, thinking *So, I got away from those two without losing a single cherry. That was neat, but they were pretty naïve.*

He reached a row of poplar trees on the south side of Route de Meyrin, turned right, flew over the customs post and a few hundred meters into France then stopped, hovering beneath the bare branches of the roadside trees, aware they would not give him shelter if George flew over but fairly certain the firefighter would not come this way.

Sofie said he's gone with Romani to the Cafeteria so I'm safe. But where the hell is that groovy party little Kata's gone to? This tunnel looks like it might be a lot of fun. Pity she didn't wait for me at the top like I told her. Now she seems to be stuck. Guess I'll have to go down after her. Count Alex Karolyi to the rescue! Don't fancy flying into that little dent in the floor. Have to fly into it pretty fast. What happens if you miss? Instant death. Don't want to go in on my own either. Needs a team of us. Who can I take to help? Gábor György would be the obvious person. He's Hungarian, he's tough, strong and he knows about rescues. Pity he's such a blind servant of CERN. There's no way he would come. He'd just want to take all my cherries and give them to Francesco Romani.

Suppose I could go and revive some other fireman some place. There must be some in the airport and there's lots in Geneva. They're always running stories about them on Léman Bleu TV. I've got enough spare crystal to revive a whole squad, but they'll probably all have the same attitude as György. They'd want to get instructions from their superiors. People don't become firemen if they've got an independent mind.

Who else do I know around here who might help? Someone who would join in an adventure and risk their lives to go into an unknown tunnel leading into a black hole? Nobody in their right mind would do it, unless they were motivated like me to get a unique business opportunity out of it. Have to admit that's still my biggest motive. Yes sure I want to save the world from being frozen and all that. Of course I do. I'd love to be a hero, but I'd really like to make some profit out of this situation as well. I'm the only entrepreneur alive on Earth at this moment, and this was why I came to CERN in the first place, to find something new which these scientists had discovered but didn't realise the commercial potential of. Scientists have no idea about marketing their own discoveries. They rely on someone like me to do it for them.

Alex took one of the bottles of water out of the plastic bags looped over his elbows and began to sip slowly.

But there's no market on Earth for crystal right now, I'm almost certain of that. Who would want to be revived to live in a frozen world? And money has no value anyway. You can take whatever you want, like I just did in the shop. I've got six crystals. What about if I take them down the tunnel and Michael Zhang restarts time? Then I'll bring him back to Earth and he'll be in my debt. With my business sense plus Michael's scientific knowledge we'll build some fantastic machine using black holes.

Alex began to get excited as the possibilities unfolded and blossomed in his mind like flowers in spring.

Danny said that Michael deliberately made ATLAS change the monopole into a black hole, he remembered. *We could do that again, but do it right this time and use a magnetic field to control the hole. Then we could do something stupendous with it. Think about the way it glowed with Hawking radiation. Maybe we could use it as a source of energy, or maybe as a weapon. Who knows what we could think of? Of course, I'd have to raise enough money to re-build ATLAS but that wouldn't be difficult. I'd be a hero, the man who saved the world, so I could easily raise billions on the capital markets, especially for a world-class project like this. Might not even need ATLAS. Maybe just a strong magnetic field and a simple proton source would do it. Of course, we'd need a magnetic monopole, but now we know they exist, so maybe we could find a way of creating them. Who knows what me and Michael could achieve together?*

Then he remembered the one person he knew in Geneva who was an expert in capital and markets and making profits.

Paul Volpone! Of course! The one man I know who would be willing to take extreme risks for extremely high stakes. And he would definitely be attracted by the weirdness of this situation. Why didn't I think of him before? He's perfect for an adventure like this. I remember that storm last November when he helped me bring the Marianne in safely. He was dead calm in that emergency.

Alex threw the bottle of water away and began to fly back along the Route de Meyrin towards Geneva.

I've struck some good deals with Paul in the past. The Banca Tuscani's got access to endless resources. Most of its obviously laundered money, probably il pizzo[8], but I've got no problems with that. My customers have no idea how my business is financed so it does me no harm. What's more important, morals or profits?

He flew through Meyrin village and rapidly on towards the city, his big bubble spanning the width of the road. As he past signs pointing out the Co-op supermarket near the airport and then the big Balexert shopping centre, he made a mental note to call in on the way back to collect supplies before he and Paul set off on their great adventure. As he approached the city the pavements became busier, the shops more numerous. Finally he

---

[8] Protection money paid to the Mafia.

flew under the railway bridge near the Cornavin station, found the Notre Dame church shrouded in plastic and turned right, flew down to the river and over the narrow bridge.

As he passed the tourist office on the island, the sign "Cité de Temps" above the little building struck him as incredibly funny. *City of Time! How ironic that this disaster should happen in the watch capital of the world!*

Flying over the broad city centre streets, Alex prepared his pitch to Paul. *Even if he isn't willing to help me rescue Kata, at least I can try to get him to invest a few millions in a black-hole machine if and when I get back.*

By the time he got to the bank, Alex was more excited by this prospect than by actually getting Volpone to go with him. But he had not anticipated how difficult it would be to get into Paul's office. It was fairly easy to get through the beautiful oak doors into the elegant front office of the Banca Tuscani and squeeze over the impressively carved wooden framed security screen guarding the tellers, but the door behind them was impassable.

Abandoning this route, Alex flew back onto the street and flew up to the second floor. Surprisingly, there were no metal grills on the window of Volpone's office. He smashed one pane with his shoe, opened the window and flew in over the thick carpet, woven with the bank's impressive medieval shield. Volpone was sitting behind his large, solid cherry-wood desk, exquisitely inlaid with the same shield in elaborate marquetry. He was about fifty, impeccable in a fine Italian pin-stripe vicuna, his plump face handsomely tanned. A black plastic rubbish bag half-full of money stood on one end of the wide desk. Piles of banded thousand US dollar bills were lined up in neat rows before him.

When he saw Alex, a look of surprise crossed Volpone's face, his hand went into a draw and came out holding a gun. From Alex's point of view, looking down the barrel, it appeared to be a rather smart Beretta Tomcat with a finely polished titanium-steel slide and barrel. Alex took a fancy to it right away, but he had other things on his mind at that moment.

'What the fuck are you doing barging in here unannounced, Karolyi?' Volpone snarled.

Not quite the reception Alex had been hoping for, but he smiled broadly and took one of the small crystals out of his pocket and put it on top of a pile of dollars.

'Calm down Paul. You ever seen anything like that?' Its glow made the pile of green-backs turn blue.

'What's happened to the light?' Volpone looked up at the ceiling and saw the big bubble curving through the air above him. 'What the fuck's that?' he said and looked at Alex with a frown.

'Don't worry, Paul. Let me explain. There's been an accident in CERN.'

'Accident? Anyone injured?' As he spoke, Paul's eyes flicked from Alex to the bubble.

'Yes, a couple, but something really exciting's happened, Paul. Just look at this crystal.'

Volpone looked at it. 'What the fuck is it?'

'It's a very special sort of stone they've made in CERN, Paul, and the beauty of it is that if you hold this crystal you're alive, but without it you're dead.'

'Dead?'

'Well not so much dead as frozen. Before I came here you were frozen, Paul.'

'I don't fucking think so, Count Karolyi.'

'I assure you that, apart from me and you and one or two others, the rest of the world and probably the rest of the Universe is frozen in time. Everything's frozen except near crystals like this.'

Paul gave him a sideways look then stared at the crystal.

'It's true, Paul, and I can prove it by doing a simple test using two watches, but listen, just humour me for a minute and suppose that time really has stopped everywhere except near one of these, okay? So what I want to ask you is, how much do you think such a stone would...'

Alex heard something, a tingle of electricity ran down his neck and he stopped and listened.

'Alex! Can you hear me?' Marianne's voice was coming from the crystal on the desk.

Paul glanced at him then back at the crystal. 'That's clever, Karolyi. Is it like a telephone?' He leaned forward. 'Oh, and I can see a woman in there too. It's a videophone, is it?' He tried to pick it up but his expression changed to fear as he began floating up out of his chair. The gun swung round to point straight at Alex's chest. 'What's going on, Karolyi? If this is some sort of fucking trick—'

'Alex, look out!' Marianne screamed.

The gun swung down, there was an explosion and a hole appeared in the desk. The recoil pushed Volpone backwards towards the ceiling. He yelled and fired again.

Alex jammed a thumb into the large crystal he was holding and flew under the desk. 'Stop that, Paul,' he shouted. There was silence. *Is his head outside the bubble?* There was another explosion and the bullet ricocheted off the bubble wall before embedding itself in the floor. *Evidently not.* Another bullet bounced twice around the bubble. *Got to stop him.*

Alex jammed his back against the desk, his feet against the floor and heaved with all his might. Bullets began slamming into the top of the desk. Alex had not been so close to death since he had been a drug dealer on the streets of Budapest. Fortunately, the heavy desktop absorbed the shots but their momentum slowed the desk's upward journey.

As the desk lifted, Alex stood and gave it one last thrust then clung to its legs and pressed the back of his crystal, giving it extra momentum. When the heavy top hit the ceiling, he felt Paul pushing the desk back. The firing stopped. *Good. He's trapped against the ceiling.*

But Paul was strong. The desk began to move back down. Alex pressed the back of his crystal as hard as he could and the desk stopped but then moved downwards again.

'Alex, are you alright?' Marianne actually sounded worried.

Paul was screaming obscenities and threatening to castrate Alex as soon as he got hold of him, a threat Alex knew was not meant as a joke. In desperation, he pressed the sides of the crystal too, making the desk rock around over Paul's plump body, looking for a weakness. The resistance increased but the obscenities sounded weaker. Taking a calculated guess at where Paul's head was, Alex turned his crystal and pushed, both his legs swung round and his feet hammered into the underside of the desk. He heard a sort of crack and the figure on the other side stopped struggling.

'Alex!' Marianne said. 'Are you all right? I think this man is dead.'

Alex pulled the desk away and let it float back down towards the floor to reveal the lifeless body of Paul Volpone, his brains splattered across the ceiling's dark oak panelling, the gun dangling temptingly from his limp hand.

Shit, Paul, why did you make me do that?

It was obvious he was dead, but it took a minute of heart-searching before Alex could come to terms not only with Paul's death but the loss of his best potential helper. The plastic rubbish bag floated slowly past with piles of dollars spilling out like so much garbage. Alex watched them for a moment. *Seems like a bit of a waste,* he thought. *Volpone's not going to need them now. Might be handy, you never know.* He collected up a few piles, wondering how many thousands were in each one, and stuffed them back into the bag. Then he flew to Volpone and gently prised the little gun out of his fingers. *Neat!* He reached in the desk draw, found a box of ammunition and put it with the gun in the bag.

Finally he flew around the room until he found Marianne's crystal. He looked into it but saw only Francesco Romani flying through what looked like the foyer of the main building. Afraid of being seen, Alex put the crystal into his pocket and used one of the others to fly.

He took one last look at Paul Volpone, his blood and brains splattered inartistically across the ceiling. *Pity about that Paul, but I guess you weren't the right man for the job. Too nervous.*

Catriona woke up shivering. The sacks had fallen off her and she was lying naked on the straw covering the low wooden bench. Women and children were asleep on other benches all around the sides of the room. She leaned over, picked the sacks off the floor, stuffed some foul-smelling straw into one of them and pulled it over herself. She curled into a ball and tried to think what to do.

The Black Death! Wasn't that the plague that killed millions of people in the Middle Ages? Spread by rats, wasn't it? Or was it fleas? How many of these people have got it? If I get it then who will help Sam? And all this because I tried to help a sick child. That's the last time I try to help anybody except Sam. I've got to get the crystal and get out of here and find the tunnel. But how am I going to—What's that?

A movement near the roof had caught her eye. She turned her head and looked up. Something was scuttling along one of the wooden rafters, passing through the beams of moonlight filtering into the barn through gaps between the roof tiles. *What is it? A squirrel? God, I hope so.* She watched it, trying to make it be a squirrel by sheer will-power. It ran below the unglazed window and the light fell upon it. It looked black. Its head had little ears and a pointed nose with long whiskers. The fur on its body stuck out all round like a halo in the moonlight. Then she heard a key turn in a lock, the squirrel stopped and her heart froze as she saw its tail.

It's not curled and furry like a squirrel's supposed to be. It's straight and thin. Like a rat's tail!

The door opened and the rat darted away along the rafter. She turned to see a human figure outlined in the doorway. It wore a cloak and mask with a long thin beak. The door closed and the figure began to move quietly around the room. *Well at least they look after the patients here,* Catriona thought with relief. She heard the hiss of air being drawn through the mask. The figure stopped. In the dim light she could see it was pouring something from a bottle onto a cloth. *Disinfectant?* she wondered.

The figure bent and touched the cloth on the arm of one of the sleeping women. Then it moved on to the next woman and Catriona caught the smell. It wasn't disinfectant. It was the smell she had smelt in the room when the woman cut open the boy's leg. It was the smell she had smelt on the track beside the cart when she bent over the dead body of the man in the snow. It was the smell of the plague. It was the smell of death.

They're deliberately putting the plague onto the patients! Catriona was horrified. *I know why. They've taken all our possessions so if we die they'll keep them, but if we survive they'll have to give us our things back.*

She lay very still, watching with a growing feeling of fear as the figure paused beside the woman sleeping on the next bench.

If that cloth touches her, she will be as good as dead. Should I speak? What should I say? I can't speak French. Anyway that wouldn't stop him. Maybe I should call and wake the others. Would they help?

The cloth touched the woman's arm and moved on, coming directly towards Catriona, moving towards her foot which was sticking out under the sack.

What should I do? I can't run. I haven't got any clothes on. Anyway where would I run to? It's the middle of the night.

The hooded figure was just a step away from her now, and the poisoned cloth was swooping towards her toes. Taking her life in her hands, Catriona yelled and kicked out, trying to knock the cloth out of his hand, but she missed and her toes made contact with the man's body. He screamed and Catriona realised it was a woman. At the same time a hubbub broke out in the barn as the other women awoke and began to moan and shout out.

It's the hospital master's wife! She's not very strong. I'm sure I can get past her.

Catriona threw off the sacks and stood up, seeing her own body white in the gloom. The woman said something and lunged at her with the cloth. Catriona ducked and stepped sideways, then shouldered the woman aside as she ran for the door.

Some of the other women were standing now, holding their children who were crying in fear and confusion. The hospital master's wife shouted at them in French but she made no attempt to stop Catriona as she yanked the door open and ran out into the snow. Her bare feet crunched as she ran across the courtyard. A bitterly cold wind whistled around her.

I've got to get my clothes back and get my crystal and get out of here and get warm.

She ran to the room where they had taken her things off her. It was locked. She ran to the hospital's front door. That was locked too. She peered back into the courtyard, searching for somewhere to hide, somewhere warm where she wouldn't freeze to death.

In the centre of the courtyard the little chapel loomed dark against the snow. She ran across to it and pulled at the door. It opened. Inside there was a musty smell of damp stone and decay, of plague and camphor, of sandalwood and death. At the far end a red light burned above the little altar. A bowl of holy water stood near the door. Catriona broke the ice, dipped her trembling fingers into the freezing water, crossed herself and walked towards the altar, naked before God, in deep humility and in total despair.

Episode 36 Wedding Feast

'Just what exactly was that ceremony in the Temple, Trissitia?' Sam stared at her ant-like face, watching her antennae waving slowly from side to side. 'It wasn't...it couldn't have been some sort of wedding ceremony could it?'

Trissitia's antennae flipped up and crossed on top of her head as her jaws began to vibrate, giving out a high-pitched chirrup of delight. 'Yes, my Husband,' she said and burst into the Argolathian equivalent of a fit of giggles.

'But that's not fair. I didn't know what I was saying. That wedding wasn't valid. You don't imagine such a stupid trick would be legal, do you?'

Her giggles subsided and her antennae settled back over the plate on the table before them as her little hands broke off a large piece of fungus which she held out to him.

'Legal, Samfitzpatrick? Are you serious? My father decides what is legal here. As his favourite daughter I think I can promise you that, should you be foolish enough to mention our secret marriage to him, he will not only decide it was perfectly legal but will be very tempted to crush and eat you for having married me without his permission. So my advice to you, my dear Husband, is to keep silent.' She raised the piece of the fawn-coloured fungus and wafted it under his nose. 'Try some of this, my darling. It's only ever served during a royal wedding feast.'

Sam took it absently and nibbled. *Crushed and eaten? Yes, I can believe that. I'll have to go along with this for now. She's out-smarted me, the cunning little devil. No, just a minute. There's one obvious flaw in her plan. Now how can I put this?*

He swallowed the fungus and took her hard little hand. It felt like a leather glove. 'Thank you, Princess,' he said trying to sound genuine, 'that food really was delicious.' Her antennae began to run lovingly over his bald pate. 'And I'm very honoured that you would choose me as your husband, Princess. I am deeply touched, I really am. But would I be right in assuming that you are hoping this marriage will produce offspring?'

'Of course, my darling,' she murmured while one antenna began to play sensuously with his ear. 'That is my dearest wish.'

'Well I'm sorry to disappoint you but I have some bad news I'm afraid. You see I'm sterile. '

Both Trissitia's antennae stopped moving. 'Sterile? How do you know?'

'Well you see I had an illness when I was a young man and it left me unable to have children.'

She pulled her hand away from his.

'I'm really sorry but I will never be able to give you a little, a little...' Sam shuddered as the offspring from such a marriage ran swiftly through his mind, its six little legs sticking out of its human body. 'If you had told me about your marriage plans before, I could have explained all this to you and saved you all this trouble.'

'Don't lie to me, Samfitzpatrick.'

'My dear Trissitia I am not lying. It's a cause of great sadness to me to have to admit this, since I would love to have children of my own, but I cannot. That is the main reason that I—'

'What is the name of this illness you claim to have had?'

'Mumps.'

'Mumps? Is that an illness? It sounds like a game.'

'It was no fun, Trissitia, I can assure you. It was during my first week of teaching. I caught mumps off one of my pupils and it developed into another disease called orchitis which was absolutely horrible.' For a moment Sam felt again the agony of his testicles swollen to the size of cricket balls. 'Afterwards the doctors told me I would never have any children. It made me very sad because I love children and always wanted a large family.'

'Have you ever tried to reproduce?' Trissitia's antennae were both hanging lifelessly at the sides of her face now. She looked totally dejected.

'No. There was no point,' Sam said. 'Since the age of twenty-two I have lived a life of celibacy, focussing all my attention on being a wonderful teacher, bringing out the best in each and every pupil. I have long-since abandoned any hope of having a family, although the pain and regret lingered with me for many years. It was only when I married the widow Brigit O'Brien six years ago that I found what my heart had been yearning for, a child to help bring up. It was Catriona upon whom I lavished all the love I had inside me.' *And anyway*, he thought, *Brigit showed absolutely no interest in me physically.*

'So those doctors might have been wrong!' Her antennae perked up and Trissitia jumped to her feet. 'Come, I will ask my father's scientists to examine you. There might be something they can do. You might not even be sterile at all. Come, Husband,' Trissitia said, pulling him to his feet. 'I'm taking you to the laboratory. We're going to have a close look at your reproductive equipment.'

Three hours later, Sam was still feeling a bit light-headed as Trissitia flew him out of the lab. It was not just the anaesthetic which was making his head swim, although that had not yet fully worn off. No, it was the news which the Argolath scientists had given him which had really knocked him sideways.

Argolathian technology was clearly far ahead of anything on Earth. Although they had never seen a creature from Earth before, the scientists had quickly determined how his reproductive organs functioned and by examining him in a scanner had proved that all his internal pipes and tubes were connected together correctly. Then they had given him a tablet which turned out to be a total anaesthetic.

When he awoke Sam got the impression that Trissitia had been closely involved in the intimate examination of his organs for she seemed bursting with excitement. 'As far as the medical team is concerned, your reproductive system is perfect, my dearest husband,' she said, her antennae quivering with joy, 'and you are probably completely fertile. Is this not wonderful news?'

'Ah yes, marvellous news,' he said, but with a good deal of apprehension.

As he sat beside Trissitia flying through the huge central hall of the palace, Sam felt utterly let down. *All these years of celibacy when I could have been having children of my own. I can't believe those Irish doctors got it so wrong. They want shooting. They've ruined my life. And now it seems I'm not only fertile but I'm going to have to resist Trissitia's monstrous plans to mate with me.*

In the hall a long table was set out for a banquet. Dozens of Argolaths were sitting around the table with King Flenkt on a throne at one end. In the middle of the table stood a white column topped by a small round blue object.

'Oh dear,' Trissitia said. 'Father's going to be angry. We're late for dinner!'

But Flenkt and his guests did not seem at all angry. They waved as the tiny plane flew overhead and Trissitia wobbled the Entroilian-flier's wings and turned a somersault that made Sam's stomach heave. Then she flew back into the laboratory.

'I thought we were going to that dinner?' Sam said.

'We are.'

She flew into one of the cabinets lining the walls which, to Sam's astonishment, contained an exact replica of the hall and table they had just seen, with models of the King and all his guests scaled-down to Sam's size. When he followed Trissitia out of the plane, Sam was taken aback as the palace guests all stood and applauded while Argolathian servants hurried forward and escorted them to the table. Everything looked so completely real that it was difficult to believe it was only a virtual projection.

Then the King himself stood, left the table and walked towards Sam. Sam could even hear his hard clawed feet clattering on the floor and when the King held out his arms and embraced Sam it felt exactly like you might expect if a large ant the size of a horse wrapped its arms round you.

'Welcome Honoured Guest and now, it seems, Honoured Son-in-Law Prince Samfitzpatrick!' King Flenkt said, and turned to his daughter who, when she heard these words, had frozen to the spot and seemed to shrink three sizes smaller. 'And did you really imagine you could keep this marriage secret from your omniscient father, my daughter?'

The tips of Trissitia's antennae quivered as they crossed themselves beneath her chin.

'And was that dirty little hole-in-the-corner wedding really what you wanted, number one daughter?'

Her antennae quickly moved up and crossed themselves over her head, indicating Yes.

'In that case I forgive you both,' Flenkt said. 'I must confess that I am totally delighted for you both and I trust that this afternoon's insemination will prove highly fruitful!' He turned and walked back towards the table. Trissitia took Sam's arm and followed him, looking rather sheepish.

Insemination? Sam thought. He could hardly believe what he had heard. Once the King was out of the way the other Argolaths left the table and rushed forward. Sam felt his hands being shaken and his back being patted and excited antennae running over his head and chest.

What insemination?

For a moment he wondered if the word meant the same in Argolathian as it did in English, but from the cheering crowd there could be little doubt what had happened.

The scientists must have taken some of my semen while they had me under the anaesthetic and used it to fertilise Trissitia! I will never trust that little minx ever again! Still, I suppose it saves me having to do the dreaded deed myself, thank God!

The Argolaths returned to the table and Sam found himself seated between the virtual King and his real daughter. He still felt robbed and cheated and fearful of what sort of creatures would be produced if this unwilling fertilisation of an alien proved fruitful, but he did not dare protest. He still remembered the threat of being squashed and eaten by the real Flenkt. He did not want to annoy the King by making a scene in front of him.

Flenkt rose to his feet and made a gracious speech welcoming the happy couple while Sam's eyes wandered to the white column dominating the table. The tiny blue object resting on top of it was no bigger than a golf ball and it took Sam a few seconds to figure out that it was the virtual image of the Universe. His heart leaped when he saw it, but also sank as he realised how tiny and fragile it was compared to the Argolaths sitting round listening to Flenkt. *Any one of them could crush that without even noticing it had gone,* Sam thought.

When Flenkt's speech finished everyone began to eat. Sam was amazed at the way reality and virtuality were integrated. He could hardly tell where one ended and the other began. As the servants came round he could easily have believed they were serving everyone, real and virtual, with the same food. There was wine too, or at least some delicious and intoxicating liquid which Sam drank greedily and felt himself begin to relax. *What's done is done,* he thought. *There's nothing I can do to change the past. Got to concentrate on the future.* He refilled his glass as the anger and fear in his heart rapidly ebbed away. He felt as if he were back in Dublin, helping Brigit to host one of her high powered dinners, rubbing shoulders with TV executives and top politicians.

'What do you think of Peshash City, Prince Samfitzpatrick?' King Flenkt said when the opening course was over. 'I trust Princess Trissitia has been looking after my honoured Son-in-Law?'

Sam smiled and nodded. 'She has looked after me very well indeed thank you, Your Majesty. I've had a very interesting day. Your city is very impressive. You are certainly much more technologically advanced than the Entroilians.'

Flenkt snorted in derision and, a few seconds later, all the other Argolaths round the table also snorted. 'Oh indeed yes,' Flenkt said. 'Entroilians are extremely primitive creatures. Except in the field of genetics they have almost no idea about any advanced technologies. For example they are even afraid of fire. Their homes are made of paper, yet they are so afraid they haven't even a fire brigade!'

'But why don't they use electricity like you do, Majesty?'

'They seem to have an aversion for all advanced mechanical things and show no desire to learn,' Flenkt said. 'Entroilian society is basically primitive and they seem happy to stay that way.'

'But they have metal weapons, Majesty, and a marvellous temple. And the Queen's Palace is almost as magnificent as your own.'

'Indeed it should be, for it was built by Argolaths! When they want any work doing they capture some of my subjects and force them into slavery. You probably saw them when you came through their mines and workshops? The Entroilians themselves are completely incapable of building with anything but paper.' Flenkt laughed as he said this and the whole table erupted in jeering anti-Entroilian mockery. 'And we make sure they stay like that by only using basic technology in their presence,' Flenkt added.

'Tell His Majesty what you told me this morning,' Trissitia said, nudging Sam's arm and beginning to giggle. 'You know, about what Queen Karolinda wants to do.'

The King looked at Sam, his antennae wafting from side to side, waiting to hear.

Sam had seen so many different things during his tour of the city this morning that it took him a few moments to recall the incident she was talking about.

It was soon after their visit to the Temple. Trissitia had just shown him round a farm, where fungus was grown upon leaves brought down from the forest on the surface, and they were flying towards the city centre to eat lunch when she said 'Oh look!' and pointed at a huge metallic worm emerging from a hole in the ground. It was enormous, its shiny segmented body wriggling while rows of metallic teeth rotated rapidly around its nose. Trissitia hovered at a safe distance as they watched the immense worm come to rest lying upon the ground.

'What is that?' Sam asked, astonished at the size of it, as the object rolled over on its side.

'It's just a Mineworm,' she said as a procession of Argolaths emerged from a door in its belly and began to work on repairing the teeth. 'It's a tunnel-making machine,' she added and flew away, impatient to eat lunch.

'Could it go right under the mountains between here and Entroilia?' Sam had asked.

'Yes, very easily. Why?'

'Queen Karolinda wants to dig a tunnel under them.'

'A tunnel? From Entroilia to Argolathia? Why?'

'Well it's top secret so I suppose I shouldn't really tell anyone.'

'Oh, come on, Samfitzpatrick. I love a bit of gossip.'

'Well, my new Son-in-Law?' Flenkt said. 'What does my rival Queen Karolinda want to do?'

'Well, Your Majesty, apparently she wants to—'

'You're not going to tell me about the tunnel she wants to dig under the mountains I hope?' the King said.

Sam nodded. 'I'm afraid I was.'

'That is not news to me, Prince Samfitzpatrick. I have close connections at the highest levels of the Entroilian command. Sedtia City is growing like a plague over the west of the island and Karolinda needs more land in the east to house her spawning offspring. I know she wants to build a new city in the fields of Argolathia directly above Peshash. She can only do that if she has some way to move goods between the two parts of her extended city. The seas are full of Zorgugdakhs so she has devised a plan to dig a tunnel under the mountains, using Argolath slaves.'

'But why don't Entroilians just fly over the mountains, father?' Trissitia said. 'That's what they do at the moment. They come over here to collect nectar and pollen from the flowers in our fields.'

'Yes, daughter, but they couldn't physically carry all the goods a city needs. Karolinda will have to dig a tunnel and build a railway under the Malordon Mountains if she is to succeed. Entroilians cannot do this themselves. Only Argolath technology is capable of such a feat. Digging such a tunnel would be easy for us, the work of only a few hours using a Mineworm, but she doesn't know that. And in any case her plan is totally unacceptable to us. The trees we use to produce leaves make no flowers, so they are of no interest to Entroilians. She would almost certainly destroy our forests in order to build her city, and we would starve. Therefore her tunnel cannot be allowed to proceed, yet she is determined to construct it. We are approaching a crisis in our relationship with our neighbours.

'We have three alternative ways of solving this problem. We could domesticate them, as we have domesticated many other animals such as the Strongarms. However Entroilians are intelligent creatures. It would take millions of Argolaths to police and control them, so that is not a practical solution.

'Or we could set fire to Sedtia and drive them off the face of our island...'

Everyone on the table began to cheer. *That's obviously a popular solution*, Sam thought.

The King raised his hand for silence. '...but they would only fly away and settle on another island, causing problems for our brother Argolaths elsewhere. And anyway Entroilians are useful to us. They provide us with honey. However there is a third solution.' The table was totally silent as the Argolaths waited to hear it.

'We will kill Karolinda and put an end to her plan.' Thunderous applause, stamping and cheering broke out at these words. When the noise died down Flenkt continued 'Most Entroilians are not in favour of the idea of a tunnel anyway. It is Karolinda's huge fertility which lies at the root of the problem. Without her, the population would stabilise and the need for expansion would disappear. There is only one reason I haven't killed her already, one thing I was waiting for, but that has now arrived.' Flenkt stood and raised his glass towards the blue object standing on the column in the centre of the table. Everyone else stood too, including Sam, glass in hand.

'Raise your glasses,' Flenkt called. 'Let us drink to the death of Karolinda and the life of the Cosmic Egg. Let us all pray that it will bring some Sons of Anting just as it has already produced the Son of Beeing for the Entroilians.'

'To the Cosmic Egg,' everyone shouted, everyone except Sam. He was too stunned to speak.

Sons of Anting. The words echoed in his head. *What does he mean, Sons of Anting?*

Episode 37 Main Building & Corsier Port

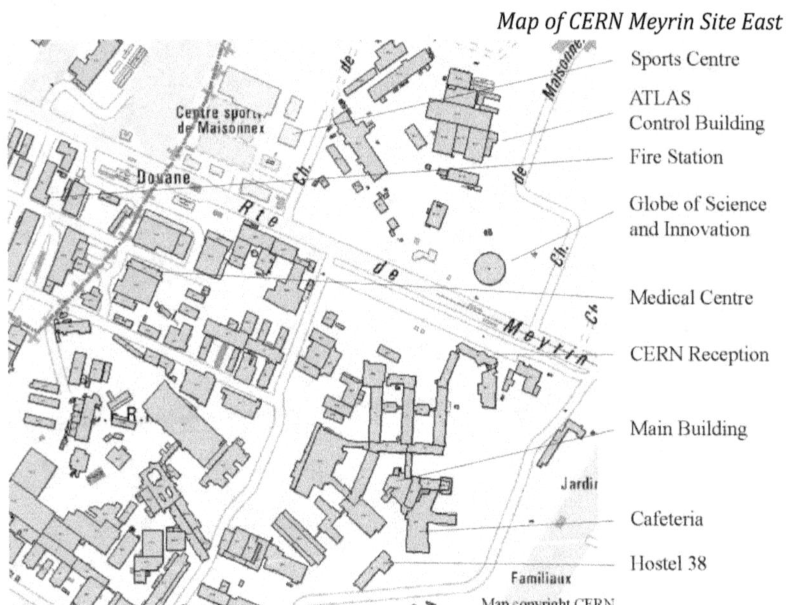

He didn't die in vain, Marianne thought as she left the Medical Centre and flew close beside Danny along the road, still glistening from the morning rain. *I'm sure of it.* She wanted to tell Danny. *Perhaps it will make him feel better. Or perhaps not. He's never shown any interest in religion, but this isn't about religion. It's about love and hope. These are two things we all need now.*

She kept glancing sideways at him, trying to remember that weird name he had given the baby. She was sure he would be more likely to accept the idea if she used that name. *If he understands, it might fetch him out of this weird state he's in.*

Danny never looked at her. He still seemed preoccupied, cut off from the world, sunk inside himself. He was obviously still brooding about what had happened, still burning up with guilt and anger.

He'll see everything in a new light in a minute when I tell him my idea, Marianne thought. *What was that name? Godorir? No, but something like that. Gridomir? No, Grodomir! Yes, that was it, I think.*

She put her arm through Danny's, letting her love flow into him. 'Mon chou, I want to tell you something very important.' His face didn't change and he didn't look at her. 'I think that Grodomir died so that we could live, mon chou.' She felt his arm grow tense and he turned a lemony face towards her, cold, hard and bitter. Her heart sank. *It's almost as if he's a stranger,* she thought, *but I have to carry on now.* 'Grodomir gave his life so that the rest of the world could live,' she said. He shot her a deep frown. 'You should be so proud of your little son, mon chou. He did not die in vain. Sometimes I think that Grodomir is like Jesus. He died to save us all. If that crystal had not hit him–'

'Dragomir,' Danny said coldly. 'His name was Dragomir not Grodomir.'

Marianne's heart sank and she slowed, pulling him round to face her. 'Ah yes, yes, Dragomir, that was it! I'm sorry I got it wrong chou, but does it really matter? Can't you see that our baby died to save the world, like Jesus?'

'He didn't die deliberately or for any particular purpose, Marianne. That is sheer emotional clap-trap and religious mumbo-jumbo,' Danny said. 'He died because of a horrible accident, and because of Michael Zhang's selfishness. The only good thing about it was that you did not die too!'

He disengaged his arm from hers as Francesco Romani and Brigit O'Brien caught up with them. Marianne felt completely defeated, abandoned and lost.

'Ah Danny!' Francesco said. 'I've been thinking about what experiments we need to do when we get to the lab. It might be best if we...'

Marianne stopped listening. She watched Danny and Francesco flying ahead of her as they followed George and Ludovico over the Library roof. Danny seemed like a different person now, professional and competent as he talked about the experiments. Marianne didn't want to watch. Francesco had been able to help him in a way she obviously couldn't. She began to feel completely inadequate.

'How are you feeling now, my dear?' Brigit O'Brien asked as she looped her arm through Marianne's. Marianne felt like bursting into tears and Brigit must have seen it in her face because she gave her a little hug. As the Irish woman's warm body pressed against her, Marianne felt the tension running away like melting butter. When she first met Brigit, dressed like an expensive prostitute and full of her own importance as she talked in a patronising tone to Francesco Romani, Marianne had taken an instant dislike to her, even more so after she got to know Catriona, but now she seemed genuinely concerned about Marianne's welfare, asking intimate gynaecological questions as they flew over parked cars towards the Main CERN Building. As a mother herself, Brigit seemed to understand exactly how she was feeling and Marianne warmed towards her. *Maybe I was wrong about you*, she thought, and was just about to start explaining her concerns about Danny when they reached the Main Building.

The electrically powered doors would not open so George had smashed a window with his hatchet and now stood by to make sure everyone went through safely. When they were all inside, Ludovico led the group across the foyer. He almost flew into a man standing in the middle and swerved up over his head. The others followed but Marianne had not had so much practice at flying and almost hit the man.

'No! In the name of God!' he called out as her feet flashed past his ears and his arm went up and hit her broken ankle. Shocking pain seared up her leg.

They all gathered near the high ceiling of the foyer and Brigit wrapped a handkerchief around Marianne's throbbing ankle. 'This is going to be a problem,' Francesco said. 'We will have this problem every time we meet people. I think this is going to lead to trouble.'

'Can't we try to look as normal as possible?' Brigit said. She flew down into a clear space and began to work out a method of flying while appearing to walk. She soon mastered the art of it. 'The trick is to point your crystal down so you keep your feet pressed on the ground,' she told them. 'It's quite easy. Come down and I'll show you.'

'I'll stay here,' Marianne said. 'My ankle hurts too much to do that.'

Left alone she began studying the crystal Francesco had given her, partly to take her mind off the throbbing pain, partly because she wanted to find Sam Fitzpatrick and ask him if he knew where Catriona was. She often thought about the poor lost little girl, her little sister, and was hoping perhaps she could bring her closer to her mother.

It was then she saw Alex Karolyi, his face floating in the centre of the crystal. It was floating above a desk with piles of money standing around it.

Typical of you, Karolyi, she thought. *You are the last person I want to see, now or at any other time. Why didn't you bring the doctor to me when I needed him? You're the one really responsible for Dragomir's death, not Michael Zhang. I hate you, Karolyi. But perhaps he knows how Catriona is?*

She called him. Another man spoke and tried to pick up the crystal. She saw a gun in his other hand. She screamed and the man began shooting. The desk lifted and the man's head was squashed against the ceiling. He kept firing and the desk began to thud into his head, jamming his head against the ceiling. She heard a horrible crack, he stopped shooting, his forehead slit open, splinters of white bone exploded around her and jets of blood spurted out. Then the desk crushed into his head once more and bloody fragments of pink brain splattered across the wooden ceiling. The desk moved away and Alex emerged from behind it, hovered before the dead man for a few seconds then began shoving piles of money into a plastic bag. Marianne watched him, utterly disgusted.

He's killed the man and now he's stealing the money.

She was still staring into the crystal when Francesco and Danny appeared below her apparently walking across the floor.

'Danny!' she called, 'I've just, I've just seen Alex Karolyi in this crystal and—'

Immediately she mentioned Alex's name, Danny snorted. She knew exactly what he was thinking.

'Karolyi?' Danny snarled. 'It's amazing what the human eye can see…when it wants to.'

'I think you're just fatigued, Marianne,' Francesco said. 'In any case I need that crystal.' He took it from her. 'I want to do experiments on a large crystal. Here, take this small one. Come along. Brigit's waiting for you.'

Marianne didn't say anything more about Karolyi. It would only cause trouble. She flew with them to where Brigit was waiting, in the corridor behind the stairs, and Danny and Francesco flew up the stairs heading for Building One. Danny didn't even kiss her before he left.

Marianne found it almost impossible to pretend to walk as she could not put her left foot flat on the ground. Finally Brigit gave up trying to teach her and helped her hobble along the corridor, past people looking in the little shop, as Marianne directed her to the Cafeteria. They flew together into the chilled food area where they found the two firefighters eating from one of the chillers.

'Where's Francesco Romani?' George said, a long thin headless sausage in his short fat fingers.

'He and Danny have gone to a lab in Building One,' Marianne said.

'They've gone to do some experiments,' Brigit said, flying to hover between the two men.

'Experiments?' George said. 'What for? Hasn't science done enough damage for one day?'

'That's exactly what I think, George,' Brigit said, looking up earnestly into his eyes. *Catriona was right about her*, Marianne thought. *She certainly likes the men.*

'We'd better go and help them, I suppose, Ludo,' George sighed. 'I wonder which lab they would use?'

'Or you could stop here and help me if you like,' Brigit said as she bent George's sausage to her lips and took a big bite out of the end, still staring into his eyes. 'Um, that's rather nice.' She reached down and took another sausage and a bottle of Cola from the chiller. 'Anyone found any straws?'

'No,' George said, flushing slightly. 'We'll go and look for some. Might as well help you ladies as anybody.'

They were still eating when Sofie and Jean-Pierre flew into the Cafeteria.

'Ah, food!' Jean-Pierre said. 'Wonderful! If only we could eat.' He held up his hands. They were deeply engrained with dirt. 'We've been digging and testing latrines outside. Give me a carton of orange juice can you?'

'Anyone seen Catriona?' Sofie asked. 'Karolyi said she was in the Sports Centre with a hundred crystals, but we couldn't find her.'

George burst out laughing. 'You don't mean you believe anything Karolyi tells you, Sofie? Are you really that naïve? I searched in the ATLAS cavern for quite a while and only found six crystals.' He handed the doctor a little carton with a short straw sticking out.

'Oh, look, is a straw on that, Brigit,' Ludovico said.

Brigit looked at it. 'I need a longer one than that.'

'I find a nice big fat one for you, gorgeous' Ludovico said with a saucy wink.

Brigit gave him a withering look then turned to Sofie. 'Where are the latrines?'

'We've dug two on the grass about a hundred metres beyond the terrace,' Sofie said. 'And we've laid out two guide ropes, one labelled Men the other Women, but I'm afraid there's no privacy when you get there.'

'Using latrines is not easy,' Jean-Pierre said. 'I suggest that we put used toilet paper and all solid waste into plastic bags, otherwise it will just be floating around and that would obviously be a health hazard. We found some carrier bags in the shop and we've left them near the latrines but I think we're going to need more, a lot more, and moist toilet tissue would be very useful but I doubt if there's much of that round here. Also it's inevitable we're going to get into a mess, so we'll need lots of antiseptic wipes to clean our hands.'

'Sounds like we need to go to the shops,' George said.

'Balexert?' Ludovico said, naming the large shopping centre near the Route de Meyrin on the way to Geneva.

'Good idea,' George said checking his watch. 'You two ready, Sofie? Ludo? Right, we can be back here by nine if we hurry. Anybody need anything else?'

'I need some straws,' Brigit said as she lifted a piece of melon from the chiller.

'I find you a nice fat one very long, Brigit' Ludovico said, nudging George's arm.

'There are quite a few things I need too,' Jean-Pierre said. 'I'll write you a list.'

'I think I'll go over to the Hostel for a rest now,' Marianne said to him.

'I'll come and find you in a few minutes when we've finished here,' he said.

She explained how he could get there, then went through the drinks area hoping it would be empty, limping along, trying to keep her feet on the ground in case she met anyone. She had almost reached the door when she bumped into a man frozen in the act of filling a cup from a tea urn.

Alex pulled the black bag full of dollars through Paul Volpone's office window, flew down to the street below and collected the carrier bags of food and water. His hands started shaking as he carried them all back to the Rhône. *Never killed anyone before. Don't think I want to do it again.* When he reached the quay he turned without thinking and followed the river headed towards the lake as he tried to decide what to do next. As he wandered among the tall masts of the yachts and cruisers moored along the lake shore his heart lifted. *At least the right man lived. Think I'll be more use in this situation than Paul. Forget selling crystal.* He transferred the gun and the ammunition from the garbage bag into the carrier bags with the food and water, then jammed the bag still half-full of money on the top of one of the masts. *Guns and water are far more important than money right now. So what's next? Suppose I've got no choice. Got to go down that*

tunnel and help Kata save the Universe on my own. Better go and pack things in a decent bag.

He flew at top speed up the shore, past Cologny and round the headland of Bellerive to Corsier Port. As the Marianne's white hull and teak decks came into the bubble, Alex felt a pang. Would he ever be able to stand behind her wheel again under forty-four square metres of schooner-rigged sail? He unlocked the door and flew through the teak-panelled saloon to the galley.

This antique oak-framed gentleman's motor yacht was more than just a luxury home he could use to impress beautiful women on short romantic cruises across Lac Léman. It was a business asset. His staff in Hungary worked long hours of unpaid overtime to earn the reward of coming here for a weekend. When they weren't living on it, his agent hired it out to local hotels and travel companies. It never made a profit, but it didn't cost him anything either, gave him free accommodation in this very expensive part of Switzerland and he regarded it as one of the best investments he had ever made.

It was also one of his greatest passions. Taking the Marianne out in a gale was better than racing in a twin-hulled catamaran. It gave him a thrill of pitching himself against the forces of nature which exhilarated him like nothing else except perhaps that night last summer, the last night with the girl whose name the boat now bore.

He transferred the water, food, gun and ammunition from the carrier bags to a rucksack, some soap, toothbrush and toothpaste, a change of underwear, a fleece, some fruit, a couple of sharp knives, toilet paper, anything he thought would be useful but not too bulky. When everything was ready, he looked at his six fragments floating above the galley table.

Maybe I'll leave one or two behind for safe keeping. No point in risking them all. How many will I need? One to fly with. Better use the big one for that. It's got a bigger bubble. He let it hover above the table like a guiding star. *And I suppose I'll need the one that can see Catriona. Looks like I'm going to have to rescue her on the way down. Nice to have the one that Marianne was in, so I can keep my eye on her. And it might be handy to take a spare.*

He started looking through each small fragment in turn, trying to work out which was which and thinking: *What should I do with the other three? Better hide them somewhere safe. Where can you hide three bubbles about three metres across so nobody else can find them? Not in this boat, obviously. Too many people know her. So where?*

After rotating the first little crystal a few times, he saw Francesco Romani's pudgy face. He was flying along a corridor with pipes and cables hanging from the ceiling, talking to somebody who was apparently flying beside him. *Looks like Romani's still in CERN. This crystal can stay here.* He put it on the edge of the table and took another.

As he looked into it, searching for something interesting among the angled edges and shining mirrored faces inside, an idea suddenly popped into his head. *I know the ideal place to hide crystals. I'll swim down to the bottom of the lake. Maybe even fly down. Nobody's ever going to think of looking down there. Be interesting to see if I can fly underwater.*

He was looking into the third face of the next crystal when he saw Catriona. The crystal was being held by somebody riding a horse and she was walking ahead with some men wearing old-fashioned steel vests like armour and another who was dressed up like a priest. The snow was thick on the ground. *Where the devil is the girl? Don't have time to talk to her right now but I'll have to take this one.* He wrapped that crystal in a piece of paper, put it into the rucksack and took the next.

He saw the top of his own head, as if he was looking down upon himself from the large crystal fragment. *So these are the two linked ones I saw in the garage shop. That could be handy. I'll take that as a spare.* He put it in the bag and took the fifth crystal. Once again, he saw the long CERN corridor, but this time he could see the sleeve of Romani's concrete-smeared blue jacket and, beyond it, Danny Schneider's unsmiling face. He was flying along the corridor beside Romani. The hatred which Alex felt at the sight of the man who had stolen Marianne shocked him, and he quickly put the crystal on the table edge and put Schneider out of his mind. He took the last of the small crystals with a tiny thrill. *This must be the one that's linked to Marianne's.*

And it was. As soon as he saw her face his heart skipped a beat. What he saw was like something out of a zombie movie. Marianne looked even worse than she had the last time he saw her, lying on that stretcher in the field under the helicopter. She still looked terribly tired, there were still dark rings round her eyes and her face was deathly pale, but now it was also creased with pain as she limped alone along a counter loaded with plates, apparently trying to look as if she was walking, although her act wouldn't have convinced anybody.

Alex's heart reached out to her. He vividly remembered the last time he had seen her here, lying naked on this very same table, her legs wrapped round his neck, groaning in ecstasy. All the passion he had felt for her that night came back, but deepened now by an acute feeling of loss. *I've got to go and see her before I go into that tunnel. She has to know how I feel.*

He twisted the crystal, trying to work out where she was. He saw a servery with rose-coloured counters on thick steel legs which he instantly recognised as the CERN Cafeteria. There seemed to be no bubble surrounding her crystal, although distant objects lacked any colour.

Further along the counter were two men, frozen in the act of filling cups from a small machine, like a black-and-white photograph. Marianne was limping straight towards them. *She can't see them! They must be hidden by her bubble.* The men were getting closer. Both wore the casual clothes of typical CERN staff, sloppy jackets and jeans. 'Stop Marianne!' he called. 'There's two men just—'

Before he could finish, one of the men suddenly changed from black-and-white to full colour, changed from frozen to active. *He's inside her bubble now!* The man's head turned, he saw Marianne and tried to move, but his feet seemed to be stuck to the floor. Marianne swerved and went flying up over his head but the man shouted and lunged up at her trying to push her away, his hand thumping heavily into her chest. She screamed in pain and the cafeteria seemed to spin round as the crystal flew away. When it came to rest, all Alex could see were yellow Lipton's tea bags.

His whole body tensed. 'You bag of shit!' he shouted, feeling a sudden cold hatred for the man whom he could no longer see.

He shoved the large crystal into the rucksack, pulled the cord closure tight, hooked his arms through the straps, took Marianne's crystal to fly with, grabbed the other two small crystals and flew out onto the deck. Without a second thought, he threw them into the lake, not even bothering to check whether they disappeared into the water, then flew along the shore to Geneva faster than he had ever flown before.

Episode 38 Engraisseurs

From his position, nailed almost naked on the crucifix behind the little chapel's altar, Jesus didn't seem any more comfortable than Catriona. His face was tilted down towards her as she stood before him, naked and trembling, but beneath the crown of thorns his eyes were closed. *Just my luck,* she thought. *Looks like he's already dead!*

Still I'll have to try praying. What else is there to do? 'Dear sweet Jesus,' she said, and meant it. Her jaws were juddering so much she could hardly speak. All the mantras she had absorbed at school came flooding back. She had never in her life prayed to Jesus before, not really and sincerely like this. In fact until this moment she had not really believed in him at all. *But if he doesn't help me I'll freeze to death.* She fell to her knees on the earthen floor before the altar, head bowed. 'I'm freezing, Lord. Is this how you want it to end for me? Have I come this far to die here, Lord? I am so weak, Jesus. So cold.'

As she said these words, with her whole body trembling uncontrollably, she looked up into his face and was overwhelmed by a feeling of awe. *There's a man who died trying to save the world. And here's me about to do exactly the same thing. But at least I'm not alone.* 'If this is your will Lord,' she managed to stammer, 'then so be it. I acknowledge your wisdom.'

The silver moonlight slanting down through the unglazed windows fell onto the unmoving face of the statue. He still hung there, a wooden statue with its eyes closed and suddenly a tiny flame of anger flared inside her. *Did you really save the world by dying? I don't think so. And anyway I'm trying to save the whole Universe not just the world. But God knows I need all the help I can get and who else is there?* 'But if it is not your will,' she jabbered through shuddering jaws, 'if you want me to carry on the struggle Lord then please give me something to keep me warm. I am so cold, Jesus. So cold.'

Tears welled up in her eyes making the moonlight dance and swim. As they overflowed and ran down her cheeks she saw two wooden candlesticks standing on a red altar cloth. She crawled forward on hands and knees, reached up and lifted the candlesticks down as carefully as she could in her jittering hands. Then she pulled the cloth off the wooden altar and wrapped it round her shuddering body. She felt no warmth. What she felt was a feeling of relief. She had given herself to Jesus. Her fate was in His hands now. The guilt of failure and the sense of responsibility left her, replaced by an inner calm. If she lived or died was out of her power to control. She had pledged her soul to Jesus just as she had secretly pledge her body to Alex Karolyi and there was nothing of her left to give. She sank slowly to the earthen floor and gave herself up to God and sleep.

'What are you doing here child?'

Catriona opened her eyes. The friar was holding a candle looking down at her. 'Come, you cannot stay there. You profane the holy altar cloth. Take it off.' He helped her to her feet, took the cloth off her and laid it back on the altar then looked at her as if he didn't even notice she was naked. 'Follow me.' He led her away from the sanctuary under the bell tower in the transept to a small vestry at the other end of the chapel. He took a cloak off a peg. 'Put this on. Now tell me, what are you doing here?'

'I ran away, Father. It was the Master's wife. She was putting plague on people's arms. Let me stop here, please. She'll kill me if I go back.'

'Engraisseurs? Are you sure?'

'Yes. She had a bottle and she put it on a cloth. I could smell it.'

'Are you willing to swear this before a magistrate?'

'Yes. Can you stop them? Can you get my crystal back?'

'I don't know. The hospital master is of the new faith. So are the Genevan magistrates. They do not have any sympathy with Catholics.' He considered the matter. 'Although technically this hospital belongs to the city of Geneva, it is outside the city wall. I might be able to get the Chatelain de Peney to hear the case. He is loyal to Rome and has taken the Prince-Bishop of Geneva into the Chateau for protection. Yes, that is possible. You must stop here. Madame de Bourgeaulx will never dare try her tricks in here. I will go to Peney on my way back to the Priory and have a word with the Chatelain. Stay here tonight. I will return in the morning.' He made the sign of the cross, wrapped his cloak around himself and walked out into the snow.

Catriona stayed in the vestry all night. It was many hours after dawn the next day when she heard banging on the hospital door. Then someone was shouting and there was more banging then the vestry door opened and two soldiers came in with long swords hanging from their belts, long harquebus guns slung over their shoulders and cloths pressed to their faces. One man had her crystal in his hand. He held it out and said something in French. Catriona tried to take it, her heart soaring. *At last I'm going to get away!* But the man withdrew the crystal and the other man said something through his face-cloth, pointing at her and then pointing at the crystal. She stared at him blankly. He repeated himself, pointing at the crystal then at her. She suddenly realised what he meant and repeated his gesture pointing at the crystal and then at herself nodding all the while.

'Yes, it's mine,' she said smiling. 'It's mine. C'est moi. C'est moi!'

The men stepped forward, took her by the arms and marched her out of the chapel into the snow. She stumbled over the long cloak. *Obviously some misunderstanding here.*

The friar was standing near the gate beside some other soldiers. They were holding the master of the hospital and his wife. They all walked out of the gate and the soldiers locked it from the outside then mounted their horses and led them along a little track away from the city.

'Thank you,' Catriona said to the friar as they walked between the horsemen.

The friar took off his mask and she saw his face for the first time, brown and elderly and with kind eyes. 'I'm sorry,' he said.

'It's all right,' Catriona said. 'It isn't your fault. I don't mind giving evidence against them.'

'No, that will not be necessary. They have admitted they are bouteurs de peste. They claim they have given themselves to the devil. In exchange he has taught them how to prepare quintessence of plague which they use to kill people to steal their clothes and possessions. [9]'

'I thought it was something like that. Why won't the soldiers give me my crystal back?'

'Have you admitted it is yours?'

'Yes of course. It is mine. Why?'

'The captain thinks the Chatelain will want to see you.'

'Who's he?'

'He's the man that runs the Chateau de Peney.'

'What does he want to see me for?'

'I'm not sure. It's got something to do with the crystal, but the captain won't tell me exactly what it is. Don't worry. I told you before; the Chatelain is sympathetic to Catholics.'

---

[9] In 1530, a conspiracy of plague-spreaders was discovered in Geneva. This included the master of the plague hospital and his wife, who confessed to acts exactly as described here. See bibliography (13) pages 44-45.

The soldiers led them quickly down the track beside the frozen river, past the wooden buildings on stilts, over a wooden bridge where the two rivers flowed together, round the meandering bends and over another bridge back into the little marina Catriona had seen before. They took her up a steep hillside with vineyards on either side. From here they had a commanding view over a broad bend in the wide river, over the landscape thick with snow to the distant icy mountains, but Catriona hardly noticed the view. She was tired, hungry and frozen. She had no sensation left in her bare feet.

A tall stone castle stood on top of the hill, wooden huts and barns leaning against its outer walls.

'That is the Chateau de Peney,' the friar said as they walked towards it.

The soldiers took the three prisoners into the Chateau and Catriona stood beside the hospital master and his wife in a large hall. Now they had taken off their masks she was surprised at how normal they looked, a balding fat man and a small mousy woman. Yet they were apparently mass murderers, willing to kill the people in their hospital for the sake of a few ragged clothes and a pocketful of coins.

'This is the Chatelain,' the friar whispered as a middle-aged, grey-haired man with a short beard came into the hall. He was wearing the usual costume, a padded waistcoat and baby's-napkin-like trousers. He seated himself in a tall wooden chair before a fire.

The captain stepped forward and spoke to him in French. The Chatelain asked the hospital master some questions, then he questioned the hospital master's wife. A sombre look crossed his face, he said something to the captain and the two prisoners were led to the end wall where their wrists were manacled to an iron ring.

The captain spoke again and held out the crystal towards the Chatelain. He stared at it then turned to Catriona and said something.

The friar stepped forward and spoke to the Chatelain who nodded. The friar turned to Catriona.

'He wants to know if that is yours, that jewel,' the friar said.

'Yes, Father,' Catriona said, nodding.

The friar spoke to the Chatelain.

'He wants to know where you got it.'

'I found it Father.'

'Where?' the friar asked, relaying the Chatelain's question.

'In a cavern. It's a hole in the ground like a cave.' She was thinking of the ATLAS cavern. How could she describe it to them? She didn't want to lie to them. She was trying to tell the truth.

'Where is this cave?'

'It was on the hillside, Father.'

'He wants to know if you can show him the cave, my child.'

'I'm not sure, Father.' Catriona's brain began to race. Perhaps they would take her back to the place where she had landed. Perhaps they would help her look for the entrance to the tunnel. She began to hope that these simple people might actually help her escape. 'Yes, Father, I think I could find my way there if you could take me back to the river.'

The Chatelain stood and they prepared to depart. Servants brought her a thick brown cloak and Catriona gratefully slipped out of the thin one the friar had lent her and put it on. They also gave her shoes and some warm thick soup and bread which tasted delicious. When she walked out of the Chateau she was feeling renewed and optimistic for the first time since falling out of the tunnel.

Three foot soldiers with rifles led the procession. Catriona walked behind them, the friar beside her. Behind them rode the captain and the Chatelain on horseback. They went down the hill to where the stone bridge ran over the brook. Here Catriona stopped. 'It's up there Father,' she said pointing along a track beside the brook.

'Along the Nant d'Avril?' the friar said. 'Very well, child. Lead the way.' She led the convoy along the little stream through the winding wooded valley. Eventually she met the track and saw the cart on her left.

'It's up there, Father,' she said, pointing up the hillside towards the cart.

The friar exchanged a glance with the Chatelain. 'Very good, child. Lead on.'

She led them up the hillside to where the cart still stood on the track, the horse frozen to death in its shafts, the dead man half-hidden in snow. The soldiers dragged him out with ropes and when the Chatelain saw him he ordered the soldiers to throw him on the cart and set fire to it. He watched until it was well alight, then he spoke again.

'Where is this cavern, child?' the friar asked.

The Chatelain and the soldiers were watching her.

She was assuming, she was hoping, she was praying that the tunnel entrance would be somewhere near where the ATLAS cavern used to be, just behind the big round wooden Globe that used to sit on the hillside. That was where she was trying to get to. That was where she thought they should start looking for the tunnel. *But where is it?*

Looking back across the valley Catriona, could see the big stone barn in village on the top of the far side. The track ran straight across the valley to the village and she was sure that this was the same road that Sam had driven them along yesterday morning, only five hundred years later, the one that cut through the middle of CERN. She closed her eyes and tried to remember what the road had looked like yesterday.

When they arrived, Sam had gone into the Reception Building with Mother, and Catriona had waited in the car park near the black and yellow crossing that led past the tram stop to the wooden dome on the far side of the road. What a long time ago it seemed. She closed her eyes and tried to imagine it.

The Globe thing was on the other side of the road and those big electricity pylons we had passed, and there were some houses and then the crest of a ridge and then this valley and then the village on the far side. She opened her eyes and looked across the valley. *I'm much too far down.* She turned round. There was the ridge, further up the hillside.

'I think it was further up that way, Father,' she said, pointing.

They followed her over the ridge. The Jura Mountains were spread along the horizon ahead of her. The hillside sloped up gently towards another ridge. *How far up should I go?* She kept going up the slope, glancing back every now and then, trying to work out where the crossing had been. When she got to the place where she thought it was she stopped and pointed across the fields to a wood on her right. 'I think it was over there, Father.' As far as she knew this was true. That was where the ATLAS offices and the other buildings had been, where that wood now stood.

The soldiers followed her across the field. To her surprise, Catriona noticed there were crucifixes crudely made out of sticks tied together and stuck in the snow of the field. There was a path through the wood, the snow compacted and trampled into the mud by the passage of many feet, including horse's hooves. *People have come this way before. Lots of them and not long ago. Why?*

More crucifixes were tied to the trees. Soon the path opened out and she found herself in a clearing. Catriona stopped and looked around. In the middle of the clearing was a cow. It was standing as motionless as the dead horse they had just passed on the path but different somehow. The horse had been obviously dead, its head hanging down, its body only held up by the shafts of the cart. But this cow had a look of life about it, as if she had been stuffed and mounted in a museum. Her head was down but not hanging lifeless. She was frozen in the act of looking down at something on the ground.

'Is this where you found the jewel?' the friar asked, translating the Chatelain's question.

Catriona didn't know what to say. She didn't say anything.

The friar repeated the question.

'In a cave somewhere round here yes, Father.'

'Where is this cave?' the friar translated.

'I'm not sure, Father. We need to look for it. Will you ask the soldiers to help me?' She was repeating the words she had been planning all the way here but, now she had arrived, she knew it was pointless looking for the cavern which was not there because it would not be dug for another five hundred years. She walked forward and nobody stopped her. She wanted to get a better look at the cow. There was something very odd about it. Just centimetres from the cow's nose, something pink was glowing in the snow. At first she wasn't sure what it was but as she moved to the side she could see it was a little pyramid. It looked like a fragment of crystal. Pink crystal.

As soon as she saw it, she knew that the pink crystal was making the cow freeze. *It's frozen in time! If I could get that I might be able to fly up and find the tunnel.* She ran forward to pick it up, still wondering why it was pink, and her forehead banged painfully against an invisible surface. She staggered back, her head reeling. When it cleared a little, she glanced back at the soldiers. They were pointing their harquebuses at her but were making no attempt to stop her.

She stepped forward again slowly, one hand on her forehead the other reaching out to feel for the invisible barrier. Something like a large glass ball curved through the air. She felt it all the way around the cow, the soldiers following her, their guns covering her every move. When she got back to the beginning, she looked at the circle of her footprints in the snow.

It's about as big as the bubble round a normal blue crystal, except that a blue one creates time on the frozen earth while this pink one is freezing time back in history. It's really confusing. So is it going to be any use to me? And how can I get it anyway if it's frozen time?

She glanced round. The Chatelain was holding the big blue crystal. It glowed in his hand. *Time obviously hasn't stopped round that, otherwise he'd be frozen.* He saw her looking and beckoned her to come to him. She walked back and stood looking up at him, the friar at her side.

'He wants to know if you can use this jewel to take the spell off the cow,' the friar said. He looked worried.

The Chatelain was holding out the blue fragment to her. *He's going to give it to me! Just like that! So easy!*

She nodded enthusiastically. *I'll take it and fly away!* He handed the crystal down to her. It felt heavy in her hand, heavy and welcome and solid. She gently pressed the bottom of it and felt herself begin to lift off the ground, but the soldiers were pointing their guns straight at her, not sure what she was going to do, and she realised that if she tried to escape they would probably shoot her down. *I'll have to wait.*

She looked at the Chatelain. 'Thank you sir,' she said and walked slowly back to the cow, still hoping to get away. The soldiers followed a step behind. She reached the circle of footsteps she had made before and felt for the glass wall. She couldn't feel it. *The wall isn't there! The blue crystal's unfrozen it somehow.* She walked straight through to the cow. She saw its head rise and suddenly the whole animal seemed to leap off the ground, its head turned and it ran off in a panic, leaving her looking down at the pink crystal.

She bent down, picked it up and hesitated, a crystal in each hand. *I need two hands to fly. What can I do with the pink one? I don't have any pockets and no bra.*

The Chatelain said something. The captain dismounted and walked towards her. She found herself looking up into the long barrels of three harquebuses and the captain's gloved hand.

'Give him the crystals, child,' the friar said. 'You are under arrest.'

'For what?' she said, staring at him in disbelief.

'For witchcraft.'

Episode 39 Return to the Universe

'That Cosmic Egg is by far the most important object ever seen in Peshash City,' King Flenkt said, staring at the Universe. 'In that tiny object resides my dearest wish and my greatest hope: to allow Argolaths to give rise to Sons of Anting.' A wave of cheering echoed round the dining room.

As the cheering died down and the guests resumed their seats, Sam flopped into his chair, totally bewildered. *What does he mean by that?*

Flenkt turned to address himself directly to Sam. 'Can you explain to me, Prince Samfitzpatrick, why your fellow emergent Michaelzhang was transformed into the Son of Beeing whilst you were not?'

All the virtual guests turned to look at Sam.

'I think so, Your Majesty,' Sam stammered, still bewildered by the King's remarks. 'When we were absorbed by the black hole, we ended up in the Cosmic Egg's pink jelly.' Sam glanced up at the image of the Universe resting on a column in the middle of the table and shuddered at the memory of nearly drowning in the horrible slimy pink of the event record. 'Michael Zhang swallowed some of it and that was what made him change. Luckily I hid inside a metal tube and so I didn't swallow any.'

'Ah,' Flenkt said. 'Michaelzhang swallowed some of the Cosmic Egg? So that explains why there is a hole in it?'

'Yes, Majesty.'

'Very good. And I understand that an Entroilian scientist has put some of Karolinda's eggs down that hole?'

'Yes, Majesty,' Sam said, thinking *He seems to know everything about the Cosmic Egg.*

'My greatest wish is that this Cosmic Egg should give rise to Sons of Anting. To achieve this I have taken the liberty of ordering my scientists to lower some of my sons into that hole. I chose the smallest ones so they fitted in easily. They will of course have to find their way to your world...' As he said this, Sam felt cold, but he froze with fear when Flenkt continued '...and I would like you, Samfitzpatrick, to go down and help them.'

It was as if a spotlight had been turned onto Sam, illuminating his deepest fear. *Go down that hole in the jelly? No,* he thought. *I never want to go back into that stuff again.*

But Sam's feeling of dread grew, as Flenkt continued 'You will need to guide them to your home planet. Once there it will be your duty to ensure that your fellow creatures co-operate in this glorious endeavour. You will show them what an honour it is to couple themselves with the sons of Flenkt.'

Sam broke out into a cold sweat as he listened to these words while everyone else, including Trissitia, cheered and banged the table. *Couple themselves?* he thought as the mad cacophony washed over him. *I don't believe this. So that's what was inside that capsule they were lowering towards the hole! I've got to lead his sons to the Earth and help them mate with human women? If that wasn't so horrific it would be laughable.*

The King sat and as the noise subsided every multi-faceted eye turned upon Sam.

'You must thank my father for the honour he has bestowed upon you, Husband,' Trissitia said, poking him in the ribs.

Sam slowly got to his feet, sweat dripping from his armpits, thinking: *I've got to convince Flenkt that his plan is hopeless.* 'I'm sorry Your Majesty,' he stammered, 'but I really don't think your plan's going to work.'

This statement was greeted by gasps of astonishment. Sam saw the real armed guards step out of the shadows surrounding the table and realised that challenging the king was tantamount to treason. He felt his head swim and he leaned against the table to stop himself falling over.

'I don't know if you're aware of this, Majesty,' he went on, thinking quickly, saying the first thing that came into his head, 'but the Entroilian eggs which Professor Itoodoo put down that hole were quite big. I think they might kill your sons before they—'

His remaining words were drowned by the howls of derision from around the table.

'Have no fear about that, Prince Samfitzpatrick,' the King roared. 'Even Entroilian adults are no match for the sons of Flenkt, and their eggs are mere playthings for us.'

'Also,' Sam went on, 'did you know that the Cosmic Egg's shell is broken?'

A stunned silence rapidly descended upon the table. *So they didn't know!* Sam thought. *That's good. It gives me a chance.*

'Broken?' Flenkt said in surprise. 'That explains why my scientists were unable to detect any activity in the Egg. How did it break?'

'Michael Zhang broke it, Your Majesty.'

'Why would he do such a stupid thing?'

'Because he was afraid that the whole Earth, the whole of my home planet would be absorbed by the black hole, Majesty.' Even Flenkt was silent now and Sam pressed home his point, speaking rapidly. 'When Michael Zhang and I first emerged from the Universe, we were floating in that pink jelly stuff and there was a sort of rain falling down from those blue crystal pipes surrounding it. Michael explained it to me afterwards. He called it the "event network". Apparently, that rain made time flow in the Universe. So he deliberately broke one of the pipes, Majesty. The rain stopped falling and that made time stop in the Universe. So you see—'

'Time has stopped inside the Cosmic Egg?' Flenkt sounded astonished.

'Yes, Majesty.'

'I am displeased, Prince Samfitzpatrick. Most distinctly and definitely displeased. Why did you not reveal this information to me before?'

'You didn't ask me, Your Majesty,' Sam said, sweating profusely, his head swimming from the wine and the tone of Flenkt's voice.

Flenkt's head turned to one of the Argolaths sitting at the table. 'Professor Nithold, can we fix this event network of the Cosmic Egg?'

'I am sorry, Your Majesty, but I do not think so. We were aware that one of the pipes was missing, of course, but we assumed this was normal. This is the first Entroilian egg which we have ever—'

'But if the Egg is not fixed,' Flenkt said, turning to Sam, 'then my sons will not give rise to Sons of Anting. Do you think your Egg can be fixed?'

Sam hesitated. *What should I say? If I tell him it can't be fixed then he's likely to destroy it, especially if he tries to get his sons back out. My only hope of saving the Universe is to make him look after it. Suppose I've got to tell him the truth. I'll have to worry about the Sons of Anting problem later.*

'Yes it can be fixed, Majesty,' Sam said. 'Professor Itoodoo told me—'

'That is the scientist who put the Entroilian eggs into the hole?' Flenkt asked.

'Yes, Your Majesty. She works at the Entroilian University. She told me that, if she could get all the crystal fragments out of the Universe, she could reassemble them and restart time. So I asked my stepdaughter to collect all the fragments and bring them down—'

'Stepdaughter? Is that some sort of relative of yours? A living being?'

Sam nodded.

'And this stepdaughter is still inside the Cosmic Egg?'

'Yes, Majesty.'

'But I thought you said time had stopped? Please explain yourself, Prince!'

'Yes, time has stopped, Your Majesty, everywhere except near fragments of the crystal pipe which Michael Zhang broke. They fell into the pink jelly and some ended up in the time I came from. Each of them is surrounded by a little bubble of time.'

'And how were you able to speak to this "Stepdaughter"?'

'Through something called "negative energy strings". Cjingha— I mean Professor Itoodoo—said they link the fragments to the event network. When I was in the Egg's shell I could see and hear people speaking on the Earth near fragments of crystal and they could hear me.'

'That's extremely interesting,' Flenkt said, looking for a long moment at Professor Nithold, then turning back to Sam. 'And how is Stepdaughter going to bring the crystals down to this Entroilian professor?'

'Well there's a tunnel. I know it exists because Catriona, my stepdaughter, she said that she has started to come down it and—'

'Is she bringing the crystals down too?'

'I don't know, Majesty. I assume so. I only saw her for a few seconds.'

Flenkt's antennae started waving up and down. 'This is indeed good news. And Itoodoo said she could reassemble these fragments and restart time? Well if she can do it then obviously my scientists can do so too. They are cleverer than any Entroilian, except perhaps Councillor Moshendiar. And once the Cosmic Egg has been fixed and time restarted, then it might be able to produce all sorts of useful new creatures which we could use to the benefit of Argolathia. Things perhaps even more powerful than Michael Zhang! So,' his head swept round to encompass the table, 'we have several tasks to achieve, my friends. We must help Stepdaughter bring all the fragments down so we can fix the "Event Network" and restart time. And, since some humans seem to be alive on Samfitzpatrick's home planet, we must of course help the Royal Princes reach it and mate with those females of his species for whom time has not stopped, so they can give birth to Sons of Anting.'

The shouts and screams of joy which followed this statement made Sam's head reel again. *What have I said?* he thought. *What have I done? Will they try to mate with Catriona as well?* Self-loathing overwhelmed. His head fell forward in shame and humiliation.

'There is no reason why we should not accomplish both these tasks simultaneously,' Flenkt went on. 'You, Prince Samfitzpatrick, will accompany my sons and guide them to the Earth. You, Professor Nithold, will investigate the communication properties of the crystal network and find out whether you can see and hear Stepdaughter and help her collect these precious crystals. Insert your detectors at the place where we found Samfitzpatrick. I want a report first thing in the morning. And you, Number One Daughter,' he said, turning to Trissitia, 'will of course accompany your husband. It is not only your place to be beside him. You must also be ready to feed your larvae with human food when you reach the Earth. I have hopes that this also might transform them into Sons of Anting, just as Michaelzhang was transformed into the Son of Beeing. So our plans are laid. Let the mission commence without delay!'

Sam sank back into his chair feeling totally defeated as the virtual guests left the table and two real armed guards stepped up beside him. *I can't stand the thought of going back into that pink jelly and helping these monsters mate with human women. But what else can I do?* His willpower seemed to have shut down. In a sort of dream he watched the King lift the Universe off its stand and carry it out of sight.

'Come on Sam,' Trissitia said.

I've failed, he thought as he let the armed guards lead him after her to the Entroilian flier. *They're going to lower me into that hole and there's nothing I can do about it. Once I'm down there I'm not going to be able to speak to Catriona. Who's going to help her then? And what will that Argolath professor do if he finds out how to see her through the crystal?*

The thought of Catriona seeing an Argolath, and even worse of one talking to her, filled him with dread until he realised this was impossible. *Of course he won't be able to speak to her. He can't speak English! Nobody here can.*

Sam grew calmer as Trissitia flew into the cabinet next door. He could see the real Universe resting on the cabinet floor. Trissitia landed on the upper platform where more armed guards were waiting near a large glass-domed silver pod fixed to the long mechanical arm. *There's nothing I can do about it anyway. Flenkt wants to put me down that hole and that's that.* He climbed into the pod beside Trissitia and looked at the boxes of provisions stacked in the back. *At least we've got lots of supplies for the journey,* Sam thought.

Trissitia controlled the arm as it lowered them swiftly down towards the Universe. Its outer blue haze gradually resolved itself into a network of individual pipes. They stood on tall stalks which emerged from the pink event record. The whole thing looked like the delicate seed of some exotic flower. The sight of it stirred his heart. *That's my home! I'm going home. Whatever happens, it has to be better than being here.*

The arm carrying the pod slipped easily through the gaps between the crystal pipes and finally descended towards the pink surface. The sight of it brought back all Sam's horror of drowning. *The last time I was this close, I was hiding inside the toroid tube.* He distinctly remembered seeing the bloated figure of Michael Zhang floating above him like an airship.

'Please put on your safety harnesses before you descend,' a voice said suddenly, startling Sam. In the control panel before them, the head of an Argolath appeared on a screen.

'Yes, Professor Nithold,' Trissitia said as she steered the pod towards the entrance to the hole. Sam's eyes looked at it, that hole winding down into the rapidly approaching surface, that deep chasm below them, descending into the unknown, his thoughts filled with an unbearable mixture of dread and longing. *How are we going to get down there safely? Michael Zhang told me it goes right back to the creation of the Universe. How are we ever going to survive that?*

Trissitia pressed a button, the long thin arm which had carried them down stopped and the pod hung just above the entrance to the hole, swinging almost imperceptibly from side to side. They both buckled their heavy harnesses, each tailored for their very different anatomies, then she turned on a headlight and Sam looked out of the glass dome at the tunnel beneath them, with a good deal of trepidation, wishing he could go to the toilet.

The hole was huge, much larger than he had imagined, and its distant pink walls glistened in the pod's strong headlight. Then the little princess advanced a small lever and the pod's nose lowered so Sam hung forward against his harness, until he was looking straight down into the tunnel. Even the headlight could not penetrate the gloom as the dwindling tunnel wound down into the depths of the Universe.

If this tunnel goes all the way back to the creation of the Universe then does that mean we're going back to the Big Bang? We'll never survive if it does. No, I've got this all wrong. I must have.

Trissitia pressed a button and two small wings opened out from the pod's sides. She flipped a switch and, with a lurch that made Sam's stomach rise into his throat, the arm released the pod which began to fall. He closed his eyes and held his breath. He could feel the harness pull him to one side as Trissitia used a joystick to fly the pod. Then, after the initial shock, his stomach settled back into its normal place and nothing more seemed to happen. He nerved himself to open his eyes and peered out through the pod's transparent dome.

The headlight was shining straight down into the tunnel, illuminating a pink oval on the wall far below them where it curved to one side. The oval patch barely seemed to be moving, although Sam knew they must be falling rapidly towards it.

'What's at the bottom of this hole, husband?' she said.

'I'm not sure but Michael, I mean Lord Michaelzhang, told me that he knew everything that had happened since the moment of creation so—'

'How did he learn all this?'

'Apparently he absorbed knowledge when he swallowed the pink jelly.'

'So it was he who made this hole?'

'Yes indeed. He burrowed his way down. I guess he must have gone to the middle.'

'So this hole goes all the way down to the creation of your Universe? How exciting!' Trissitia pressed a button and the headlight swung round to illuminate the hole's curving side wall. From this distance the pink surface seemed perfectly uniform and featureless. 'What's this Universe of yours made of, husband?' she said.

'I'm not sure. Michaelzhang told me it was made by a sort of rain falling from the pipes. He called them "time quanta". I think they were sort of little drops of time. And he said the pink jelly was a sort of geological record of the history of my Universe. I think that as we go down the tunnel we must be going back in time. Don't you think you ought to check how close we are to that bend below us?'

'Very well, husband. Thank you, Samfitzpatrick!'

'What for?'

'For giving me this new life, and the chance of going on a great adventure. This is the most exciting thing that's ever happened to me. Life in the Palace was pretty boring before you came along. So thank you, husband.' Her hard claw squeezed his hand for a moment then she pointed the headlight down the tunnel. The bend below them was much closer now, and she pulled on the joystick, pointing the pod's nose away from the wall into the centre of the hole.

As she flew around the first bend, another came into sight, then another and another. At first Trissitia was able to follow the tunnel's curving trajectory quite easily, but as they fell further and their speed increased, she found it more and more difficult to stay in the centre.

The bends also seemed to be getting closer together, their twists and turns tighter as if Michael had been searching for something as he ate his way down through the pink jelly. And there was another problem.

'Do you think the hole's getting narrower?' Trissitia said as she struggled to keep away from the circular pink wall.

'I'm sure it is.'

'But why? If Lord Michaelzhang was swallowing the jelly he should have been getting bigger, so the tunnel should be getting wider shouldn't it?'

Sam thought about it although it was difficult to think clearly as he swung from side to side in his harness faster and more violently in response to her steering round the corners. *She's right*, he thought. *Michael started out even smaller than me. As he went down he was swallowing the event record, and he must have been getting bigger. So why isn't the tunnel getting wider?* It took him a couple of minutes of heart-stopping flight before he figured it out.

'This is the tunnel he made when he came up...' he gasped, barely able to speak because of the pressure of the harness on his chest, 'If he was still swallowing...as he went back up...then the tunnel...would be getting bigger.'

But Trissitia wasn't listening. She was concentrating on flying. The walls were very close now.

'Queh!' she said under her breath, swinging the joystick around rapidly. 'Queh, queh, queh! I can't—'

The pod hit the wall and bounced off. Sam had assumed the pink stuff would be soft, like jelly, and was surprised how violent the collision was, but as far as he could tell the pod was unharmed.

'The tunnel's too narrow to fly,' Trissitia shouted as she pressed a button. The pod's wings folded back into its body. 'Hold on Samfitzpatrick! We'll have to slide down from here.'

Without its wings, the pod began to tumble and spin. Sam was thrown violently against his harness and held on, trying to stop the straps digging into him. Soon they were spinning erratically, bouncing from one side of the tunnel to the other with nauseating violence, the collisions growing more frequent until suddenly the spinning stopped altogether and after a short period of violent vibration the pod started sliding backwards down the tunnel wall.

Then began a breath-taking descent down the winding tunnel which would have tested the nerve of an Olympic skier. All Sam could see was a short stretch of the tunnel above them, wriggling in the beam of the pod's headlight.

What's going to happen when we hit the bottom? Sam thought as he clung to his harness and closed his eyes.

Episode 40 Balaxert & The Lab

As Sofie reached the ceiling of the central hallway in the Balexert shopping centre, a large packet tucked under her arm, she heard Ludovico say 'She fancy you, George. She slobber every time she look at you.'

'Who fancies him?' Sofie said as she unfolded a large duvet cover from the packet. 'Surely you don't mean me?'

'You, Sofie?' Ludovico sniggered. 'No be stupid! I mean Her Excellency the Irish Ambassador, of course, the magnificent Brigit O'Brien.'

'Brigit?' George said, taking a list from a pocket of his uniform. 'No, she's out of my class I'm afraid, Ludo old chap. Let's just check we've got everything. Then we'd better go. It's nearly time for Francesco's meeting. Right: carrier bags?'

Ludovico and Sofie began searching through the cloud of booty floating beneath the skylight where they had forced their way into the Balexert shopping mall. There had been too many people milling around the doors for them to get in safely any other way. Ludovico found the box of carrier bags he had retrieved from the Migros supermarket. 'Yes,' he said and pushed it into the duvet cover.

'Toilet rolls?' George called.

'Yes,' Ludo said.

'Moist toilet tissues?'

'I've got them,' Sofie replied, trying to push the large pack into the duvet cover.

'What this?' Ludovico said, pulling them out and reading the pack. '"Two hundred toilet wipes for clean little bottoms"? These no good, Sofie. They for children. They no big enough for your big ass!'

'I couldn't find any bigger ones,' Sofie said.

'They will do for now, Ludo,' George snapped. 'Have we got matches?'

'Yes George,' Sofie said.

'Straws?'

'Oh yes!' Ludovico giggled as he shoved them into the cover. 'Nice long ones.'

'Biscuits?' George said, turning a sour face on Ludo. 'Batteries? Torches? Camping stoves? Gas canisters...'

When they had checked everything on his list, George tied a rope round the cover's mouth and they pushed their giant shopping bag through the hole in the skylight then heaved it over the Balexert roof and down to the Route de Meyrin. George had already taught them that the best way to navigate, given the limited visibility allowed by their bubbles, was to follow the arrows painted on the road lanes. Their knowledge of Genevan geography made it fairly painless to navigate, and in this case it was very easy since the Route de Meyrin went straight past CERN.

George led the way, pulling the rope, while Sofie and Ludovico followed behind, each holding one corner of the duvet cover to stop it dragging on the road. As they passed the row of stumpy street lights, where the road ran beside the airport, Sofie glanced up, wondering whether there could be a plane hanging suspended in the air above them. *There are planes flying in and out of Geneva all day,* she thought. *If this disaster really has affected the whole world then people must be frozen in all sorts of dangerous situations. Not my problem, thank goodness. We've got enough to worry about just keeping ourselves alive and healthy.*

They had just reached the taller street lights beyond the airport when another bubble merged with theirs and Sofie saw something yellow hurtle overhead before disappearing out of their bubbles. All she could think of was aeroplanes but George shouted 'Karolyi! Come on!' He let go the rope and flew on at top speed.

Neither Sofie nor Ludovico had as much experience of flying as George and they only caught up with him in Meyrin village. He was hovering in front of a tram stop. 'Get back you two!' he shouted as they flew into his bubble.

They stopped and Sofie saw Alex Karolyi, his back against the stop's rear windows, both arms held out towards George.

When he saw the new arrivals, Alex swung his arms round to point at them, saying 'Stay right where you are!'

Sofie's guts contracted as her eyes saw the gun in his hand. 'I knew you were a swine, Karolyi,' she shouted, 'but I didn't know you were a gangster too!'

'Shut up Sofie,' George hissed. As far as Sofie could see, George was not injured and of course he was not frightened, just furious. Sofie could see his massive chest pumping oxygen into his lungs as he prepared himself for action. 'You're never going to get away with this, Karolyi,' he snarled.

Alex swung the gun and pointed it straight at him. 'My friend here says different, György. I don't want to hurt you, but you can't arrest me for stealing crystal. You don't have the right and anyways it's just stupid. I'm trying to help Kata save the world, for Christ's sake! Now listen, Gábor György, Marianne's in big trouble right now. I've seen her. Some clowns have grabbed her.'

'Grabbed Marianne? Where?'

'In the Cafeteria.'

'Which Cafeteria?'

'The one in the Main Building, for Christ's sake.'

'Don't give me that crap, Karolyi! You've just come up from Geneva so how the hell could you know what's happening in the Cafeteria?'

'Through the crystal, György.'

'What? What are you talking about?'

'It would take too long to explain. Just believe me, she needs help. Now are you going to stop here and talk about it or are you going to do your job and help me rescue her?'

'You're not going anywhere with that gun, Karolyi. Hand it over. Then we'll come and see what's happening.'

'Okay, György. You win.' Alex tossed the gun back down the tram stop, back towards Geneva. When George flew after it, Alex pressed his crystal, flew out of the other end of the stop and vanished from sight.

George paused for a moment as he checked the gun, then jammed it in a pocket, shouting 'Come on, Green Team!'

They flew along the Route de Meyrin, past the church and the old barn, assuming that Alex was heading for CERN.

'If these crystals are radioactive then we might as well just give up now, Professor,' Danny said as he flew with Francesco through the maze of narrow, wood-panelled corridors towards the little laboratory in Building One, gas pipes and data cables hanging overhead. 'We might already have had a fatal dose of radiation, and even if we haven't I don't see how we would be able to protect ourselves and use crystal at the same time.'

'Don't be so pessimistic, young man,' Francesco said. 'If crystal emits radiation then it must be fairly gentle. We have been in contact with it long enough for our skin to have been burnt by now if it was strong. Ah, here is the laboratory.' He led Danny into an office, flew past the filing cabinets and reached the little laboratory at the back. 'The first thing to do is find a Geiger counter.'

They soon found a yellow hand-held Gamma-Scout with an almost fully charged battery. Danny turned the ray selector to alpha plus beta plus gamma, checked the window was fully open and pressed the count button.

'What's the background level?' Francesco said, moving the large crystal out of the way.

Danny waited for the reading to stabilise. '2.73,' he said.

'2.73 microSievert per hour?' Francesco said, feeling relieved. 'That's not as high as I feared, but still, it's high.'

'It's nearly thirty times higher than normal background for Geneva,' Danny said, looking grave.

'Yes, but it's not dangerous. It's only about the same level as you would receive flying away on holiday.'

'But you don't spend days or weeks on a plane,' Danny said, giving him a sour glance.

'Pilots do. Listen, Danny, according to the Euroatom directive[10], workers are allowed to take a maximum of 50 milliSievert per year—'

'That's exceptional,' Danny interrupted him. 'The standard is 100 milliSievert over five years.'

'Okay, so 20 milliSievert per year is regarded as a safe level. So if we stayed in a bubble for a year at 2.73 milliSievert per hour, that would be...' he pulled out his mobile phone and pressed the screen a few times '20.8 milliSievert per year!' he said, smiling and looking relieved. 'You happy with that?'

Danny nodded. 'I just hope this doesn't go on for five years,' he said.

'Yes, so do I. This radiation must be coming from the bubble. So now for the real test. Check the radiation from this.' He held the large crystal before the Geiger counter's window, gripping it delicately between thumb and first finger, and held his breath.

'2.79,' Danny said after a pause.

Francesco started breathing again. 'So, no significant difference. Crystal isn't radioactive! It could have been much

---

[10] For a discussion of radiation levels see bibliography (11).

worse. It seems that only the bubble is creating the radiation. I'd like to understand why.'

They did some more measurements, Danny carefully recording everything, then Francesco left him making basic observations on the large crystal while he flew with the small one to the library.

Half an hour later he flew back along a corridor feeling pretty pleased with himself. At first he was so eager to tell Danny Schneider the results of his research that he even forgot to walk-fly until he met a couple of scientists coming down the corridor and narrowly avoided a collision. From then on he pretended to walk but met nobody else before reaching the small lab.

Danny was floating horizontally peering into a microscope.

'I think I understand the pattern on the bubble now, Danny,' Francesco announced proudly.

'Oh really?' Danny sounded preoccupied.

'Are you not excited? This is a very important discovery. It is very simple, really. Come over here and I will show you how it works.'

Danny sighed as he took the crystal out of the microscope and followed him across to a white-board on the lab wall.

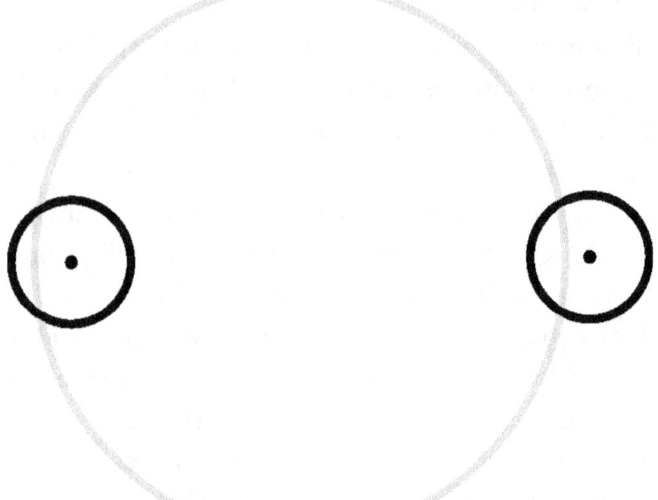

'This is the bubble,' Francesco said, drawing a big green circle. 'Now let's think about the atoms of gas in the air whose electron shells are partly inside the bubble and partly outside. There are two cases we need to consider.' He added two small black circles overlapping the big one with dots at their centres. 'For this atom,' he pointed at the left atom, 'the nucleus is inside the bubble and most of its electrons are also inside so, as the nucleus moves, they will move with it. But any electrons outside the bubble will be frozen and left behind.'

Danny nodded. 'So you accept the theory that time has stopped outside a bubble Professor?'

'I think I have to. All the evidence points that way. What Einstein would say about this I dread to think. I have no idea how the laws of relativity work at the bubble wall but that is a different question. It's just one of the many problems we will have to work on in the future. I assume that the boundary between the inside and the outside of the bubble is very narrow. It might even be a discontinuity in space-time. But for now I just want us to think about these atoms which are cut by the bubble wall. Right, so this nucleus is inside the bubble and it will keep moving, so what happens when it moves away from the bubble wall, young man?'

'Well, as you say, any electrons outside the bubble will be left behind so I suppose the moving atom will be ionised[11].'

'Precisely! Like this.' He drew a red circle inside the bubble, also with a black dot at its centre. 'In the same way this other atom,' he pointed at the atom on the right, 'might have its nucleus outside the bubble. Then the nucleus will be frozen, but any electrons which happen to be inside the bubble will be left wandering in free space. So what is the result?'

'I suppose these free electrons would get attracted to the ionised atoms,' Danny said thoughtfully.

---

[11] An "ion" is an atom or molecule which has lost or gained one or more electrons.

Francesco drew an arrow

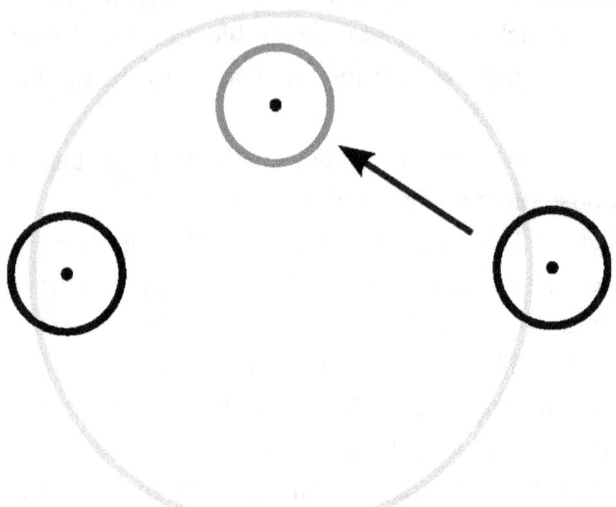

'Correct!' Francesco drew an arrow to show an electron being captured by the ion. 'And as they are captured they fall through the atomic energy levels—'

'And so emit the radiation we measured!' Danny exclaimed.

'Indeed, and also creating the colours in the bubble wall. I've just been to the library to check the spectroscopy and of all the molecules in the air, oxygen has the strongest visible spectrum dominated by red and green lines. In fact the Corona Borealis is often precisely those colours because of the emission from oxygen.'

'The Northern Lights? So that explains why we see the red and green colours but what about the patterns, Professor? Why are the colours arranged in these patterns?'

Francesco glanced at the pattern, considering the question. Fields of red and green were constantly appearing, drifting about like the surface of a soap bubble, then merging into the black areas which separated them. 'I'm not sure about that yet,' he said thoughtfully, then shrugged. 'It's probably stimulated emission of radiation, a sort of cascade process. I still need to do some more work on that problem, but I'm absolutely sure the bubble wall is full of ionised atoms. That would also explain why you get a small electric shock when you touch it.'

'And why is it that the bubble feels hard to touch yet, when we fly, things can pass straight through it?'

'I think that has something to do with the way space-time is configured at the bubble wall. We need somebody to solve the relativistic equations at the bubble boundary to fully understand that question. That is a task for an expert in gravitational theory. I doubt we will find many people with those skills in CERN. There is still so much work to do, so many exciting things to discover! I've been thinking about this situation, Danny. I know that this is a disaster, with two men absorbed by a black hole and ATLAS badly damaged and the world being frozen in time, but I also think this is an incredible opportunity for us to learn a huge amount about science. Completely new knowledge will emerge from this experience, Danny, knowledge we could not have gained any other way. Maybe, in the end, the world will be a better place for having gone through this disaster. And, after all only two people have been killed. It could have been worse.'

'Three,' Danny said. 'My son was also killed.'

'Ah yes, quite. I'm sorry, you are right. That was sad. Very sad. Oh yes, and there was that other firefighter, what was his name? Can't remember. So now then, how have you got on with measuring the basic parameters of that large crystal?'

'I've almost finished.' Danny took a piece of paper out of his jacket pocket. 'I've measured its size, refractive index, electric and magnetic fields. I haven't found anything very interesting at all, apart from one thing.'

'Oh yes? And that is?'

'Come over here, Professor Romani, and look through this microscope. Actually you can see this with the naked eye but a microscope makes it much clearer, since the objects are so small.'

They flew back to the bench and Danny placed the large crystal into a wire cage he had constructed on the microscope's stage and spent a long time slowly rotating it until finally he grunted and moved aside so Francesco could look.

Francesco hesitated. 'It's not plugged in.'

'You won't need a light to see this, Professor.'

Francesco handed his small crystal to Danny and looked down the two eyepieces. Something blue flashed inside the crystal. A striped object was waving from side to side with a regular rhythm. He adjusted the focus, the striped object seemed to shrink and he saw a tiny fish swim slowly across from one side of the crystal to the other. Its mouth was opening and closing as if it was feeding. Its two pectoral fins began pushing against the water and the fish rotated, the scales on its head glistening in the reflected blue light. 'Merda!' Francesco said. 'What's this?'

'It's a fish.'

'Yes I can see that, Danny, but where is it? And how can we see it in this crystal?'

'I have no idea, Professor Romani. I've looked through all eight faces of that large crystal and I have seen two different fish and the bottom of a pond or river. Can we try looking through this one now?'

Danny took the large crystal off the microscope stage and placed Francesco's smaller one onto it. Then he backed away, offering Francesco the first look.

'I just see internal reflections and refractions from other faces,' Francesco said.

'You need to move it so you are looking exactly into the centre of one of the outer faces.' Danny said. 'You might need to look into several of them until you find the right one.'

Following these instructions, Francesco suddenly saw a long, narrow white corridor with many green doors leading off both sides. The bronze carpet was moving past him as if he were flying and Brigit O'Brien was just ahead of him, pretending to walk. Every time she reached a door she tried the handle and banged, calling 'Marianne'. Most doors seemed to be locked. Occasionally one opened and she went in shouting Marianne's name.

Francesco looked up at Danny feeling stunned. 'Can you hear anything?'

Danny shook his head with a puzzled frown.

'I saw Ambassador O'Brien. I could hear her too. She was searching for Marianne and calling her name. I think she was in the Hostel. Here, see for yourself.'

Danny frowned again then bent and looked into the microscope. 'Yes, it's definitely one of the hostels.'

'This is absolutely incredible Danny. Incredible.' Francesco was more amazed by this than anything else he had seen today. 'What physics is involved in this? How is it possible to see and hear out of another crystal? I don't understand this. Do you, Danny?'

Danny shook his head. 'I don't understand anything that's happened here today, Professor. I don't know what this crystal is made of or where it's come from. The whole thing is not understandable to me at all. It's out of my domain. I'm just an engineer. But I'd like to complete my basic observations and find out what else we can see in this crystal, Professor.'

'You expect to see something else?'

'Perhaps. By looking into two different faces of the big one I saw two different fish, so I guess we might see something else in this one too if we look into a different face.' He flipped the crystal over and peered down the eyepieces, slowly adjusting the crystal. 'Maybe we will be able to see Marianne or—Good God! I can see her! That swine Karolyi is holding her in his arms!'

Without another word, Danny grabbed the large crystal which was still floating beside the microscope and flew quickly out of the laboratory.

'Stop Danny!' Francesco shouted. 'Where are you...' But it was too late. Danny's bubble had separated from his and Francesco knew he would never be able to find him in the maze of corridors in Building One. Mystified, he looked into the microscope. Not only was Alex Karolyi holding Marianne Schneider in his arms but the bald firefighter was pointing a gun at him. They appeared to be in the CERN Cafeteria. Francesco heard Alex say something about the Medical Centre then fly away at top speed. Francesco lifted the small crystal off the microscope stage and flew out of the lab, heading for the Cafeteria.

If the two men hadn't been holding her Alex wouldn't have known who the woman in the grey firefighter's uniform was as his bubble surrounded the tableau at the tea bar. They were frozen, one man holding her arm and another pulling her long dark hair. Alex let out a howl of outrage and flew at the nearest man, thumping him in the face. He let her go. The other man screamed and let go too.

Alex had only just lifted Marianne in his arms when the three firefighters flew into the aisle. Alex ignored them and looked down into Marianne's face. What he saw made him want to cry. Her eyes were closed and surrounded by dark rings, her cheeks gaunt, their greyness emphasised by the uniform she wore and the blood trickling from a gash on her forehead.

'Are you all right kedvenc?' he whispered.

'Put her down slowly, Karolyi,' George growled.

Reluctantly, Alex's eyes left Marianne's face and turned to George. His arms were straight; he was holding the gun in both hands aiming it at Alex's head.

You are pathetic, Alex thought. *A little boy with a new toy.* 'She needs a doctor, György,' Alex said, gathering Marianne's limp body to his heart with one arm and gripping his crystal in the other hand. 'I'll be in the Medical Centre if you need me.' The firefighters watched him in disbelief as he flew out of one end of the servery just as Danny Schneider flew in at the other.

Alex was flying past the traffic island on the Route Pauli when Marianne revived. She looked at him and a frown flickered across her face, followed quickly by a look of recognition and a smile, her old smile, the smile she hadn't given him for almost a year. But it was immediately replaced by a wince.

'I've got a terrible headache,' she said.

In spite of her weariness and her bleeding face she was still the most beautiful woman Alex had ever known. He kissed her forehead, tasting the salt of her blood and sweat. All he wanted now was to carry her along this road out of CERN and down to his boat. It wasn't for sex. He wanted to look after her, to nurse her, to protect her, to show her how much he loved her. He had never felt this way about a woman before. Until this moment he hadn't even known it was possible to feel like this.

'You were hit on the head, kedvenc.'

'Was I?'

'I just rescued you from the bastards who'd grabbed you.'

'Did you? Thank you, Alex,' she said distantly, as if it was painful to speak.

Alex reached the junction with the Route Einstein and stopped, cradling her body against him, feeling her full breasts pressing through his shirt. The nearness of her thrilled him, even in the pitiful state she was in.

'Do you remember that night, Marianne?'

She didn't answer.

'On my boat?'

'Just forget about that, Alex. It was a long time ago.'

'I've renamed her after you, you know.'

'Have you? What did you call her? The Fool?'

'The Marianne.'

'Why?'

'Because I fell in love with you that night, kedvenc.'

'Don't call me that! It was a mistake.'

'A mistake? What, all night? I don't think so. It was a wonderful night, kedvenc, and you know it.'

'Forget it, Alex. It never happened. Where are we going?'

I can't take her to the boat, much as I'd like to. She needs medical attention. 'We're going to the Medical Centre,' he said and began to fly up the Route Einstein.

'Where's Danny?'

'He's in the Cafeteria.'

'I want to go back.'

Alex stopped.

'You'd be better off in the Medical Centre honey. I'm hoping the doctor will be there.'

'He isn't there. He's in the Cafeteria. I want to go back, Alex.'

'All right honey. I'll take you.'

'No! I'll go on my own. If you meet George he won't be very pleased with you.'

'Nobody is very pleased with me anymore kedvenc, including you.'

'There he is,' George said as he flew into Alex's bubble, quickly followed by the other two firefighters. 'We'll take her off your hands now, Karolyi. And no funny business.'

Alex looked up to see the wrong end of the little Beretta for the third time that day.

Episode 41 Virtual Reality Chamber

The little room off the Palace's Main Hall rang with the cheers of the night-shift engineers as they watched the images on the scanner screen showing the pod slip away from the probe's arm and fall down the hole into the Cosmic Egg. Professor Porqoi Nithold cut their celebrations short. 'Enable the Virtual Reality Chamber!' he barked as he stamped across the makeshift laboratory, entered the Chamber and slammed the door closed with a vicious flick of his abdomen.

The magnified head of Rudok, the Senior Control Engineer, appeared on the Chamber's far wall, his antennae quivering. 'Anything wrong Professor Nithold?' he said nervously. In the other walls Nithold saw other Argolathian heads briefly leave their screens and glance up at his virtual three-dimensional image floating in the laboratory above them.

'The emergent Samfitzpatrick made me look completely incompetent before His Majesty,' Nithold snapped. 'It seems that time has stopped inside the Cosmic Egg!'

'What?'

'That's right. And I had no idea. I didn't even know that one of the Cosmic Egg's blue pipes had been broken! Yet it seems that some stupid Entroilian academic called Professor Itoodoo knows better. A female, no less!'

'By the Anting!'

'Sickening, isn't it? Apparently, when time was functioning in the Egg, some sort of rain was falling from the pipes. This Itoodoo creature told the emergent that the missing pipe could be fixed. So His Majesty wants me to help something called "Stepdaughter" to collect the fragments of the broken pipe and bring them here so I can restart time in the Egg.'

'How are you going to do that, Professor?'

Nithold hesitated. 'Nobody has told me that.'

'Well at least His Majesty has confidence in your abilities, Professor! That must be some satisfaction?'

'No, I don't think he trusts me now, after the emergent made me look so stupid. His Majesty has ordered me, yes *ordered me* to place detectors in the crystal cavern where we found the emergent. It's appalling. He clearly has no confidence whatever in my ability or judgement. As His Majesty's senior scientific advisor, decisions about how to accomplish this task should be mine alone.' Nithold turned on the hand-held flight controller. 'Reactivate the Cosmic Egg scanner and position this chamber on the departure platform!' After a moment the walls of the virtual reality chamber grew dark, Nithold pulled the controller's joystick to one side and the edge of the small platform at the top of the Cosmic Egg's cabinet swung into view, dark grey against the deeper blackness. He pressed the lever forward and the edge came closer, giving him the impression of moving forward. Surrounded by images projected onto every wall it was easy to believe he was actually inside the little cabinet, especially as he moved over the edge of the platform and out into the inky blackness.

'But wouldn't it be good to make contact with this stepdaughter, Professor?' the disembodied voice of Rudok echoed around the chamber. 'What a marvellous opportunity to explore the biology and culture of Prince Samfitzpatrick's—'

'Marvellous?' Nithold snapped as he tilted the controller and saw the tiny pink Cosmic Egg far below him, its blue transparent shell shimmering in the bottom of the cabinet. 'The most important task is to understand the mode of functioning of the Cosmic Egg.' The professor clicked the flight controller and began to descend towards the egg. 'These little creatures are of very minor significance compared to the whole Egg. And don't forget, Rudok, that we have to report back to His Majesty by morning. There'll be no sleep for us tonight!'

As Nithold flew rapidly towards it, the Egg seemed to grow larger. By the time he reached the network of blue crystal rods it seemed huge, as if he was hovering on the outside of a gigantic planet surrounded by a delicate blue cobweb. In spite of his anger he was astonished at its beauty. The laser beams which Rudok was using to scan the Egg reflected and refracted through the crystals. They were arranged into groups, several dozen radiating from a central point like a starburst, all curving away and joining with other similar groups in an intricate and apparently random pattern. The whole thing seemed to have grown organically.

Crysorganic? he thought. *That's what Moshendiar called them.*

'Are you ready, Professor?' Rudok said. 'The co-ordinates are 52.4094 South—'

'Just put a marker there and I'll find it.' Nithold said absently as his eyes swept the network, searching for any patterns there might be in the arrangement of the starbursts. A moment later a huge white virtual pole appeared on his left, emerging from the far side of the Cosmic Egg and tapering away into the distance. Nithold clicked the controller and began to fly around the Egg towards it. *I wish Moshendiar had explained how crysorganic materials function,* he thought. *It obviously has both organic and inorganic properties. If this network is crystalline, surely there should be some regularity in the pattern of these junctions, but I can't see any. Investigating the properties of this substance alone would be a major research project. How can I possibly get any useful results by morning? It's not feasible.*

Nithold still had not seen any sort of pattern by the time he reached the virtual white pole. He looked down but could not see where the pipe was missing from the network.

'Is that marker on the spot where we found Prince Samfitzpatrick?'

'Well no, not exactly, Professor. It's not far away, but unfortunately I didn't note the exact co-ordinates of the place so I've put the marker in the hole where we dropped the pod.'

'What?' Looking straight down Nithold saw the white pole vanishing into the deep hole in the pink ocean. 'You fool, Rudok! Didn't you realise the place where we found the emergent was of major significance?'

'I'm so sorry, Professor,' Rudok blustered. 'There was a lot happening at the time. But I could easily search the records to find where we put King Flenkt when he first visited the Cosmic Egg.'

'No no no, there's no time for that! Oh well, I'll just have to do a visual search. Turn the marker off so I can see all the network around here.' The white pole vanished and Nithold hovered above the hole in the pink surface, scanning the crystals below him. It took him a while to find the gap, but when he did he gasped 'By the Anting!'

'What's wrong Professor?'

'But of course, it's obvious! I should have realised this before! What a fool I've been. Come into this chamber and see for yourself, Rudok.' Nithold flew down, passing the outermost crystal pipes until he was hovering inside the crystal network. The blue-green pipes formed a thick layer all around him. *It's like a web woven by a swarm of rilomis!* he thought. A few moments later part of the virtual image swung back as the engineer opened the door and came into the chamber. Nithold pointed a heavy clawed hand at one wall. 'There's one gap.' In the wall's centre was a starburst with a hole where one pipe was obviously missing. 'And there,' he said, pointing at the opposite wall where lay an exactly similar starburst with an exactly similar gap, 'is another one!'

Rudok looked from one wall to the other, his antennae hanging limp in astonishment. 'There are two gaps, Professor!'

'Of course there are! It makes sense, can't you see? One is the place where we found Prince Samfitzpatrick.'

'And the other one?'

'It must be where the other end of the broken pipe used to be. There's no other possible explanation.'

'By the Anting! I wonder why we never noticed before?'

'Yes, I wonder why *you* didn't notice it before, Rudok! Weren't you in charge of the scanner? Hmm. Now to fulfil my orders from His Majesty I have to put some sensors into the gap where we found the Prince. I don't suppose, Senior Engineer Rudok, that you are able to tell me which of these two gaps that would be?'

Rudok's antennae went as limp as two pieces of string but he said nothing.

'No, I thought not. Well we have to start somewhere. Let's examine this one.' He chose one of the two gaps at random and flew down towards it. The Virtual Reality Chamber was too large to fit in so he pressed the scale button on the controller and the crystal starburst seemed to expand around him until the gap was large enough for him to enter.

'Prince Samfitzpatrick said he could see and talk to people on his home planet when he was in the gap, but he did not explain how he did it. All I know is that the fragments of the broken crystal pipe are joined to this network through things called negative energy strings, and it was these which allowed him to talk to people on his home planet. So now I must try to talk to somebody called "Stepdaughter". I have absolutely no idea who that is. The only thing I know is that her name is Catriona and that she has started to go down some sort of tunnel.'

'Could it be that hole?' Rudok said, pointing at the hole in the pink surface below them.

'I have no idea. But in any case the Prince and Princess are investigating that hole so I will leave that to them. His Majesty's *order* was to investigate this gap, or maybe the other one. I wish I knew which one Samfitzpatrick was in when we found him. How stupid of you, Rudok, not to have recorded its co-ordinates.'

'I'm really sorry, Professor. I suppose we'll need to check them both.'

'Yes, and since we've only got one Virtual Reality Chamber, you'll have to use the micro-probes.'

'Yes of course Professor Nithold.'

As the engineer returned to the lab, Nithold began to dictate into the voice recorder. 'Recording by Porqoi Nithold. Inspecting one of two holes in the event network of the Cosmic Egg as instructed by His Majesty King Flenkt. Engineer Rudok inspecting other hole. Holes apparently made by breaking of a crystal pipe. My location,' he clicked a few buttons on the flight controller and some figures appeared floating in the air before him, 'is 52.40972 South, 1.55219 East.'

There was a short break in the recording as he counted. 'There are sixty faces making up the walls of this hole. Each is formed from the end of a long regular prism. Prisms are regular in shape but with various numbers of sides, from three to seven. Far end of each prism attached to a set of similar prisms forming a junction similar to the one I am in. The material of these prisms is believed to be crysorganic. No! Erase last sentence! These prisms are made from some form of crystalline material which is semi-transparent and of a blue-green colour.' As he spoke, Nithold saw a cluster of probes descend from the top of the cabinet on the end of a slender articulated metallic arm. The cluster entered the other hole through the gap where the broken pipe had been.

'How many faces has that hole got, Rudok?' Nithold asked over the intercom.

There was a pause. Nithold could see the probes turning as Rudok counted the crystal faces. 'Sixty, Professor, if you don't count the gap.'

'Same as mine. Hmm,' he muttered, wondering *Coincidence? Or do all crystal junctions have sixty pipes coming in? Or no, sixty one! One is missing here. We need to check that later. Not a priority at present.* 'Okay,' he said. 'I assume that the emergent must have seen the creatures of his home through the faces in the hole he was in, so let's both do a quick scan of them all. Only spend a maximum of two minutes on each one. Even that will take us two hours and we don't have much time.'

'Okay, Professor. Should I attach a virtual number to each face?'

'Oh, so you've decided to use your brain at last, have you Rudok? Good idea.'

Nithold chose one of the faces in his hole and flew the virtual chamber towards it but as he came close he saw the number "27" appear in one corner of it. He flew around until he found the face with the number "1".

'Face One pentagonal,' he dictated quickly into the controller's voice recorder. 'Appears to be perfectly planar and regular. Each edge is...' he activated the laser pointer and ran it rapidly along one edge, '...approximately 1.502 cuads long.' *This isn't the right time for accurate measurements*, he thought. *My priority is to look into these crystals. That must have been how the emergent saw and heard Stepdaughter. How else could he have done it?*

Looking into the long thin body of the crystal prism he could see its edges tapering away into the distance until it curved round towards another junction. 'Crystalline structure appears flawless,' he dictated. 'Can't see any defects.' It tinged the blackness of the scanner cabinet with a pale blue glow, and where two crystals overlapped the blue colour was stronger. The complex overlapping patterns were all straight edges and flat sheets of colour. 'Can't see anything of interest,' he dictated and flew slowly across the face, staring into it, scanning it from all angles. The pattern changed but still nothing of interest appeared, no promise of anything which might be the image of another emergent.

Nithold moved to the crystal marked "2" and repeated his observations, dictating his results into the voice recorder. This crystal appeared to be very similar to the first except that it had six faces. He moved from crystal to crystal with a slowly rising sense of anxiety. *What will the King say if I have nothing to report in the morning? "You are completely incompetent, Nithold! I obviously need to find a new scientific advisor!"* His anxiety growing, Nithold began to spend more time looking into each crystal, experimenting not just by varying his position and the angle of view but also his distance from the face, but still with the same negative result. Rudok too reported finding nothing as he scanned the crystals in the other junction.

After an hour, while inspecting crystal twenty-seven, Nithold had the sudden idea that he might be able to hear something even if he could see nothing, so he turned up the recorder's amplifier and pointed it at the crystal as he flew across the face then played back the recording hoping he might hear something. The recording was silent.

It was about twenty minutes later, while scanning across crystal thirty-five, that he thought he saw, deep down inside the crystal, something with a lighter shade of blue. He stopped and stared but saw nothing. *Optical illusion?* he wondered. *I don't think so.* He flew slowly back, staring into the flat blue sheet of colour. The five edges of the prism looked almost identical as they tapered together before they curved away, showing that he was very close to the centre of the crystal face. He flew a little further, watching the vanishing perspective of those edges change but not seeing anything else in the crystal. *Perhaps I was at the exact centre when I saw it?* Trying to get a fuller view of all five faces, he flew away from the crystal and suddenly saw it again.

'Rudok!' he shouted into the intercom. 'I can see something in one of the crystals!'

'Thank the Anting! What is it, Professor?'

Nithold peered into the crystal. 'It looks like a rope.' It was clearly made up of smaller threads. It reminded him of one of those tangles of creepers he sometime saw hanging from the trees in the damp and steaming forest near the foot of the Malordon Mountains in summer. But all that was too much to explain right now.

'Can I come and have a look?' Rudok sounded excited.

'No, I want you to try something. Take another look into one of the crystals in your junction and make sure you're looking into the exact centre, Rudok. Let me know whether you see anything.'

'Okay, Prof. Oh, and just to warn you, the King's come into the lab. Not sure what he wants.'

'Oh really? Excellent! Please ask His Majesty if he would be so kind as to come in here straight away.'

As Nithold waited for the King, he dictated his observations of the rope floating in the crystal face before him, feeling satisfied, almost elated. *I've certainly got something to show Flenkt now!*

Each of the pale yellow creeper-like strands was quite thin, but dozens of them were tangled together to make the thick rope. It was impossible to count them. It began not far from the flat, near end of the crystalline pipe and snaked away down the middle. Its central section was bright, but too far away to see clearly. It finally faded away as it approached the bend in the pipe, as if going out of focus.

The idea flashed into his mind: *Could they be those negative energy strings which the emergent told the King about at the wedding feast?* This thought stimulated his scientific curiosity so strongly that it drove out everything else. *The discovery of such strings would be a breakthrough of major proportions.* He flew closer to the crystal, trying to get a better view, and was astonished when the image moved rapidly towards him, growing larger, the individual threads becoming clearer until the rope appeared to be floating just below the crystal's smooth surface. It was so close Nithold felt as if he could reach out and touch it. He was just about to fly even closer when the door opened and he turned to see the King walk in.

Before Flenkt's inquisitive bright-green eyes, Nithold's confidence evaporated. *He's going to ask me whether I've found any of the emergent's fellow-beings,* he thought. *He won't be satisfied with just seeing these strings. I've got to persuade him they are important.*

'Well, Nithold?' Flenkt said. 'What is it? What have you found?'

Nithold took a step back and bowed, using the controller's laser to indicate the spot on the floor which he had been occupying. 'Please stand there, Majesty,' he said, trying to sound confident. 'I have found something which I believe is of the highest importance.' He helped the King to place his head correctly and was gratified at Flenkt's initial enthusiasm.

Flenkt waved his antennae in approval, then turned to the scientist. 'Yes, well I'm glad my sons are safe and having a good meal, Nithold, but where is Stepdaughter?'

Nithold stared at him in dumb incomprehension. 'Sons, Majesty?' he gasped. 'You...you can see your sons?'

'Of course. You seem surprised, Nithold. Wasn't that what you wanted to show me?'

'Yes, yes, of course Your Majesty. It's just that I also saw the negative energy strings, at least that's what I assumed—'

'What are you gibbering about, Nithold? You can see my sons in that blue pipe as clear as your own antennae. Yes I agree that's important and very gratifying but—'

'I'm sorry to interrupt, Your Majesty, but may I perhaps have a look?'

Flenkt's antennae quivered with anger but he graciously moved aside and let Nithold stand in the viewing spot. When he looked into the crystal Nithold cried out loud in surprise.

'What's the matter now, Nithold? It's just my sons eating the remains of some larvae—'

'No, Majesty, not at all. I can't see any of that, but I can see the pod, and there are flames shooting out of its rocket!' He stared at the pod in amazement. Its rear end was slowly moving towards him, the rocket's brilliant light reflecting off the twisting silvery negative energy strands and illuminating for the first time a pink circular wall.

'Let me see,' Flenkt said and pushed him aside.

Nithold's mind was working overtime as the King looked once more into the crystal. 'If Your Majesty can see your royal sons eating larvae and I can see the pod then clearly we must be looking at things in the hole in the Cosmic Egg.'

'Well that's pretty obvious, Nithold.'

Nothing is obvious in this situation, Nithold thought. 'This proves that the negative energy strings must go down the hole too,' he said, trying to control his injured feelings.

'But why do you see things that I can't see, Nithold?' Flenkt said. 'I can't see the pod at all. Just my sons and a sort of rope. It goes up to...' Flenkt leaned to one side, apparently trying to get a better view. 'Ah yes, I can see it now! The pod's coming towards me. I can almost smell its rocket!' He leaned back the other way. 'Sucklin Rodbel! It's frying one of my sons! Stop it, Nithold. Don't just stand there, you idiot! Stop it!'

Episode 42 The Trial

When the old man came into the Great Hall everyone stood. His obvious affluence was in stark contrast to the ragged poverty of the peasants and soldiers standing beneath the tall wooden-panelled walls. The elaborately woven golden stole hanging round his neck, the beautifully embroidered white cassock and, most of all, his tall, pointed golden mitre only enhanced Catriona's sense of unreality.

'That is the Prince-Bishop of Geneva,' the friar whispered. 'You are very lucky to have him to hear your case. He is an expert in trying witches.'

The Prince-Bishop walked to the table and sat beside the Chatelain who was untying the lace of a little black leather pouch. Catriona's frightened eyes watched as he up-ended the bag and a shower of heavy golden coins clunked, rolled, and spun across the solid pine table. When all was silent he let fall two more objects from the bag. The blue and pink crystal pyramids clattered onto the pile of coins. The Chatelain looked at Catriona and said something in French. Standing beside her the friar translated: 'Do you admit that those Devil's Jewels are yours?'

A hush descended over the crowd in the Chateau de Peney's Hall. All the farm-hands and the soldiers and the women and even the children had cheered after the first trial, when the hospital master and his wife had confessed everything. Now it was Catriona's turn and they were all looking at her, even the two murderers who stood shackled to the wall.

'Tell him to be careful,' Catriona whispered to the priest. 'I think the pink one's only safe as long as it's close to the blue one.'

The friar passed on the warning and the Chatelain pulled out a dagger and pushed the crystals closer together then pointed it at Catriona's heart and repeated his question.

'Do you admit that those Devil's Jewels are yours?' the friar said urgently.

'Yes, they are mine, father,' she said, thinking *What else can I say? The blue one is mine and I'd like to have that pink one as well even though it's obviously a bit dangerous. Sam told me to take all the fragments down the tunnel but I only brought that blue one so he'll be a bit happier if I can take another one too. If I ever manage to find the—*

'Does God exist?' the friar said and immediately he had her full attention. He was staring at the Prince Bishop who was staring straight at Catriona with a sombre expression on his wrinkled, care-worn face.

'Answer the question, child. The Prince-Bishop wants to know if God exists. And think hard before you answer. Your life depends upon it.'

Does God exist? I don't think there's a God up in the sky but I'm sure there's something inside us all, a sort of spirit. And didn't I put myself in Jesus' hands in that chapel in the hospital and didn't he save my life? And isn't he the Son of God? So how can I deny him now?

'I think...' She could hardly speak her mouth was so dry. *My life depends on this answer.* She swallowed hard and tried again. 'I think God does exist, father.'

The friar relayed her answer. A murmur of approval went round the hall. *I seem to have got that right anyway.*

The Prince-Bishop spoke again. 'Does the Devil exist?' The friar translated.

This one's a bit more tricky. If I say "Yes" then it might seem like I'm confessing to being in league with the devil. That's what witches are supposed to do isn't it, be in league with the devil? But if I say "No" then it might seem like I'm trying to cover up for him. What should I say?

'Does the Devil exist?' the friar repeated.

Best just tell the truth, she told herself. *But what is the truth? What do I really think? Does the Devil exist? You could say that there's a little devil inside all of us, just like there's a little bit of God inside all of us. There's certainly a devil inside Alex Karolyi. I never met anyone who could cast a spell over me like he has. But is that really the—*

'Does the devil exist?' The tension in the air was like a fog filling the Great Hall, making it hard to breathe.

'Yes Father,' Catriona said, her voice sounding very high and tense.

'Oui,' the priest translated and once more a sigh of approval rippled round the room.

The Prince-Bishop spoke again.

'Do witches exist?' the friar translated.

'No,' Catriona said without any hesitation and smiled. *I know I got that one right.*

There was a silence which seemed to last for an eternity, then gasps of disbelief and shocked cries of outrage went up from the peasants crowding the hall. The Chatelain shouted and banged the table and the crowd fell silent. He conferred with the Prince-Bishop who took something out of his pocket.

'You are very lucky,' the friar said. 'They could have sentenced you to death for that answer but they are going to give you one more chance. The Chatelain says that, as you are a foreigner, you might have misunderstood the question so they are going to make sure you are really a witch. Take off your clothes.'

'What? Why?'

'The Prince-Bishop is going to search you.'

'Search me? What for? I haven't got any more crystal.'

'For the Devil's Mark.'

'For what?' Catriona felt utterly confused, and a wave of panic began to rise up from her stomach as two soldiers came towards her with ropes. A ripple of excitement echoed round the Great Hall and Catriona felt herself tremble.

'The Devil's Mark,' the friar continued. 'It's what a witch uses to feed milk to the Devil. It can be a scar, a mole, a birthmark or an extra nipple[12].'

'But I've got moles,' Catriona said as the soldiers stood before her. 'That's not a crime!'

'Don't worry child. The Devil's Mark is no ordinary mole. It is insensitive to pain and will not bleed. You will be tested by the Prince-Bishop himself. He is a very experienced witch-pricker. You will be in very good hands.'

She looked at the man in the golden mitre sitting at the table and saw he had a bodkin-like thing in his hand with a very narrow blade sticking out of its silver handle.

'Take off your clothes child, quickly,' the friar insisted. 'If you are innocent you will come to no harm.'

In a panic Catriona looked at the people crowded into the hall, every face watching her intently, then looked at the soldiers standing before her and realised she had no choice. *If I've either got to do this or die I suppose I'll have to do it.*

She slipped off the cloak the Chatelain had given her and put one arm over her chest, one hand over her groin. The crowd watched in rapt silence as the soldiers gripped her arms and escorted her to the long table. The Chatelain put his money and the crystals back into his bag then he and the Prince-Bishop stood, scraping back their heavy chairs.

---

[12] The Devil's Mark was believed to be an anaesthetic scar somewhere on a witch's body where she had been scratched by the Devil's claws at the moment of the initiation. See for example bibliography (13) page 25.

The soldiers let go her arms and motioned her to get up onto the table. It was high and the wooden surface was rough. When she did not move, one of the soldiers grasped her arm again. She shook him off, jumped up onto the table and quickly lay herself face down upon it, her arms tucked in at her sides, her eyes shut tight. The wood beneath her was hard and cold. The fear of splinters just added to her sense of impending disaster.

She heard the Prince-Bishop walking slowly round her. There was no sound from the crowd. She heard a man breathing above her, the sound moving slowly down the table. She felt him touch her back and she jumped. *If the Devil's Mark can't feel anything then I'd better make it obvious that I can feel something.* He touched her bottom and she jumped again. *God, what's he going to do now?* But nothing happened and she felt him touch her leg.

Then he said something.

'Turn over,' the friar said quietly.

She felt relieved to know he was nearby, but she didn't move. She couldn't. She felt as if she was tied down to the table.

'Turn over child or you will be found guilty and burnt.'

She forced herself to turn over and stared up into the Prince-Bishop's eyes. He had taken off his mitre, revealing the face of an old man with grey hairy eyebrows and a very serious expression. *If he's getting some sort of thrill out of this, he's not showing it.* His eyes ran slowly over her face, down her neck and he moved away down her body.

He paused when he reached her chest. She lifted her head and looked at him, then down at her own body. Her sense of unreality grew at what she saw. The arms were hairy, the stomach was plump, the hips were wide and the breasts were large and sagging to the sides. *That isn't my body*, she thought, and the panic rose up from her chest and began to race round and round inside her head as the old man moved down towards her groin. She couldn't bear to watch and let her head fall back on the table with a thump.

He's going to tell me to open my legs in a minute. What will I do? Shall I make a run for it? Which is better, to be publicly humiliated or—

There was a gasp from the crowd. Catriona's head lifted and she looked down again. The Prince-Bishop was pressing the bodkin against her foot. The narrow blade seemed to have gone into her flesh all the way up to the silver handle, yet she felt nothing. As he moved it away the blade seemed to come out but still she felt nothing. Then she heard a faint metallic click. The Chatelain began to speak. The Prince-Bishop put his bodkin into his pocket with a tiny smile.

'It's a fraud,' Catriona shouted, sitting up. 'It's a trick. That bodkin thing must have a retractable blade or something.'

But the friar wasn't listening. The Chatelain was speaking and the friar began to translate as he handed her back her cloak, his voice sounding full of grief. 'It is written in Exodus 22 verse 18: Thou shalt not suffer a witch to live.'

'For as much as in this Court of Justice held by me, Nycolas d'Orsières, Chatelain of Peney within the Republic of Geneva, upon this twenty-first day of May in the year of Our Lord 1536;'

The Chatelain paused and the friar translated, but Catriona couldn't really follow what he was saying. All she could do was to hold in her hands the cold iron chain which shackled her wrists to the wall, trying to stop the heavy manacles from cutting into her flesh, quietly sobbing over and over 'I've failed, Sam. I'm sorry.'

'The three accused persons,' Nycolas d'Orsières continued, reading from the large book that lay on the table beside the two Devil's Jewels. 'Claude de Bourgeaulx Master of l'Hôpital de la Peste, Brisette de Bourgeaulx his wife and Catriona O'Brien, native of Ireland, are hereby found guilty by this court of the several articles of witchcraft specified in the indictments given against you. You will be taken from here to the place of execution and your bodies shall be dismembered and then rendered into quarters and you shall be burned—'

'Seigneur d'Orsières!' somebody shouted outside the Great Hall. The Chatelain stopped speaking, the friar stopped translating and Catriona stopped sobbing. She held her breath, listening, hoping somehow somebody would rush in and tell them it was all a mistake. And indeed it did seem as if something was happening outside because she could hear the noise of gunfire and people shouting. The women in the Great Hall started screaming and everyone was running out.

Shackled to the wall beside Catriona, the hospital master rattled his chain and let out an insane roar of laughter.

'What's happening, Father?' Catriona asked, hoping against hope that somebody had come to rescue her.

'The General Council of Geneva has confirmed the adoption of the Reform throughout the City,' the friar said, 'and decreed that this Chateau shall be destroyed[13]. I'm sorry child. It seems there is no hope.'

He made the sign of the cross over her then turned and ran for his life. In a few seconds everyone who was not chained to the wall had gone and Catriona was left with the other two prisoners.

Smoke began to billow down from the roof and the snap of burning timber echoed around the Hall's panelled walls. Claude de Bourgeaulx started yanking at his chain but the iron manacles only cut into his wrists making them bleed. The roaring of gunfire grew louder, delicate tongues of flame began

---

[13] For an account of the siege of the Castle of Peney, see bibliography (17) page 119ff.

to lick at the roof joists and the tiles above them began to crack, their fragments falling to the floor around the prisoners. The hospital master started lashing out at Catriona with his feet and jumping about in an insane dance as if he couldn't feel the pain in his wrists. *He obviously blames me for what's happened, the stupid man!*

She moved away as far as her chain would allow but he grabbed it and started to reel her in like a fish on a hook, his wife shouting and screaming behind him. Catriona wondered if somehow the crystal could protect her and whether she could reach it but when she looked at the Chatelain's table it held only the book. The Devil's Jewels had disappeared.

She tried to brace her bare feet against the hard stone floor. 'It's your own fault,' she screamed at the hospital master in English. 'You were deliberately spreading the plague but I'm completely innocent. I was only convicted by a wicked trick. This isn't fair.' But Claude hauled on the chain again, her feet slipped across the smooth stone and she stumbled towards him.

The roof was well ablaze now, with smoke drifting down behind the wooden panels and out over her ankles. And through it swarmed little animals squealing in terror. *Oh no, not more rats!* As she stepped sideways, trying to avoid them, Catriona felt one of them beneath her foot. Her whole body shuddered in revulsion as she slipped and crashed to the ground. A rat ran inside her cloak, its claws scratching her skin. She tried to hit it with the manacles round her wrists but only managed to hurt herself. She tried again but her arms were jerked away as Claude dragged her towards him. She screamed as she had never screamed in her life before and rolled over, trying to crush the animal. Her rolling brought her within Claude's reach.

He grabbed her arm and lifted her bodily off the ground. With a horrible curse he wrapped his hands round her throat and began to squeeze, shaking her, giving full vent to his fury.

Catriona went limp. She had been through too many traumas in the past few days. She couldn't take any more. All the fight had gone out of her. Everything went black.

Nycolas d'Orsières left the three witches and ran out of the Great Hall. They would either perish in the fire or be slaughtered by the Genevans. Justice would be served either way, and Nycolas had greater matters on his mind. He went through the archway into the tower and began to run up the spiral stairs.

For years he, almost alone among Genevans, had supported Catholicism when the rest of the City-State was moving towards the Reform. He alone had offered shelter to the Prince-Bishop when he was attacked in his Palace and chased out of the City. And after Genevan soldiers attacked the Chateau de Peney last year, Nycolas had strengthened his ties with the Catholic Duke of Savoy, hoping he would come to his aid when the next inevitable attack came.

But now the Duke has more to think about than my little Chateau. Everyone knows that France is about to invade Italy. Savoy is the first place they'll attack. No, Charles won't help me, but by God I won't give up my castle without a fight.

Nycolas emerged onto the battlement in the gathering evening gloom to survey the disposition of the besieging Genevan soldiers. Fire was lapping up the wooden buildings leaning against the Chateau's outer wall and some of the timbers in the roof of the Great Hall had caught fire. *They must be extinguished immediately!* Nycolas stepped across the top of the thick wall, leaned over and peered down into the darkness of the inner courtyard.

Men were standing around with torches, uncertain what to do. 'Bring two wooden buckets and a long rope up here!' Nycolas shouted. 'Fetch water out of the well. Fill the horse-trough.

Quickly now!' The men began to run around. In the gloom he could just make out the Prince-Bishop's purple cloak near the stables. He and the friar were saddling a horse. Then a deafening boom rent the air immediately followed by the sound of splintering wood.

Nycolas stepped across to the castellation on the outer side of the wall and looked down. In the light from the fires he saw the hole which the cannon ball had blasted in the Chateau's heavy wooden door. He heard the crack of a gun and something whistled past his head. He sheltered behind a merlon[14] in the battlement and carefully peered over a crenel. On the muddy snow, an arc of red points of light glowed from a dozen harquebusiers' smouldering matchcords[15]. Beyond them the axe heads of dozens of halberds glinted in the pink light from the clouds above the distant Jura Mountains. *If the Prince-Bishop tries to escape now he'll be cut to pieces. But he's got the Devil's Jewels. I saw him take them off the table. What will happen if the Genevans get them? Could they use them as weapons against me?*

An idea sprang into Nycolas' mind. Keeping his head low, he ran back along the top of the wall to the tower, down the stairs into the Great Hall. The little Irish witch was hanging limp in the hospital master's hands. As Nycolas ran across to them, Claude threw her to the ground and raised his foot above her stomach.

Nycolas drew his sword and swung the steel blade. Claude's head tilted to one side and a fountain of blood spurted up and splashed down on the Irish witch's body, then he slowly toppled sideways like a felled tree and crashed to the floor. His wife

---

[14] Merlons were the raised sections in a battlement behind which archers sheltered as they fired through the crenels or gaps.

[15] A harquebus was a long gun similar to a rifle, ignited by a glowing string called a matchcord. Halberds were axes with long pole-like handles.

screamed, turned on Nycolas and began to rain curses down on his head. Ignoring her, he bent and examined the girl. She was still alive. He quickly unlocked the iron padlock on her manacles, picked her up and carried her out to the courtyard.

The Prince-Bishop and the friar were still trying to saddle the horse. Nycolas threw the girl onto a bale of straw and took the horse's headstall off the friar. The friar ran to the horse-trough, brought water in his hat and tried to revive Catriona.

'The Lutherans have us surrounded,' Nycolas said to the Prince-Bishop who was still trying to tighten the saddle on the terrified mare. 'There's no way out. Do you still have those Devil's Jewels?'

'Out of my way you fool,' the Prince-Bishop said. 'I'm going to ask the Duke of Savoy for help to get my bishopric back.'

'Charles won't help you. You must have heard that France is about to invade Savoy?'

The Prince-Bishop paused in tightening the saddle. 'King Francis? Never. He's got his hands full persecuting the Huguenots.'

'So you haven't heard? Charles has set his son up as the Duke of Milan. Francis is furious. He's going to invade Italy. Savoy will be the first place he'll go.'

'Well if the Duke can't help me,' the Prince-Bishop said, pulling himself up onto the mare, 'then I'll have to go to Rome and get instructions from the Holy Father himself. I'll give him these Devil's Jewels,' he patted a bag hanging from his belt, 'and he'll give me a good diocese.'

Nycolas took out his dagger and sliced through the cord. The bag fell open, gold and jewels cascading down the horse's flank onto the cobbled floor. Ignoring the Prince-Bishop's howls of protest Nycolas knelt down, picked up the two Devil's Jewels and held them under Catriona's nose. She was just starting to come round. He looked at the friar. 'Ask the witch if she can use these to freeze the cannon. Tell her if she can save my Chateau I'll spare her life.'

Episode 43 Planck Epoch

'Did you know you are frying your brothers, Princess Trissitia?' The voice of the Argolath sounded relaxed, almost amused, in sharp contrast to the urgency of his words.

It's Professor Nithold, Sam thought as he looked at the pod's screen. Nithold's antennae were dreamily waving from side to side. *He's enjoying this!*

'My brothers?' Trissitia squealed and pulled back the rocket's power lever. For the past thirty seconds she had been blasting the jet of hot gas down the hole in the Cosmic Egg to retard the pod's breakneck rearward descent. The pod had never been designed to go backwards and there were no cameras in its tail, so they had no idea what lay below them. All they could see, in the beam of the headlight pointing back up the way they had come, was a sort of braided silver cable winding up the centre of the hole receding above them.

Sam was still trying to work out what that cable was when the rocket died and he felt his stomach lurch. *The pod's accelerating backwards*. After a few second's free-fall he was suddenly and violently pressed into the back of his seat. A moment later the pod slowed to an almost complete halt.

'I think you only killed a couple of your brothers, Princess,' Nithold said. Sam thought he could hear the equivalent of an Argolath giggle.

'It looks like we've reached the bottom of the hole, Samfitzpatrick!' Trissitia said with relief. 'Are we inside your Universe now? Is this what it was like when it was created?'

Looking out of the transparent dome, Sam saw the pod's headlight, now tinted amber, slowly panning down the tunnel's surface. He guessed that the pod was slowly tipping over.

Everything appeared calm. The tunnel had widened out into a sort of bulbous cavern.

'Created?' he said. 'No, I don't think so. As I understand it the Universe began with the Big Bang. It was a sort of huge explosion. It must have been very hot, not calm like this.' He began to worry what would happen if they did manage to get inside, but dismissed the idea. *We'll have to deal with that when we get there*, he thought. *There must be a way to survive, otherwise why would Cjingha have put those Entroilian eggs into the hole?*

'So how do we get inside it? And what do you think is making that yellow colour?'

'I really have no idea unless…Could it be the honey?'

'What honey?' Trissitia said.

'Cjingha put some honey into the Cosmic Egg.'

'Cjingha? Is that the Entroilian you told my father about? The one who works at the University?'

'Professor Cjingha Itoodoo, yes.'

'That would make sense,' Trissitia said. 'If she put some honey into the hole it would have run down to the bottom and that must be what has stopped us. But why did she—What's that?'

Sam turned to where her claw was pointing. A little larva was wriggling rapidly up the pod's dome, thrashing about as it tried to escape from a small Argolath whose jaws were sunk into the larva's rear end. It seemed to be eating the poor creature alive as the segmented maggot dragged it over the slippery transparent surface.

'Ah, that's Prince Sulkim,' Trissitia said proudly, waving her antennae indulgently towards the Argolath. The prince let go of the larva for a moment and bowed towards his sister, then crawled after his prey and recommenced sucking the juices out of it. 'He's one of my brothers! Looks like the eggs which your Entroilian professor put down here have hatched just in time for breakfast. Hmm, he's making me feel hungry. That larva looks rather delicious! I presume that's what this honey is for, to feed these larvae?'

'Yes,' Sam said weakly as he watched green liquid ooze from the wound and float away into the honey pool, thinking: *I need to keep those larvae alive at all costs. Once they grow into Entroilians, they can help me stop these monsters reaching the Earth!*

'Ah, she sent them down here to be transformed into Sons of Beeing, did she?' Trissitia said. 'Well my brothers will soon—'

'Transformed?' Sam said. 'No! Oh no, not at all. The Entroilians don't want to make more creatures like Michael Zhang. She put them down the hole so that they could help Catriona, my stepdaughter, to collect all the fragments of crystal.'

'Aw, you are so naïve my dear Husband. That might be what she told you but in reality she must have been hoping they would be transformed into Sons of Beeing.'

'I don't think so. She just wanted to help Catriona restart time in the Universe.'

'Yes of course she did. She wanted Stepdaughter to restart time so that the Cosmic Egg would give rise to more Sons of Beeing. It's obvious. How like a larva you are, Husband. Guileless and innocent as a newly hatched egg! But don't worry. My brothers will soon dispose of these irrelevant little objects. I suppose they must be doing that right now. Let's see if I can find them. Maybe I can eat one myself. I'm ravenous!'

She pressed a button on the control panel, a small propeller unfolded from the pod's nose, it began to rotate and the pod turned, its amber headlight running rapidly down the cavern's curving wall until it was pointing straight down.

I don't like the sound of this, Sam thought as four or five more Argolaths came into view directly below the pod. They were crawling down the braided cable, now coloured blue. A short distance below, at the bottom of the honey pool, the cable disappeared into a small mound of writhing Entroilian larvae. They too were lit by the pale blue light which filtered up from somewhere underneath them. Several of the Argolath princes had already reached them and were biting at them in a frenzy of excitement.

Sam was appalled. *I've got to stop those Argolaths killing the larvae! If they die then who is going to help me? If I can break that cable, maybe the Argolaths won't be able to reach them.*

'Let me have a go at steering this pod,' he said and snatched the joystick away from Trissitia.

'Ah, you are becoming more masterful, my Husband,' she said as she let him take the control. 'I like that!' He felt her three fingered claw gently caress the back of his hand, the little hairs which covered its surface making it feel soft and warm despite its crinkled, rubbery covering. 'But do look out, Husband. You're going to cut that rope if you're not careful and then my brother's won't be able to...' But she was too late. Sam had deliberately aimed the propeller at the cable and now it struck the inter-twined blue fibres. They bent and splayed out around the blade but to Sam's huge disappointment they did not break. Instead they wrapped themselves around the blades and soon the propeller was completely entangled. It stopped turning and, with its propeller fixed, the whole pod began to rotate.

'You are making a real mess of steering, Husband. The propeller's trapped now. What is that rope anyhow?'

'I have no idea,' Sam said as he increased the power to the propeller, still hoping to break the cable and stop the other princes reaching their prey. The cable began to bend.

'I think I know what it is,' a male Argolath voice said. Sam glanced at the screen for a moment in surprise, having forgotten Nithold was watching them.

'Yes Professor? Trissitia said. 'What is it?'

'I think it's probably made up of negative energy strings.'

As soon as he said this, Sam had a sudden and vivid recollection of Cjingha standing in her laboratory saying to Councillor Moshendiar: "Negative energy threads are microscopically narrow. They have a repulsive gravitational field which could hold open a tunnel like that."

Sam let go of the accelerator and pulled the joystick over, thinking: *Oh my God! If I had broken those negative energy threads then this hole in the Universe would have collapsed and we'd all have been crushed to death!* He broke out into a cold sweat as he watched the princes crawl quickly past the trapped propeller and head down the cable towards the defenceless larvae. *If I could get this propeller free I might still be able to kill some of them with it*, Sam thought, and he struggled desperately to free the blades which were now thoroughly enmeshed with the negative energy strings.

Trissitia leaned forward in her chair and one antenna began lovingly to stroke his bald patch. 'You've got yourself into a bit of a mess there, my Husband. Would you like me to help you?'

'Yes please, Trissitia,' he said feebly, abandoning his efforts to free the propeller.

'Very well, my masterful Husband,' she said, 'but please won't you call me something a little more affectionate? After all, I am probably bearing the eggs you fertilised.' She giggled and rubbed her rear end in a lascivious way. 'My father used to call my mother Sashamida. It's the name of a sweet sort of fungus he loves to eat. It sounds so much nicer than "Trissitia". Won't you call me Sashamida, please Husband?'

'Look Trissitia,' Sam snapped as he renewed wrestling with the joystick, 'right now I've got enough to worry about just trying to survive without learning new words.' But, though he tried for several minutes, it was impossible to free the propeller. Finally, taking his hand off the control, he said 'Okay, Samashida. You go ahead.'

'Sashamida,' she corrected him gently as she jabbed her claw into a button on the control panel and the blades of the propeller folded up under the weight of the surrounding strings. 'The word is "Sa-sha-MI-da". I'll deploy the rearward propeller.' She pressed another button, Sam heard something click behind him and heard a whirring sound. The pod moved slowly backwards and the blades of the front propeller slipped out easily from the entangling cable. She clicked again, it retracted into the front hatch and the doors closed. Finally the second propeller fell silent and the pod stopped, floating beside the cable.

The Argolath princes had reached the pile of larvae and now began biting at them, sucking out the juices which ran from their wounds.

'So what do we do now, my masterful Husband?' Trissitia said as she casually watched her brothers. 'How do we get into your Universe?'

With growing anxiety Sam stared down at the massacre that was taking place before him. A faint blue glow diffused through the writhing bodies of the larvae and reflected off the strings which wound their way between them. 'Look,' he said. 'I suppose those larvae must be covering up the bottom of the tunnel. Can we push them out of the way and see what lies below them?'

'Yes, I think so, but I would have to interrupt my brothers' breakfast. Ah well, they can finish it later.' She turned on the rear propeller once more and the pod moved forward, parallel to the cable. The princes scuttled to one side as she used the pod's rounded nose to gently nudge the blind, wriggling larvae out of the way. It was not easy. The squirming mass of creatures seemed to be attracted downwards towards the blue light and kept fighting with the pod to stay close to it. As she pushed the last larva aside, the source of the blue light was finally revealed.

Below them, lying at the very bottom of the honey-pool embedded in the curving cavern's pink wall, was a large blue crystal. Its beauty was breath-taking and for a moment they both stared at it, awestruck.

The whole crystal glowed with its own blue light. It was huge, almost as wide as the pod itself, and spherical in shape with many flat faces like a massive blue diamond. As soon as he saw it, Sam was sure this crystal was a piece of the event network. From each face emerged a fine blue negative energy string which all wove themselves together to form the cable.

'What is that thing, Sashamida?' Trissitia said.

'It must be a fragment of the pipe Michael broke,' he said. 'Cjingha said that a piece of it might have fallen down the hole.'

'I wish you'd stop talking about "Cjingha". Do you fancy your chances with her?'

Sam's temper flared. 'What an outrageous suggestion! Why do you think everyone's motivated by sex?' Her antennae stiffened with anger and Sam made himself breathe deeply. *She's obviously infatuated with me and I'm going to need her help to collect all the crystals.* 'I'm sorry, Sashamida,' he said. 'I didn't mean to…Of course I don't fancy Cjingha.'

'Oh thank you, Husband!' she said and there was a little catch of emotion in her voice. 'Do you really and truly love me as I love you?'

'I…I don't think this is the right time to talk about serious matters like love now, Sashamida. We need to get into the Universe and find the tunnel that my stepdaughter will be coming down. If we can find it and go up the tunnel, I'm hoping it will lead us straight to the Earth. Only problem is, that crystal's in the way.'

'I wonder if we can vaporise it?' she said, reaching for a switch marked "Laser canon".

'No!' Sam shouted, holding her arm. 'You mustn't harm it! We have to collect all the fragments and take them to…er, to your Argolath Professor, so he can fix the event network and restart time! Isn't there anything else the pod can do, apart from vaporising it?'

'Oh yes, I'm sorry Husband. I'm so stupid. Let's see if we can push the crystal out of the way without harming it.' She pressed some buttons and two slim arms unfolded from the front of the pod. Each arm was capped with a grip which looked remarkably like an Argolath's claw. One held a thick pad, the other a small cylinder. One arm pressed the pad against a crystal face, then the other smashed the pad with the cylinder, squashing the negative energy thread flat.

'Be careful!' Sam whispered breathlessly. 'You mustn't break those threads. They're holding this tunnel open. Push it on a corner, not on the flat part.'

She moved the pad to a corner and Sam was much relieved to see the negative energy string spring back. *Thank God it's not broken. I wonder why I never saw these threads when I was in the crystal cavern?* Then he remembered Cjingha in her lab explaining to Councillor Moshendiar why he could not see them in the projector:

"Negative energy threads are microscopically narrow."

So how come I can see them now? Sam wondered, but before he could work it out, his thoughts were disturbed by a series of hammer-like pneumatic clunks. The cylinder was vibrating and hitting the pad which then thudded against the crystal. Soon the stone began to move, bit by bit, through the pink wall into the universe. After a minute's hammering it suddenly slipped through altogether, leaving a gaping hole from which a bundle of negative energy threads protruded.

The honey began to drain into the hole, slowly at first but gathering momentum, carrying the pod with it after the crystal. 'Hurrah!' Sam shouted. 'I'm back in the Univer—' But the words died on his lips as, through the pod's transparent dome, he saw the crystal inexplicably shrink and seem to vanish before his eyes. 'We need to find that crystal,' Sam shouted, turning to Trissitia. 'We're going to need it to restart ti—.'

What he saw stopped his mouth and made his mind reel. Trissitia's head was being stretched and warped, bloating out towards him as if he were looking at a video projected on a distorting rubber sheet. He could see every detail of her two jaws quivering beside her mouth as her head bulged. The next second her head enclosed him completely and for a moment it was dark. Then he saw soft green tendons linking vividly pulsating purple membranes and the next moment there was a light to his left and he found himself looking out past her moving jaws at the pod's control panel. *I'm inside her mouth!* He could not get his mind around what was happening. This distortion was so far beyond his experience all he could think was: *Is she going to swallow me?* As he looked out, something blue moved past the space outside and he saw, to his horror, the back of his suit and then his own head stretching as if it too were made of rubber. A moment later he both saw and felt the whole rubbery scene collapse down from the top. *I'm being squashed flat! I can't breathe.*

Sam wanted to scream but screaming had no meaning. The next moment he felt himself being rolled up into a cylinder, then stretched out into a very long thin line. All that was left of Sam Fitzpatrick now was his mind, floating in a sea of honey that was distorting everything, pulsating with a life of its own like a beating heart. Sometimes he felt flat. Other times he was solid but distorted, as if his head was sticking out of his own backside and his arms and legs were all knotted together. And sometimes, just for a moment, things went back to normal and he was sitting in the pod beside Trissitia. This gave him hope. He waited for these glimpses of normality, thinking *I wonder what Michael Zhang made of all this?*

Sacred Book 1: The Planck Epoch[16]

Dictated with Divine Wisdom by His Holiness the Son of Beeing to High Priest Glagnump Koddlezine[17]

When the Universe had not yet come into existence;
When the Laws of Nature were still unformulated;
Then did her glorious Majesty Karolinda,
Queen of all Entroilia,
Lay the wondrous Cosmic Egg.

This Egg, this miracle of unrealised potentiality, contained within itself a manifold of sixty dimensions[18]. In that era, before the ovum had been fertilised, before growth had started, then were all sixty of these dimensions curled up

---

[16] Author's note: Michael Zhang's so-called "Sacred Books" form part of the corpus of documents in my possession which establish the basic authenticity of the events described in Time Crystal. I have taken the liberty of inserting these "Books" at appropriate places within this story, to facilitate reader comprehension. W.S.

[17] This heading, written by a different hand from the rest of this "Sacred Book", was evidently added by Princess Uskabellu at a later date.

[18] The reader should note that, while much of the information contained within subsequent "Sacred Books" would probably not be disputed by many scientists, none would agree with the description given here. There is no evidence that there were sixty dimensions in the primeval universe. The origin of the universe is currently one of the greatest unsolved mysteries of science. Indeed, the whole concept of a Cosmic Egg, and everything else connected with Entroilia, would no doubt be regarded by all scientists as total fantasy.

infinitesimally small into a point without size. Into a nothing within the domain of the forthcoming. These sixty co-located points of potentiality were the foundations upon which the Cosmos would be constructed. And time itself was one of these unmanifest dimensions.

This was the condition that the Cosmic Seed[19] found when, beneath the clear blue skies of Entroilia, the primary sperm did penetrate and impregnate the Cosmic Egg. Men sometimes call this "the Big Bang" but it was neither big nor did it bang, so I will denominate this event as the "Fertilisation"[20].

That fertilisation — praise the wondrous event — introduced a single scalar field into the manifold[21], a field hereby denominated the "Primordial Field". Its bounteous presence caused the sixty curled-up dimensions within the ovum to unwind into a linear form. Being a scalar field, the Primordial was represented at every point along each uncurled dimension by a single number.

There was a timeless moment, pregnant with possibilities, when each dimension uncurled at random, all acting independently of the others, then curled up again. These unwindings manifested themselves differently in different regions of the cosmos. It was as if the legs of a billion newly hatched primeval arthropods were momentarily stretching

---

[19] The "Cosmic Seed" is evidently the same thing as the "Cosmic Monopole" mentioned in Michael's diary, but that term is not used in the Sacred Books.

[20] See "Sacred Book 3" for further discussion of the term "Big Bang".

[21] For details of the manifold, see bibliography (20).

and reaching out for their mother, and when they failed to find her their legs re-contracted in an elaborate solo dance.

To the fanciful mind it might have seemed that the Egg was in the process of conducting experiments with different physical configurations, trying to find one that fitted the Primordial Field seed which it had been given. This dance might have ended in failure and the Egg might have remained forever infertile but — by the divine Grace of the Beeing — it happened that one particular set of uncurled dimensions exactly fitted the inherent properties of the Primordial Field.

There were four dimensions in this perfectly matching set and, like the legs of a predator snaring its prey, they entangled themselves around the Field. Was it pure co-incidence — even the mind of the devout might question — that there existed exactly four uncurled dimensions none more, none less? And the faithful in their wisdom would surely respond "Indeed no!"

For the Field itself also contained exactly four separate but interdependent components[22]. Furthermore — believers in their wisdom will explain — one of the Field's four components was different from the others and in a similar fashion — matched perhaps by divine providence — one of the uncurled dimensions was different from the other three. The fit was perfect and now there became manifest within

---

[22] Michael Zhang is suggesting there is a link between the facts that space-time has four dimensions and "Unified Field Theory" (see bibliography entry (18)) contains four fundamental physical forces.

the Cosmic Egg a basic physical property hereby denominated the "metric tensor"[23].

One of the four uncurl dimensions was the one mankind calls "time". The first manifestation of this dimension produced the smallest possible granule of time. This phase of history, denominated the "Planck Epoch[24]", ended — by the divine Grace of the Beeing — when the four dimensions of space-time came into existence which happened at the smallest possible interval of time after the fertilisation: 5.39106 times ten to the power minus 44 seconds, a period denominated with divine wisdom the "Planck Time[25]".

---

[23] For details on the metric tensor, see bibliography (19).

[24] For a standard scientific description of the Planck Epoch, see bibliography (21).

[25] For more on Planck Time, see bibliography (22).

Episode 44 The Map

'Ah, here they are at last,' Professor Romani said when George and his group finally found the corner of the Cafeteria where Francesco was floating in a large bubble between a row of cream table-tops and a circle of white ceiling tiles. Danny Schneider was waiting there too, as well as Ambassador Brigit O'Brien and Dr Jean-Pierre Plaisent. Danny looked first at Alex, then his eyes went straight to Marianne and his look of loathing was transformed into one of utter disdain.

He hates us both! Marianne thought. She flew quickly across the open space formed by the cluster of their bubbles and took Danny's arm. 'How are you, mon chou?' she said, but she knew he wouldn't answer. She squeezed his arm and began talking, not even sure what she was saying, just trying to get some reaction out of him.

'So now I can start the mee...' Francesco said, then a startled look crossed his face. 'Dio santo fireman! What is that gun for?'

George stopped pointing the gun at Alex's head and put it in his pocket. 'Don't worry, Professor,' he said with a grin. 'It isn't loaded.'

Alex struggled and said something in Hungarian but Ludovico tightened the hammerlock he had on Alex's right arm, twisting it up his back and pressing his head against his wincing prisoner's cheek with a look of glee.

Marianne turned away, afraid her expression would reveal to Danny what was in her heart. *Alex was only trying to help me in his own stupid way, and now he's suffering for it. But Danny comes first. I must show him how much I love him. I must prove that Alex means nothing to me.*

'What do you want us to do with Karolyi now, Professor Romani?' George said.

Before Francesco could speak, Danny said 'I suggest you tie him up.' He glanced at Marianne and added 'You cannot trust him.'

Marianne felt as if he had slapped her face. *He means me! He doesn't trust me anymore. Oh Danny, mon pauvre chou confus.*

'I have no authority to tie anybody up,' Francesco said. 'Has he committed any crime?'

'Well,' George said, 'he stole a bunch of crystals from—'

'I saw him kill a man,' Marianne blurted out. *It doesn't matter if I get Alex into trouble,* she thought. *I have to prove to Danny I don't care about him. What better way than this? All I want is for mon chou to trust me and give me a cuddle and stroke my hair like he used to when I first knew him.*

All eyes were on her now, filled with astonishment, waiting for an explanation.

'When was this?' Francesco said.

'When I was in the foyer, Professor. You were talking to Danny. I looked into the big crystal and I saw him. He was pushing a desk into a man and he killed him. Then he stole some money and that gun.' A voice inside her was screaming *it was self-defence* but she ignored it, just as she ignored the sad look on Alex's face and the slow shake of his head.

'In that case, I suppose you'd better tie him up,' Francesco said. 'Then maybe I can start my meeting.'

At last Danny smiled. It was like the sun breaking through after a storm. Hope came back into Marianne's life. She bathed in the glory of it and squeezed his arm while they watched the firefighters tie Alex to one of the metal struts bridging a skylight in the Cafeteria ceiling. This was Marianne's favourite spot in CERN, the place where she and Danny had hosted their quiet little wedding reception two months ago. She loved to linger here over lunch, looking out of the long windows at people sitting on the terrace or strolling along the broad lawn, although now she couldn't see—

'I heard you were looking for me, Marianne,' Jean-Pierre said. He had flown over and was hovering beside her. 'I was very surprised when I heard you had come here without consulting me. I went with Brigit to look for you in the hostel. How are you, my dear? I need to check your condition. And what did you mean just now about seeing Alex kill a man? How did you see him? Where was he?'

Danny's head turned at the mention of Alex's name.

'I'll tell you about it after this meeting,' she whispered to Jean-Pierre.

When George and Ludo had tied Alex to a beam in the Cafeteria ceiling, Francesco cleared his throat and said: 'Now I need to call this meeting to order.' He waited for everyone to go quiet, then went on: 'This is an historic event. It seems that every human who is alive in the Universe is probably here—'

'Except Catriona,' Jean-Pierre said. Marianne nodded and glanced at Brigit. Catriona was never far from Marianne's thoughts, but Brigit looked surprised at the mention of her daughter's name, as if she couldn't quite remember who she was.

'And one or two others,' Alex said.

'I don't know what you mean by that remark,' Francesco said, 'but you can have your say in due course, Count Karolyi. First I would like to say on behalf of myself and CERN how sorry I am for what has happened. As Director General, I must take personal responsibility for it. However, I would like to emphasise that the chances of this event, caused by a cosmic monopole being trapped by ATLAS, the chances were so remote that nobody could possibly have predicted it would happen. Nevertheless it has and I very much regret it.'

Marianne's heart went out to Francesco. *He looks devastated*, she thought as he went on 'Now I think we should all give a short report on what we have been doing and what we've found so far. Anyone object? No? Then I'll start the ball rolling.'

Francesco reported at great length on what caused the pattern on the bubbles, drawing diagrams of atoms on a table-top, the only place he could find where his felt-tip pen would work.

Finally Brigit said 'Do we really need to know all this Francesco?' She had flown across to the other side of the big bubble and was hovering near George.

'Marianne is tired,' Jean-Pierre said. 'I was hoping we could keep this meeting short.'

'I don't think that's possible, Doctor' Francesco said. 'There's a lot to discuss. Marianne can go if she wants. No? Then perhaps you'd like to give your report next, Doctor Plaisent?'

Jean-Pierre and Sofie together explained where the latrines were, how to find them and how to use them hygienically.

'We've got the antiseptic wipes and other stuff you asked for, doc,' George said. 'Unfortunately we had to abandon them back near the airport, but we'll go and collect them when this meeting is over.'

Danny spoke next. His report was the most important of them all, Marianne thought. 'I made basic measurements on the two crystals,' he said. 'I found no radiation or any other fields from either crystal except light. They are not radioactive—'

'So crystal isn't dangerous?' Jean-Pierre said. 'That's very good news.'

'No, doctor. I also found one other thing. I was able to see out of crystals. I suppose this is the same phenomenon that Marianne found.' He spoke about her without looking at her, as if she were in a different universe. 'For example, through the small crystal I could see your and Ludo's crystal, doctor. In the large one I saw two fish.'

'What do you mean?' Jean-Pierre said, 'see out of my crystal? I do not understand this.'

'No, me neither,' Brigit said. 'What the hell are you talking about Danny?'

'Danny can you demonstrate this?' Francesco said. 'Give me that large crystal, Danny, and take this small one. That's it. Now turn away, please.' Danny turned his crystal and spun round so he was facing away from the group. 'Now doctor, please hold up some fingers on your hand. That's right. Now Danny, how many fingers is he holding up?'

Danny looked at the small crystal he was holding, studying it as if he were reading a book. 'Three,' he said. There were gasps all round.

'That's right!' Jean-Pierre said, and curled down one of his fingers. 'How many now?'

'Two,' Danny said.

'Right again,' Jean-Pierre said with a puzzled air.

Marianne hugged Danny saying 'Well done, chou.' He didn't try to stop her. Instead he showed everyone how to hold their crystals close to their eyes and turn them slowly until they were looking straight into one flat face, warning them the image was very tiny. The others became very excited and spent a long time looking into their crystals.

Francesco started drawing a diagram on another table top to map out which crystal could see through which. 'So what can you see, my dear?' he asked Marianne who happened to be nearest to him, writing her name at the top of the table.

Marianne looked through the small crystal which Sofie had collected from the tea bar and restored to her. After seeing Alex kill the businessman earlier, she knew exactly how to hold it. 'I can see Jean-Pierre.'

Francesco wrote "Doctor" on the table and drew a line to it from Marianne's name.

'And the other way?' Danny said.

'What do you mean, chou?'

'Look into the other faces. I saw two different fish through the big crystal and I can see two different things through this little one so I suspect you should be able to see something else through yours.'

Marianne rotated her crystal peering into its other sides, feeling much happier now Danny was actually talking to her. *Maybe he's beginning to get back to normal at last. I really hope so.* Two of her crystal's faces just seemed to show its inner edges and reflections. *I can't stand much more of his strange behaviour on top of losing the baby. I'm starting to feel a little crazy myself.* But when she looked into the fourth face her heart sink. 'I can see something yellow,' she said as if she didn't know what it was, 'What do you think it is, Danny?'

Danny took her crystal and turned it slowly. 'It's HIS pocket,' he snarled, handing it back to her. 'George!' he called. 'Karolyi's got some more crystal in his shirt pocket.'

George and Ludovico flew up to the ceiling and George took the little crystal out of Alex's shirt pocket, then the two men began to search his other pockets while Francesco wrote "Alex" on the map and added a line joining it to Marianne. The simple little picture, showing her linked to the Doctor on one side and to Alex on the other, made her want to cry.

'So then, Dr Plaisent,' Francesco said. 'What can you see through your crystal?'

Jean-Pierre was holding his crystal close to his eye. 'I can see you, Marianne! This could be very handy. We might even be able to do a remote consultation!'

Francesco drew an arrowhead on the table at each end of the line joining "Marianne" with "Doctor". 'And the other way?' he said.

Jean-Pierre turned the crystal. 'I can see Danny.'

'Oh,' Marianne said, 'can I swap with you then, Jean-Pierre, so I can see Danny and talk to him?'

'Talk to him?' Jean-Pierre said. 'Can you talk through—'

'Oh please don't start swapping crystal around!' Francesco said. 'You will ruin my diagram.'

Jean-Pierre stared at Francesco then turned to Marianne. 'Of course we can swap, my dear,' he said, exchanging his crystal with hers. 'You need to be able to see Danny for the good of your health. I can perfectly understand that, and I'm sure everyone else does too.'

Francesco sighed and changed his diagram, smudging out their names with a dampened paper serviette then swapping them over so "Doctor" was at the top and "Marianne" now lay between "Doctor" and "Danny". 'And I assume you can now see Marianne through your crystal, Danny?' he said. 'This could be the second scientific prediction about crystal. The first was the ionisation of gas and now I predict that, if A can see B through a pair of crystals, then B can see A. This prediction is based upon the postulation that crystals are linked together in pairs by some sort of invisible two-way communication system. Well, Danny? Can you see Marianne or not?'

'Yes Professor.'

Francesco beamed broadly and drew another arrowhead on the table to indicate the communication was indeed two-way.

Danny reported that he could see Ludovico through another face of his crystal, and Ludovico stopped searching Alex's pockets, looked into his crystal and duly confirmed that he too could see Danny.

'Splendid, splendid,' Francesco said. 'And whom can you see the other way, fireman?'

'I see out of the lovely Brigit O'Brien crystal,' Ludovico said and gave her a big grin, then continued searching Alex.

'Oh really?' Brigit said, sounding a little put out and peering into her crystal. 'Well it's a damn good job nobody looked while I had it in my bra!' Everyone laughed.

'Pity she no keep it in her knickers,' Ludovico whispered loudly.

Even the normally sombre Jean-Pierre smiled and everyone else, except Brigit, laughed even louder, but she became so indignant that Francesco had to calm her down. Everyone was laughing so much that nobody heard Alex's howl of pain as Ludo plunged his hand deep into Alex's trouser pocket and viciously squeezed his testicles.

Finally, Francesco added "Brigit" to the diagram and asked her to confirm she could see Ludovico.

'There's no way I'm keeping this bloody crystal, Francesco, if that sex-maniac can see through it. Anyone want to swap?'

'Yes, I'll swap with you, Ambassador,' Sofie said. 'I've already seen you through this fragment so I know they are linked. It would be a good idea if Ludo and I could see each other, and Marianne said you can talk through crystals as well.'

'Yes, can you show us how that works?' Jean-Pierre said.

'Oh please, not now!' Francesco said. 'I really must insist that we finish the diagram of the crystal connections. It is vital that we have an accurate picture. It is basic evidence. I have no doubt we will need this to help us investigate crystal. So...' he changed the diagram so Ludovico was linked to Sofie and Sofie to Brigit. 'So which crystal can you see through, Brigit, apart from Sofie's?'

'Well I'm not sure. All I can—Oh, I can see you, George! That's handy.'

'Coucou Madam Ambassador,' George said, waving as he looked into one of the little cloud of crystals floating before him. 'I can see you too!'

'Lucky bastard,' Ludovico said as he began searching Alex's rucksack.

'Where did all those crystals come from?' Francesco asked, staring at the pile before George.

'They're my spares, Professor.'

'Spares? I did not know we had any spare.'

'No? I found them after you left the ATLAS cavern.'

'How many do you have?'

'Two that I found there and this one Karolyi had in his shirt pocket. Ludo's just searching his bag to see—'

'I find another two here,' Ludovico said, looking up from Alex's rucksack, holding two crystals in one hand and with his other hand in his pocket. 'One of them he is pretty big. Look!'

'My God!' Francesco said, 'it's another double crystal. Where did that come from?'

'Better you ask Karolyi, Professor Romani,' Ludovico said. 'Shall I put these with you, George?'

'No, stop fireman!' Francesco shouted, flying towards him. 'Do not mix them up! You are destroying valuable evidence if you mix them up.'

Ludovico looked at him blankly, then at George.

'Better do as the Professor says, Ludo,' George said in a sing-song voice.

'It is basic scientific evidence to know the provenance of these crystals,' Francesco insisted. 'It might be very important to know exactly where they were found. It is like archaeology. At the moment we don't know whether this information is important or not, so we must record as much as we can. And if people are going to swap crystals around, I won't know which one is which, since they all look identical. At the very least, we need to label each one of them, so I can identify them on the diagram. I need some sticky labels...' He looked around as if he expected to see a supply of labels floating towards him through the air and frowned when he could not find them. 'Can one of you go upstairs to my secretary's office and fetch some sticky labels? There are some in the stationary cupboard.'

'You go, will you, Sofie?' George said.

'Where is it?' she asked.

'Fifth floor,' Francesco said. 'Room fifteen.' He carefully arranged the spare crystals in two groups, those which George had found in the ATLAS cavern and those which Alex had found. Then he and the firefighters began working out which one could see out of which other one. By the time Sofie returned, they had laid three of them on the table beside the words "George1", "George2" and "Black".

Francesco flew round with the labels, writing a letter or sometimes a letter and a number onto them and sticking one on each crystal, ensuring that he did not cover one of the two faces through which they could see something interesting. 'It doesn't matter if we cover the other faces,' he said. 'I'm not interested in seeing reflections.'

'I think you should just explain what this means,' Jean-Pierre said, looking at the table top. 'What do these numbers mean, George1, George2 and so on?'

'If somebody has more than one crystal then I've number them,' Francesco said. as he flew back to the table. 'I had to abbreviate the names on the labels because there's not enough room so George1 is labelled G1. It's all perfectly simple.'

'And Black?' Brigit said. 'What does that mean, Francesco?'

'Through George2 all you can see is a sort of black spot,' he said and changed the word "Alex" to "Alex1". He linked it to "George3" with a double-headed arrow, and "George3" to the word "Fish".

'What's Fish?' Brigit asked.

'You can see it in here,' George said as he handed her a crystal labelled "G3". Brigit took it, held it close to her eye and said 'My God, it's alive!'

'Is this the same fish Danny saw in the big crystal?' Jean-Pierre said. 'What kind of fish did you see, Danny?'

'How should I know?' Danny shrugged. 'I'm an engineer. I can't be expected to be a fish expert as well.'

'I see some coins in this one.' Ludovico was looking into one of the crystals he had taken out of Alex's rucksack. 'They looks quite old.'

'Let me see,' George said and looked into the crystal. 'You're right, Ludo. They're very old. This one says "FRANCIS:DEI:GRA:FRANCORVM:REX". Anyone know what that means?'

'It sounds like Latin,' Jean-Pierre said. 'Let me see. Yes, it says "Francis by the grace of God King of France".'

'Francis?' Francesco said as he wrote "Coins" on the table top. 'King of France? When was the last time there was a King Francis?'

'They could be in a museum somewhere,' Jean-Pierre said. 'Geneva's full of them, but I don't understand how a crystal got in there.'

George passed the crystal round and everyone had a look at the old coins. When Marianne looked, she thought one of them moved, although it was hard to be sure. They seemed to be inside a leather pouch and, like the fish, were lit by a pale blue light, although she thought there was also a pink light shining on some of them.

'I think there were two kings called Francis in the 16th century,' she told Danny. He seemed totally disinterested.

'Two things are obvious about this diagram,' Francesco said as he looked down at his handiwork. 'Communication is mostly two-way. For example Marianne can see the doctor and he can see Marianne. The second thing is that most crystals can only see two others. They form a sort of chain. Look.' Everyone gathered round the table.

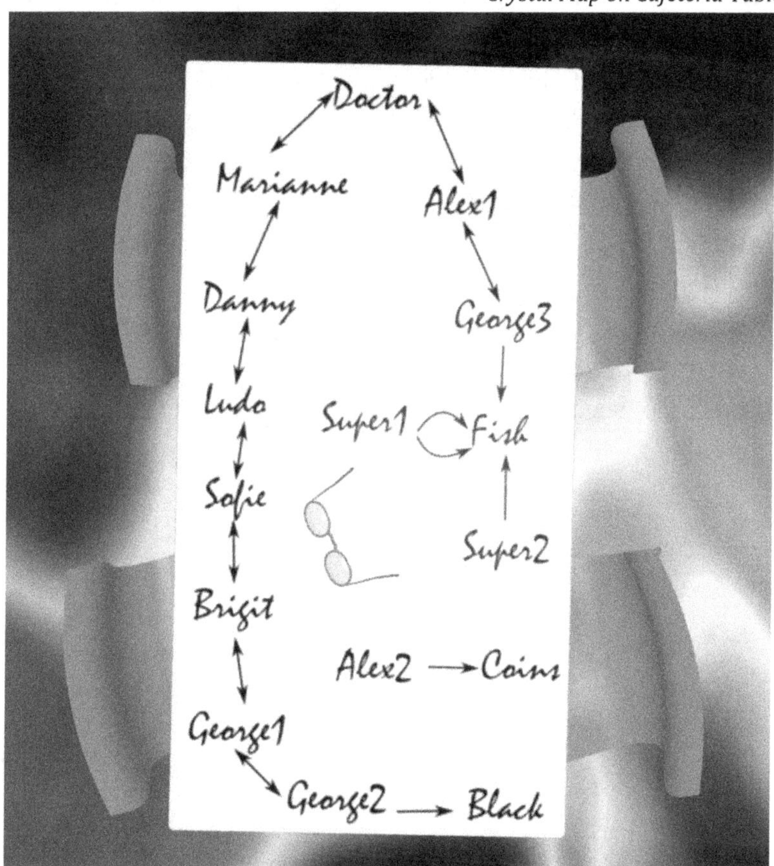

'And what are Super1 and Super2?' the doctor asked.

'They are the two large fragments. Now, there are some very interesting features of this map. The "Fish" is the only thing that has more than two arrows.'

'I know this kind of fish,' Ludo said looking into one of the crystals. 'Is a perch, the sort they catch in the lake. Serve up in the fancy restaurants in town.'

'And notice that there are four arrows going to the Fish,' Francesco said, 'two from Super1 and one each from Super2 and George1. That is most interesting.'

'Not to me it isn't,' Brigit said. 'This is taking so much time. Can I give my report now?' She explained that there was enough food and water in the Cafeteria to keep them alive for months. George told them what the firefighters had collected from Balexert and finally Francesco turned to Alex. 'Would you like to give your report now, Count Karolyi?'

Alex spoke quietly but immediately he had everyone's full attention.

'Catriona told me she saw Sam in a crystal she found in the ATLAS cavern.'

Francesco seemed to explode. 'That is utterly and totally impossible!'

Episode 45 Battle of Peney

'The Chatelain wants to know if you can use the Devil's Jewels to freeze the cannon,' the friar said.

Still dazed from the hospital master's attack and with her neck and head throbbing with pain, Catriona had no idea what he meant. Her eyes could barely even focus on the two crystal fragments glowing blue and pink on the Chatelain's palm.

'Can you make the pink one freeze the cannon like it froze the cow in the wood?' the friar insisted.

Realisation dawned gradually through the fog of pain and with it came fresh hope of escape. She nodded feebly then winced. 'Yes, Father, I think I can.' It hurt to speak and her voice sounded thick, as if her assailant's murderous hand were still wrapped around her throat.

The Chatelain didn't wait for the translation. He shoved the crystals into a pouch at his waist, yanked her to her feet and dragged her out of the courtyard, through the Great Hall and up the spiral stairs. Smoke drifted across the battlement, yellow light flickering on its underside. People below were shouting on both sides of the wall. Archers were hiding behind the tall merlons on its top, occasionally leaning over the low crenels to shoot down at the besieging enemy outside the castle.

The Chatelain dragged Catriona behind a merlon, took the pink crystal out of his leather pouch and offered it to her, talking rapidly in French, while pointing over a crenel. She peeped down and saw soldiers, black against the snow outside the castle, working to reload the huge cannon. There was a crackle of gunfire and the hiss of bullets overhead. She crouched behind the merlon, looking at the pink crystal on the Chatelain's palm. *He wants me to use that to freeze the cannon, like it froze the cow,* she thought. Neither it nor the big round blue crystal glowing inside his leather bag betrayed any sign of the two invisible bubbles which, she was certain, still surrounded them. She had thought about this a lot while waiting for the trial to start.

Both crystals must have a bubble, she had decided. *In CERN, where time is frozen, a blue fragment's bubble gives you life. But here, where time is still going, the pink crystal's bubble stops time and freezes things, like it did with the cow. But if you bring the two of them together then the blue one's big bubble cancels out the little pink one and time works normally.*

The Chatelain shoved the pink crystal under her nose, shouting now and looking seriously angry.

'I don't want that!' she shouted in English, shaking her head, knowing he could not understand but angry with him because he seemed to be so stupid and angry at fate for getting her into this stupid situation. 'Don't you realise that it freezes things? Yes of course you do, because you want me to freeze the cannon.' The Chatelain listened to her, an uncomprehending look on his angry face. 'So how do you expect me to fly if I'm frozen?' Catriona went on. 'Is it because you think I'm a witch and can do anything I want? Well I can't! I can't fly without...'

Suddenly an idea popped into her head like a light being turned on. She closed her eyes for a moment. *It's a terrible risk, but my only hope of escape.* She grabbed the pink crystal out of his hand and pointed at the blue one flickering like a living flame in his pouch and looked him straight in the face. 'I need that one too. Yes, that one. Give it to me!' She held out her other hand.

A bullet ricocheted off the merlon and whizzed past the Chatelain's head. He drew back, took out the large crystal and shoved it into her hand, grunting and hissing in French.

Her heart leaped as she felt it heavy and solid. She held them both for a moment, terribly afraid lest she should lose them again, wondering how she could carry them both.

I'll have to use the blue one to fly. Need two hands for that. So what shall I do with the pink one?

There were no pockets in the cloak she wore. She hesitated for a moment then opened her mouth and tried to pop the small pink one inside. To her surprise, it was difficult to get it in. She had to twist it, the Chatelain shouting at her and making her nervous, until she managed to insert it, the back resting against her tongue, the edges clutched between her teeth and with one sharp corner sticking out between her lips. *At least I won't swallow it. It's far too big.*

She glanced at the Chatelain then at the gap between the castellated merlons, grasped the blue crystal in her two hands and pressed her thumbs against it.

Nycolas d'Orsières was utterly astonished as he watched the little Irish witch lift up into the air, like a bird without wings, and fly over the parapet. *So it's true: witches really can fly!* In the past few years he had condemned dozens of women to death, usually after torturing them, for putting spells on their neighbours' cows or other maleficia[26] but he had never really believed the stories of those who confessed to being strigae[27]. Take that one last month for example, Jeanette Clerc[28]. After a few drops of the rope she'd readily confessed to killing her neighbour's cow with a herb she had cut on Saint John's Eve and that would have been enough for Nycolas, but once she started her confession all the details poured out of her like foulness from a sewer: how a black devil with a piercing voice called Simon had come to her at night

---

[26] Plural of maleficium, Latin for "malevolent act".

[27] Plural of striga, Latin for evil spirit or witch.

[28] The trial of Jeanette Clerc is recorded in bibliography (13), pages 56-57.

and given her a bag of money to become his servant; how, when she agreed, he gave her a small white stick and a box of grease; how she rubbed the grease on the stick and said 'White stick, black stick, carry me where you should. Go, in the Devil's name go!'; how she flew with him to his sabbat to join her sisters dancing naked in the wood, lit by a blue-green light; how she kissed Simon unnaturally and how his seed was ice-cold.

Nycolas shivered as he watched the Irish witch fly down off the battlement towards the river. He hadn't believed any of Jeanette's confession at the time, condemning her to death just to keep the Prince-Bishop happy. Every month Monseigneur was sending to Rome a list of the number of witches killed in his bishopric and wanted to make it look as impressive as possible. In fact, Nycolas had felt a little sorry for Jeanette. Simon had made her promise to pay him one chicken every year and when she got home she found all the money had changed to leaves. But apparently it had all been true. This Irish witch was using the Devil's Jewel to fly and he could see with his own eyes the blue-green light glowing in her hands, the pink one in her mouth as she flew out over the Genevan soldiers arrayed before his Chateau.

Although he was frightened by this demonstration of the Devil's power, Nycolas was also delighted. She had not confessed to being able to fly. He had not known about this power of the Jewel when he asked her to help him. *This is better than anything I dared dream of. She'll fly down and drop the pink Jewel onto the cannon and freeze it.*

But as she flew over the row of harquebusiers they saw her and began shooting up at her. Crack! Bang! She swerved upwards. Crack crack! Nycolas' heart stopped for a second. *If they kill her I'm finished.* A moment later the guns fell silent. Looking down he saw their red glowing matchcords moving rapidly around their dark silhouettes against the snow. *They're reloading!* He looked up. *She's still flying. They all missed! Their guns aren't accurate enough at this range. Arrows would have been more effective.*

'Fly down,' Nycolas shouted, leaning over the battlement, safe now, confident of victory. 'Put the pink jewel on the cannon.' He pointed down at it, his heart soaring.

Once that cannon is frozen my Chateau will be safe, he thought. *The Genevans will have to go back to the city to get another. Then I will make the witch take the spell off the cannon and my soldiers will pull it into the Chateau. We might even be able to hoist it up onto this battlement. Yes, that will be a real defence against them when they come back. But where's the witch?*

He glanced up but could not see her. He scanned the sky and was shocked to see that, instead of flying down, the witch was flying over his head, heading north. He ran along the top of the wall shouting at her. 'You're safe now. Fly down you fool! Put the pink Jewel on the cannon.' *Is she stupid? Didn't she*—But then he remembered: *She doesn't speak French!*

She flew higher. *She's going to escape!* A fierce anger began to burn in his stomach as he ran along the wall until he crashed into a soldier who was standing pulling water up on a rope. Nycolas was cursing the man's soul when he saw the bow slung across his chest. 'Give me that bow, quick!' Nycolas was a better shot than any of his soldiers. 'Shoot her down!' he called to the other archers who were standing on the battlement staring up at her open mouthed.

He strung an arrow, raised the bow, drew the string and aimed at the witch's pink head. For a second he swung the bow to follow her movement, then pointed the arrow ahead of her and, with God's name on his lips he let slip the string, still swinging the bow. The shaft whistled as the white tail feathers arced upwards. There was a scream from the sky, the blue jewel flew up into the air and began to arch towards the ground. The witch began to fall, her head glowing pink against the darkening sky.

Then Nycolas heard the gate of the Chateau open and a horse's hoofs thudded across the snow. 'Close the gate!' he roared and leaned over the parapet. The figure riding down the path below him had to be the Prince-Bishop. Nobody else would be so foolish as to risk his life to escape, but the Prince-Bishop of Geneva had nothing to lose. He must know that if he was caught by the Genevans he would be imprisoned at the very least.

As Nycolas looked down, the witch tumbled past the Chatelain heading towards the path. She spun as she fell, her outstretched arms and legs as rigid as a dead tree, her head still glowing pink, her cloak stiff, rotating with her. It wasn't natural, the way she moved. *So that is what a dead witch really looks like,* Nycolas thought. A moment later she hit the path, bounced over the Bishop's head and began to roll down the hillside towards the river. Looking down Nycolas saw the bright blue crystal land on the snow not far ahead of the galloping horse. The Prince-Bishop must have seen it too because he reined in and half-jumped, half-fell from his horse onto the snow as the Genevan soldiers began racing towards him.

In a flash the old man was on his feet, grasping the blue jewel as he ran back towards his horse. The soldiers quickly caught up with him, braying like a pack of wolves, and the Bishop ducked between his mare's legs, trying to escape their clutches. What happened next was extraordinary. Looking down Nycolas saw the old man suddenly shoot out from beneath his horse as if he had been kicked sideways. He flew through the air just like the witch had, although with a good deal less grace, and crashed heavily into the stone wall of the Chateau. He lay on the snow, groaning in pain, as the soldiers ran to him.

The cannon fired again and with a sickening crack the Chateau's door swung open. Genevan soldiers began swarming through. Abandoning the Bishop to his fate, Nycolas ran along the battlement to the tower. As he ran down the spiral stairs, the roar of a huge explosion within the Chateau rent the air. By the time he reached the courtyard, flames were shooting up walls, the stables and all storerooms were alight and smoke was pouring through the Great-Hall's roof.

With no hope of saving his Chateau now, Nycolas ran to safety through the smashed gate into the welcoming muzzles of a dozen harquebuses.

It still lacked a few minutes to six, yet the morning streets of Geneva were already bustling when a small procession of the soldiers escorted Nycolas and the Prince-Bishop into the town. Too polite to jeer or throw stones, the Genevan citizens were nevertheless fascinated and many followed the soldiers as they escorted their two well-dressed prisoners up the hill, past the Temple of Saint-Pierre which stood on its summit and towards the Chapel of Notre Dame la Neuve, which everyone was now calling "Calvin's Auditorium[29]".

The captain of the guard left his prisoners near the door and Nycolas watched him approach a gaunt figure in a flat cap and long black fur-trimmed cloak who was sitting quietly preparing for the Bible Study at seven. A crowd of silently excited citizens pushed past the prisoners and gradually filled the white stone Chapel as the two men conversed in an arched alcove. Finally the dark figure emerged into the central space, held aloft a black

---

[29] Author's note: While it is true that Notre Dame la Neuve stopped being used as a church in 1536, it was not called "Calvin's Auditorium" until 1556, when, at Calvin's suggestion, it was made available as a place of worship to the large numbers of protestant refugees who were then flooding into the city. See bibliography (23) page 6. W.S.

Bible and beckoned the prisoners to come forward. Two soldiers escorted the Prince-Bishop towards him but left Nycolas and the other soldiers at the back of the Auditorium. The dark figure pointed at the Prince-Bishop whose knees were being pushed onto the stone floor by the soldiers.

'Doest thou, Pierre de La Baume[30], admit that thou didst erstwhile hold the title and position of "Prince-Bishop of Geneva"?'

'Aye, that I did,' the Prince-Bishop said, 'and proud I was and still am to hold the post.'

'And doest thou further admit,' the dark figure continued, his deep voice echoing around the Chapel, 'that whilst in that role thou didst abuse and betray the power and authority entrusted thou thereby, and didst commit heinous and grievous sins against the people and State of Geneva in the holy name of God and of His son Christ the Lord?'

'No, in the name of Our Lord I most certainly did not.'

'How then doest thou justify thy support of the Savoyard tyrant Charles, never once protesting against his wicked and invidious suppression of the liberties of the citizens of Geneva but on the contrary aiding and abetting in his infamous conduct?'

'I could not protest against what was lawfully imposed.'

'Enough. The citizens evicted thee twice from the City of Geneva and that is proof enough of thy guilt. And dost thou further admit, Pierre de La Baume, that thou didst follow and obey and promulgate the word and teaching of the Antichrist?'

'I certainly do not. To whom do you refer, stranger, by name of "the Antichrist"?'

'I mean him whose servants do transform themselves, by Satan's guile, into what seemeth, to the unwary, as angels of light. I mean him whose disciples useth the delusion of Satan to

---

[30] See bibliography (17) page 38.

draw the people away from the true worship of God to vanity. I mean him whose pastors will corrupt and abuse the simple and the naïve and the innocent and the pure, turning them into the very creatures and servants of Hell.

'I mean he who pretends to teach but who cannot tell the difference between what the Lord does, and what Satan and the ungodly design to do. I mean he who holds wicked instruments under his hand which he can turn as he pleases. They, as they are wicked, give effect to the iniquity conceived in their wicked hearts and bodies and minds. I mean that man of sin who situates himself in Rome, that same son of perdition of whom Paul speaks and whom the innocent call "the Holy Father". Yes, it is he, even the Pope, whose shepherds should protect their flocks and yet ravish and destroy them like carnal wolves, filling their own pockets as they suck away the purity of the souls of their lambs.

'I do not deny that there are good men amongst his pastors, but he, the Antichrist, puts the power and glory of himself and his Church above the sanctity and purity of those foolish enough to follow him. And while the Roman church remains under his tyranny, that church will be filled with the sacrilegious impiety he has profaned, with the cruel domination he has oppressed, by evil and deadly doctrines and pastors whom he has defended like portions of plague smeared by engraisseurs on the arms of innocent patients. It is he whom I declare is the Antichrist. Doest thou deny it?'

'Yes, I deny it all! By God, Pope Paul III is the Father of the Holy Roman Catholic Church who—'

'Alessandro Farnese,' the dark figure interrupted, 'is a corrupt Italian who is abusing his position to advance the power and wealth of his family by nepotism. He is the perfect example of the type of corruption of which I speak.'

'Who are you, stranger?' Pierre sounded overawed in the presence of such self-assurance and conviction. 'And pray what title or position do you hold which gives you the right to interrogate me?'

'My name is Calvin. John Calvin. I am in Geneva by the invitation of William Farel. Clearly thou art too corrupted by attachment to the Catholic Church to admit of its corruption so let me ask thee another question. It is for this matter I have been specifically asked to interrogate thee.' Calvin turned to one of the Genevan soldiers. 'Thou, Captain, doest thou say thou didst see this man fly?'

'Yes indeed, Councillor. He picked up a blue thing dropped by a witch into the snow.'

'A witch? And where is this witch now?'

'She flew off down towards the river, Councillor, and we lost sight of her.'

Nycolas knew where she had gone. He remembered seeing the Irish witch bouncing down through the leafless trees and crashing through the ice that covered the river, but he said nothing.

'Very well,' Calvin said. 'And who else hath witnessed this flight of the Bishop?'

Most of the soldiers raised their hands.

'So,' he said, turning to face Pierre. 'Doest thou admit that thou art a witch?'

'No! That is complete nonsense. I was pulled along by the Devil's Jewel which the witch had dropped from the sky.'

'Devil's Jewel?' Calvin sounded slightly astonished. 'What is that? Who hath this object now?'

'It's here Councillor,' the Captain said, offering it to him.

Calvin looked at it for a moment, resting it on his hand, then took it gingerly between long fingers and examined it closely. 'It is indeed a beautiful object. Truly this could be the work of the

Devil himself. And dost thou deny that thou flewest with this Jewel?'

'I do deny it,' the Prince-Bishop said. 'It pulled me along. It was not my intention or wish to fly. I merely wanted to mount my horse and carry the Jewel to Charles.'

'It pulled thee along? But behold, it pulleth me not. I am not pulled. The Captain was not pulled. Nobody is pulled by any force of evil except he who wisheth to be pulled. Thou clearly wished to be subject to this force of the Devil just as thou wished to be pulled by the evil of the Antichrist. Thou wert a willing accomplice in this act of evil. Doth thou deny it?'

'I deny it again and I will deny it forever.'

'Thou knowest, for thou art a veteran of witchcraft trials, that those who are accused of witchcraft and yet deny it will be subject to interrogation. I ask you once more, do you deny it?'

The Prince-Bishop simply glared at Calvin.

'Very well. Thou leavest me no choice. Interrogation is repugnant to me, hence I will not perform the act myself, but there is one among this company who hath kindly volunteered to undertake this disagreeable task. Will that person step forward?'

The crowd of soldiers parted and into the centre of the Chapel stepped a small figure wearing a long brown cloak whom Nycolas could not at first recognise. It was not until the figure threw back its hood that he saw the grinning, malicious face of the hospital master's wife.

Episode 46 The Meeting

I'm sorry but I cannot accept any of this,' Francesco Romani said, shaking his head until his jowls wobbled.

I didn't expect you would, you fat dogmatist, Alex thought as he stared down at the little meeting ranged in a circle below him, his arms aching from the ropes which trussed him like a Christmas turkey to a beam in the Cafeteria ceiling.

'Mr Fitzpatrick cannot possibly be alive,' Francesco went on. 'Nobody can survive being absorbed into a black hole. As everyone knows, they would be torn apart by gravitational tides as they passed through the event horizon. This concept is universally accepted within the scientific community. All this nonsense about people surviving in a black hole is pure science fiction. And even if he did survive by some process unknown to science, there is no way he could ever communicate with us. A black hole is called black precisely because nothing can come out of it.'

'You think I don't know all that, Professor Romani?' Alex said with growing exasperation. 'I would have said exactly the same myself before this happened, but Catriona definitely told me she spoke to Sam and he told her to take all the crystals down a tunnel so Zhang could restart time.'

'Michael Zhang?' Danny Schneider gasped. 'Is he still alive?' But before Alex could answer Francesco asked 'Did you hear Sam say this yourself, Count?'

'No,' Alex sighed, 'it's what Kata told me, but I believe her because afterwards she told me she had gone down the tunnel herself—'

'So that's where she disappeared to,' George said.

'—and she said she was stuck' Alex went on, ignoring him, 'and needed me to go down and help her. And she certainly wasn't anywhere round here, because I saw her walking through some deep snow behind two men in armour. Don't you understand, all of you?' He looked around at the upturned faces with a growing feeling of desperation. 'She needs our help! She needs your help and my help. She—'

'So you never actually saw Sam yourself?' Francesco insisted.

'Well no, I've not actually SEEN him, but I heard him when Marianne found me and little Kata on the balcony. And Marianne heard him too.'

Francesco looked at her. 'Is this true, my dear?'

'Oh yes, Professor Romani. I heard Sam when I first woke up in the stretcher. He saved my life by helping me to get out. And when I reached the balcony he told me that Catriona and Alex were there when I could not see them. I think I would probably be dead now if it was not for his help.'

'And his voice came out of a crystal?' Francesco asked.

Marianne nodded.

'Which one? Which crystal was it, my dear?'

'The one I gave to…to him.' She clutched Danny's arm tighter and nodded towards Alex without looking at him.

'So this was presumably the same crystal you heard him in, Count Karolyi? But we have just looked through all of these crystals,' Francesco pointed at the diagram he had drawn on the table top directly below Alex, 'and nobody reported seeing or hearing Mr Fitzpatrick. How do you explain that, Count?'

'I have no idea.'

'Hmm. So exactly which crystal was it you heard him in?'

'How should I know, Professor? A hell of a lot has happened since then! Let me think. I guess it must have been the one I gave to György.' Marianne looked around, wondering who György was. 'But does it matter? The fact is that Sam DID survive. You've got two witnesses here to prove it, and we have to go down that—'

'No!' Francesco said passionately. 'What we've got are two people who believe they have heard a voice. This is not unusual in moments of extreme stress, and it proves nothing. Am I right, Dr Plaisent?'

Jean-Pierre nodded slowly. 'Stress can cause delusions, yes, but if Sam was a delusion, how do you explain the fact that he told Marianne about Catriona and Alex being on the balcony before she could even see them?'

Francesco thought about this for a moment, then said quietly 'We have no proof that this happened. Alex was frozen at that time and Marianne was obviously in a distressed state.' He turned to Marianne and patted her arm. 'No offence intended my dear but you were probably not exactly calm at that moment, I'm sure you will agree. You might have misremembered what happened. But whatever it was, it could not possibly have been Sam. Don't you agree, Danny?'

Danny Schneider looked distinctly uncomfortable as he shook his head and said: 'Nobody knows what is possible in this situation Professor Romani. Nobody has ever travelled into a black hole before. We are working with things beyond the known laws of physics. We know that we can see from one crystal into another, yet no known process can explain that. We are dealing with things we don't understand. For example I would have said that it was impossible to freeze time, yet that has definitely happened. We must at least consider the possibility that what Karolyi says is true and I for one hope that Michael Zhang is alive. I would very much like to meet him again.'

Marianne glanced at her husband, then stared with frozen eyes at a nearby chair.

'Do you think it might be useful,' Jean-Pierre said, 'if Alex tried to speak to Mr Fitzpatrick again now? We could see if we all suffer the same delusion.' There was a strong hint of irony in his voice but Francesco did not seem to hear it.

'Yes,' Francesco said, 'excellent idea! Are you happy to try this experiment, Count Karolyi?'

'Well I never actually spoke to him myself, I only heard him, but Kata did, so if you'd care to untie me I'll try it, and in fact you can speak to him yourself.'

'That would be extremely interesting. Please untie him, fireman.'

'Hold on, Professor,' George said. 'Can we trust him? What about this gun and the man Marianne says she saw him kill?'

'Well?' Francesco said. 'Is any of that true, Count?'

'I'm sorry to say it's all true, Professor, but I can assure you it was purely self-defence. Paul was a friend of mine. I went to ask him to help me rescue Kata. Unfortunately he panicked and started shooting. I had no option. I certainly never wanted to kill him.'

'So why did you take his gun?' George said, fishing it out of his pocket.

'Simply as a precaution. I thought it might be useful when I went down that tunnel.'

'And the money Marianne saw you steal?' Danny said. 'Why did you do that?'

'I guess that was a moment of madness in the shock of having killed him. I threw it away soon afterwards. I realise now it was a stupid and pointless thing to do. Money has no meaning any—'

'But why did you point this at me, Karolyi?' George said, waving the gun at him.

'I was trying to get over here to rescue Marianne, György, and you were trying to stop me. What else could I do?'

Francesco hesitated then said 'I think we have to trust him. Untie him, if you please, fireman.'

George and Ludovico flew forward and began to untie Alex. 'If you put one finger out of place I'll tear your balls off Karolyi,' George whispered.

'And then I shove them up your arse,' Ludovico added sweetly.

Alex shrugged off the rope, rubbed the circulation back into his arms, his shoulder still aching from Ludovico's earlier hammerlock, and took the crystal George was offering him. A little label was stuck on one side bearing the legend G3. 'Is this the one I gave you?' Alex asked him.

George shrugged. 'Who knows, Karolyi, and notice this.' He took the magazine out of his pocket and slipped it into the Tomcat's handle. 'It really is loaded this time.'

'Then you better check that the safety is on, György, else you'll be shooting your own bollocks off.'

George frowned and began to examine the gun as Alex flew down to the centre of the group where one large fragment and several of the small ones were floating together. He let the small crystal fragment George had given him hover before him and the circle of people gathered around it. Then he hesitated.

'Look, Professor Romani. Exactly what's the outcome going to be of this little demonstration? Suppose I do manage to get Sam to talk. Do you agree that I can take all your crystal fragments down the tunnel?'

There was a moment of shocked silence then Brigit said 'You're certainly not taking my crystal, Count Karolyi', Ludovico said 'No way!' and George said 'Not mine!'

'But that's what Sam told Kata to do,' Alex said. 'As I understand it, Michael can't restart time unless he gets them all. So what are the terms and conditions? I'd like to agree the deal before I go any further.'

'Just get Sam Fitzpatrick in there, Karolyi,' George snarled. 'We need to talk to the organ-grinder, not the monkey.'

'The fireman is quite right,' Francesco said. 'We cannot agree what we will do until we understand exactly what has happened. There are so many unanswered questions here. We first need to talk to Mr Fitzpatrick, or even better to Michael Zhang, and prove they are still alive. This is the future of mankind we're talking about. We cannot agree to give you all the crystal without a lot more information.'

Alex sighed, turned to face the crystal and began calling: 'Sam! Can you hear me?' He felt like a stage magician trying to conjuror a sleepy rabbit out of a hat. There was no answer. After five minutes he gave up and picked the crystal out of the air, turning it over to look at the label Francesco had stuck onto it. 'This is G3. To be honest I have no idea which one I was holding when I heard Sam speak. What about if I try to find Catriona? I saw her in my...not long ago. Let me try one of the crystals I was carrying.'

Francesco checked the labels on the spare crystals which were floating near the diagram on the table. 'Try this. It's one of yours.'

'Give me mine back first, Karolyi,' George said. As he took it he added, 'and by the way I'm pretty sure this really was the one you gave me originally, so bad luck, Gypsy Rose Karolyi. Looks like Sam's disappeared.'

Alex looked at the crystal Francesco had given him. The label said A1. 'This might not be the right crystal but I figure I should be able to see her in one of these. So what will happen if I do manage to call her, Professor Romani? Sam told her to take György down the tunnel to help her. Will you at least let me and György go back to ATLAS and try to get down the tunnel? And if you won't let me take all the crystal then at least you can spare me two so we can bring Sam and Michael back up the tunnel. What do you say?'

Francesco thought about it. 'Give me that crystal,' he said. 'I see no reason why we need have you to perform this experiment. If all you do is call then I can do that myself.'

Francesco held out his hand. Alex hesitated.

'What's your problem Karolyi?' George said holding the little gun in his huge fist.

Alex handed over the crystal.

'Wise decision, my friend,' George grinned. 'I'll just tie him back up, Professor.'

'Now hold on Gábor György!' Alex said.

'Yes, tie him up fireman,' Francesco said. 'He has admitted robbery and murder. I will need to consider how to deal with him when I have more time. Now then, let's see.' Francesco began to call into the crystal looking rather embarrassed. 'Catriona! Catriona! Is that how you do it?'

Alex's eyes flipped up to the ceiling then back to Francesco and he nodded as he let George tie his arms behind his back. Francesco kept calling. Gradually other people began to call as well. George even pulled Alex across until all nine were clustered around the crystal, their heads close together, chanting Catriona's name like the chorus in a Greek drama. When that failed, people began calling into their own crystals. It was deafening as their cries echoed around the little honeycomb of bubbles, but still nobody heard or saw her.

Eventually Francesco clapped his hands and they gradually fell silent. 'I hear nothing,' he said. 'Anyone hear anything? No? Then I propose we move on to the next item of business. I would—'

'Hold on Professor,' Alex called. 'This doesn't prove anything. The fact that she isn't replying probably just shows how much she needs our help. You can't just leave her—'

'I cannot do anything else, Count Karolyi. We need evidence here, not hearsay. And there is an important matter which needs everyone's agreement. I'd like to discuss that now.'

They all moved away to a more comfortable distance, George pulling Alex, and the group formed a circle around the two large crystals and several small ones which hung just above the map on the table. Francesco restored the A1 crystal to its correct place on the map, then said:

'As you know, four crystals have fused together so far to make two larger ones,' Francesco said, 'and large crystals have large bubbles. This is very important. Danny and I measured the diameters of a small and large bubble. The small one is three metres across but the large one is over eight metres, almost three times bigger. Now as you know volume increases with the cube of the diameter and this means that the large bubble has a volume twenty times bigger than the small one. In other words, twenty times as many people can live in a large bubble than a small one.'

'I don't think so,' Brigit said, her eyes running over the big bubble that surrounded them. 'Twenty people living in a bubble this size? That's utterly ridiculous, Francesco! This one feels crowded now and there's only nine of us.'

'I agree,' said Jean-Pierre. 'There would be no privacy, and hygiene would be—'

'Well maybe not twenty but certainly more than two,' Francesco said. 'If two fragments are separate then only two people can live. If they fuse together then we could easily have four or more people in a bubble this size. I agree we need to think about privacy and hygiene, but they are not impossible problems to solve. Agreed? Right, so while we were doing our experiments on crystal, Danny and I tried to fuse the two fragments we had, but we failed. I suspect that only certain crystals will fuse together.' He pointed at the diagram on the table. 'Looking at this map my hunch now is that crystals which are adjacent are the ones that will fuse and I want to try fusing three to make a triple.'

'And what,' said Brigit, 'would be the point of this fusion Francesco?'

'If my prediction is correct then its bubble will be twenty-two metres across and its volume will be four hundred times bigger than the bubbles of three separate crystals. Just imagine that, ladies and gentlemen. With four hundred times as much space we could easily build partitions or maybe erect tents and gain some privacy. And not only would we have far more space but we would then have lots more spare crystals which our scientists could use to start doing research. You have to realise that right here in CERN we have some of the world's best physicists and I want our best people to work on the problem of crystal, to find out as much as we can about it as quickly as we can. I think this is our top priority. I am hoping that eventually we can create a bubble big enough to revive the whole of CERN. Imagine what that will be like. Instead of just nine people alive we will have thousands. I'd like—'

'You must be raving mad, Francesco,' Brigit said, a little cloud of concrete dust puffing out of her blond curls as she tossed her head in disbelief. 'That is absolutely preposterous. You have no idea what would happen, or even if it's possible to fuse these crystals. Don't you think that science has caused enough damage without you setting out to create more havoc? There is no way you are going to fuse my crystal with anyone else's. It's out of the question.'

'But why not, Madam Ambassador? Don't you want to create a bigger bubble?'

'It doesn't matter what I want. It doesn't matter what you want, Francesco. It doesn't matter what any of us here wants. This is a problem that affects the whole world. As far as we know the whole world is frozen in time, isn't that right?'

'As far as we know, yes.'

'So what happens next must be a political decision that is taken as far as possible by everyone on Earth. Now as it happens, Francesco, as it just happens, we have a body right here in Geneva which represents almost all the nations of the world. The United Nations has more agencies and offices here than in New York. Things could not have turned out better in that regard. I believe we must get the UN involved in this. I propose we should use the spare crystals to revive representatives from states belonging to the Security Council, or at least the permanent members if we haven't got enough for all of them, so they can form an emergency committee. Those nations all have ambassadors here. What is needed here is a political decision about what to do, and that requires a politically organised body which can take charge, not a bunch of scientists. Scientists have caused this problem and now it's down to the politicians to decide how to solve it and it's the Security Council which determines international law. No other body is capable of doing that.'

Murmurs of approval rippled round the group.

'I must object,' Francesco said vehemently. 'It was not science that caused this problem. It was the laws of nature. CERN merely happened to create the circumstances in which the disaster could happen. It was inevitable—'

'I'm sorry Professor but I disagree,' Danny said, his whole face deathly pale. 'I'm perfectly certain that Michael Zhang knew what was happening. He knew that ATLAS had captured a cosmic monopole but he kept it secret. He deliberately engineered that black hole.'

'That is irrelevant now!' Francesco burst out. He was beginning to turn red in the face. 'CERN owns all these crystals. They were made in CERN. They belong to CERN. As Director General I have the authority and the responsibility to decide what will happen to them. This is not a matter for the United Nations. Where are the spare crystals now?'

'I've got them Professor,' George said.

'Excellent!' Francesco held out his hand. 'I'll take them.' George did not move. 'Come on, fireman! Hand them over.'

'No,' George said. Everyone was looking at him. 'Sorry Professor Romani. I can't do that.'

'What? Why not?'

'Because I agree with Brigit. I don't think we should be doing any more experiments with crystal at this time. On the contrary I think we should be using these spare fragments to revive people who have the authority to decide what to do.'

'Thank you George,' Brigit said.

'I agree,' Jean-Pierre said.

There was a long silence.

'I'm sorry Professor,' Danny said, 'but I don't think crystal really belongs to CERN. What is CERN? It's an organisation that belongs to its member states, to the countries that pay for it. I think if this crystal belongs to anyone it belongs to its member states.'

'Well I'm not so sure about that, Danny,' Brigit said, 'although I agree that it doesn't belong to CERN. But Ireland isn't a member of CERN. Does that mean the Irish people have no rights regarding crystal? And what about Russia? Is that a member?'

'Not a member, no,' Francesco said, 'although it has observer status.'

'The United States?'

Francesco shook his head. 'The same.'

'China?'

'We have a co-operation agreement.'

'Wonderful. India? Oh, don't bother. It's obvious that CERN membership does not even include all the major countries, and it seems to me that crystal belongs to all people on Earth. I'm certain that the UN is the only possible place to discuss what we do next.'

'I have to agree with Brigit,' Jean-Pierre said, 'although for different reasons. If you revive thousands of people then how will we feed them? Where will they sleep? Have we got enough bottles of water for them? And the latrines we dug certainly wouldn't be adequate for thousands. No, I think it would just turn a bad situation into a humanitarian disaster.'

'That's right, Francesco' Brigit said. 'Haven't you ever heard of sustainable development? I've heard enough of all this. I'm tired, I'm filthy, I'm fed up. I want a bath and a change of clothes and a good sleep. I propose we reconvene this meeting tomorrow. But I give you notice now, Francesco, that I will be tabling a motion that we immediately revive representatives of the permanent members of the UN Security Council and let them decide what to do. Perhaps you'd all like to sleep on that motion? In the meantime, George, I wonder if you could show me where I might be able to find some decent clothes?'

'Wait a minute,' Alex called. 'What about Kata and Sam? Aren't you going to let me try to rescue them? Don't you want Michael to restart time? Don't you want to save the Universe? You can't wait for the United Nations to do it! That's just not going to happen. They'd be talking about it for a month and by that time Sam could be dead. You don't seem to understand the urgency of the situation. Maybe it's my fault. Perhaps I haven't explained it properly. We have to go down the tunnel now. Right now. Kata said she's come out of the tunnel and is stuck down there some place. She needs help. Sam needs our crystals to restart time. Can't you see what I'm saying? We've got to do something. Now!'

Episode 47 Unification & Inflation

During one of those rare moments when he was not being curled up into a ball or squashed flat or stretched out into a long thin line, when for a few seconds space and time seemed to be normal, Sam saw some of the Entroilian larvae come plopping through the hole into the pool of honey. Once he caught a glimpse of a beautiful blue tunnel curving away into the distance, and knew immediately that it was the tunnel he would have to follow. And one time he saw a bundle of negative energy threads, tangled together into a thick rope, trailing away up the centre of the tunnel.

'Can we follow those strings?' Sam shouted, but a moment later he was rolled up into a cylinder. After an eternity of deformation, he came back to normal and heard Trissitia exclaiming:

'It's no good, Husband. The propellers aren't working.'

'Can we make this pod pull itself along that cable?' Sam asked, pointing at the tangled negative energy strings.

'Yes, I think so,' Trissitia said. She played with the controls and a moment later Sam saw one of the pod's claws reach out and grip the rope. As the arm bent and the pod slid up the rope, the second claw reached ahead and began to repeat the operation. The honey pool slipped behind them and they moved quickly into the blue tunnel inside the Universe.

'There's that blue stone again,' Trissitia said.

Sam could see it too, the big blue crystal ahead of them, hanging in the middle of the blue tunnel, suspended between two bundles of negative energy threads. One bundle went winding up the blue tunnel into the distance, shrinking rapidly until it was almost invisible. The other bundle threaded down through the honey pool and, Sam assumed, out of the universe and back up the pink tunnel they had just descended.

'I hope we get away from this chaos,' Sam said, for there were still awful moments of complete distortion.

'Yes, and I hope those strings don't break!' Trissitia replied, then for a moment they were stretched and rolled up like a ball of wool. 'But I think it's working, husband,' she continued as they returned to normal. The arms had pulled them almost up to the crystal. 'The warping doesn't seem so bad now,' she added.

She was right. The distortion had nearly ceased. Sam could hardly believe what had just happened. The whole experience had been so completely unreal, weird, fantastic. The sense of unreality was only enhanced by the beauty of the huge round crystal which floated before them, one negative energy string emerging from each of its many faces.

'Can we capture that crystal somehow, Sashamida?' Sam said. He felt closer to her now that they had survived the nightmare together and emerged apparently unscathed, thanks to her prompt action. 'I know ultimately it has to come out of the universe so somebody can use it to restart time, but at present I think it might be useful to us, although I'm not sure how. But it seems a shame just to leave it here if we can take it with us.'

'Yes, husband. No problem.' Trissitia's antennae curled with pleasure as she made the arms manipulate some flexible strapping to secure the crystal tightly against the pod's rounded nose, obviously please that Sam had used her pet name. 'Wasn't that horrible?'

'Awful. I never want to go through anything like that again,' he said as he examined the crystal. He felt that gaining possession of it was some sort of compensation for what he had just experienced.

'Are, here are some of my brothers,' Trissitia said. 'Thank the Anting they survived.'

Looking out of the dome, Sam saw three large Argolaths and in their long front legs they were each gripping a terrified-looking Entroilian larva.

'Oh good,' Trissitia said. 'They're dealing with those miserable little larvae straight away. Well done, brothers!'

Sam was appalled as he saw the Argolaths biting the wriggling larvae unmercifully. 'Stop them!' he shouted. 'You've got to stop them, Trissitia!'

'Have I, Husband? Why?' She sounded amused by his urgency.

Sam watched in alarm, trying to think of a good excuse for helping the larvae, an excuse which did not include killing her brothers. 'Because this is my Universe and you will have to share it with the Entroilians in peace. Otherwise I won't help you.'

'But my brothers do not need your help now, Samfitzpatrick. You've already told me this tunnel leads to your home planet so they should be able to find it easily.'

The Entroilians were thrashing about, their pale green blood oozing out of a score of cuts in their flanks with six huge Argolaths tearing one poor larva to pieces in a frenzy of blood-lust and cramming the pieces into their mouths with evident relish. Each one was much larger than the larva, larger even than the pod in which Sam was sitting.

I've got to stop them somehow, Sam thought. *If they don't grow into Entroilians, who else can help me stop those monsters mating with women? I've got to find an undeniable reason that the Entroilians have to be allowed to live!*

He shuddered and turned back to the little Argolath upon whom the fate of humanity now seemed to rest.

He studied Trissitia trying to think of an argument that would convince her. She lay back in her seat, fully relaxed, her antennae waving languidly from side to side as she looked out of the pod's dome, watching the slaughter, her head tilted to one side. *It's as if she's watching a TV comedy! She's nothing more than a child, really. I'd better treat her like one.* He reached out and took her claw-like hand. Her head turned towards him, her antennae still wafting contentedly.

'Sashamida,' he said, stroking the back of her hard hand and nerving himself for the lies he was about to tell. 'You know that you're my best friend as well as my wife, don't you my dear?'

Coyly her antennae wrapped behind her eyes and she squeezed his hand. 'Oh Sashamida, I am so happy to hear you say this. It fills my heart with—'

'So then would you mind if I gave you some advice?' Sam interrupted her.

'No of course not, my Husband. What is it?'

'Well my dear, I know those silly little Entroilian larvae are of no use to us now, but I think you might find they could come in quite handy later on as we go up to the Earth. Don't you remember your father saying that we must help Catriona bring all the fragments down so his scientists can fix the event network and restart time?'

Her antennae crossed, signifying she did.

'So we've got to find all those crystals and take them to him. I'm sure that would be easier if we had these Entroilians to help us, once they emerge as adults.'

Her other claw began tapping thoughtfully against her jaws. *I've got her full attention now*, Sam thought.

'Help us?' she said. 'How?'

'Well Entroilians can fly so they'll be able to carry the crystals down the tunnel very quickly, then fly back and collect more. We really have no idea how many crystals there are my dear, but they seem to be very small and the pipe which Michael broke was huge so there must be thousands of them, millions maybe. It would take us ages to carry them all in this pod. But if we had those Entroilians as slaves to do this work for us, then your

Professor could get on and fix the Universe while you and your brothers got on with…with your work.'

'Entroilian slaves…' she said thoughtfully. 'That's quite an amusing idea.'

'So don't you think it would be better if your brothers spared those Entroilians' lives and we made them do something useful instead of just eating them?'

Trissitia's antennae crossed over her head. 'That's a really good idea, my Husband. It would be a suitable revenge for the slavery which Entroilians have put Argolath miners into.' She flipped a switch on the control panel and lifted a microphone out of its cradle. 'Attention my brothers! This is Princess Trissitia. I believe those Entroilians will be very useful to us later in our mission. They can be slaves carrying crystal down the tunnel and back to Argolathia. I would respectfully ask your highnesses to spare their miserable little lives.' Sam saw the Argolaths pause in their murder of the larvae whose bloody fragments hung from their jaws. 'If you agree,' Trissitia continued, 'I will carry the remaining ones up the tunnel in this pod, since they clearly will not be able to walk.'

The princes conferred among themselves and, after a short while, a heated disagreement began. *But at least they've stopped the killing*, Sam thought as he looked around, feeling like an accused man waiting for the verdict of a jury and trying to find something to take his mind off the possible verdict. He was surrounded by the blue tunnel, and to his surprise he was able to see something churning around outside it. It seemed as if he was floating inside a boiling witches cauldron. *Michael Zhang must have been down here*, Sam thought. *I wonder what he made of all this?*

Sacred Book 2: Grand Unification Epoch

Dictated with Divine Wisdom by His Holiness the Son of Beeing partly to High Priest Glagnump Koddlezine and partly to the Princess Uskabellu and deposited in the Sedtia Library.

The uncurling of four dimensions from the cosmic manifold — may the divine Beeing be forever praised for His wisdom in ordaining that these events should come to pass — and the concomitant appearance of time within the Cosmic Egg, caused the Primordial Field to degenerate into two distinct sub-fields.

One field is denominated "Gravity". It permeated everywhere throughout the Cosmic Egg, propagating at the maximum speed possible within the constraints of the metric. This caused the remaining three uncurled dimensions of the manifold to crystallise into the sub-manifold we recognise as space.

The other sub-field, known to mankind as the "Unified Field", contained the remaining three fundamental forces latent within the Primordial Field. At this time, denominated the "Grand Unification Epoch", all three forces were of exactly equal strength. Men say they were "symmetrical". But, it seems, nature hates symmetry and the three forces fought among themselves for supremacy.

This was an age of uncertainty within that tiny insignificant speck which would eventually grow into the Cosmos. The three fields were like three equally matched divisions of an army at war with itself. The battles involved the temporary manifestation of the three fields in different configurations and differing relative strengths, as if nature were again experimenting, this time searching for a combination of the three components of the Unified Field which would be stable.

These battles raged at every point within the tiny embryonic Cosmos, small in comparison with the Universe of today, but nevertheless large enough for millions of battle-experiments to be conducted simultaneously. The three fields fought bitter battles among themselves, warring for supremacy, churning the uncurled dimensions, contesting which would be first to become actual.

Most battles ended in mutual defeat. The fields failed to find a stable configuration within the uncurled dimensions and, lacking substantiality, they collapsed upon themselves in preparation for the next battle.

The Cosmic Egg was growing, the uncurled dimensions elongating, creating more space out of nothing, as the battle raged within. This stretched the Unified Field, reducing the density of its energy, cooling the Cosmos. It was as if the three divisions were growing weary of battle, each enfeebled by their futile efforts to gain supremacy over the other two.

This phase of history — denominated with divine wisdom the "Grand Unification Epoch" — ended at ten to the power minus thirty-six seconds after the fertilisation of the Cosmic Egg.

Finally, to Sam's relief, the Argolath princes must have decided Trissitia was right because they let go their captives. Sam quickly helped her pull the half-dozen surviving Entroilian larvae into the pod. *God knows whether they will be any use in the long run,* Sam thought, *but at least I have some potential allies.*

'We're going to need some food for them as well,' Trissitia said. She emptied one of the boxes of supplies from the back of the pod and scooped some of the honey into it then she shut the dome and shoved the box and the larvae behind the seats. 'Thank you, brothers,' she said into the microphone as the Argolaths drifted away in the churning ocean. 'I will take these larvae up to my Husband's home planet. It is at the top of this tunnel. I wish I could give you a lift, but you are too big to fit in my pod. You're going to have to walk, but I'm sure it won't take too long.'

She strapped herself into her seat, turned on the engine and began to fly the pod up the tunnel. Looking back, Sam saw the Argolath princes starting to crawl slowly and carefully up the slippery blue tunnel wall. Suddenly they seemed to shrink and it took him a few moments to realise the wall they were crawling up had receded because the whole tunnel had increased enormously in size. Sam watched the detailed pattern on its surface blurring into a uniform blue as it carried the princes far away.

What's happening? Why's the tunnel getting bigger? Where's the honey gone? Where have the negative energy strings gone? My God, this is my Universe, my home, but really I know almost nothing about it.

Sacred Book 3: Inflation

Dictated with Divine Wisdom by His Holiness the Son of Beeing to the Princess Uskabellu

The Grand Unification Epoch ended — praise the wondrous event — when the expanding Cosmos cooled below a critical temperature – of the order of ten to the power twenty-six Celsius. Now the energy had fallen below a level at which the battle could continue. The three fields were too weak to fight, but still they were unable to decide which one was stronger. There existed then a precarious balance, a state in which no force was victor and all the combatants were exhausted.

While these three warring forces were thus enfeebled, the force of gravity – which had materialised earlier – began to take a key role in reshaping the Cosmos.

The battlefield appeared deserted. The Cosmos was at its lowest possible energy level; but it was not completely empty. Space-time still contained something – denominated by mankind the "Higgs Fields", which possessed some energy. The Cosmic Egg was incapable of sustaining a completely empty region.

Men sometimes say: "Nature abhors a vacuum". This statement might or might not be true in the world of mankind, but it was absolutely true in the young Cosmos. A complete vacuum containing nothing was not possible. Higgs fields appeared spontaneously within empty space.

This state of a vacuum containing some energy is designated the "False Vacuum" and it had a very extraordinary property; within the false vacuum, gravitation was negative! Each piece of false vacuum repelled all the other pieces. This repulsion made space-time expand and this, in turn, created more false vacuum which thereby increased the force of repulsion.

The space inside the Cosmic Egg grew in a runaway process from the size of a tiny dot to the size of a whole galaxy in a matter of moments. The cosmos expanded faster and faster, exponentially, in a process called "Inflation". This was the event which gave rise to the expression "Big Bang" which men sometimes use, but that term compounds all the events from the creation of my Universe to the process of Inflation, and is no longer useful.

Before Inflation, the energy density was not uniformly distributed. There were tiny dense regions, formed by chance quantum fluctuations, and with Inflation they became hugely magnified. They would later form the bases for the large-scale structures of the Cosmos. During Inflation, the space inside the Cosmos expanded by a factor of roughly ten to the power eighty. The wise worshipper will note that this dramatic expansion was only apparent inside the Cosmic Egg; from the outside, the Egg appeared totally unchanged. There was no physical problem with this, no shortage of space-time, no overcrowding within the Cosmic Egg, for it had been designed to allow an almost infinite expansion within whilst remaining, on the outside, a simple Egg, small and finite, one of thousands of such eggs within Entroilia.

This "Inflation Epoch" ended — by the divine Grace of the Beeing — at ten to the minus thirty-two seconds after the fertilisation of the Cosmic Egg.

Episode 48 The Boutique

When Alex Karolyi finished his appeal it was Ambassador Brigit O'Brien who spoke first.

'Listen, Count Karolyi,' she snapped. 'Sam Fitzpatrick is my husband so I think I have the right to express my opinion and in this case I completely agree with Francesco. We can't risk people's lives, not to mention losing precious crystals, by chasing after him without some evidence that he really is still alive!'

'But he IS still—' Alex said.

'Shut up Karolyi,' George growled. 'Just listen.' He was floating beside Alex, holding the rope which tied his arms behind his back.

'And as for Catriona,' Brigit went on, giving George a tiny wink then glaring at Alex again, 'she's my daughter so don't you go telling me what we should be doing to help her. You think your opinion is more important than the voice of the people of the Earth? Well we've had enough dictators in history, thank you very much, and we don't need another one now. In fact we have to avoid that at all costs. It would be so easy for some little bully to take power now and impose his will upon the rest of us.' She turned and glared to one side as she said this. George's eyes followed her gaze. Francesco Romani's face had turned beetroot.

'We have entered a new age now, young man,' Brigit continued, turning back to Alex, 'an age in which the very foundations of civilization and everything which humanity has achieved are now in grave danger. I believe we must put the United Nations at the centre of everything we do. It is the only institution on Earth which can give power where it belongs, to the people of the Earth. Because I believe that something good can actually come out of this disaster. Now, at last, the world has a chance to unite under a rational form of governance, and I will fight until my dying breath to ensure that it works.'

'Bravo!' George Gabor cried, then stared straight at Francesco Romani, silently daring him to disagree. There were murmurs of agreement from all around the little circle of people, and Francesco said nothing, looking downcast but deeply uncomfortable. George looked again at Brigit feeling pride, admiration and awe at the wisdom and inner strength of this woman. She was looking straight at him and smiling. Hitherto George had regarded Brigit as somewhat superficial, but now he realised what an intellectual and moral strength she had. For a moment their eyes met and a silent message of mutual admiration passed between them. When she spoke again her voice was as gentle as a caress. 'Are you ready to go now, Georgie? I want you to help me find some new clothes.' To his embarrassment he felt his cheeks tingle and realised that, for the first time in his life, he was blushing. With that realisation his discomfiture grew and a sweat broke out on the back of his neck.

'Sure,' he said, trying to sound casual. 'I just need to sort out when we're meeting again and what to do with this young man here,' he added, yanking Alex's rope. 'What do you want me to do with him, Professor?'

Francesco cleared his throat. 'Can you keep him somewhere secure until the next meeting? And I need a crystal to fly with. I don't suppose anyone will object if I have a large one? I have more measurements I need to make before tomorrow's meeting.'

George scooped up the five small fragments and the two doubles which had been floating above the map. He put one of the small ones in his pocket and, since nobody seemed to object, pushed one of the two large ones towards Francesco saying

'Well, I suppose we could lock Karolyi up somewhere, if that's what you want, Professor Romani. Ludo, you and Sofie take him over to the Fire Station and leave him in the Lecture Room without any crystal. Should be safe enough up there. And while you're at it, find a safe place to keep these.' He passed the remaining five crystals to Ludovico, four small and one double. Then he took the gun out of his pocket and gave it to him as well. 'You better take this too. Then I want you and Sofie to go back to the airport and fetch the goods we left behind when we chased Karolyi. I'll meet you in the Fire Station in about an hour. I'm just going to escort the Ambassador to Balexert.'

Ludovico grinned. 'No forget to show her where the straws are, George. She might want a longer one.'

'Yes, thanks for that advice, Ludo. Shall we go, Madam Ambassador?'

'Wait!' Francesco shouted as they began to fly away. 'We have not agreed what time we will meet next. Look, it's ten thirty-seven now. I propose we meet here in six hours, say at five o'clock tomorrow—'

'No way can I be ready in six hours,' Brigit said. 'I need some clean clothes and a bath and some sleep. I'll need at least ten hours.'

'Ten hours? Really? We have some very important matters to...Oh, all right Brigit. So nine o'clock again. Everyone agree it is now thirty-seven, no thirty-eight minutes past ten? Can you check your watches? At least we should be able to agree on that if nothing else!'

'Come along Marianne,' Jean-Pierre said as the group dispersed. 'I want to check your temperature and blood pressure before you have the next antibiotic. Danny are you coming too?'

'Yes, I am. I just want to ask George something before he goes. You two go on. Which hostel are you going to, Marianne?'

'Thirty eight, chou. It's closer.'

'Okay, I'll come over in a minute.'

'Balexert is just here, Madam Ambassador,' George said at last, as they reached the slip-road leading from the Route de Meyrin towards the shopping mall.

'Balexert?' Brigit gasped. 'Don't be silly, Georgie. I want some decent clothes. Come on. You can help me find the boutique I normally go to. It's near the Madeleine Church. You must know it. And for God's sake call me Brigit.'

They flew on towards Geneva in silence. Since they had spoken to Danny and left CERN, Brigit had been talking about herself non-stop, about her television career and about how she had resigned to help her political party gain an overall majority at the last election. George hadn't said much on the journey so far. He felt unsure of his position.

'Where do you come from, Georgie?' she said after a while.

'You don't need to be polite, Brigit. I'm sure you don't really want to know.'

'If I didn't want to know I wouldn't ask, believe me.' She flew closer to him, her arm brushing his. 'So tell me about yourself.'

'All right. I was a senior fire officer in Budapest, in Hungary. Then I had some problems.'

'What kind of problems?' He could feel her eyes studying him. It was flattering that such an attractive and distinguished woman should take any interest in him, but also puzzling. It had never happened before. Yet it was a relief to be able to talk. Ever since seeing the dead face of Robert Moore in the ATLAS cavern, he had been haunted by flashbacks of an even older disaster.

'My marriage broke up at about the same time that I lost seven of my men in a big fire.' That was about as much as he could say on the subject. He didn't want to go into the details for fear of making the flashbacks worse. 'And I sort of broke down for a while I guess. Anyway I left Hungary three years ago and got a secondment here to CERN. They have a scheme to do that for firefighters.'

'I'm sorry to hear that, Georgie. But you're happy here, are you? I mean, before this disaster happened today, were you happy?'

'Not really. I didn't have a real firefighter's job. It's too technical here. I want to fight fire. It's what I was born for but you hardly ever get any fires here. Rescuing people stuck in lifts takes most of my time.'

'Oh that's sad. So what's kept you here?'

'The mountains. I love climbing. I'm a volunteer with several mountain rescue services. There aren't any real mountains in Hungary but here we've got the Alps and the Juras.'

'So at least you had something you were passionate about. That's good, it's important. Have you got any children?'

It was a very surprising question but he saw no harm in satisfying her curiosity. 'Yes, two. They're both grown up and left home now.'

'You don't look old enough.'

'I'm forty-three. I'm not sure why you're asking me these questions, Brigit.'

There was a pause before she said: 'When something like this happens Georgie, a disaster like this, I suppose it makes you stop and think. Quite honestly it's making me rethink my whole life. This morning—God, was it really only this morning?—this morning I was all set for a career in politics. I was planning to spend a few years here as the UN Ambassador and then go back to Ireland and run for President. That was my plan. I'm good at planning, George. I've planned out almost everything in my life. The only thing I didn't plan for was Catriona. She was an accident, but then I was very young. Anyway, normally I plan things out in life and then I make them happen.'

They had reached an intersection and George stopped. 'Can we just plan out this route for a moment? I'm pretty sure this is Avenue Wendt. I come here every few days to indulge myself at McDonalds. Let me just check.' They flew to the building on the corner, found Migros and McDonalds, then followed the car lane down the Rue de la Servette towards Geneva, George trying to ignore his rumbling stomach.

'But everything's changed now Georgie, and I mean everything. And I keep trying to work out what's going to happen next. Where's my life going now? Where's the whole bloody world going if it comes to that? And I really haven't got a clue. I don't like that, Georgie. I'm the type of person who likes to know exactly where she's going and, when I don't know, I hate it. It makes me feel lost, like a little boat tossed about in a storm on a big ocean. I'm afraid of what might happen, I suppose, but I'm also angry. Very, very angry. I mean, look at these poor bloody people.'

Below them people were waiting in line to board an orange and white striped trolleybus. One woman was trying to fold her push-chair with one hand whilst holding a child with the other.

'Those people are as good as dead now, Georgie. What have they done to deserve this? Well I'm determined that something good has to come out of this mess. We've got to learn from this disaster, George. If we don't then the whole thing has just been bad. But if we can learn from our mistakes then at least something good will come out of it.'

They flew under the railway bridge and followed the dotted line down the middle of the road, narrowly missing a motorcyclist. 'Which way's the Madeleine from here?' Brigit said, slowing down.

'Where are you trying to get to exactly?'

'Septième Etage. It's near the Madeleine Church.'

'Oh yes, I know. Uhh, down here.' George turned right at a yellow striped pedestrian crossing painted on the road and they flew along the Rue de Cornavin towards the river. 'But I still don't know why a woman like you is asking about a man like me, Brigit. We're from completely different worlds. We have absolutely nothing in common.'

'You don't think so? I'd say the complete opposite, myself. I think we're very similar kinds of people, George, you and I. We both know what we want out of life and we both have the strength and determination to go and get it. We both want to help make the world a better place. Isn't that true?'

George shrugged. 'I just want to save people from fire. Or mountains.'

'I don't believe that, George. Have you never wanted to change the world?'

George thought about it. 'My father did. He was a staunch Communist, one of the few left in Hungary when I was a child. He was always busy protesting against the economic reforms being introduced by the government. He wanted to create a world that was fair to all people, including the poor, and yes, I agreed with that for sure, but I didn't think that Communism was the answer. To me it seemed that reform was required.'

'So you never got involved with Communism?'

'Not with any sort of politics.' They reached the river and followed the tram lines which crossed the bridge. 'I turned away from all politics and just decided I wanted to help people in some direct way, some practical way.'

'So you became a firefighter.'

'Eventually, yes.'

'And here you're the Chief of the Fire Service.'

'What? The hell I am! I'm just a humble team leader.'

'Why? Don't you want to be the leader?'

'No. Not after what happened in Hungary.'

'What was your role there?'

'I was a station chief.'

'Exactly! We're both leaders, you and I, and that's what the world needs right now.' They had crossed the river and now she seemed to recognise where she was. 'This way,' she said and led him with confidence up the narrow Passage de la Monnaie. 'But I don't think you realise how much the world has changed since this disaster, George. You're still in the CERN mind-set. I think I can help you with that and I think you can help me too. Now what was I saying? Oh yes, when a disaster like this happens it makes you rethink your whole life and I've been doing a lot of thinking. I've been looking at everyone and looking at myself too and thinking about us all. People are incredible things when you think about it, aren't we? There's so much going on inside our heads and in our hearts that normally we aren't even aware of, but something like this happens and suddenly Bang! You see everything that's going on and it all looks completely different. Is this the Rue de la Confederation? Oh yes. This way.' She flew across the road, found the little monumental fountain and turned left, keeping close to the shops. 'Well as I say I've seen things in a new light including myself.'

'And have you come to any conclusions?'

'Yes. Two. The first is that we have to get the United Nations involved in this problem as soon as possible, as I said in that meeting.'

George stopped, hovering above the tram lines on the road. 'I counted thirteen crystals in that meeting today. How many countries are there in the United Nations?'

'About two hundred.'

'So that's not going to work,' he said, flying on.

'And that's why I want to get just the major players involved. Anyway that's the first thing I decided. We need to turn right here somewhere. Come on.' She flew to the right side of the road and followed the shops.

'And the second thing?'

'I want to have another baby.' They passed the entrance to the Confederation Centre and reached the cinema. 'Come on George, this way, up this alley.'

She flew up the alley, crossed the road at the top and turned left, keeping close to the restaurants and shops. George followed a little way behind. His heart was pounding and he was having trouble keeping up with her although she wasn't flying fast.

'Yes, ever since you came and revived me and Francesco in that so-called Safe Room I've been just burning for sex. It's as if my body's saying *"Quick, we need to make more babies as fast as possible and save the world".*'

'But we aren't short of people, Brigit. We've got millions of those, billions for all I know. What we're short of is crystal.'

'I know. This isn't a logical thing, Georgie. It's an emotional response. I'm a woman. It's my instinct I suppose. I've lost my daughter. Now, to be honest, she and I didn't always get on, but when you lose your child, it's a terrible thing. I've always loved sex anyway, and when a disaster like this happens the first thing you want is to make love and try to make another baby. Don't you feel like that?'

'Well no, to be honest I haven't noticed my sex drive put on any sudden burst of speed recently. I've sort of got used to doing without it during the past few years, if you want the truth.'

'But that doesn't mean you're not interested does it? Or does it? Ah, we have to go up here.'

They had reached a curving bank of steps and she flew up, over the heads of people who were sitting frozen in the act of enjoying the spring sunshine.

George followed, trying to digest what she was saying. *Looks like Ludo was right about her*, he thought. *How did he know?* He found her hovering outside a shop door.

'This is Septième Etage,' she said. 'Come on, Georgie. Don't worry, I don't bite. Well not hard, anyway.'

He followed her into the boutique. The shop was empty. Brigit began to pull jackets and jumpers, dresses and trousers off rails and throw them at George. 'Bring them out here, George,' she said flying back out into the paved area in front of the shop. George followed her out and found her taking off her concrete-stained red suit as she floated above the pavement. 'Give me that Mike & Chris wrap-jacket, Sweetie,' she said, floating before him in her red bra and pants. 'No, the beautiful grey one.' He held it out. 'Bring it over here. I told you, I won't bite. Come on George.'

He flew over and she took the jacket off the pile in his arms then reached down and ran her hand over the front of his trousers. His body instantly responded to her caress. 'Mmm, that feels nice, Georgie. You see, you do still have a sex drive. You just needed someone to start the motor. Put those things down for a minute. Come here, honey.'

She put her arms round his neck and kissed him. Their mouths opened and their tongues met like old friends. George was amazed that he could still remember how to kiss, it had been so long. Her arms went behind her back and she unhooked her brassiere and flung it away. 'That's better,' she whispered and carried on kissing him as her hand reached down and massaged him through his trousers. George's hands moved up her rib cage and he shuddered as they closed around her warm heavy breasts, the nipples pressing firmly into his palms.

She pulled at his belt. 'Do these things come off or are they attached to your body?' He unbuckled his belt and she opened his fly and began to slide his trousers over his buttocks then suddenly she stopped. 'I want to take a bath with you first George,' she said.

George froze. His heart was pounding and he was more eager to have her than he had been about anything for a long time. He wanted to feel her hand holding him but now she had stopped. He felt confused, frustrated, slightly angry. Surely she wasn't just—

'I don't want you touching me without washing your hands at the very least, and I don't want you to make love to me without touching me first. Do you know where we can have a bath together?'

It took a fair amount of effort for George to force his mind to focus on the question. 'What about the lake? It's pretty clean.'

'That sounds fine. Come on, George. We've got the clothes. Let's go and find some soap and towels. Then I want to give you the best sex you ever had in your life, fireman.' She kissed him again, scooped her new clothes together and flew topless down the steps into the streets of Geneva.

Episode 49 Strappado

'Are you a witch?' the voice on the other side of the cell door said for the third time. Again there was no answer. Nycolas d'Orsières stood and looked through the grille. The smell of human excrement filled his nostrils. In the candlelight he could see the wrinkled, grey-skinned figure of the Prince-Bishop lying naked on the stone floor in a pile of his own filth. 'Hoist him again,' the Magistrate said.

Until a few weeks ago, the hall where the Magistrate sat had been the refectory of the Convent of Poor Clares[31]. Then the Genevan mob had driven the nuns out of town and now the convent had become the new Palace of Justice. Beside the Magistrate sat the clerk to the court. On the table before them lay a Bible, a ledger, a quill pen and an ink pot, a leather bag and a perfumed handkerchief which the Magistrate lifted to his nostrils occasionally to mask the smell.

The naked Prince-Bishop lay face down on the floor before them. A rope was tied to his wrists which were held together behind his back by a leather strap. The rope went up over a small pulley tied to a beam in the ceiling and down to a heavy wooden windlass. Two soldiers sat at a table beside it, playing dice.

Brisette de Bourgeaulx, widow of the late Maître de l'Hôpital de la Peste, was sitting on the bench beside them. When she heard the Magistrate's command she grinned and spoke to the soldiers who reluctantly stood and heaved at the levers on the windlass. The drum rotated and the strappado rope tightened. The pulley in the ceiling creaked and the rope dragged the

---

[31] See bibliography (17) for the diary of one of these nuns.

Prince-Bishop across the stone floor, pulled his arms up behind his back at an unnatural angle then lifted him up once more into the air. When he was hanging a metre off the ground the soldiers dropped the windlass' ratchet and resumed their game.

'Confess that you are a witch,' the Magistrate commanded. The clerk dipped his quill pen in the inkpot and made a note in his ledger. The suspended figure gave no response. His head hung down, facing the stone floor with unseeing eyes. There was a long pause.

'Pull him,' the Magistrate commanded.

The thinner of the two soldiers sighed, threw down his dice and said something to the fat one. They both bent and lifted a heavy yellow stone. An iron chain joined the stone to a shackle. Brisette took the shackle and closed it around one of the old man's ankles, picking the least besmirched leg. At a nod from her the soldiers let go and the stone dropped, pulling the Prince-Bishop's left leg. Both his shoulders dislocated with two loud cracks, the shoulder-blades sticking out of his back like handles, and he let out a scream of agony.

'Now,' the Magistrate said, 'do you confess that you are a witch?'

'Never!' the Prince-Bishop gasped as more excrement drained out of him and splashed onto the floor.

'Bring in the first witness,' the Magistrate commanded.

The thin soldier walked to Nycolas' cell, opened the door and escorted him across the Refectory to stand before the Magistrate's table. The stinking old man hung beside him like a rotting carcass.

'State your name and position,' the Magistrate said.

'Nycolas d'Orsières. Until the Genevans burnt my Chateau down, I was the Chatelain de Peney.'

The Magistrate gestured towards the Prince-Bishop. 'Did you see this man fly?'

'Yes, your honour.' There was no point in trying to protect him now. The Prince-Bishop was as good as dead already and Nycolas had his own skin to think about. He had been accused of rebellion against the Reform. His trial would begin tomorrow and would almost inevitably end in a death sentence.

'State what happened.'

'I was standing on top of the Chateau with the Irish witch. She flew off carrying the blue Devil's Jewel and—'

'Was it this?' The Magistrate took the blue crystal out of the leather bag and held it up to show him. The soldiers stood and stared at it, obviously enthralled by its brilliance and the way it glowed in the dark.

'Yes, that's it.'

The Magistrate looked at it, resting on his palm. 'What is this stone? It is indeed very beautiful. Whence came it hither?'

Nycolas too gazed at it for a few moments, remembering its power. When he had given it to the Irish witch, standing on the battlement, she had pressed it with her thumbs and that was what had given her the power of flight. He was sure of that. As he looked at the gorgeous stone, hope stirred once again in his mind. He had nothing to lose by trying to escape and if that meant using the Devil's Jewel or even going into league with the devil himself, so be it. 'The Irish witch said she found it in a cave on the hillside near Meyrin village, your honour.'

'A cave? Have you seen this cave?'

'No, she could not find it but I believe her because she led us to where the other Devil's Jewel had turned the cow to stone.'

'Cow, what cow? Nobody told me that an Irish witch had put maleficia on a cow.'

'No, she didn't your honour. She took the maleficia off the cow. It was the other Devil's Jewel, the pink one, which turned the cow to stone. The Irish witch brought it back to life.'

The clerk dropped his quill pen and the Magistrate stared at Nycolas for a long time.

'So are there two Devil's Jewels?

'Yes your honour, a pink one and that blue one. The pink one is much smaller.'

'And what happened to this Irish witch? Did you kill her or is she still at large?'

'She too was turned to stone by the pink Devil's Jewel. I saw her fall down the cliff near my Chateau.' Once again Nycolas remembered seeing her bounce down the cliff, her head glowing pink, and disappear through the ice into the Rhone. He was sure that nobody else had seen this, for the river had been visible only from his position on top of the Chateau wall.

'I must question this witch,' the Magistrate said as he put the crystal back into the bag. 'Continue with your evidence.'

'The Irish witch flew away, using that blue stone, but I shot her down and she dropped it. The Prince-Bishop picked—'

'There is no Prince-Bishop. The accused is Pierre de La Baume.' The Magistrate nodded at the naked man hanging beside Nycolas. He was whining under his breath like a dying dog.

'Ah, yes, Pierre de La Baume picked it up and he began to fly as well, and that was when the Genevan soldiers caught him.'

'I demand...' a voice overhead wheezed slowly, 'the right...to question that witch.' Nycolas looked up to see the agonised face of the hanging Prince-Bishop staring down at the Magistrate. 'She can prove...I am innocent.'

The Magistrate conferred with the clerk then nodded. 'Bring him down gently.'

The soldiers lifted the windlass' ratchet and began to lower the Prince-Bishop. When the stone attached to his ankle reached the floor, his shoulders snapped back into their sockets with two small thuds as he groaned in agony.

'Do you know where the witch is now?' the Magistrate said to Nycolas.

'I saw where she fell, your honour. I presume she is still there.' He did not think it wise to mention that she had fallen into the frozen river and so was most certainly dead now.

The Magistrate turned to the soldiers. 'It is too late to do any more today. In the morning, I want you to escort this prisoner and let him lead you to find the Irish witch. Bring her back and I will question her tomorrow.'

'May I respectfully suggest that the Devil might come to collect her during the night?' Nycolas said. A plan was forming rapidly in his febrile mind. 'Would it not be better to secure her as soon as possible, your honour?'

The Magistrate considered, then turned to the soldiers.

'Put Pierre de La Baume in a cell then take Nycolas d'Orsières and see if he can find this witch. If you find her bring her back here.'

'If I might suggest also, your honour,' Nycolas said, 'we will not be able to do anything unless we have that blue Devil's Jewel to release her from the spell of the pink one. She has turned to stone in the same way as the cow.'

The Magistrate stared at him, evidently astonished. 'If you do that you will be accused of witchcraft yourself.'

'I'm willing to take that chance, your honour.'

'But why? Why would you risk your life to retrieve this jewel?'

Nicolas paused thinking furiously for an excuse, then said 'I too have been a magistrate, your honour. I want to see justice administered for all. So now I hope, indeed I pray that, by helping you to find the truth and deliver justice in the case of Pierre de La Baume, I too might hope to obtain justice in my own trial tomorrow.'

The Magistrate was clearly impressed. 'Very well.' He handed the bag to one of the soldiers. 'Let him use this to try to release the witch from the spell, but observe carefully what transpires.'

The fat soldier took the bag and hung it on his belt. As they turned towards Nycolas, they glanced at each other and both grinned broadly.

Episode 50 Big Bang

'What's that bright light?' Trissitia said. 'It's hurting my eyes.'

Sam stopped staring at the receding princes crawling up the wall behind them and looked where she was pointing with one claw as she controlled the pod's flight with the other. A brilliant light was shining in through the blue wall ahead of them, getting rapidly brighter as they flew up the tunnel.

'Slow down Trissitia!' Sam cried. 'I think—' But he was too late. One moment the pod was flying up the tunnel and the next it was hurtling through a hailstorm of missiles bombarding it like rocks. Sam could hear them pounding on the outside of the pod. A moment later the transparent dome gave way and, not having fastened his seat belt, Sam was immediately swept out of the pod by the hurricane and went hurtling away, blinded by the painfully bright light, alone and terrified, leaving Trissitia still strapped into her seat pitifully calling him to come back.

Sam lost sight of her amidst the cloud of missiles slamming into him from all directions, some as gentle as butterflies, others as heavy as cricket balls. Sam curled himself up, trying to protect his head with his arms. Each heavy impact knocked him sideways and sent him shooting away in a new direction whilst the smaller objects forced their way up his trouser legs and down his shirt collar. He could even feel them vibrating around inside his clothes as if they were frantically trying to get out.

One of them's going to crack my ribs soon, he thought. In the hope that the pod would offer some shelter he lowered his arms and peeped out, searching for it. What he saw was horrific. Missiles of all sizes were emerging from a fog of white smoke and hurtling around him as if he was in the centre of a battle between a dozen stone-age tribes. And through the torrent of missiles there flew strange bird-like objects with multiple wings which they flapped as they flew by or collided gently with him and bounced lightly away. Sam had no idea what any of these things were.

'What is all this?' Sam's terrified mind silently shouted. 'And where's that bloody pod?'

Sacred Book 4: The Big Bang

Eventually, by random fluctuations — and the divine grace of the Beeing —, the Higgs fields attached themselves to the three fundamental forces within the Unified Field, each part of which now acquired its own strength and individual nature. This dramatic change is denominated a "Phase Transition" and the three fields inherent within the Unified Field were able to become manifest. The symmetry of the Unified Field had broken and the Cosmos would never again be so simple.

The first to appear was the "Strong Nuclear Force" and in succession the other two came into existence, the "Electromagnetic Force" and the "Weak Nuclear Force". Their properties were very different from each other, and from the force of gravity, but together these four forces would shape the future, from the smallest particle to the largest structures of the Cosmos.

These newly manifest forces effectively converted the latent energy within the Higgs fields into real, material, physical particles which burst into existence as if by magic. The false vacuum decayed and the energy of the Higgs fields was gradually converted into particles: tiny bundles of energy with exotic names such as quarks, gluons, electrons, neutrinos and photons made from the different types of fields. They emerged from the parts of the Unified Field each with different properties.

As more and more energy was released by the Higgs fields, the particles moved faster and faster until the Cosmos was transformed from a vacuum into a cauldron of ultra-hot particles boiling in chaotic profusion and colliding at extreme velocity and the Inflation Epoch came to a dramatic end.

The Cosmos was now hotter than ever before. The war was over, the fundamental forces had been defined, but peace had not yet been achieved. A dramatic new phase of history was about to begin.

This moment is sometimes called "Reheating" but the wise denominate this phase as the real "Big Bang". It occurred — by the divine Grace of the Beeing — some ten to the minus thirty-two seconds after the fertilisation of the Cosmic Egg.

But Michael was not there to explain any of this. All Sam knew was that he could not survive much longer under this massive bombardment[32]. For a moment he glimpsed a blue light. *That could be the crystal!* he thought as an impacting quark pushed him away, but soon he saw the light again and this time one of the pod's arms flashed out and a pincer caught his jacket as he drifted past in the storm. The arm lifted him over the crystal strapped to the pod's nose. A metal shield had been placed over the hole left by the shattered transparent dome. This shield opened and Sam was pushed quickly inside the pod before the shield closed safely behind him.

---

[32] Author's note: Neither Michael's "Sacred Books" nor his diary nor any other document I can find, nor any scientist I have consulted over this, has any explanation for how Sam, Trissitia or the pod were able to survive in the appalling conditions of the Big Bang. My own theory, for what it is worth, is that they had all shrunk to roughly the same size as particles. I think this theory is supported by the fact that they could see particles, although they are far too small for any current human device to see. W.S.

The noise was deafening, a continuous thunder as thousands of objects battered the outside of the pod. Trissitia hurled herself onto him, wrapping both arms and all four legs round him and rubbing her antennae over his bruised and battered body checking for broken bones as she shouted 'How are you my dearest Sashamida Husband?'

Sam could barely hear her above the din, but this show of affection touched him profoundly. It was obvious that this little alien creature, who had tricked him so cruelly over the marriage and the insemination, actually cared deeply about him. Sam felt hugely grateful to her for saving his life, and for her obvious love. *She is my only friend now. I think perhaps it was her love for me which made her do those terrible things.* Sam didn't know whether to be thrilled or appalled. *I'm certainly going to need as much help as I can find, but can I really trust her? Will she help me stop her brothers abusing humans? I'm not sure. After all, she's already abused me herself, in a way.*

'We've got to get the pod out of here as soon as we can, Husband,' she shouted still clinging to him, her huge ant-like head only inches away from his. 'I've put up the protective shield but the rest of the bodywork was never designed to withstand this kind of continuous pounding. Some panels are already beginning to buckle. I believe we have come out of the tunnel. I have used all the pod's scanners and cannot find any trace of it.'

'Can't we fly around and look for it?' Sam too had to shout to make himself heard.

'No, the motors are completely clogged with these stone things. We have no power. What can we do?'

'If you are right,' he said, 'and we have come out of the tunnel, then those stones must be part of my young Universe. As I understand it, the Universe began with a sort of big bang. Looks like we were protected from it while we were in the tunnel.'

'Well we aren't protected now, Husband, so what can we do?'

Sam stared at her, but gained no inspiration. He looked around at the inside of the pod, equally without success. The Entroilian larvae were gently feeding on the honey, unaware of any danger. He closed his eyes, forcing himself to stay calm and desperately trying to envisage the situation outside the pod. He saw missiles flying around, smashing into its thin outer skin. He saw the big blue crystal strapped to the nose and began to worry it might be knocked off and they would lose it forever. He knew that would be a disaster. Then he suddenly remembered looking through the crystals when he was trapped inside the event network and seeing people using their crystals to fly. Hope surged in his heart.

'Can we use the pod's arms to press the sides of the crystal, Trissitia?'

'Perhaps, but why?'

Sam explained how people on Earth could fly by pressing the faces of their crystals.

Trissitia became excited and turned the camera on. An image of the big blue crystal outlined against the hailstorm appeared on a small screen. She pushed a joystick; one of the pod's arms retracted into a little opening and emerged equipped with the padded plate she had used before. Trissitia controlled it, making it press the pad against one face of the crystal. Nothing happened.

'You need to press harder,' Sam said. 'I just hope we don't break any of the strings.'

'But Husband, can't you see?'

Sam frowned and peered at the camera screen. 'See what? I can't see anything.'

'That's what I mean. The strings aren't there! I suppose they must have been broken by all these stones hitting them.'

Sam's heart sank. He looked at the screen, fear and panic rising within him. *She's right!* The blue crystal's faces where perfectly smooth now, showing no signs of the threads which had emerged from their centres. 'But Professor Itoodoo said it was those negative energy strings which hold open Michael's tunnel. If they've all broken then the tunnel must have collapsed.'

'So how are we ever going to get back to Argolathia?' There was fear in Trissitia's voice, but it was as nothing compared to the terror which filled Sam, as he stared at her, thinking *And how am I ever going to get back to Earth?*

Trissitia was gripping Sam's hand, looking at him with antennae limp from fear, waiting for him to find an immediate solution as they listened to the missiles drumming on the skin of the pod and the metal shield which had replaced the broken dome.

'If the negative energy strings have all broken and the tunnel has collapsed then I don't know how we're ever going to get out of here,' he shouted, shaking his head. Trissitia's antennae collapsed completely and her claw trembled in his hand. 'Don't worry, my dear,' he said, patting it reassuringly. 'I'm sure everything's going to be all right. Don't let's worry about those strings right now. Let's just see whether we can fly, shall we? Can you make the arm push the crystal harder?'

There was a long, breathless pause during which Sam was thinking: *I suppose it's not all bad news. If there is no tunnel then at least the Earth will be safe from invasion by Argolaths!*

Finally Trissitia said: 'We're moving Sashamida!'

'Are we? I can't feel anything.'

'It's very slow, but you can see it here.' She pointed at a dial on the control panel. The needle was barely registering. Gradually it moved across the scale. 'We're going faster! Wonderful, Sashamida! Now, how do we steer?'

'You have to push the crystal in the direction you want to go.'

It took her a little while to master this, but eventually she was able to steer it and go anywhere she wanted.

'That's brilliant, Sashamida! Well done!' Sam was genuinely impressed with her dexterity and began to feel a little more optimistic. 'Now, can we use the scanner to find the tunnel?' Her answer deflated all his hopes.

'No, Sashamida. I already told you. It doesn't show up on the scanner at all.'

'Show me.' Sam had never seen the scanner image before but it was not very informative. It merely showed a haze of rapidly moving dots. There was nothing that looked like a tunnel anywhere. The only odd thing he could see was a little round group of dots near the edge of the screen. They weren't moving.

'What do you think is happening there, Princess?' he said, pointing at the group.

She examined them. 'I don't know. That wasn't there before. Oh, but we've moved since the last time I looked at the scanner. I'll fly closer so we can get a better view.'

She made the pod's arms turn the crystal again and the static cluster of dots moved into the centre of the scanner screen, then she began to fly towards it. Sam watched it slowly getting bigger, his ears ringing from the increasingly intolerable thunder of particles battering the fragile pod as it accelerated forward.

'I'll change the resolution,' Trissitia shouted and the finer details of the cluster of unmoving objects became visible on the scanner. The contrast was dramatic between the storm churning around the pod and the group of completely stationary objects on the screen. They seemed to form a perfect little sphere.

'I think we're close enough now to use the camera,' she shouted, then slowed the pod's movement and pressed a button. The image on the camera screen revealed a collection of thousands of stationary objects, some large and round like stones, some small with wing-like projections, all statically arranged in a neat round tableau somewhat like an exhibition in a museum, a spherical haven of calm in an ocean of chaos.

All around the outside of this group, objects were bouncing away. *It's as if the stationary ones were surrounded by some sort protective sphere*, Sam thought, deeply puzzled. The whole tableau was lit by an inner pink light. The scene reminded Sam of the autumn Sun rising through the mist over Dublin Bay. He moved closer, peering at the middle of the pink circle, and what he saw made him gasp. 'There's another crystal at the centre,' he shouted. 'A pink one!' As soon as he saw it, Sam felt elated. 'We've got to get that crystal! I don't know why, but I'm sure our lives depend on it!'

'Ah, you are truly decisive, my masterful Husband. I like that! Let's take a closer look!' Trissitia pressed a button and the camera zoomed in on the pink crystal in the middle of a tranquil sphere of unmoving particles surrounded by a hectic storm of flying objects. On the screen, the crystal looked like a pyramid with four flat triangular faces, very different from the almost spherical blue one strapped to the front of their pod. 'I wonder why it's pink?' she shouted.

'No idea.' Sam was concentrating on the camera screen, uncertain of what would happen when they reached the sphere of unmoving objects, trying to make sure the pod did not crash into it. 'Does the colour really matter? It's a piece of crystal so we've obviously got to try and collect it. I just hope that somehow it's going to help us to find that tunnel. We're getting very close. Slow down.'

Trissitia pulled on the joystick, the padded arm pressed the front of the blue crystal and the pod slowed. As they approached the group of objects, the nearest one began to move, suddenly springing into life and hurtling away. As they came closer, more particles moved away, leaving a curving indentation in the sphere of frozen particles.

Glancing at the scanner screen, Sam saw the sphere now looked more like an apple with a bite taken out of it, and the bite was growing bigger. *These things are frozen like Catty and Alex were on the balcony,* Sam thought. *When Marianne moved towards them they started moving, and it's the same here.*

'Why are some of those things starting to move, Sashamida?' Trissitia sounded puzzled.

'I think it's because this blue crystal is unfreezing them somehow.' The noise of missiles battering the pod had diminished and Sam could speak now without shouting.

'But why were they frozen?' Trissitia said. 'Is it that pink thing that's doing it?'

'It must be.' He watched the objects evaporating away from the growing indentation with understanding gradually emerging from the confusion in his mind. 'On the Earth time has stopped and everything is frozen except near little fragments of blue crystal. Here it seems to be the opposite. If time has only stopped around that pink crystal then maybe this blue one is unfreezing it somehow, giving time back to it perhaps.'

'Yes, I see that. And the blue one can only unfreeze things which are close to it?'

'Apparently. Yes, that makes sense. One of the people on Earth, somebody called Marianne, said she was surrounded by something she called a "bubble". She couldn't see anything outside it.'

'So do you think there are bubbles here too, Husband? I suppose that would explain the round shape, if the pink crystal has a bubble, a bubble without time, a bubble of timelessness?'

'Yes, I think you've got it exactly. This blue crystal seems to be surrounded by a big invisible bubble of time and it's pushing its way into that little timeless bubble round the pink one.'

'And that's why only the nearest things are getting unfrozen?'

The bite on the scanner screen had almost reached the pink crystal at the centre of the frozen circle. Sam suddenly became worried. 'Stop!' he shouted.

Trissitia stopped the pod. 'What's wrong, Husband?'

'I'm not sure what's going to happen when the blue bubble reaches the pink crystal itself.'

'Well I imagine the pink crystal will begin to move, Sashamida.'

'Exactly! But if it goes shooting away like all these stone-things, then we might lose it.'

'But it will still show up on the scanner, won't it?'

'I suppose so, but I really want to collect that pink crystal. I'm hoping that somehow it's going to help us find the tunnel again.'

'But you said the tunnel has collapsed because the negative energy strings have disappeared.'

'Well now I'm not so sure. I'm hoping that it still exists. Maybe the strings are still there, just invisible. Remember we couldn't see them before we went right down to the bottom of the hole in the Cosmic Egg. Now we've come a little way up the tunnel inside the egg, maybe they have become invisible again. Don't worry about that now. We've got to catch that crystal when it starts to move! Have you got a net or something we can use to catch it?'

'No husband. This is a flying pod, not a fishing boat!'

'Okay, then I guess we've got to just take a chance and see what happens. Move forward very slowly, please.'

One of the pod's arms pressed the back of the blue crystal and the pod began to move. A moment later the pink crystal shot sideways a short distance, then stopped.

'Wait a minute!' Sam said. 'Let me think.'

Trissitia stopped the pod then zoomed the camera onto the crystal. The image looked almost the same as it had before, like a half moon. There was the smaller circle of frozen objects with a large curved slice taken out of them by the blue crystal's invisible bubble.

'This is going to keep happening,' Sam said. 'Every time we move close to it the bloody thing will just move away from us.'

'Don't swear like that, Husband! I won't have it! Let me think.' She tapped her jaws with a clawed hand. 'Why did it move? Why didn't it just stay where it was?'

'I suppose it must have been moving at some time in the past. When we unfroze it, it just carried on moving. That's going to happen every time.'

'And will it always keep moving in the same direction every time?'

'I suppose so.' Sam was beginning to remember some of the physics he had learnt at school. 'I suppose it will have to, since we're not pushing it. It will only change direction if something pushes it sideways. Maybe if it collides with something—'

'It doesn't need to collide with anything,' Trissitia said. 'If it keeps moving in the same direction every time we unfreeze it, then all we need to do is move ourselves so it moves towards us and we can catch it. It's obvious, Sashamida!'

'You know, I think you're right!' Sam said. He was so delighted and pleased with her that he gave her a hug, saying 'Well done, Sashamida!' It felt a bit like hugging a long, thin leather armchair with spindly legs. Her antennae fluttered with delight, then she backed the pod away from the pink crystal until the half-moon had expanded into a complete circle, manoeuvred the pod so that it was facing in the direction she thought the pink crystal had moved, and once more she began to approach it cautiously.

Just before the blue crystal's large bubble reached the little pink crystal, Sam shouted 'Stop! For God's sake stop!'

Trissitia stopped the pod. 'What's the matter, Sashamida?'

'I just realised what would happen when we unfreeze the pink crystal, Trissitia.'

She looked at him, her head on one side. 'It will come towards us. Isn't that what you want?'

'Yes, I want to catch it, but if that pink crystal comes flying towards us at high speed then what will happen? It's much bigger than any of the other things around us. If it hits our pod it could seriously damage it!'

'You are right, wise Husband! I never thought of that.'

'We've got to catch it but somehow make sure it doesn't hit us. You say this pod hasn't got a net? Well how about a spare shield, like this one?' Sam's knuckles knocked on the shield she had used to cover the hole left by the smashed dome.

'No. There's only one of those.'

Sam swallowed the curses which arose in his throat. 'So have you got anything which could catch that crystal when it comes towards us?'

'I have the pod's arms.'

'They might not be fast enough!' Sam said. 'That pink crystal moved really quickly.' He was beginning to despair.

'True,' Trissitia said and her antennae crossed over her head. 'And in any case the arms might not be strong enough to stop it. It is not worth the risk Sashamida. There has to be some other solution.'

Man and Argolath stared at each other. Trissitia's antennae uncrossed themselves and began wafting from side to side, moving in perfect harmony. Sam stared at them and suddenly had a vision of the two crystals flying directly towards each other. Then, as he watched, the big blue one turned around and flew away in the opposite direction, the little pink one flying after it. They did not crash.

'What about if you move this pod away as soon as the pink crystal begins to move towards us?' he said. 'Then you could use the arms to—'

'But I don't think the pod could move fast enough for that, Sashamida. The pink crystal was moving very quickly and it is much smaller and lighter than this pod. And anyway if we move away from it how are we ever going to catch it?'

'Once we match its speed we could gradually let it come closer to us until we caught it.' The image of the two crystals moving in harmony was so strong in Sam's mind that he was sure this must be the solution but Trissitia was not convinced.

'I don't think we can match its speed, Husband. It's moving too fast, and if I get it wrong it might hit us and punch a hole in the pod.'

There was a silence, a long thoughtful silence. Trissitia began to run her antennae over Sam's bald patch. 'Come on, Husband. I know you are a wise…a very wise…er, what kind of creature are you did you say?'

'I'm a human being,' Sam said with a wry smile. This conversation, this whole situation, seemed utterly bizarre.

'Yes indeed, you are a very wise human being. I am sure you can think of a solution. Would you like to mate with me now? It might inspire you.'

This suggestion was so silly that Sam just shook his head and focussed his entire attention onto the two crystals on the screen, picturing the pink one as a small, fast missile which was flying towards a big, slow-moving blue jumbo jet. In his mind he saw the pink one hurtle towards the blue one and it exploded. He shuddered and ran the movie again, this time trying to move the jumbo jet away from the missile, but it was too slow and got hit again. *She's right*, he thought.

He closed his eyes and with an effort he forced the blue jumbo jet to fly around the pink missile back to where it had been in the beginning. He gave each of them a bubble, then he started the movie again. The jumbo moved forward, the missile flew off to the side and stopped. He turned the jumbo so that it was flying in a line parallel to the missile but still the missile flew faster and got away. And then, as if it had its own little pilot, the jumbo went round behind the missile and slowly flew towards it. When the two bubbles overlapped, the pink missile hurtled a short distance away then stopped. The jumbo flew after it slowly and caught up with it, accelerating as fast as it could. The same thing happened, but now the jumbo was moving slightly faster. He watched in astonishment as the jumbo gave chase, getting gradually faster and faster, the missile repeatedly leaping forward and stopping until finally the jumbo was flying just behind it at the same speed. Immediately he knew he had found the solution to the problem.

'Okay, Sashamida,' he said. 'I've got the solution! Turn left!'

Episode 51 Freedom

'Poor Francesco didn't get much out of that meeting,' Jean-Pierre said as he slid one of the key-cards he had found in the hostel's reception office into the lock of door 018. 'I'd say Brigit O'Brien's going to be the leader of our little group, wouldn't you, Marianne?' She didn't say anything. She was thinking about Danny. 'Just wait here,' he said, pushing the door open. 'I want to make sure the room is empty.

How will Danny find me? Marianne wondered as she waited by the green bedroom door. *I hope he won't be long. What did he want to ask George Gabor about?*

'Yes, it's empty,' Jean-Pierre said as he flew back to Marianne. She followed him into the room, leaving the door ajar so it would be easy for Danny to get in. The doctor opened his bag as they floated above the crumpled duvet of the narrow, single bed. The room had obviously not been cleaned since the last occupant left that morning. 'Give me your arm,' he said. 'I'll check your blood pressure.'

'How will Danny know where I am?' Marianne said as she slipped her arms out of the grey firefighter's uniform and pushed up the sleeve of the medical gown she wore underneath.

'I'll go back and put a note on the front door in a minute. How are you feeling now?'

'I'm absolutely exhausted, Jean-Pierre. I don't know how I managed to stay awake during that meeting.'

'I thought I saw you nodding off a few times,' he chuckled as he wrapped the cuff round her arm.

'I'm still worried about Danny, Jean-Pierre. He's so preoccupied with Michael Zhang. You heard what he was saying in that meeting about Michael deliberately creating the black hole? And it's not just that. He blames Michael for killing the baby. He called him a murderer! Did I tell you that he said that if Michael Zhang was still alive he'd kill him? Did you see his face after Alex said that Michael was still alive? He was smiling! Do you know it was the first time I've seen him smile since the disaster happened? I've never seen him like this before, Jean-Pierre. He's almost like a stranger.'

He nodded, told her to relax and waited while the machine measured her blood pressure. 'I understand you're worried my dear,' he said as he unwrapped the cuff, put it back in his bag and took two tablets out of a little box. 'Look, here are some sedatives. Try to get him to take them. And your blood pressure is still very low, Marianne. Are you drinking enough fluids? You need a lot of water and lots of rest.' He took out another box and gave it to her. 'Here are your antibiotics and I brought this for you as well.' He handed her a bottle of water. 'You need to have a tablet every eight hours. Have you got a watch?'

'Yes.' She showed him.

'Has it got an alarm?'

'No.'

'Don't worry. Mine has. It's nearly eleven o'clock now. I'll come round at seven to make sure you take it on time.' As he set the alarm, Marianne took a tablet out of the box and began to open the water bottle. He looked up when he heard the seal breaking. 'Just a minute. Let me take your temperature first.' He took an electronic thermometer from his pocket and pressed the button. 'Here, pop this in your mouth.' It felt cold under her tongue.

'That's it. I think you'll sleep well tonight Marianne. I know I will. This has been the most amazing day of my life! I know there has been a terrible disaster, of course, for you especially, and I realise this might sound strange but I wouldn't have missed this for anything. It's not every day that a doctor plays such an important part in the world. In the University Hospital I'm just a little cog in a very big machine. Yes, I help people in the accident and emergency department. When I go out with the helicopter I occasionally even save somebody's life, but apart from when I vote in a referendum I never actually get to play any part in helping to decide anything important.

'But here, in this weird situation, it's totally different. I'm not just helping you and the others as they become sick—and I'm certain that they will, given our lack of basic hygiene. But as well as that I've got a chance to actually help take really important decisions. We all have. There's a huge weight resting on our shoulders, Marianne, and that's going to hit people when they've had the chance to think about what it means. It won't just be Danny who will be acting strangely, I can assure you.'

The thermometer beeped. 'Right, let's read that.' He took it and read the little display. 'Hmm, 37.2. Slightly higher than normal. Looks like you might be developing a temperature, young lady. Here, take your antibiotic.'

Their eyes met as she swallowed the tablet. She wanted to say *Please don't leave me, Jean-Pierre, not until Danny gets here*, but it would have sounded so selfish. She could see he was tired too. So she just swallowed and tried to smile.

'Now then, have you got everything you need?'

She nodded. 'Thanks for all your help.'

'That's okay, Marianne. Well, I'll see you tomorrow. Have a good sleep and don't worry about Danny. I'll have a talk to him after the next meeting and see what I can do. Good night.'

After he had gone Marianne flew to the wardrobe, opened the doors and looked inside. Then she flew to the little bathroom and searched in the shower and on the floor. It was only when she found herself looking down the toilet pan that she stopped. *You've got to stop doing this, Marianne. It's silly. Drago isn't here.*

This was not the first time she had found herself looking for him. Every time she went into a new room she caught herself looking around, searching everywhere, as if she might find her baby floating around somewhere, bundled up in the tiny blue clothes she had bought for him, with his fat little face peeping out, smiling at her, warm and pink. She could almost see him, almost smell him, the milky sweetness of him, and it broke her into tiny pieces every time she looked for him without finding him. And to find herself looking down the toilet, that was mortifying.

She turned away and saw the green door standing ajar as if it too was waiting for Danny to come in. She felt her heart would break if he didn't come soon and look at her with his sombre, grey face and maybe even give her a cuddle. And suddenly she felt angry, angry with Danny for the very first time. *Why aren't you here? Is the fireman more important than your wife? Is your pain at losing ATLAS more than mine at losing our son? What's happened to the love you said you felt for me last summer? Has it all faded like the heat of the Sun?*

She flew back to the bed, pulled herself down onto it and began to sob into the pillow.

Marianne awoke when something hit her back. At first she didn't know where she was. It always took her a long time to wake up properly. She took the crystal out of her pocket and spun round. Behind her was a rough-textured wall with a round lamp sticking out. It took her a few seconds to realise where she was. *It's a ceiling lamp. I'm in the hostel, in a bedroom. I must have drifted up here in my sleep.* She looked at her watch. *Three minutes past five. Where's Danny?* She flew around the room and into the bathroom but he was not there. She paused by the open door and looked into the corridor.

Where is he? Could he still be with George? Surely not! What was it he wanted to ask him in the Cafeteria? In a flash it came to her. *He wanted to know how to get into the tunnel! He wants to go down and kill Michael Zhang!* Instantly she was wide awake. *Nothing else it could have been. So where is he now? I know! He's already gone down the tunnel, I'm certain of it. He wouldn't come and tell me because he knew I would try to stop him. Either that or go with him. Oh my poor chou. I'm sorry for being angry with you. I've got to go after him. I've got to stop him doing something terrible. How do I get down there? Can't ask George. He'd try to stop me. Have to ask Alex. Where did George tell Ludo to put him? The Tyre Store. Should tell Jean-Pierre what I'm doing. No, I can't do that. He'd try to stop me too. I'll leave him a note.*

She flew around looking for something to write with but could find nothing except a little bar of soap in the bathroom. She picked it up to write a message on the mirror over the sink, but when she saw herself she stopped.

I look exactly like grandma, just before she died!

She threw the soap away and flew out of the room and down the corridor. It never crossed her mind to collect the box of antibiotics.

She got lost twice on her way to the Fire Station. The bubble was so disorienting. Marianne had searched every room in the Station before she finally found the Lecture Room, hidden away up some metal stairs at one end of the large garage. At first she could not open the door, but finally found a key hanging on a hook beside the glass door. She unlocked it and pushed it open. 'Alex?' she called as she flew in. 'Are you in here?'

Alex was floating near a flip chart at the front of the room, still tied up and without a crystal. She had to get close to him to make sure he was inside the bubble. His dark eyes grew large when he saw her, lit by the blue glow from her crystal.

'How do I get into the tunnel?' she said fiercely.

He looked puzzled. 'The tunnel? Why do you... Has Danny gone down there? Is that it? How do you know?'

It was as if he could read her mind and that made her angry. *What right does he have to do that? Danny can't do it, so how can he?* 'I just know,' she snapped.

'And you want to go after him? Don't be stupid kedvenc! That's preposterous. You're not fit to go anywhere except maybe to hospital. Look at yourself, girl.' There was genuine anxiety in his eyes.

'It's all right,' she said bitterly. 'I'll find it by myself, don't worry. Goodbye Alex.'

'Wait sweetheart! If I tell you how to get into the tunnel will you promise me you won't go down there on your own?'

'Of course I won't! You think I'm totally stupid? Now tell me.'

Alex sighed. 'I saw little Kata fly into it. The tunnel entrance is exactly where Sam said it was.'

'Where? Tell me.'

'There's a dip in the ground near one of the feet of the beam pipe shield support.'

'A dip?'

'Yes, just a tiny one but my guess is that the tunnel entrance is very small.'

'Thank you Alex. Good night. I'm sorry for disturbing you.'

'Please wait Marianne. You're not up to this, darling. It would kill you, the state you're in.'

'That's not your problem Karolyi.' She stared at him coldly.

'I know. All right,' he said softly. 'I can't stop you but I'm coming with you. There's no way I'm letting you go on your own. Untie me.'

It wasn't until he said this that she realised she wanted him to say it. The thought of going down the tunnel on her own had petrified her. She shrugged, pretending to be nonchalant. 'It's up to you. I'll untie you but no funny business. You promise me?'

He nodded and grinned his stupid, lop-sided grin. 'No funny business, sweetheart.'

She began to untie him. As she struggled with the knot his hand waved around, trying to touch hers. 'Stop doing that!' she snapped but at the back of her mind she was glad. She knew with utter certainty that this arrogant fool still loved her and it made the pain a little less hard to bear, made the world a little less lonely, even though she truly and utterly despised him. 'Don't get the wrong idea, Karolyi,' she said as the first knot began to unfold. 'I'm only doing this because I'm going to need someone to help and you're the only person available. Frankly I wish it was somebody else.'

'Thanks, kedvenc. That makes me feel so much better.'

'It's nothing but the truth. You're desperate to go and save Catriona. You like her. I'm still not strong and I'll need someone to help me. That's all there is to it. Okay?'

'Sure honey, I get the message. Look, we're going to need two pieces of crystal so we can both fly,' Alex said as she struggled with a knot.

She stopped, her heart sinking. 'But I've only got one.'

'No worries, kedvenc,' he said. 'I've got a secret stash.'

'That's so typical of you, Karolyi, keeping secret crystals when you know they could help others!' She yanked at the rope thinking *Poor Catriona! How could she love a man like you, you selfish swine?*

As the final coil of rope slipped away from his arms, he sighed and began rubbing his wrists, saying 'Ah, that's better. Okay, so I'll fly shall I?'

She hesitated then gave him her crystal. He turned her round, handling her body as if he owned it, and pulling her to him, her back against his chest, her bottom in his groin. As he caught her in his arms she caught his heavy smell in her nostrils and something moved inside her. She was shocked at the strength of it, as if she had been caught by a little earthquake. And when his hands came together near her chest, holding the crystal just inches from her breasts, something suddenly happened that made Marianne gasp.

'Sorry, kedvenc, have I hurt you?'

'No, it's okay. Let's go.' She couldn't tell him what had happened. She looked down, just hoping he wouldn't notice the two damp patches where her milk had started to flow.

They had just left the Lecture Room and were flying past some lockers in the garage when they met George Gabor and Brigit O'Brien coming towards them.

'She's let him out!' Brigit said.

'Going somewhere Mister Karolyi?' George said.

Alex stopped. 'Hi György. I'm just taking this young lady out to a bar for a night cap. You two care to join us?'

Before George could reply Marianne said 'Did Danny ask you about the tunnel, George?'

'Yes Marianne,' he said.

'And you told him how to find it?'

George nodded. 'I did. Why?'

'I think he's gone down there, George. I'm going after him. He's going to kill Michael Zhang.'

'What?' Alex said letting go of her and turning her round to face him. 'How do you know that?'

'It's what he told me in the Medical Centre. He said it was a good job Michael was dead because if he was still alive he would kill him. I'm certain it's what he's going to do now he knows Michael is still alive. It's not Danny's fault. He's not himself.'

'You should have told me about this before, kedvenc. It would be a disaster for all of us if he killed Michael Zhang. Kata said he's going to help Sam restart time.'

'But why does Danny want to kill him?' George asked. 'I know he thinks Michael deliberately created the black hole but that doesn't—'

'He holds him responsible for the baby's death as well,' Marianne said. 'I think he's flipped to tell you the truth. He's just not himself anymore.'

'We've got to stop him,' Alex said.

'Sounds like it,' George said.

'But *you* can't go down the tunnel, Marianne,' Brigit said. 'You're not well enough.'

'I have to go.'

'I'm going with her,' Alex said.

'Quite right,' Brigit said.

'I'll go too,' George said. 'But you're definitely not well enough, Mari—'

'My place is with Danny,' she exclaimed. 'He's got to be talked through his problem. He needs somebody who understands him and I'm the only one who even comes close. You can't do it, George.'

'If you go down that tunnel you'd be more of a hindrance than a help, Marianne Schneider,' George said sternly, 'whereas if you stay here you can, um…you could…er'

'You could help me, sweetie,' Brigit said, taking Marianne's arm. 'I want to get the United Nations Security Council involved in deciding what to do. Your language skills will be invaluable.'

'That's right,' George said. 'Listen, Marianne. I promise you that when we find Danny we'll bring him back here and you can talk to him for as long as you want.'

Marianne hesitated.

'He's right, Marianne,' Brigit said. 'I need you here and in a few days you're going to be much stronger than you are now and we can think about it again. Just let the men find him and bring him back for you while you get well. You know it makes sense, sweetie.'

Marianne looked at her. Brigit had washed her hair, changed into some smart new clothes and looked clean and confident.

Marianne knew in her heart they were right. *I'm not really strong enough. There's still a pain in my abdomen, and there's still the threat of infection. Jean-Pierre said I had a bit of a temperature and I've forgotten to bring the antibiotics.* 'I suppose you're right,' she admitted.

'Wise decision,' George said. 'Look Alex, Brigit and I have been talking about what you said at the meeting.' He glanced down then looked straight into Alex's face and said 'I realise now you're right. I'm sorry for the way I've treated you.'

Alex stared as if George had just grown another head.

'It's true,' Brigit said. 'We were just coming to let you out. We think you're absolutely right. I can't understand why we didn't agree with you at the meeting. Somebody's got to go down the tunnel and help Catriona take that crystal to Michael.'

'And I brought you this,' George said as he gave him the rucksack filled with all the things Ludovico had taken out in the Cafeteria.

'I don't know what to say György.' Alex held out his arms and the two men embraced, thumping each other on the back.

'Perhaps you might want to pay him back by telling him about your secret stash of crystal,' Marianne said bitterly. For some reason which she could not understand, she suddenly felt both angry and relieved at the same time.

Alex stared at her with a blank expression, then his broad smile slowly came back.

'Good idea Mrs Schneider,' he said and turned to George. 'I guess if we're making a fresh start I'd better come clean. There are two more crystals. I threw them in the lake near my boat.'

'Oh, so that's why we saw the fish? It's obvious really. Thanks for telling me. I'll keep your secret for now. Two more crystals might come in very handy later on. No need to go to the lake. We've got spare crystal here in the Fire Station. I'll ask Ludo what he's done with them. And I need to let him know what's going on.'

They found Ludovico and Sofie floating asleep in a big bubble in the kitchen below the Lecture Room. When George awoke Ludovico and asked him about the crystal, he said 'I put everything in Laron Parfait's office,' then he saw Brigit and a sly smile crossed his face. 'Hello your Excellency,' he said. 'Had a nice bath?'

'Yes wonderful wasn't it Georgie?' she said taking George's hand. Ludovico's eyebrows elevated up his forehead.

'Fantastic,' George said as he put his arm round her and kissed her, then grinned at Ludovico, whose eyebrows rocketed upwards until they almost disappeared off the top of his head.

Episode 52 Return to the Tunnel

'We're getting closer, Samfitzpatrick,' Trissitia shouted excitedly 'Well done Sashamida! But I don't think this pod will take this battering for much longer, Husband,'

Sam could hardly hear her above the roar of particles thundering onto the pod's outer skin, but he thought she sounded really worried. Sam was too. The noise had grown gradually louder as she had accelerated after the pink crystal until now it was an almost intolerable crescendo, like a hundred simultaneous storms thundering onto the front of the pod. Even the Entroilian larvae were obviously disturbed by the noise, thrashing about in the pod's cramped store, pushing into the back of Sam's seat and toppling boxes in their futile attempts to escape from the din.

As she had followed the pink crystal, gradually going faster and getting ever closer, the camera screen had fogged up, showing nothing but the impenetrable particles hurtling into them, so they had both been watching the crystal's image in the scanner. Now they had caught up with it and the camera revealed the pink tetrahedron, hanging apparently stationary just ahead of them as they hurtled after it through the hailstorm.

'Trissitia,' Sam shouted, 'get that blood...that blinking crystal!'

She pressed a button, pushed a joystick and the scanner screen showed one arm extend forward from the pod's nose towards the pink crystal. Within a few moments the arm had grasped it securely.

'Fantastic, Sashamida,' Sam yelled. 'Now slow us down before these stones make a hole in the pod.' He saw the pod's other arm press the front of the blue crystal and he was thrown forward in his seat as the pod slowed and the noise of impacting objects reduced to a more tolerable level, like very heavy rain. Finally, one arm lifted the strapping and the other slipped the pink crystal in beside the much larger blue one.

'Can we take a closer look at that new crystal?' Sam said.

She rotated the camera until it was looking straight down at the pink stone. It was clearly visible on the camera's screen, with the white fog in the background. He was struck by the similarity between the two crystals. Both had flat sides and straight edges. Highlights sparkled within them both, light reflected and refracted off their inner surfaces. But the similarities were no less profound than their differences. The pink one was small, so small that Sam was sure he could have held it in his hand if only it were inside the pod, whereas the blue one was many times larger so he was not even sure he could have lifted it. But the most outstanding difference, apart from their colour and size, was the number of their faces. The pink one clearly had only four whereas the blue one had dozens, too many for Sam even to—

'What's that blue thing?' Trissitia said. She was studying the two crystals on the camera screen.

'What blue thing?' Sam said, puzzled at her question.

'This.' The tip of one of her hairy antennae reached towards the screen and pointed at a spot near the edge of the pink crystal but before she could touch it her antenna stopped and she said 'Oh, it's gone. Wait, I'll go back.' Her hand pushed the joystick back a little. 'There it is again.'

Sam leaned forward and squinted at the screen but his short-sighted eyes couldn't see anything until his nose was almost touching it. A tiny bright blue beam of light was refracting through the pink crystal. 'I don't think its inside,' Sam said, 'I think it's behind the crystal and the light's passing through it. Go forward again.'

Sam studied the screen as she pushed the joystick and the dot of light moved past the crystal's edge into the white mist. 'Stop!' he cried. 'It's disappeared again! Go back a bit.' She moved the pod back and the blue dot came back into view within the pink crystal. 'It's really weird. It's only visible when it's on the far side of the pink crystal. When you look straight at it, it's invisible!'

'What do you think it is, Husband?'

'I suppose it's another blue crystal. It's pretty far away but I'm positive it's on the far side of the pink one. Look, Trissitia, I want you to fly towards it. I'll control the camera and make sure we keep it in view.'

'Okay Husband. Good idea.'

'Left a bit,' Sam said, moving the camera so he could still see the distant blue light through the pink crystal. 'Up a bit. Okay, a bit faster…' It took many minutes before Sam was able to say 'It's getting bigger. It looks like a triangle.'

'Is it another crystal?'

'I don't know.'

'How are we able to see it through this fog?'

'Yeah, I was wondering that myself.'

The white fog still surrounded them, hiding everything from view, yet when he looked through the pink crystal Sam could see this distant blue sparkling light. It was very puzzling.

'It doesn't show up on the scanner,' Trissitia said, 'unless…' She changed the resolution. 'There it is. I've found it! It's a very long way away, Samfitzpatrick.'

They flew on for a long time, the blue light getting brighter, Trissitia making small adjustments to their course but afraid of going faster because of the possible damage to the pod. It took nearly an hour before Sam saw it clearly on the scanner screen and when he did he was astounded.

'It seems to be… My goodness, it's a sort of funnel. And it's big!'

'Why is the noise of particles getting louder, Husband. I haven't told the pod to go faster.'

'Slow down a bit!'

Trissitia pulled on the joystick, the arms pressed the front of the blue crystal, but still the hail of colliding particles grew louder. She pressed the joystick with increasing force, making worried noises. Finally she said 'I can't do anything to stop it, Husband! There's some sort of external force pulling us forward. This pod doesn't have sufficient counter-force to stop the motion.'

Once again, her voice was almost overwhelmed as the thunder of particles grew deafening and, as before, the Entroilian larvae thrashed about behind them in obvious alarm. 'We're going into it!' Trissitia screamed and she wrapped her arms and legs round Sam for safety, shouting into his ear. 'Look, there it is!'

On the camera screen, looming behind the blue crystal, Sam saw a huge circular cone shining with a crisp blue light and narrowing to a point in the centre. 'My God!' he shouted back. 'It must be the entrance to the tunnel! There's nothing else it can be! Wabadoobah!!' He felt as if he had just seen the US cavalry riding over the hill to save him from the red Indians.

'There's another one!' Trissitia screamed. Her antennae were pointing to one side of the scanner screen. Two cones were clearly outlined there, one ahead of them very close, one further away behind them but moving rapidly towards them. Then several things happened at once. Warning lights started flashing on the control panel as dents appeared in the pod's skin and the sound of tearing metal joined the ever louder thundering noise accompanied by Trissitia's screams of panic. Sam's eyes were glued to the scanner as the second cone hurtled towards them, getting larger and then, with a sudden rush, the two cones met, their yawning mouths clamped together, enclosing the pod like a tiny fish caught in the kiss of two whales and the noise instantly fell silent.

And when he looked at the camera, with the noise still ringing in his ears, to his astonishment and enormous relief Sam saw the familiar blue tunnel wall surrounding them. Trissitia saw it too. As the realisation dawned on them both that they were safely back inside the tunnel, she nestled her head on his chest and Sam gave her another hug.

'What a horrible place your Universe is, Samfitzpatrick. Wouldn't you just love to be back in Peshash City and spending the night together in a nice warm bed?' Sam was just about to put her straight on this matter once and for all when she said: 'Oh look, Husband, it's turned blue!'

'What has?'

'The pink crystal.'

Sam looked at the camera screen. Both crystals now glowed bright blue. 'I wonder why?'

'I'll ask my scientists shall I?' a friendly voice said behind them. Both their heads spun round to see King Flenkt's virtual image perched on a packing case with the mass of Entroilian larvae writhing around his feet. He appeared to be sitting on the edge of a large table covered with computer terminals. It stretched up through the pod's dented metal shield and around it sat a dozen more Argolaths.

'Oh Father, how kind of you to visit us,' Trissitia exclaimed, squeezing Sam's hand so hard it hurt. 'What an unexpected pleasure!'

Sam's initial surprise at seeing Flenkt did not last long. He realised that his sudden appearance was not really too surprising. *It's like when I first saw him in that crystal cave in the event network,* Sam thought. *It's probably taken them some time to work out how to project his image down here. The Argolaths certainly have some remarkable technology.*

'Greetings my daughter.' The King waved an imperious hand around the table. 'These are the greatest scientific brains in Argolathia. They're going to be monitoring everything that happens to you on your trip. It's a great piece of research for them and best of all it costs me nothing!' He began to laugh and all the scientists echoed him with hollow, sycophantic laughter. Flenkt waved his hand again and they immediately stopped laughing and returned to working at their computer screens.

I guess they're going to be watching us all the time from now on, Sam thought, *and Flenkt could pop up anywhere. That's going to make my job a lot more difficult. He'll be able to see anything he wants. How the hell am I ever going to defeat his sons if they've got a spy like that hanging around all the time?*

Flenkt too turned to the scientists. 'My honoured friend Prince Samfitzpatrick would like to know why the pink crystal has turned blue.'

Their computer screens flickered, the scientists' heads leaned over and they whispered to each other. Finally one stood up. As soon as he spoke, Sam recognised Professor Nithold's voice.

'We believe that this crystal, and all the others, are fragments of the Cosmic Egg shell, Your Majesty. We also think that they are joined together by strings of negative energy and it is these strings which hold the tunnel open. And as I'm sure Your Majesty also knows, the pink crystal was found at a break in the tunnel. This must have been coincident with a break in the strings.'

'Makes sense,' Flenkt nodded. 'String makes tunnel so no string, no tunnel.'

'Indeed, Your Majesty. And the fact that the pink crystal was frozen in time is strong corroboratory evidence that it had lost contact with the string.'

'How's that?'

The professor's triangular head tilted to one side and his hands clasped together as if he were explaining that one and one makes two. 'Because this string is in fact made up of higher dimensions of space-time which are curled up very tightly. One of these dimensions is time itself. If contact with the string is lost then time obviously stops.'

'So the fragment was pink and frozen in time because its string had broken?'

'All the strings had, Your Majesty.'

'All? What do you mean, all the strings?'

'There are many strings, Your Majesty, which are woven together to form a sort of rope. The crystals are strung out along the rope like beads on a necklace. It seems that the whole rope had broken at the break in the tunnel. When the pink crystal came back into the tunnel, I believe it regained contact with the two ends of the broken rope which must have fused back together. This allowed the pink crystal to regain contact with time and that's why it turned blue again.'

'So blue means it has the time, pink means it's lost it?'

'Exactly so. Your Majesty is most wise and understanding.'

Flenkt turned to Sam. 'So that sorts that out, I think.'

Sam nodded but inwardly he was confused. Cjingha too had talked about these negative energy strings, in the Entroilian University, so it was probably true. But she also said that it was vibrations in the strings which had let him see and hear people on Earth while he was back in his little crystal cave high above the pink ocean of the Universe. *So how could the strings vibrate if they were broken?* He wanted to ask Flenkt's scientists about this, but it was too late.

'Hurry up daughter and go up the tunnel,' Flenkt was saying. 'I want to see what delights Samfitzpatrick's fellow creatures will provide for my sons when they finally arrive.'

Then the table, King Flenkt and all the scientists rapidly dwindled away and vanished like mist.

Good riddance, Sam thought. *I don't trust Flenkt any further than I trust his daughter.*

'Goodbye Father!' Trissitia called then turned to Sam. 'Right then, Husband. Now that we are back in the tunnel I need to check this pod is not damaged too much. If necessary we can make some repairs and then we'll go find your home planet.'

'Good idea. I really want to get a close-up view of that new crystal as well.'

With some difficulty they forced open the battered metal shield and Sam used the pod's arms to lift the small crystal, now glinting blue, into the cabin while Trissitia crawled around on the outside of the pod, her claw-like feet easily gripping the metal case as she inspected the damage. By the time she returned Sam had disappeared.

She began to call for him, throwing the Entroilian larvae around in anger, then she began screaming 'Sashamida! Sashamida!' at the top of her voice in a most distressed way until Sam was forced to fly down to comfort her. She threw her arms round him and hugged him as if she had not seen him for a week. 'Where have you been, Husband?'

'I've just been learning how to use the little crystal to fly. It's great fun, really. You'll have to try it, but you'll have to use the little one. The big round one is too large to hold.'

'I wish you had told me what you were doing, Sashamida. I thought you'd been attacked by those wretched larvae or something.'

'No, I'm fine,' Sam said, feeling guilty for upsetting her so. *She really seems to be in love with me,* Sam thought. *That's good for me at the moment, but things might turn difficult if she finds out I don't feel the same about her.* He shuddered and put the thought out of his mind, saying 'So what state's this pod in now?'

'It's not too bad. I've programmed the arms to do a bit of welding. They won't take long. Let's have something to eat while we're waiting. Then we should just be able to fly up the tunnel. If we use the crystal to fly then it will save our pod's fuel.'

They had some of the delicious dried fungus from one of the crates and Trissitia fed the larvae with honey, even though it was obvious she hated them. When the pod had finished repairing itself, they strapped themselves into their seats, Sam shoving the small blue crystal safely in his jacket's inner pocket.

'I've stowed the shield back in the underhold,' Trissitia said. 'I don't think we'll need it inside this tunnel. So which way do we go, left or right?'

Sam looked both ways along the tunnel. They appeared exactly the same. 'I don't know.'

'What happens if we go the wrong way?'

'We'll end up back at the honey pool, I suppose.'

'Well we haven't come far from there, so it won't matter will it? You choose which way, Sashamida.'

'Okay, I'll be the captain.' He chose one way at random and she piloted the pod along the tunnel, the wind whistling past their heads as if they were driving an open-topped coupe. The blue wall of the tunnel was still protecting them from the storm of particles outside but the light got rapidly brighter. It was soon so bright it hurt Sam's eyes. 'I think we're going the wrong way,' he said as the head of an Argolath appeared around a bend in the tunnel, crawling towards them. Also he noticed that the tunnel was getting narrower.

'You're right Husband, we're definitely going the wrong way.' She turned the pod round and flew rapidly in the opposite direction, eager to get away from the blinding light. It dimmed and before long faded into complete darkness. She stopped again.

'I can't see where I'm going. I don't want to hit the tunnel wall. Why's it gone dark?' Trissitia asked.

'I suppose we must have left the Big Bang behind,' Sam said.

'Yes, but it wasn't dark like this the last time we flew up the tunnel. Wait, I'll turn the headlight on so I can see the blue wall.' She flipped a switch and a beam shone out into the darkness. 'Where is it? Can you see the tunnel, Husband?'

'No, Sashamida.' All Sam could see was a haze of tiny dots sparkling in the headlight. 'Try turning the pod round. It must be here somewhere.'

She pressed the blue crystal and the beam swept through more dots, but there was no visible wall. Her head turned towards him, her antennae hanging limply down her face. 'You don't think we've come out of the tunnel again, do you Husband?'

Episode 53 ATLAS

'Ludo, you're in charge here now.' George said, letting go of Brigit and grinning at the expression of astonishment on Ludovico's face as he floated in the Fire Station kitchen. 'Alex and I are going—'

'You've let him out!' Sofie said, shocked at seeing Alex, then she saw Marianne and was even more shocked at the sight of her. *She looks like a living corpse,* Sofie thought as she flew to her, put her arms round the poor fragile young woman and kissed her. 'What are you doing here?'

'I'm okay Sofie. Don't worry.' Marianne's tone was cold, almost as if Sofie were a stranger.

Sofie felt hurt. *Does she blame me for not saving the baby?* Sofie thought. *I wish we could talk about it.*

'There's been a change of plan,' George said. 'Marianne thinks Danny Schneider's gone down the tunnel to kill Michael Zhang and—'

'What's that?' Sofie said, spinning round. It was as if new problems were bombarding her from all sides.

'I told you what Danny said, Sofie,' Marianne said squeezing her hand feebly. 'He's in such a strange mood and now he's disappeared. He was supposed to follow me to the hostel but he never arrived.'

'If he kills Michael it will be a disaster,' Alex said, 'so György and I are going to find Schneider and stop him and then find Kata and take the crystal down to Michael.'

'When was all this decided?' Sofie was astonished.

'A few minutes ago,' Brigit said.

'What does Francesco say about it?'

'Francesco?' Brigit shook her head. 'We haven't told him yet. Look, there are six of us here. Why don't we vote on it?'

'Would that be fair?' Sofie said. 'Francesco's not here.'

'No, nor Jean-Pierre,' Marianne said.

'It might not matter if enough of us vote in favour,' Brigit said.

'True,' Sofie said. 'But what are we voting about?'

'Whether to do what Alex just said,' George said. 'All in favour?'

'Just go over it again George, please,' Sofie said. 'I'm still confused.'

'George and Alex are going down the tunnel,' Brigit said slowly, 'to stop Danny killing Michael and help Catriona take her crystal to Sam and Michael.'

'But in the Cafeteria Alex couldn't prove that Sam was still alive!' Sofie's head was spinning with this sudden change of plan.

'That didn't prove anything,' Brigit said. 'Sam could have been asleep or anything.'

'Like dead maybe,' Ludovico said.

'Well if he and Michael are dead then the world's going to stay in this freaking frozen state forever,' George said. 'Is that what you want, Ludo old chap?'

'It could be worse,' Ludovico said. 'We could maybe send the spare crystals down the tunnel and never see them again and get nothing out of it.'

'And anyway this sounds like a big job you're taking on, George,' Sofie said. 'Are you sure two people will be enough?'

'And why Karolyi he is going?' Ludovico said. 'Is he suddenly turn from murderer into hero or something?'

'Look,' George said, putting on his authoritative voice. 'I want you two to stay here and help Francesco Romani. No point risking the whole of Green Team! Karolyi's expendable and he's dead keen to go. If he's killed it doesn't really matter.' Sofie thought she saw George give Karolyi an eyelid-flickering wink.

'All right. You ready to vote now Sofie?' She nodded. 'All in favour?' George said.

'Wait a minute,' Ludovico said. 'I want you take me too. I think Sofie she is right. Is too big job for two peoples.'

George shook his head. 'I'd rather you stay here, Ludo. Romani's going to be furious when he finds out what we've done and Brigit's going to need support. She's got this plan to get world politicians involved and that's important. I want you to stay here and help her.'

Ludovico looked sideways at Brigit and a sly little smile creased his face. 'Oh, alright then boss. If you insist.'

'So,' George said, 'all in favour please raise your hands.'

Five people raised their hands. Five pairs of eyes turned on Sofie.

'Against?' George said.

Sofie raised her hand. 'I'm sorry but I think that if you're voting we should let Professor Romani and the doctor have their say first. I'm not sure that Karolyi or Catriona ever really saw Sam, and I'm positive Romani would vote against this if he was here. I guess I'm voting on his behalf really. But it won't make any difference, will it?'

'No,' Brigit said. 'The vote's carried anyway.'

'Right Ludo,' George said, 'where did you hide the crystals? We'll need three, one for Karolyi and two for Sam and Michael.'

'What about the gun?' Alex said.

'Hmm,' George said. 'That might come in useful.'

'You're not going to shoot Danny!' Marianne sounded horrified.

'Of course not kedvenc,' Alex said, 'but we don't know what we're going to find down there. It's just a precaution.'

'And we'll need that big crystal too,' George said pointing at the double crystal that floated between Sofie and Ludovico.

'Why?' Sofie said.

'You never know what's going to happen while we're down there,' George said.

'But you can say the same about up here,' Ludovico said. 'We might need it too.'

'That's true, Georgie,' Brigit said. 'It'll be very helpful when we have our UN meeting.'

'Has that been decided as well?' Sofie said.

Brigit looked at her. 'Marianne and I are going to organise it, yes. You don't have to help if you don't want to, Sofie.'

'It's not that I don't want to help, Brigit, it's just that I'd like to be told what's going on and maybe asked what I think about it.'

'We'll talk about it when the men have gone, if you don't mind.'

'Well I'd still rather like to have that double crystal Brigit,' George said. 'Surely the main thing now is to find Danny and make sure he doesn't do anything silly and I think it might help.'

'Umm, okay Georgie. I suppose you're right,' Brigit said. 'And if the worst comes to the worst we should be able to make another one if what Francesco said was correct.'

'Give me the big crystal, Ludo,' George said. 'Do you need this to fly?' He offered him the small crystal he had been flying with.

'No, I got one. But if you taking this big one, then why you no give that little one to Karolyi?'

'That's true,' George said. He handed the small crystal to Alex and took the double one off Ludovico. Alex gave the crystal he had been flying with back to Marianne. 'Right,' George said 'Let's go and get the other things.'

They flew through the garage into the Fire Station and up to the office marked "Fire and Rescue Service Chief". Ludovico flew in and pulled open the desk drawer, the others followed him and clustered round the desk. Ludo took out two of the four crystals and handed them to George, then began to feel in the drawer for the gun. He pulled the drawer out as far as he could and bent to look inside it.

'Something wrong, Ludo?' George asked.

'The gun she is no here.' Ludovico began pulling open all the drawers and throwing out the papers. They fluttered around inside his bubble. Eventually he stopped and looked at George. 'Is gone.'

'Who knew where it was?'

'Only me,' Ludovico said. 'Sofie she was in the kitchen.'

They stared at each other in silence.

'Are you sure—' Brigit began.

'Who can see through your crystal Ludo?' Alex said. 'Anyone remember the diagram?'

'When we were looking through our crystals Ludovico could see out of mine,' Brigit said.

'But then he swapped with me,' Sofie said. 'I can see out of Ludo's crystal but I didn't see where he hid those things.'

'No,' George said. 'So who else can see out of your crystal, Ludo?'

'Danny,' Ludovico said, then looked straight at Marianne.

'You think he's taken the gun?' she whispered.

'I no see who else can do it,' Ludovico said.

'He must have seen you putting it in here,' George said.

The silence which filled their bubbles was more frightening than a scream.

Professor Francesco Romani floated in the Cafeteria feeling crushed, defeated, humiliated. He pushed his spectacles up over his black-tinted hair and wiped his face with his handkerchief.

That was the worst meeting of my life. In the course of a few hours I've gone from being one of the most important scientists on Earth to being nothing, ignored even in my own institution, my staff in open rebellion against me, my orders refused, my scientific advice spurned. Worse still I have presided over CERN during the moment of its most complete failure, the failure to anticipate and prevent this disaster. Ultimately the responsibility for that failure is mine. Danny Schneider is probably right. It does look as if Zhang deliberately engineered the black hole. And during the moment of crisis, while we were down in the Electronics Room, I supported Zhang and agreed that ATLAS should be left running. That was unforgivable!

Come on now, Francesco, he told himself. *The world needs the calm voice of reason and science more than ever, now that everyone else is in a panic, hearing voices, refusing to perform essential experiments, unable to follow the dictates of common sense. You must just carry on alone. There is no way that Sam and Michael could have survived. That is simply mass hysteria. The world needs you, Francesco! Find out as much as you can about the science of crystal. Eventually reason will prevail.*

He pulled his glasses down onto his nose, took the large fragment that floated before him and looked at it. The label said "Super2". He looked at the diagram on the table-top. *I've ended up with the crystal Karolyi made. Good! Danny and I examined Super1 before. If I now examine Super2 and compare the results I can start to answer some basic scientific questions.*

The questions flooded into his mind in a torrent, and as each one came, as each exciting new challenge presented itself, so his self-confidence returned.

Will this have the same sized bubble as Super1? What about its refractive index and electric and magnetic fields? He remembered seeing Danny throw away his results before he went to talk to the fireman. He searched the Cafeteria floor and eventually found the piece of paper under a table. *Extraordinary that he should just throw these away. Incredible. Doesn't he realise how important they are? But then he's an engineer, not a real scientist. Doesn't understand that it's only by carefully measuring, recording and piecing together these details that the big picture of science emerges, like a fascinating jigsaw puzzle, only far more interesting and useful.*

He smoothed out the paper, turned it over and copied the map of crystal connections from the table-top onto the back of it, then flew out of the Cafeteria, through the foyer, up the stairs, across the bridge to Building One and into the lab feeling excited. He immediately began searching for the Geiger counter.

Without Danny's assistance it took much longer to make precise measurements of all the previous parameters. He recorded all his results in a notebook he found in the lab's office. He also worked out a method of measuring the crystal's inertial mass using an ingenious system which he devised comprising vibrating springs. This was the first time Francesco had done such basic science since his student days and he loved every minute of it. By twenty past five he had almost completed his examination and was beginning to feel very tired. The only thing remaining was to examine the crystal under the microscope. The first thing he saw was a fish.

Ah yes, the fish, he thought. *That's important. It's the only thing that can be seen through three different crystals. And Danny said there are two different fish. Can I see them both in this crystal?*

He turned the crystal round, looking into each of its six faces in turn. Apart from the fish, he saw something in only one other face, but what he saw shocked and appalled him. There was a pair of heavy-duty gloves lying on a shelf in a small metal cabinet lit by a pale blue light. Taped to the cabinet's back wall was a photograph of a naked woman doing what, to Francesco, seemed the most disgusting act of self-degradation. He felt injured and insulted that he was obliged to look at such an image, and quickly made a note on the page for Super2: "Face 6 shows gloves and photograph in metal cabinet".

He pulled the crumpled piece of paper containing his crystal map out of his pocket, considered it for a moment then flew to the whiteboard and wiped it clean. Then he carefully copied the map onto the board, wrote "Cabinet" and drew a line to it from Super2.

Crystal Map on Whiteboard

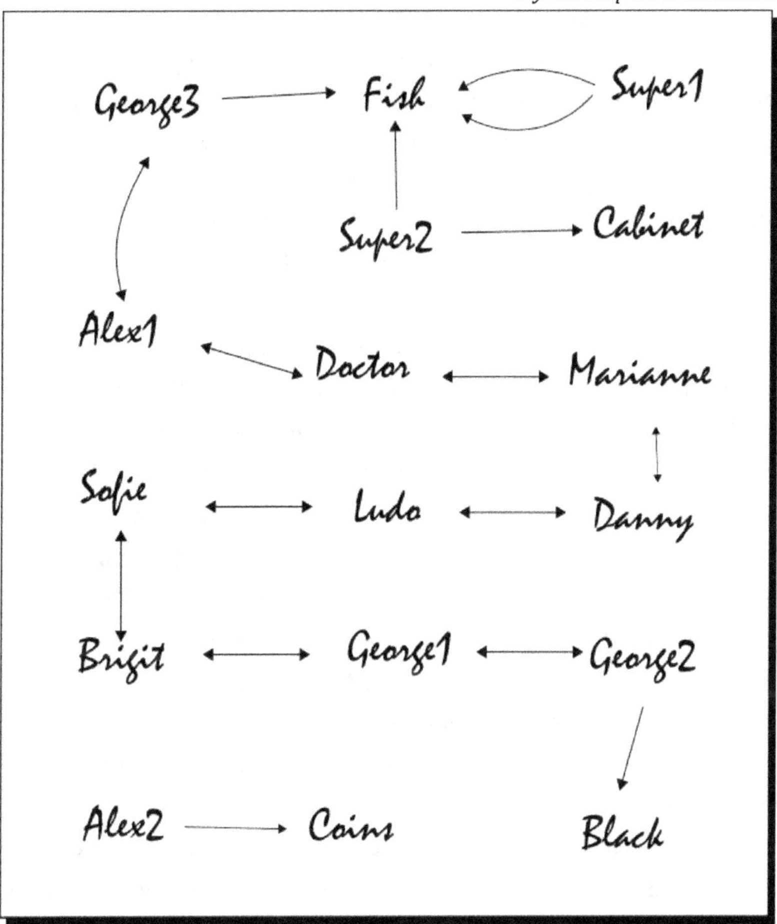

He flew back to the microscope and looked into the crystal again, checking the faces once more, hoping that, with a bigger crystal, he might be able to see things in more than two faces, but found nothing new.

He watched the fish for a while. It was clearly alive. *From what the fireman said it's probably in Lac Léman.* He watched it swimming round, apparently attracted by the pale blue light that reflected off its scales as it turned. *That light's the same colour as this crystal. Could there be a crystal in the lake? Can't imagine how...*

Suddenly he remembered a party on Alex Karolyi's boat late last summer. Karolyi had obviously been trying to drum up business. *I did not stay long. Music too loud and young people getting drunk, but I remember that boat; very impressive. Could this fish be somehow connected to that? Might Karolyi have taken a crystal to his boat and left it in the lake? Hidden it perhaps? If he can kill a friend, then he's probably capable of anything.*

Where was that boat? Near that little port I think, just past Bellerive. If I flew up there, I could get that crystal right now! And if my theory is correct, it should fuse with Super2! Yes, I have to go and get that crystal! It's my duty as Director General. CERN owns it. But it's a big lake. Karolyi could have put it anywhere. Easiest thing would be to go and ask him where it is. He's an intelligent man. He would know that telling the truth would go in his favour in any future murder trial. In the worst case, I could offer him his freedom in return for showing me where this crystal is. If I can produce a treble crystal, and its bubble is really as big as I think it's going to be, then I bet all opposition to my fusion plan will just melt away! Where did the bald fireman tell the other one to put him? Ah yes, the Lecture Room.

It was because Super2's large bubble almost spanned the Route Einstein that Francesco saw Marianne and Sofie coming the other way as he flew towards the Fire Station.

'Marianne?' he said, in some surprise. 'What are you doing here my dear? I thought you were in the hostel.'

'I'm just taking her back there now, Professor Romani,' Sofie said. 'I think you should know that George and Alex are going down the tunnel.'

Francesco saw Marianne give her a frown of annoyance but he was too astonished at her news to wonder why. 'Alex Karolyi?' he said. 'But I need… I thought he was locked up in the Fire Station?'

'There's been a change of plan,' Marianne said. 'I'm certain that Danny's gone down the tunnel to kill Michael Zhang, so I let Karolyi out.'

'You had no right to do that. I'm surprised at you, Marianne. Very surprised. Where is he now?'

'They've gone into the ATLAS cavern to look for the tunnel.'

'Tunnel? Surely you don't mean Karolyi's ridiculous story about a tunnel leading down to Sam and Michael? But that's all madness, Marianne! This is utterly unacceptable! I gave an order to keep Karolyi locked up. You cannot let him out without my permission.'

'We had a vote,' Sofie said.

'A vote?' Francesco was almost shouting now. Sweat broke out on his face. 'A vote? What about? I never voted.'

'Nor did Jean-Pierre,' Marianne said, 'but Brigit said it wouldn't have made any difference. Five of us voted in favour of finding Danny and then—'

'Brigit?' Cold rage burned inside Francesco now, rage amounting almost to hatred. 'I am in charge here,' he thundered, 'not Ambassador O'Brien. Votes,' he paused to breathe deeply, trying to calm himself, fearing the consequences for his heart. 'Votes,' he said again, 'are only valid if they are preceded by a discussion and I never had any chance to express my opinion. Now look. You are both CERN employees. I order you not to take any further actions without my express permission. Do you both understand?'

Sofie nodded but Marianne frowned. 'Things have changed, Professor,' she said. 'The whole world has changed, you must see that. Your position has changed too. You cannot expect us to act just as CERN employees any longer. There are much bigger questions at stake and we all have to do what we think is best.'

'I am shocked and astonished at you, Marianne Schneider. You always seemed to me to be the model employee: diligent and obedient, but I have to say you never appeared exceptionally intelligent. That impression is confirmed now because you are coming to some totally erroneous conclusions. It is precisely because there are bigger issues at stake that we need to maintain discipline, Marianne. Discipline, reason and science! That is what the world needs now. We are in danger of the world falling into chaos. The world needs science more than ever, not impulsive searches for non-existent tunnels.' He turned round and began to fly back down the Route Einstein. They quickly flew after him and caught him up.

'What are you going to do, Professor?' Marianne said.

'Stop them, of course.'

'Then we're coming with you. Come on Sofie.'

But Francesco soon left them behind as he flew back down the Einstein and over the main road into the northern site. As he flew down the shaft into the ATLAS cavern he heard Danny Schneider say 'You lied to me,' and a moment later Francesco found himself inside a honeycomb of bubbles. Danny was floating near the blue beam-pipe shield between the two big brown wheels. There was a wild look in his eyes and a gun in his hand. He was pointing it at George. Behind George were Alex, Brigit and Ludovico. Brigit saw Francesco and held up one hand like a cop stopping the traffic while pressing one finger of her other hand to her lips. Francesco stopped and floated above the scene.

'No Danny, I didn't lie to you,' George was saying. 'Now just tell me Danny, what's the problem?' Behind George's back, his finger was rotating in a circular motion.

'I can't find the tunnel.'

'Where have you looked?'

'Everywhere,' Danny said.

'Have you looked where I told you?'

'Of course I have, man!' Danny shouted. 'Do you take me for a bloody fool? There's just a little dip in the concrete. There's no tunnel there.'

'Well that's where Catriona disappeared, Danny.' George's fingers were still sending out the semaphore signal. Ludovico began slowly moving to one side as George said 'Come with me and I'll show you exactly where it is.'

Ignoring the gun, George flew past Danny towards the floor. When Danny followed him, Ludovico flew quietly out of Francesco's big bubble round the back of the beam-pipe.

Suddenly George stopped and turned around. 'Of course I suppose you've tried flying into it at full speed?' George said.

'No, you never told me—'

I've heard enough of this nonsense, Francesco thought. *Danny Schneider is a highly skilled engineer. He's a rational person. He isn't really going to use that gun. He's just trying to frighten the fireman. It's probably because of the shock at having ATLAS damaged during his shift. He's like me. He feels guilty, poor fellow.*

Francesco flew down and floated between the two men. 'Now Danny just stop all this nonsense and give me that gun, then we can just forget about all this.'

Danny swung the gun and pointed it at him. 'Go back, Romani. I'm going down to find Michael Zhang, and when I do I'm going to kill him.'

At that moment Marianne and Sofie arrived, flying into Francesco's bubble. Sofie stopped when she saw Danny but Marianne started screaming 'Danny! Danny!'

'Stay back Marianne,' Danny said.

When she saw the gun she stopped too, horror and compassion mixed on her face.

Danny flew round Marianne so he had a clear view of Francesco. 'Listen, Romani. Zhang deliberately engineered this disaster to satisfy his own ego,' he said, 'and you helped him. You persuaded me to leave ATLAS running when we could have stopped it and prevented this catastrophe. You're as much to blame as he is and you deserve to die as well.'

'No Danny!' Marianne screamed and began to fly towards him at the same moment that Ludovico flew into the bubble from the side. Danny saw him and swung the gun round towards him. With a curse, George flew at him and grabbed the pistol. For a moment there was a struggle between the two men, then an explosion echoed round their bubbles and George twisted away towards Ludovico, blood streaming from his chest as Danny flew past him down towards the cavern floor.

Francesco watched as everything seemed to happen in slow motion. Marianne flew down past George screaming 'Danny, Danny.' Alex flew after her calling 'Stop! Wait Marianne!' Ludovico flew to George and pressed his hand to the wound in George's chest trying to staunch the blood. Sofie and Brigit flew to help him, Brigit screaming 'Georgie, for God's sake!'

Francesco seemed to awaken from a dream and he too flew down, his crystal's big bubble reaching the floor. He caught a glimpse of Danny Schneider disappearing at high speed into the ground. He seemed to shrink and then vanish. Francesco could hardly believe his eyes. Marianne sped after him.

'Marianne no!' Alex called, putting on a burst of speed.

Francesco stared, trying to record everything in his memory, as both of them followed Danny. As they shrank and disappeared into the concrete floor Francesco was thinking *I am witnessing a scientific phenomenon of the highest importance*. But he felt no impulse to follow them.

Episode 54 Search for Danny

Marianne pushed on the back of her crystal as hard as she could, flying as fast as she could head first towards the floor of the ATLAS cavern but wanting to go even faster, wanting to catch up with Danny, to tell him how sorry she was. She kept thinking: *This is all my fault. If only I hadn't fallen on those stairs and lost the baby he wouldn't be doing this now.*

In the junction where her bubble overlapped with Danny's she could see a red label stuck to the bottom of one of his shoes. The sight of that sale price label still stuck to his sole only confirmed to her what an inadequate wife she was. 'I'm sorry chou,' she screamed. 'Please stop!' But even as she did Danny hurtled head-first into the floor.

She saw first his muscular hands, next his long arms and then his noble but troubled head, each shrink and vanish into a tiny dip in the concrete. Then a wave of disappearance travelled rapidly up his chest, his hips and along his legs as if his body had turned to water and was being pulled down the plug-hole of some invisible sink.

For a moment, all she could see were the soles of his shoes. All that was left of the husband she wanted so much to help was that shameful little red label, staring her in the face, mocking her with its brazen redness, red like his blood which every moment she expected to splash into her face, red like a beacon leading her willingly to her death, a death she knew she deserved for being such a bad wife. She pressed the back of her crystal even harder and prayed for both their souls as even that label shrank and the crystal in her outstretched arms finally reached the floor.

But she did not die. Instead, to her utter amazement, the dip opened up and ballooned out around her. She found herself flying into a deep funnel-shaped hole. There was a bright blue light at the bottom of it. She could see Danny a short way ahead, flying quickly down the funnel towards the light. She flew after him as fast as she could, screaming 'Stop Danny! Please stop Danny!' But he didn't stop. He was flying away from her, getting rapidly smaller as he descended towards the blue light. Then something pulled her arm and she heard Alex Karolyi saying 'Stop kedvenc!'

In a rage she tried to shrug him off, still screaming at Danny at the top of her voice, but Alex's grip tightened and she saw her husband dwindle away and vanish into the blue light ahead. In a fury she spun round. 'Now look what you've done, you fool. He's gone! Let go of me!'

'If you go down there he'll shoot you, Marianne.'

A shock passed through her as if he had slapped her face. 'Don't be ridiculous. He's my husband!'

'Yes and he shot George. How do you know you won't be next?'

'That was an accident!' She shook her arm again, trying to get free. She hated this horrible, vain meddler more than she had ever thought it possible to hate anybody. 'Danny didn't mean to shoot him.'

Alex frowned. 'You must have seen him pointing the gun at Francesco and saying he deserved to die.'

'No! I don't remember that. You're lying!'

'Danny's flipped, kedvenc. You said so yourself.'

'He's...He was defending himself. George and Ludovico attacked him.'

'You're fooling yourself, kedvenc.'

'Don't call me that!' she screamed, and with a painful wrench managed to snatch her arm away from his grip. Turning and pressing her crystal she flew rapidly towards the distant light.

She couldn't see Danny at all now. It was only as her eyes scoured the rocky funnel walls, desperately searching for him, that she suddenly realised: *The bubble's gone!*

Seeing distant objects after living inside that little bubble for hours, constantly surrounded by its glistening soap-like surface, felt almost like being liberated from prison. In spite of her anxiety about Danny and her fear of this strange funnel and her exhaustion and grief after losing the baby and her loathing of Alex, yet still she felt a tiny thrill of exhilaration. *I can fly wherever I want and see everything now that horrible bubble's gone. I'm a free spirit. This must be what it's like being an angel. Oh, how I wish I was an angel! I wish I had died when my baby died and gone to heaven with him. Instead I have to try to stop Danny killing Michael. I know this is my duty. If he kills him then the world will stay frozen in time for ever. Nobody else can do this, only me. I suppose God saved me for this purpose, but I wish there was some other way of doing it. This funnel feels like the road to hell!*

She had looked all around the sloping rocky walls now but had not seen Danny anywhere. Her eyes turned towards the blue glow at the bottom of the funnel. *I suppose he must be down there somewhere, hidden by the light.* She headed towards it and the funnel seemed to move away out into the shadows until she was flying in almost total darkness. This frightened her. *How can something which seems to get narrower actually grow wider when I go down? It doesn't make sense. But then nothing makes sense any more. The whole world has gone mad.*

The only light now was the blueness ahead and more blue light playing on the backs of her hands. She glanced behind and saw Alex Karolyi still following her, his eyes fixed upon her, a sombre expression replacing his normal conceited grin. She saw him now with clarity, her vision unclouded by the passion she once had felt for him. The light from his crystal cast shadows across his face, exaggerating his features, making his nose large, his eyes depressed into his skull; he looked grotesque. *How could I ever have thought he was handsome? Why doesn't the beast just go back and leave me alone? He's the real murderer, not Danny! I saw him murder that banker and steal his money.*

With a shudder she turned towards the blue light and tried to get away from him, pressing both thumbs into her crystal so hard she felt they would snap off, but the light from Alex's crystal stayed with her. *Well, I suppose I can't stop him. And it might be useful to have somebody around to help, even if it is only him. I really do feel incredibly weak and I don't think he would ever hurt me. I think the monster loves me in his own pathetic little way.*

'It's a long way down there kedvenc,' Alex said over her shoulder. 'You want me to help you go faster?'

She hesitated then shrugged. 'If you want.'

He linked his arm through hers and pressed the back of his crystal. She could feel the wind begin to ruffle her hair and soon it was flapping around her face as they sped down towards the distant light.

'Have you noticed our bubbles have gone? 'Alex said. 'I wonder whether that means time's working again down here?'

A thousand thoughts filled her head as they sped down towards the distant blue light, Alex telling her she should turn round and go back, Marianne trying to ignore him, thinking *Where's Danny? Did he really threaten Romani? Is he really crazy enough to shoot me? I suppose I deserve it anyway.*

The blue light grew larger, finally opening out into a huge tube, a gigantic cylinder several kilometres wide with a circular mouth. Marianne felt awestruck by its magnificent size and beauty.

'This must be the tunnel,' Alex said. 'The one Kata was talking about.'

It snaked away into the distance and finally disappeared around a bend. It was vast, frightening her, overwhelming her mind with endless questions. *Where did it come from? How was it made? Where does it lead?* And, above all, *How far down has Danny gone?*

As they flew into it, Marianne could see that the tunnel's blue wall was slightly transparent, revealing a changing pattern outside. The tunnel partly obscured the scene, making it appear dull as if shrouded by mist, but after watching for some time she realised she could see the sky, flickering rapidly, and a mountainous landscape, which was changing more slowly.

Every few seconds the scene turned white, the forests and rivers and mountains blurred together, then the whiteness gradually darkened and the details returned. The mountains which lay between land and sky were divided into two ranges, like the gaping jaws of some gigantic dragon, their ragged peaks biting into the sky. A bright wide band of light arched across the sky between the ranges, as if someone was trying to tie up the dragon's mouth with a thick white rope.

She flew on, ignoring her fears, hoping to see Danny round the bend ahead. But when they reached it, all she saw was another bend. The tunnel seemed to snake about in different directions as if trying to find its way into the bowels of hell. She began to look around, searching desperately for her husband, peering out through the wall at the landscape below. *I suppose he could have got to the bottom of the tunnel already and be out there somewhere. But even if Danny's down there I wouldn't be able to see him. The scene is changing too fast.* She slipped huner arm out of Alex's and pressed the front of her crystal, trying to bring herself to a stop.

Alex flew past her, then slowed and returned, saying 'What are you doing kedvenc?'

'I want to look for Danny.' Her eyes were studying the land outside the tunnel as its pace of change slowed. She was awestruck by the arch of light curving across the sky. As she slowed down it too had changed from an arch to a waving line oscillating rapidly back and forth within a narrow band, as if a lasso was spinning around the Earth. The flickering slowed, becoming painful to watch, making her want to shut her eyes but too fascinated and afraid of missing Danny.

As she moved slower, the flicker changed to a clear alternation between light and dark, and the line of light changed into a single point moving rapidly across the sky, visible only during the light periods. She had almost stopped now and for a while the scene remained in darkness. Finally the point of light moved slowly up from the mountains into the sky and stopped at the same moment she did. She squinted at the bright disc shining down through the tunnel wall. *It's the Sun!*

The landscape below had also stopped changing and she could make out the greens of a wood below and the intensely blue sky reflected in a huge curving lake not far away. Its body swept around the foothills of the mountain range on her right like a slumbering blue serpent from whose mouth issued the long winding tongue of a river.

'I'm pretty sure they're the Juras,' Alex said nodding towards the other mountain range from which the Sun had just arisen.

She turned her crystal to the right but stopped when she saw a long low bulge not far away. 'We must be near Geneva,' she said and pointed at the familiar shape. 'Isn't that the Salève?'

Visible from many parts of the city, the Salève Mountain always reminded Marianne of a sleeping giant. From up here she could clearly see his head, neck and body, although curiously there was no trace of the white quarries which normally scarred his shoulders.

'Yeah. Geneva must be down there,' Alex said, pointing at the little hill where the river emerged from the lake. Atop the hill she could see Saint Peter's Cathedral but, to her surprise, its spire was in a different place and smaller than she remembered, and the rest of the city looked strangely flat[33]. She could not see any of the taller buildings or even the water jet which normally dominated the city's sky-line.

'I figure we ought to be more or less above the CERN site here,' Alex said, 'but I can't see it.'

'What about Danny?' she said. 'Is he down there?'

They both looked down and for several minutes they surveyed the curving pine branches and beech crowns in the wood below them as they hovered side by side in silence, like a pair of eagles searching for a stray lamb.

Eventually Alex said 'Well I can't see him, honey.'

'No,' Marianne said. 'I can't either. It's no good hanging around here.' She turned, ready to fly on, but Alex caught her arm.

'What are you going to do, Marianne?'

She shrugged off his hand. 'I'm going to find Danny of course.'

'Listen sweetheart, you're not strong enough for all this. Don't you think it would be better if you just went back up the tunnel and let me and György—'

'No! If you don't want to help me then just go back on your own, Karolyi. I'm the only one who understands Danny. Nobody else can save him.'

---

[33] The medieval spire of St Peter's Cathedral, visible in the view of Geneva drawn by Nicolas Manuel drawn in 1548 (shown in bibliography entry (15) pages 18-19) stood at the summit of the nave. After the Reformation, it was reduced to a stump which was removed in 1895 and the current copper-clad spire was erected above the transept, as described on page 61 of bibliography entry (14)

She flew away from him down the blue tunnel. The Sun immediately began moving once more across the sky. It arced overhead and slipped behind the Alps. Night fell and stars twinkled overhead. She stopped, suddenly afraid of flying in the dark.

Alex caught up with her again and when he spoke, awe and disbelief echoed in his voice. 'The Sun's moving the wrong way!'

'What do you mean?'

'It normally rises over the Alps and sets over the Juras, right? But now it's going the other way. You know what? I think we're going back in time! Look, just humour me a second and wait there. Okay, kedvenc?'

She nodded. She didn't want to fly on alone in the dark and it was important to understand if they really were going back in time. She watched him return a short way up the tunnel, back the way they had come.

It puzzled her to see that he was now lit from one side by a blue light which grew in intensity and rotated around him as he flew. It stopped moving when he stopped flying and turned to face her. 'The Sun's back up now,' he said. 'It's come up over the Alps like it normally does. Going up the tunnel must be forward in time, going down is backward.'

'But it's still dark here,' she said, feeling afraid. 'We are at different times and yet we can talk to each other. How can that be?'

Alex flew back to her. The light rotated around him in the opposite direction, then faded away as he reached her. 'It's okay kedvenc. Don't worry. I figure this is a sort of time tunnel. Come on, let's go and find Mr Schneider.'

They began to fly down through the darkness side by side, the stars spinning quickly overhead.

How did he know I was afraid? Marianne thought as the Sun rose over the Jura Mountains. *What right has he got to look into my heart and see my fear so easily? I wish I was brave enough to fly without him, but I dare not.*

Yet as the daylight returned her anger was replaced by reassurance. Just giving a name to this tunnel he had made it seem less frightening. *This is the Time Tunnel*, she told herself. *We are going back in time as we go down, that's all. We can always get back to CERN if we go back up.*

Every moment she was hoping to see Danny round the next bend. The sky recommenced to flicker, slowly at first but with quickening pace as they flew faster. As they rounded the bend they saw a long straight section of tunnel dwindling away into the distance. Marianne's heart sank. 'I can't see Danny along there,' she groaned. 'Where is he?'

'Come on, sweetie, he must be down there somewhere,' Alex said, linking his arm through hers and pulling her forward. 'There must be a bend at the far end of this straight stretch. Come on! Be brave.'

She allowed him to pull her onward, but as soon as they entered the straight section, everything changed. The flickering stopped. The blue tunnel wall disappeared. The previously misty landscape now looked clear, the mountains sharply outlined black against the pink western sky. Marianne felt ice-cold air biting her face, the wind pulling her long dark hair out behind her as they hurtled downwards towards the little wood far below.

'We're in free fall!' Alex shouted. He pressed the bottom of his crystal with one hand, pulling Marianne with his other arm, and immediately their rate of descent slowed. Marianne copied him. The biting rush of cold air grew weaker and then stopped. They were floating high above a grey landscape which was turning rapidly darker as the twilight dwindled into night.

'The bloody tunnel's disappeared!' Alex said, looking upwards. She could see his face in the blue glow from the crystal he held in his hands. She looked up too. A few bright stars sparkled in the darkening sky. The setting Sun cast pink highlights on the underside of the clouds fringing the nearby Jura Mountains, but there was no sign of the tunnel. She looked down hoping to see Danny but she could only see a brown track near a small wood, the tops of its trees poking out of the greyness which covered the hillside.

'I can't see any landmarks down there,' Alex said. 'I think the whole place is covered in snow!'

'How am I ever going to find him in all this?' she groaned. She began to shiver and suddenly remembered she had forgotten to bring the antibiotics. 'Anyway it's too dark now. Let's go down and try to get warm.'

'No, wait a minute kedvenc. This darkness could actually help us. His crystal must be glowing like ours. I learned a trick yesterday while I was in the BP garage. I think it might show us where Danny is. Let me try something, honey.'

He disengaged his arm from hers and she watched as he lifted his glowing crystal close to one eye, still pressing the bottom to stop himself falling, and looked through it. He had to squint to protect his eye from the glowing light as he rotated it and spun slowly in the air, scanning the landscape, rocking it so he could get a view as far as the horizon. When he was facing towards the slumbering hump of the Salève he stopped. 'There it is!' he said.

'What is it? Can you see Danny?'

'I don't know if it's Danny or Catriona or maybe even Sam or Michael, but I can see a crystal over there. Crystals glow when you look through another one. Have a look through yours honey. You should be able to see it if you hold it at the right angle. No, not like that. Don't look straight into a face. You have to look at it obliquely. Let the light bend through your crystal. Here let me show you.'

'Don't bother, Karolyi,' she said as she turned to face in the same direction. 'I can manage without your help.' She adjusted the crystal so she was not looking straight into it, trying to find the light from distant objects. She could see the silhouette of the Salève, then she found the squat city, and to its right she saw a dome of blue light shining upwards, illuminating an otherwise totally dark patch of countryside. Its source was glowing brightly behind a bank of trees. It was only visible when she was looking through her crystal.

'And there's another one,' Alex said excitedly. 'A pink one!'

He had turned further to the right towards where, in the far distance, the Juras seemed to meet the Alps. Looking through her crystal, Marianne could see it too, a pink glow near a broad sweep in the pink river, the last of the light from the setting Sun reflecting off the water's surface.

'Isn't that just the sunset?'

'I don't think so, kedvenc,' Alex said. 'There's something else down there, behind the near bank.'

'Do you think one of them is Danny?'

'No idea. Listen honey, we haven't tried looking straight into these crystals yet. You know, when Francesco was drawing his map in the CERN Cafeteria and you could see Danny through your crystal. Maybe if you look into it you can see him now.'

Mother of God, he's right! she thought. *How could I have forgotten that?* She excitedly held her crystal further away from her eye and began to look straight into each face in turn, searching for the tiny image of Danny floating inside it among the inner reflected edges and faces, glinting like mirrors and shards of broken glass.

In the darkened wood, eight hundred metres below them, a thin man in a green jacket was sitting on a fallen tree-trunk, sheltering his blue crystal in the palms of his hands so its glow would not reveal his position to the couple floating above him. He peered into it, watching them through Marianne's crystal, listening to their conversation with a feeling of hatred burning in his heart, but also a glow of satisfaction, knowing that the time for revenge was near.

When he had first fallen out of the Time Tunnel, Danny Schneider had searched the frozen landscape for Michael Zhang. When he failed to find him, he had looked into his crystal. In one face, he saw the firefighter Ludovico Narkosa trying desperately to staunch the blood spurting from George Gabor's chest and in that moment Danny realised his fate was sealed. There was no going back now. But he felt no remorse.

It was Zhang's fault I shot him. It's even more important now that I find Zhang and kill him.

But then, searching the other faces of his crystal, he had seen Marianne flying down the Time Tunnel with Alex Karolyi at her side. Jealousy and hatred burned in his heart, and he resolved he had to kill Karolyi as well. It was only a matter of time before they followed him out of the tunnel.

He had waited, watching and listening through his crystal, to discover whether Marianne too would condemn herself by uttering words of love to Karolyi, in which case it would have been his duty to execute her also. She had not done so, but by watching them he had learned the vital information that it was possible to find other crystals by looking obliquely through one of them. *I must try this for myself,* he decided.

Keeping his crystal covered, Danny flew up until he was hovering above the tops of the trees. Then he peered obliquely into one of the other faces and saw their two blue crystals floating high above him, glowing against the night sky and, some distance away across the southern landscape, the distant blue and pink glows exactly as Karolyi and Marianne had described.

Leaving the pleasure of killing Karolyi for later, and still not having yet decided whether to also execute Marianne, Danny flew silently and low across the landscape towards the brightest of the two distant glowing objects, the blue one which, he had no doubt, belonged either to Sam Fitzpatrick or to Michael Zhang.

Episode 55 Saving George

'He can't breathe!' Brigit's scream brought Francesco back to the present.

He had been trying to remember every detail of the incredible scientific event he had just witnessed. Not the way Danny Schneider had threatened Francesco's life and shot George Gabor. Nor the way Brigit and the two firefighters had rushed in to try to save George's life. These things had shocked him, of course, but in a way they were mundane, ordinary and totally unremarkable from a scientific point of view.

No, what had touched the deepest part of Francesco and enthralled his curiosity, was the extraordinary way that first Danny, then Marianne and finally Alex had flown, one after another, headfirst into the concrete floor. Each one had shrunk, obviously entering a warped region of space-time, and finally disappeared from sight. At first Francesco had assumed that the black hole must still be there, but a moment's reflection had convinced him this was impossible.

If the black hole was really buried in the floor, he had mused, *it would be absorbing the concrete and the surrounding rock. A visible hole would be opening up. No, the black hole cannot still be there. Either it's still floating around somewhere or it has evaporated by Hawking radiation. I just hope the latter is correct. In which case, where did those three people go? There is only one explanation I can think of. The wormhole[34] theory must be*

---

[34] Author's Note: Michael Zhang briefly discussed wormholes in his Diary entry "The Black Hole". But note that the wormhole discussed by Michael and the one observed by Francesco were not necessarily the same. For more information about wormholes, see bibliography (24).

correct! And that must be the tunnel that Alex Karolyi was talking about in the Cafeteria.

He was still trying to commit to memory every detail of the event he had observed, so he could write down an accurate description at the first opportunity, when Brigit's scream of 'He can't breathe!' brought him back to the present.

Francesco flew to the little huddle of people clustered near the massive beam pipe shield. Ludovico was pressing his hands over the gunshot wound in George's chest while Sofie and Brigit supported his body as George gasped for breath.

'I know some first aid,' Francesco said, keen to be seen showing leadership after his total humiliation in the cafeteria. He began desperately trying to remember the training he had received as a conscript in the Italian army thirty years before.

'Bene,' Ludovico said, speaking Italian. 'You take over, professore. I go down the tunnel to get the bastardo Schneider.'

'No fireman,' Francesco replied in English. 'That's too dangerous. Danny is obviously in an unstable mental condition. He can shoot anybody. I think he was going to shoot me before you came into the bubble.'

'He's right Ludo,' Sofie said. 'You're not even armed and it would take more than one person to bring him back.'

'I don't like that sucking sound,' Brigit said, looking at Ludovico's hands still pressed on George's chest, 'nor those bubbles coming out.' Every time George breathed in, air was sucked into the wound; when he breathed out bubbles of frothy blood seeped out around the firefighter's fingers.

'Are you all right Georgie?' Brigit said stroking the injured man's bald head.

George smiled and nodded but pain was written all over his face.

'His lips are turning blue,' she said with a rising note of fear in her voice.

'That means he's not getting enough oxygen,' Francesco said, remembering an army poster showing lungs shrinking as air filled the chest cavity around them. 'His lungs have probably collapsed. We have to stop the air getting into that hole. Anyone got any plastic?'

Brigit shook her head. Sofie searched her pockets but had nothing.

Feeling in his jacket, Francesco found a cigarette packet. 'Can you open his tunic, Brigit?' he said as he began carefully unwrapping the cellophane, flattening it out without touching the inside. She unbuttoned the top of George's overalls. 'Now lift up his T-shirt,' Francesco said with growing confidence. 'We need to put this onto his skin.' Sofie helped her tear the uniform and pull it away from around Ludovico's hand.

'Right, fireman.' Francesco said to Ludovico. 'Hold this over the wound. When he breathes out let the air out but press down hard when he breathes in. Don't let any more air get in there.' Ludovico took the cellophane with one hand and quickly slipped it over the gunshot wound.

'Firewoman,' Francesco said to Sofie, unable to remember her name. 'Can you go and get the doctor and bring him here? He should be in the Hostel.'

'Can't we take George there?' Brigit asked, her pale, drawn face watching Ludovico.

'No,' Francesco said, feeling able at last to re-exert his authority, 'I don't think we should move him until he's stable. I'll go to the Medical Centre and fetch some dressings.'

'Equipment also in ambulances, Professor Romani,' Ludovico said as George breathed out and he let the air bubble out under the cellophane. 'Is probably one up in SX.'

'Okay, I'll check up there first.'

Brigit stroked George's head. 'You're going to be all right, Georgie,' she said. 'Just try to relax. Here, let me take that off you.' She squeezed his hand and pulled at the double crystal he was still clutching. He let it go, closed his eyes and his face relaxed.

Sofie and Francesco were just flying away when Sofie said 'Oh my God!' and stopped. Francesco stopped too. 'I just thought,' she said. 'Why don't we just take all his crystal off him and leave him frozen? That's what I did with Marianne after she had the baby. God, I wish I'd thought of this before!'

Francesco stared at her for a moment then nodded and turned back. 'Right. We have to be very quick. We don't want him breathing without somebody pressing the plastic on his chest. Everyone except you...' he glanced at Ludovico's name badge, '...except Ludovico must fly away first. Then you must follow as fast as you can, Ludovico.'

'Wait,' Ludovico said. 'He still got crystal in he pocket.'

'Why?' Francesco frowned at him.

'He is take them down the tunnel. He want give them to Sam and Michael.'

'They must be taken out.'

Ludovico reached forward with one hand but, when they saw his bloody fingers, Brigit and Sofie put their hands into George's pockets and pulled out the two spare crystals.

'We're going to leave you here until we can bring the doctor to you, Georgie,' Brigit said stroking his face. 'Do you understand?'

George nodded. 'Good idea, sweetheart,' he gasped.

Francesco was shocked. At first he thought George was simply being over-familiar but when Brigit kissed George on the lips he realised that something was going on between them. He watched her glancing back as she flew up through the ATLAS cavern between Francesco and Sofie. When the window between their bubbles closed, Brigit hesitated but Francesco led them up to the top of the shaft and they waited for Ludovico to follow them.

'D'you think he'll be all right, Francesco?' Brigit asked. She seemed deeply worried.

'Oh yes,' Francesco said, 'once Ludovico leaves him, he'll be frozen in time until the doctor arrives, so his condition cannot change. Well done for thinking of this, er, Sofie,' he said, reading her name and trying to memorise it. She was obviously an intelligent young woman. She might be useful to him in the future. 'And he didn't have any blood coming out of his mouth,' he went on, trying to sound optimistic, 'so I think the bullet missed his lungs. If the lung itself is punctured, then it's much more serious.'

'I'm so glad you know about first aid, Francesco. You did a very good job. I think you probably saved his life.' The tone of her voice was conciliatory and genuinely grateful, in marked contrast with her antagonistic attitude during their previous meeting.

Perhaps I can get some benefit from this unfortunate situation, Francesco thought. 'I'm happy I was able to help—'

'I leave him as fast as I can,' Ludovico said as he flew up the shaft and joined them.

'Right,' Brigit said. 'Well I'm going to fetch the doctor.'

Merda! Francesco thought. *I'm going to lose this opportunity if she goes.*

'Sofie, can you show me where the hostel is?' Brigit said.

'Just a moment, Brigit,' Francesco said quickly. 'I understand you had some sort of vote about George and Alex going down the tunnel? I'm sorry, but I feel that was inappropriate, since I did not have an opportunity to express my opinion.' Brigit looked at him with a frown, but she listened despite her obvious impatience. 'As Director General of CERN I have special responsibilities for the safety, not just of my staff, but of the people of Geneva.' Brigit nodded and began to speak but Francesco continued: 'And what is more, I wanted to ask Alex something. I believe that he has hidden a fragment of crystal in the lake and I wanted to—'

'Yes he has,' Brigit said. 'Two, of them actually. He told us about them after Marianne let him out of the Lecture Room.'

'I knew it!' Francesco was elated. *Now the truth is coming out at last!* 'Did he say where they were?'

Brigit shook her head. 'I don't remember.'

'He said he threw them into the lake near his boat, wherever that is,' Sofie said.

Francesco's heart beat a little faster. 'I know where it is. Well he won't need them now he's gone down the tunnel so I will go and search for them. I would like to make some measurements on them, unless anyone objects?'

'I might need them,' Ludovico said. 'Karolyi he need help. What he know about rescue or dealing with dangerous situation? I going to get a gun and go after him and help him find Danny Schneider.'

'No!' Francesco said. 'I am strongly against anyone else entering that tunnel until we know a lot more about it. I believe it could be what is called a wormhole, but theory says that people would never survive entering it. However, I have to admit that, until a few minutes ago, I was absolutely certain Michael Zhang and Sam Fitzpatrick could never have survived being absorbed by the black hole, but now having witnessed with my own eyes two people shrink and vanish into the floor, I am not sure about anything.' He looked into the eyes of each of them in turn, Ludovico, Sofie and above all Brigit, making sure they were listening to him. He felt this was perhaps the most important speech of his life. *I have to show I am conciliatory and open to new ideas*, he thought.

'Please, just let me explain something, Brigit. George is frozen in time so he is not going to get any worse. There is no urgency about getting the doctor, but we have an important decision which needs to be made.'

'And that is what?' she said.

'All our scientific assumptions are now open to question,' he went on. 'Perhaps Michael and Sam really have survived. Perhaps Alex really did speak to them. It is clear that whole new realms of scientific research have opened up here, research for which the skills of CERN scientists will certainly be needed. I want to start doing this research now, and to revive some of our leading scientists so they can help me. Because, before we do anything else, we first need to examine crystal scientifically and understand as much as we can about it.' He glanced at Brigit and was relieved to see she was nodding in agreement. 'We need to put our scientists to work as soon as possible,' he went on, feeling cautiously in control. 'Therefore I would like to collect all the spare crystals and give some of them to our principal scientists so they can make measurements upon them and begin to work out the theory underlying what is happening. Does anyone have any objections to that?'

'I no think that George he would want you to—' Ludovico began.

'Oh for God's sake,' Brigit snapped. 'Francesco's just saved his bloody life. You think Georgie would be arguing about a few bloody crystals now? And anyway what difference does it make who looks after them for now? Here, Francesco.' She gave him the big crystal she had taken out of George's hand and the little one she took from his pocket. 'Now I'm going to find the doctor. I'm not happy about just leaving Georgie without any medical attention, even if he is frozen. Now Sofie, can you please show me where the hostel is?'

'The doc, he might need some help,' Ludovico said. 'If I no going down to help Karolyi then I come with you if you no mind, Brigit.'

'Yes I do bloody mind, actually,' she said coldly. 'Sofie can show me where the hostel is. I can do without your help, young man.'

She obviously doesn't like him, Francesco thought. 'You can come and help me find those crystals in the lake,' he said to Ludovico. 'Sofie, before you go, can you please give me the spare crystal you took off George?'

Sofie took the crystal out of her pocket then hesitated, looking at Brigit.

'It can't harm just to measure it, Sofie,' Brigit said.

Sofie handed it to Francesco.

He glanced at his watch. 'It's nearly seven now. I think we'd better cancel that nine o'clock meeting, Brigit.'

'I agree, but I still want to make a decision on taking the spare crystals to the United Nations and letting them decide what we do next. What about this afternoon? Three o'clock in the Cafeteria?'

Everyone nodded. Brigit and Sofie flew off towards the hostel as Francesco carefully wrapped his three new crystals in his handkerchief and put them in his pocket. He followed Ludovico towards Geneva feeling as if he had just won the Lotto.

There was a note taped to the outside of the hostel's mirrored door:

Marianne Schneider Room 018
Doctor Plaisent Room 021

'He's on the ground floor,' Sofie said and led Brigit past the reception desk and along the corridor thinking *I'll be glad to see Jean-Pierre again.* She pushed open door 021 and Brigit followed her in. The single bed was unoccupied.

'He isn't here,' Brigit said.

'He could be anywhere,' Sofie said. 'He might have floated away in his sleep.'

They began to search the room for him, Sofie looking under the pine desk and even opening the door of the wardrobe, while Brigit looked in the tiny bathroom.

'He's definitely not here,' Brigit said when they met again near the door. 'I wonder if he's with Marianne? Which room was she in?'

'018 I think,' Sofie said. 'It's just along the corridor.'

They found Jean-Pierre still searching Marianne's room, baffled at not finding her there. They explained to him what had happened and he took it all in, his sombre Swiss face showing neither surprise nor alarm.

'But why has Marianne gone down the tunnel?' he said. 'She's very weak and needs complete rest.'

Brigit explained what had happened.

'And why was Karolyi let out?'

Sofie told him how Marianne had let him out to help her find the tunnel, but that in the end they had held a vote to decide what to do. 'I'm sorry you couldn't vote too Jean-Pierre,' she said, 'but it wouldn't have made any difference. There were six of us.'

'It's all right, Sofie. I would have voted the same way. I thought about it after the meeting and decided Karolyi was probably right. We ought to help Catriona take the crystals down to Michael Zhang if there's any chance he can restart time. After all, who wants to live like this for the rest of their lives? So now George is injured and Marianne has gone down the tunnel without her antibiotics,' he said, holding up a little box. 'I've lost one patient and gained another. Sounds like I'd better go and see him. I'll need to scrub up first and collect some equipment from the Medical Centre. While we fly over there I want you to tell me exactly what you can remember about George's injury.'

'No, Jean-Pierre,' Brigit said. 'I can't go with you. I can't face seeing George again in that state. Do you think he's going to be all right? Can you save him?'

'You say he was shot in the chest? Was he coughing up any blood?'

'Please don't talk to me about blood. It makes me feel ill. Sofie will tell you about it.'

Sofie reassured the doctor that George was not coughing up any blood.

'In that case I think there is a very good chance I can save him. It sounds as if his lung is not punctured so it's just a matter of getting all the air out of his chest and sealing the wound.'

'I'm so glad to hear that!' Brigit said. 'Frankly I'm devastated about this shooting. I've lost my husband and my daughter and now Georgie's been shot. I...I want you to know, both of you, that I've fallen in love with George.'

Sofie felt distinctly uncomfortable and Jean-Pierre said 'That's none of our business, Brigit.'

'No. Anyway I can't help you with Georgie, I'm sorry. I'm going to visit a friend of mine in Geneva and get some advice about how to handle the UN. Sofie, can you help Jean-Pierre with George?'

Sofie said she would be glad to.

'It's a pity I gave my crystals to Francesco,' Brigit said. 'I would like to have a spare one just in case I need to lend one to my friend. I could kick myself now for giving all the spares away.'

Sofie hesitated for a second then said 'There are two spares in the Fire Station, Brigit. I'm sure George wouldn't mind if you took one of those. I'll show you where they are. There's no hurry with George. He's frozen.'

Ludovico and Francesco flew rapidly down the Route de Meyrin, across the river Rhône and up the southern shore of Lac Léman to Corsier Port, where Count Alex Karolyi's boat had been moored the previous summer when Francesco had gone to the party. It was easy to find the port by following the coast but not easy to locate Alex's boat with their view limited to a few metres by their bubbles.

Francesco finally recognised the magnificent teak cabin of Alex's classic gentleman's sailing yacht and they agreed to each search the water on one side of the boat. It took Francesco only a few minutes, flying low over the flat surface, to find the frozen ripples which began to spread out as soon as his bubble enclosed them. There were two intersecting sets, each spreading from a splash-surrounded hole where a crystal had entered the water at high speed.

The two men met on the deck of the boat a few minutes later and discussed their plan. Although Francesco was reluctant to enter the water, Ludovico was eager and rapidly stripped, giving Francesco his clothes to hold and, once he was naked, giving him also a cheeky wink and a little waggle of his buttocks. Then he flew head-first over the side and into the water. Francesco held his breath too, floating in the air above the foaming water waiting for the young Italian to emerge, thinking about his plan.

If my theory is correct then one of the crystals in this lake should fuse with one of the big ones in my pocket. Pity I said I would give them to other scientists. Ah well, too late now. Whom should I revive first? Of course! Martin Salinger! Why didn't I think of him before? He's the one person who could solve all my problems at a stroke!

Episode 56 The River

'This is far enough, isn't it Hans?' the fat soldier wheezed in German as he yanked on the rope tied round Nycolas d'Orsières's wrists. 'Why don't we just kill him now and take that jewel back to Bern?'

Hans did not reply. He was listening to the roar of the wide river beneath their feet. Walking on the frozen Rhône was dangerous enough in daylight, and could be deadly on a moonless night like this, but the Chatelain had told them the witch had fallen into the icy water below Peney and Hans had decided this was the shortest route. Yet the ice creaked beneath them, especially under Heinz's enormous weight, as they followed the current out of Geneva.

They had passed the little stilted river houses on the outskirts of the town and were now rounding a broad bend. There was almost no light from the sky except the twinkling of countless stars, but Hans was holding up the huge glowing blue crystal like a lantern, trying to see the places where the ice was thin enough to show the churning water beneath. The crystal was so bright it cast shadows among the trees climbing up the steep right bank towards the stars. The snow-covered pines and leafless bushes swept around them like an amphitheatre.

'I'm not going any further,' the fat soldier protested and yanked the rope again. 'Let's just kill him now!'

Pulled off balance and shocked by what he was hearing, Nycolas slipped and fell heavily onto the ice. There was a loud cracking noise and he lay still for a moment.

Hans stopped and waited for the prisoner to get up. 'We can't kill him yet, Heinz,' Hans said, also speaking German. 'He's still got to show us where the Irish witch fell with the pink jewel.

Then we'll kill him, get the pink jewel too and divide the booty by casting the die.'

'But gentlemen,' Nycolas said as he lay on the ice, speaking fluent German. 'You don't seem to have thought this matter through!'

'Gott im Himmel, he speaks German!' The long barrel of Heinz's harquebus glinted in the crystal's light as he spun round to face the prisoner and drew his sword.

'I'm already a dead man, gentlemen,' Nycolas continued calmly, 'Tomorrow I stand trial for rebellion against the Reform. As you know that is a capital offence and I will inevitably be found guilty. I have nothing to lose by taking to the grave the secret location of the devil's pink jewel. However I am willing to show you where it is in return for my freedom.'

The two soldiers began animatedly discussing whether to kill him now, later or not at all. Nycolas looked up at them, making no effort to get to his feet. *Why waste energy if they're going to kill me anyway?* The ice was surprisingly warm and he felt astonishingly relaxed. *If I manage to get away then it will be a bonus. If not, well, I've had a good life.*

He rolled his head, surveying the world for perhaps the last time. On his left, beyond the low river bank, he could see the humped white back of the snow-covered Salève Mountain. Behind it the black dome of heaven arched upwards and across to the steep bank on his right. He was just admiring the beauty of the stars when he saw a blue light drift over the high bank and stop, hovering in the air above the two soldiers' heads. They clearly had not seen it for they continued looking down at him, animatedly discussing what to do.

Nycolas's heart was thumping so hard he thought they might hear it, although he felt no fear, only intense excitement and hope. Against the black sky he could just make out a person's head lit by the blue crystal he was holding, a head with short hair. *It's not a witch. It's male. It must be the Devil himself! He'll kill these soldiers and take his jewel. Perhaps he'll spare my life if I help him.*

'I'm sorry to interrupt you, gentlemen,' he said calmly, 'but my friend the Devil has come to collect me. You see, I am a witch and if you harm me he will certainly kill you in revenge.'

'What the hell are you talking about?' Hans snapped.

'Just look up gentleman. Look up and greet the Devil incarnate.'

Both soldiers looked at each other, then up at the sky.

'Where is Michael Zhang?' the Devil called down in German.

Hans dropped the jewel onto the ice, Heinz threw down the rope and both soldiers unslung their long harquebuses from their shoulders.

Nycolas felt the rope tied to his wrists go slack as they began to load their guns. He reeled in the rope. The far end slithered past the blue crystal like the tail of a snake. *That jewel is what the Devil has come for*, he thought. *I have to get it and give it to him. I have to prove I am his servant.* He began to crawl awkwardly towards it on his knees, keeping his head low, using his bound hands as a third leg, trying to avoid the soldiers' attention. Then he heard a woman's voice overhead calling 'Danny! Danny!' and a man's voice shouting 'Come back Marianne!' although Nycolas could not understand the foreign language he spoke.

'Look out Heinz, there's more!' Hans said as he raised his gun towards the sky.

So the Devil has brought more witches to help him! Nycolas thought as he crept towards Hans' legs. There was an explosion above him, a witch screamed and the butt of Hans's harquebus crashed to the ice only centimetres from Nycolas's head as the soldier began to reload, pouring powder into the gun's muzzle. The blue crystal was almost within his grasp now.

'Be careful Hans!' the other soldier called, still looking up. 'One of them's coming at you!'

Nycolas lunged forward with both hands, still tied at the wrists, and grasped the large blue crystal between his palms. A moment later another hand descended from the sky and tried to wrench the jewel from his grip. *The Devil's hand!* It was as delicate as a woman's, a moist white hand which had obviously never wielded a sword or drawn a bow. The Devil tried to take the jewel but Nycolas resisted, thinking *I have to make sure he will carry me away.*

The Devil's hand was slippery with sweat and as he struggled to free his jewel, Nycolas tightened his grip and felt it pull him forward. To his delight he found himself sliding along the ice, the rope trailing behind him. The Devil grasped the rope and, still floating in the sky above Nycolas, was dragged along after him. He held the rope in one hand, a blue jewel in the other. The light from their two glowing jewels shone down into the ice, revealing the river water flowing not far beneath.

'Stop!' Hans shouted and began running after them. 'Come on Heinz!'

Although icy water was seeping through Nycolas's quilted hacketon jacket, yet he felt no discomfort, only elation at the prospect of escape. *This must be how the Irish witch flew off the battlement of my Chateau! If I learn to control it, I too might be able to fly!* His fingers pressed the crystal, trying to work out how to fly upwards, and he swerved towards the middle of the river where the ice was thinnest.

Behind him he could hear the soldiers running in pursuit, then there was the cracking of ice and splashing in water and screams of fear and swearing in German. With a feeling of ecstasy and still trying to fly, Nycolas turned the jewel and found himself facing back towards Geneva. The witch called Marianne and the other one in the yellow chemise were hovering in the air just above a black hole in the night-grey ice. The heads of both soldiers were sticking out of the hole as they bobbed in the icy water, screaming for help. At first Nycolas assumed the witches were trying to drown them, as was only natural, but it soon became apparent that instead they were trying to pull the soldiers out! Nycolas was shocked.

The Devil called Danny was still hovering in the air above Nycolas, looking back at the extraordinary scene.

Nycolas was still holding the devil's jewel, wondering what to do with it. He looked up at the Devil. *If I give it to him he will fly away and leave me here*, Nycolas thought. *Then those soldiers will catch me and I will be condemned for witchcraft. I have to fly away with the Devil.* 'Can you teach me to fly?' he called up to the Devil in German.

The Devil called Danny looked down at him and for a moment their eyes met. Danny looked just like a normal person, strained with fatigue and with anger, almost hatred burning in his eyes. His face looked surprisingly young. He wore strange attire, a green tunic over a white chemise. He was not at all what Nycolas had expected the Devil to look like.

'Where is Michael Zhang?' Danny said again in German.

'Who is Michael Zhang?' Nycolas asked. He felt absolutely no fear. 'Teach me to fly and I will help you find him, Oh wonderful Devil,' Nycolas said. 'Just teach me to fly and I will be your most faithful witch and make you greatest of all Satan's servants.'

A look of diabolic hatred suddenly crossed the Devil's face and he bent his legs and stamped viciously on Nycolas' back. The ice below him cracked and he plunged into the freezing river water. Once again he felt the Devil pulling at his fingers, trying to free the large jewel. He locked his hands around it as the Devil's feet swung again and the water closed over his head. Only his hands were still above water, held up by the rope. The undertow of the river was strong and he felt his body being pulled beneath the ice. Only the rope round his wrists stopped him being swept away. The turbulent current was pushing his body up against the covering ice sheet, pressing the air out of his lungs. Then a searing pain shot through his hands.

In desperation he opened his eyes and looked up through the ice. In the jewel's blue light he saw the blurred image of the Devil standing on the ice still holding the rope and stamping on Nycolas's hands trying to make him let go of the jewel. He could feel his fingers breaking as the shoes battered them into the ice and then the jewel slipped from their grip. The Devil let go of the rope and the current began to carry Nycolas away. The last thing he saw, before the freezing water entered his lungs, was the Devil flying away and the two witches flying after him, the one named Marianne calling pitifully 'Danny! Danny!'

Alex and Marianne had not been able to save the two men in the river. The light from their crystals showed they had been dressed in heavy armour which had pulled them down into the water and the current had swept them away into the blackness under the ice. It seemed that Danny had acquired another crystal from the third man, for Alex could see two blue glowing lights as he followed Marianne up the steep wooded bank after her husband. Danny flew much faster than his wife and soon disappeared over the ridge. As Alex caught up with Marianne, her crystal suddenly swerved to one side and she plunged into the ice-covered trees.

Alex followed the light of her crystal and found her tangled in a pine branch. She was covered in ice shards. He pulled her gently out and brushed them away. When his hand touched her skin it burned. 'You've got a fever Marianne,' he said. He scooped up a handful of snow and pressed it onto the back of her neck. 'You need your antibiotics, kedvenc. We've got to go back to CERN and get them, otherwise you're going to be seriously ill.'

'Where's Danny?" she moaned, pitiful as a child. 'I want to see Danny,' she said and began to cry.

'Okay Marianne,' he said, feeling his heart flutter with anxiety. *You might want to see Danny, my love*, he thought as he carried her up the high river bank, *but he's more likely to kill you than help you. What you need is to see Dr Plaisent.*

When they reached the top he paused, resting on top of a tall pine with Marianne beside him like a pair of roosting crows, and took the crystal from her limp burning fingers, afraid she would drop it. She offered no resistance. He lifted it and looked through it at the black sky, hoping to see the tunnel entrance in the same way they had seen the distant glowing crystals. He scanned the sky but saw nothing but the stars. With a sigh he broadened his search to view the whole landscape and saw again the pink glow, low down beneath the black Jura Mountains outlined against the slightly pink western sky. *Perhaps that's the tunnel entrance!* he thought and his heart leaped, but then he saw two blue spots of light moving rapidly towards the pink and his excitement died. *Danny must have seen it too. Guess I'll have to follow him. What choice have I got, if it's the tunnel entrance?*

He moved the crystal aside and the blue and pink lights vanished from sight, but there was a curious red glow, slightly higher than the level of the frozen landscape. Looking through Marianne's crystal again he confirmed that the pink and red lights were in exactly the same direction. *That's good*, he thought. *I can use that as a beacon.*

He put Marianne's crystal in his pocket and checked her condition. She had passed out. He pressed her to him, afraid she would fall out of the tree. She hung like a rag doll against his body. *She needs help urgently.* This was the closest he had been to her' for almost a year. Telling himself he was checking her temperature, but feeling his lust for her stirring, he let his hand push into her grey firefighter's uniform, under the cotton robe she wore, and cup itself lovingly around one breast. It was full and heavy, bigger than he remembered, and as hot as a cup of coffee. His mouth watered and his body stirred more strongly at the touch of her flesh, her nipple in his palm. Then he felt a cooler dampness in his hand. He lifted it and put out his tongue, tasting the milky sweetness. *The milk for my baby,* he thought with a feeling of profound grief deep in his stomach. *I wonder if she knows it was mine and not Danny's. And would Danny be so determined to kill Michael Zhang if he knew the truth? Maybe I'll get a chance to tell him before too long.*

He slipped one arm around her waist, clasped his crystal in the fist of his other hand and pressed his thumb into it, flying towards the red light, keeping low over the rolling ice-covered landscape of forest and field and broad meandering river. When they reached the hilltop, Alex found the red smouldering remains of a burned-out and deserted castle. He landed beside it, warmed his rigid fingers near the glowing embers, then checked his crystal, looking for the pink glow. He saw it shining up from the bottom of a steep wooded bank leading down to a sharp bend in the frozen river.

Excited but cautious, he carried Marianne down, keeping close to the bank, hiding the light of his crystal among the trees whenever possible. He found Danny near the river, outlined against the glow from one of his crystals. He was sitting on a fallen tree-trunk, his back towards Alex, and seemed to be talking into the crystal which he held close to his face. Alex flew closer, trying to hear what he was saying.

'How will that help, Professor?'

Alex assumed he was getting advice from Professor Francesco Romani and pressed the bottom of his crystal, hovering to listen. There was a period of silence and Alex guessed Romani was talking. Looking down at the river, he clearly could see the source of the pink glow. There was a large hole in the ice at

Danny's feet and, about ten metres downstream, a pink light was illuminating the underside of the ice.

Then Danny said 'Oh really, Professor?' He felt in his pocket then suddenly stood up, spun round and pointed his gun at Alex. The light from his crystals clearly revealed Alex's position. 'Come down here, Karolyi!' he barked. 'Don't try to escape or you're a dead man.'

'I've got Marianne here, Danny,' Alex said. 'She needs her antibiotics.'

'Just do as I tell you, Karolyi. Come down!' Danny raised the crystals in one hand, brightening the scene, and raised the gun in the other, aiming it at them.

Alex flew down thinking *He doesn't give a shit about his wife. The man's a complete maniac.* He landed and stood before Danny, still holding Marianne in his arms.

'What a handsome couple!' Danny sneered. 'I never thought I would ever say this, Karolyi,' he said, 'but I am really glad to see you. I need your help. Put her down. Over there.' Danny nodded at a fallen tree nearby.

Alex didn't move. *How can you talk about Marianne like that, Schneider, as if she was a bag of shopping instead of your wife?* Alex stood for a moment with the burning, unconscious woman in his arms and a feeling of hatred in his heart for this man who had taken his love and yet seemed to feel nothing for her. As calmly as he could, he said 'She needs to see a doctor urgently, Danny.'

'I said put her down, Karolyi!'

Alex had never heard such maniacal obsession in another man's voice. Carefully he laid his precious burden on the tree-trunk.

Danny showed no interest in her whatsoever. 'Now put your crystal beside her,' he said, still pointing the gun at Alex.

Alex did as he was told.

Danny lifted one of his own crystals and stared at him through it. Alex recognised it as the large one Catriona had been flying with just before she disappeared into the tunnel in the ATLAS cavern. *So little Kata must be here somewhere!* he thought

'And the other one,' Danny said.

He's seen the crystal in my pocket, Alex thought. He took Marianne's crystal out and laid it beside the first, saying 'What help do you need, Mr Schneider?'

'Step back,' Danny said. Alex retreated. Danny moved forward, picked the two crystals off the bank and put them into his jacket pocket. Still ignoring Marianne, he nodded towards the pink glow under the river ice. 'There's a pink crystal down there. I need it. Unfortunately I cannot swim. But I think you can, Karolyi. I believe you and my wife spent some time together in the swimming pool last summer. That is so, is it not?'

'Yes it is,' Alex agreed, 'but that was before she started seeing you, Mr Schneider.'

'I suggest you strip off before you go in,' Danny said, ignoring him.

'Marianne needs a doctor, Danny. She's burning with a fever.'

'Well there are no doctors here. We seem to have gone back in time, Karolyi. To get back to CERN you need to get back into the tunnel and I have just learned that the only way to do this is by looking through the pink crystal which is lying at the bottom of that hole in the ice. Now strip off and go and get it!'

Alex stripped down to his underpants, hanging his clothes on the branches of the fallen tree, and paused for a moment to look down at Marianne. She was still unconscious. *If I don't see you again, my darling*, he thought, *I kiss you goodbye.* Then he turned and walked past Danny towards the black circle that marked the hole in the ice-covered river, his feet chilled by the snow on the bank.

'No funny business, Karolyi. Look at me.'

Alex looked back. Danny was pointing the gun at Marianne.

'You wouldn't kill your own wife, Schneider!'

'I advise you not to gamble on that, Karolyi. Now go and get it!'

Alex stepped through the hole in the ice into the freezing water. His feet and legs began to throb with cold but he hardly noticed. He was thinking about what Danny might do to Marianne while he was gone. *I'm leaving her with a homicidal maniac. But I guess if the only way to find the tunnel is to get this pink crystal then I just have to do it. I wonder how Professor Romani found out about this? He must have found some pink crystal himself, I guess.*

He sat on the ice, pushing aside the floating fragments of smashed ice with his feet. *Wonder what could have caused a hole this size?* It was about three metres across and almost perfectly round. He lowered his body into the river. He knew it was going to be cold, but even so the shock of the icy water took his breath away. He sat on the sloping bank under the water with just his head sticking out as he got his breath back. The source of the pink light lay a few metres away downstream. *I've got to go under the ice and then get back to this hole. If I can't find it, I'm dead. Wonder how fast the current is? Got no choice with that maniac waving Volpone's gun around.*

Feeling his body begin to shiver, he breathed in deeply twice then took one last big gulp of air, turned to face the current and ducked down under the steel-grey ice. He let the black water carry him backwards towards the pink glow, swimming against the current to control his speed as he watched his escape-hole drift away, replaced by a ceiling of solid ice lit from above by Danny's blue crystal. He had an urge to go back, to make sure he could get out, but couldn't face the idea of coming back into this ice-bath a second time. *Hope to Christ I can find my way out.*

He squinted down through the cloudy water, searching for the source of the light. The pink glow drifted under him. It seemed to be surrounded by something grey which extended to one side, but it was difficult to see in the gloomy river. He increased his stroke and swam back to it.

Danny said the pink light was another crystal, he thought, *but that thing's much bigger.*

As he swam down towards it, blinking and peering, ignoring the first little complaints from his lungs, he saw the grey thing was triangular in shape. He descended through the cloudy water and the shape became clearer. It was a sort of cloak. At one end was the head of a girl with ginger-coloured hair. The pink crystal was in her mouth and in its light her features were clearly outlined. Her eyes were wide open and unmoving. *It's little Kata! She's dead!*

Catriona's body was floating on its back about a metre above the river bed. Strangely, she looked perfectly dry. The cloak was not moving. Neither was her hair.

How's she floating like that? Squeezing crystal between her teeth?

His muscles were quivering now, trying to generate some heat, and it was difficult to control them, but he managed to swim down, intending to get the crystal out of her mouth. With a sharp pain, one hand hit an invisible barrier. Confused, with his lungs beginning seriously to complain, he tried again but once more he met the smooth glass-like wall. He swam to the side but the barrier curved around her. She was floating above a gully in the river bed which the fast-flowing current had cut into the rock as it rounded the bend beneath the hill.

He swam down, eager to keep moving and so get warmer, trying to get underneath the obstruction. It seemed to be spherical, like a gigantic ball of glass, completely surrounding the inanimate girl. It rested firmly on the river bed and he could not get under it. The size of it struck him immediately. *Same size as bubble in CERN. Why solid? Don't understand. Never mind. Have to push whole thing. Upstream! And lift out. How heavy is it?*

He jammed his feet on the river bed and pushed. The unseen ball was slippery but not heavy. As he lifted it out of the depression, the strong icy current immediately gripped it and pushed it towards him, away from the hole in the ice. Alex was shoved aside and the ball rolled a little way downstream, Catriona's feet rising over her head, then she stopped again, head down.

With his lungs demanding immediate air and his body demanding heat, he checked her situation. She lay deeper inside the gully. Confident that the river would not carry her away, he swam upstream past the frozen girl. He could see the blue light from Danny's crystal glowing down through the ice and, further, the hole he had come through, a jagged black shape clearly outlined against the blue ice. He swam to it and pushed his head through into the air above, gasping for breath, with the chill beginning to bite into his bones. Finally he heaved himself onto the frozen bank and lay at Danny's feet, unable to stand, his whole body shivering uncontrollably.

'Where is it?' Danny barked. 'Have you got it, Karolyi? Give it to me, you bastard!' With a vicious kick to the stomach he knocked out what little breath there was in Alex's lungs. Alex's mind was numb with cold and pain but hot with hatred for this inhuman devil.

When he had got his breath back and calmed himself down, Alex explained with shivering jaws what he had seen as Danny held the gun to his throbbing head.

'It was really strange, as if she had been p-p-preserved in f-f-formaldehyde and b-b-bottled inside a giant goldfish b-b-bowl. Look Danny, I'm f-f-frozen to death. Can't I go up to that b-b-burning castle and t-t-try to get warm?'

'No,' Danny snapped. 'Just wait, Karolyi.' He picked up the big blue crystal and began talking into it again, explaining what Alex had told him and asking what to do next.

Why ask Romani? Alex wondered as he turned to check Marianne. In the light from Danny's crystal he could see that her face was still burning with fever. *She needs to cool down as much as I need to get warm. If only I could take her clothes off and lie next to her, like we used to do last summer.*

He walked over to her, his teeth chattering almost uncontrollably. Checking that Danny was not watching he unzipped the front of her thick heavy firefighter's overall and opened the front of the white hospital gown she wore beneath. Picking up a handful of snow he pressed it between and under her burning breasts, letting his hand linger there lovingly, feeling her heart pounding with fever as the melt-water trickled through his fingers and down her belly. At the touch of the snow she started groaning.

If she doesn't get her antibiotics soon she's going to die, Alex thought as his body began to tremble uncontrollably. *Danny says we need the pink crystal to find the tunnel entrance. Okay, so I've got to get it out of the river as soon as possible. If I don't get it soon I'm never going to get it.*

He stood up and turned to stare at the man who had stolen this precious woman from him. Danny was still talking into the big blue crystal, his back towards Alex. An overwhelming feeling of hatred surged through Alex's whole being. He lifted a heavy rock and staggered along the frozen river bank. It was an effort even to walk. Danny was still staring at the big blue crystal. As Alex raised the rock high above Danny's head, he caught a glimpse of something floating inside the crystal, its image reflecting off the internal faces. It was the head of a white ant.

Episode 57 The Operation

It was while Ludovico was still holding the cellophane to the wound that George had left his body and begun floating outside himself. George watched with interest as the bloody bubbles seeped out of his chest around the plastic. He felt no alarm, only elation and a profound sense of release. *At last I'm free!* he thought.

Ludo did not seem to notice George's mind floating over his head. He took his hand off the plastic on George's chest, pressed his crystal and flew rapidly backwards. The bubble moved with him, leaving George's mind and body both suspended in space and time. It seemed only a moment later when Dr Jean-Pierre Plaisent and Firewoman Sofie Dialektaki flew down and hovered before his body.

The doctor quickly assessed the situation then pressed his hand on the plastic covering the hole in George's chest while Sofie began cutting away the top of his overalls and his T-shirt with a pair of scissors. They were both wearing surgical gloves and both seemed to assume their patient was unconscious. Indeed, from the way his own head was flopping onto his chest, George too thought he looked unconscious.

Then everything changed and for a moment George was looking down, not at himself, but at a climber hanging from a rope below a slab of granite.

I remember you! George thought. *On the Jungfrau last January. Helicopter couldn't reach you so it dropped my mountain rescue team onto the ice above and we climbed down.*

George remembered the sudden and overwhelming feeling of jealousy he had felt when he saw the climber swinging in the wind, his arms frozen to the rope, hanging over the void. Here was a man on the edge of death, of escape, of peace, and George just wanted to swap places with him. This vision lasted only a moment and then George was back in the ATLAS cavern floating outside his body.

So this is what it's like when you die, he thought. *I've got here at last! I've been waiting for this since the disaster in Budapest. What sweet release!*

He was surprised to notice he felt no pain. The heart-clutching agony in his chest and the breathless suffocation had been replaced by a feeling of peace. He watched Sofie working with efficient calmness, as she always did, and a huge wave of affection and respect welled up inside him. *You're the first firewoman I've ever had in any of my teams,* George told her, although he knew she couldn't hear him. *I am tremendously proud of you Sofie. You are at least as good as any of the men I've ever trained. So much better than little Robert Moore. And the way you helped Marianne Schneider was truly amazing. God bless you, Sofie.*

George smiled to himself. *Why am I asking God to bless her? I don't even believe in God! And yet here I am, floating outside my body! So are the stories about ghosts and spirits and angels really all true? I've heard about this kind of thing before but I never believed it. What do they call this?*

George thought about it, racking his brain, trying to remember. After a moment, as if in answer to his question, a voice said "It is an out of body experience". It was a familiar voice, a man's voice but not his own. George nodded. *Yeah, that's it. Out of body experience. Well for sure I'm not in my body any more. So am I dead?* "No," the voice said. "If you were dead, Dr Plaisent would be trying to resuscitate you." George knew the voice was right and he felt terribly disappointed. He felt angry and looked down at his own body floating below him with a feeling of loathing, a big bald man with a bloody chest, willing that man to die.

His chest was completely bare now. Jean-Pierre had replaced Francesco's little cellophane patch over the wound with a sterile waterproof plastic dressing taped down on three sides. *I wonder what are the chances he will save my life? Don't bother, Dr Plaisent*, he called. *Just let me die!* But the doctor obviously couldn't hear him.

'I couldn't find a chest drain,' he said to Sofie, 'not even a flutter valve, so I'll have to improvise one. Have you ever seen this done before?'

Sofie shook her head, looking slightly astonished.

'No, I've never done it before either.'

George watched as the doctor took a paper package out of his bag, tore off the end, extracted a long thin transparent plastic tube and handed it to her. *You really don't need to bother, doc*, George told him as he tore open another package and took out a scalpel, which he used to cut some holes into one end of the tube. *It doesn't matter if this guy dies*, George said but the doctor just looked at the other end of the tube and said 'I really need a one-way flutter valve. How can I...'

Jean-Pierre looked at Sofie, searching her face for inspiration. 'I know,' he said. He cut the finger off a surgical glove and slipped it over the end of the tube. 'That might work,' he said, examining his handiwork. 'We'll find out when I've inserted the other end.'

So is this experience some sort of mental effect? George wondered as he watched the doctor. *Something people often get when they're near death? But how can it be caused by my brain if I'm outside my body, outside my brain? Because sure as hell I'm still me, still Hungarian firefighter Gábor György. Wish I could tell the doctor what's happening and ask him for a diagnosis of the condition. I'm sure he'd be interested in this.*

But the doctor was busy. He was injecting something into George's chest with a hypodermic syringe. Sofie screwed up her mouth as she watched him push the needle deep between his ribs, his thumb pushing the plunger down hard. *He's going to operate,* George thought. *I wonder if I can will myself to die before he saves me? It's now or never. If he succeeds then I'll have to begin the torment of living all over again. That's the last thing I want.* He tried to let himself go. It required an heroic act of willpower and concentration, a Herculean feat of bravery to force himself to die, but he made himself sink inside himself and the whole scene turned black.

George was sliding down some sort of long tunnel. Everything was black, utterly and totally black. *Is this the tunnel Alex Karolyi was talking about? No, it can't be. This isn't a physical tunnel. I'm not taking my physical body with me. I've done it! I've left my body behind. I must be dying now!* George had never experienced such intense happiness. He was hurtling along the black tunnel at incredible speed. Ahead of him he could sense a white light. It was as if he was going home, as if he was returning to Budapest but with the welcoming adulation of his friends awaiting him instead of the feeling of utter failure and self-hatred which had driven him away. The whiteness was growing brighter, becoming overwhelming, and suddenly he emerged into a huge, open, endless space.

"Welcome György," a voice said. He opened his eyes and looked up. He was floating before a Being of Light. He sensed himself as a tiny dot. He did not know who or what the Being was, but he felt no fear. He immediately abandoned all his previous ideas about religion. *All religions are wrong,* he thought, *and they all have an element of truth. Other people must have experienced this and lived to tell the tale. That must be how religions get started.* Here, before his eyes, was the complete truth, the living Truth. *At last.* From those two words, "Welcome György," he knew, with a conviction which he had never felt in his life about anything, that this Being loved him. Loved him completely and utterly. Loved him to a degree which embarrassed George because he knew he was not worthy of such love.

All around him there were uncountable numbers of other dots like himself, but the Being was talking only to him. George knew this was a tremendous privilege, that the whole of this place was waiting for him to answer and he felt guilty. Guilty for being such a failure. Guilty for making such a mess of his life. Guilty for not knowing what to say.

"You have a lot to learn, György," the Being said. "It is time for you to find out who you really are."

One of the other dots moved towards George. Then a mist arose around the Being, around George, and he lost sight of everything. A moment later the mist began to clear and he looked down at himself. He wasn't a dot any more but he wasn't a man either. He was a little boy, maybe four years old, wearing short baggy blue trousers and a green jacket. The mist blew away. The Being had vanished and all he could see were trees. He was walking through a cherry orchard on a hillside. Instantly he recognised the place and his heart began to pound. It was utterly familiar and vivid. He remembered his father telling him to wait in the farm but George had got bored and had walked down the lane to the orchard searching for him.

George had never been in a cherry orchard before. He was a town boy and his father rarely brought him out into the countryside. He looked up into the trees. The Hungarian Sun was shining down through the cherries. Each one of them gleamed with their own soft succulent vermillion light like tiny red lamps. George stared at them in wonder. How could these trees produce so many beautiful cherries and let them all just hang there waiting for the farmer to come and reach up and pick them? What was it that created such bounteousness on this hillside so far from home?

He looked around, searching for the farmer, and saw his father kneeling by a cherry tree in the middle of the orchard. A bag was resting on the ground against the trunk of the tree. His father had taken his hat off. There was a cigarette smouldering in his hand. Little George could smell it.

Gábor Ignác touched the cigarette onto a thick white cord protruding from the bag. It began to smoulder and the red smoking point burnt quickly along the cord. Ignác stood up and ran.

'What are you doing, papa?' George called as he ran after his father. Ignác turned, saw him running towards the bag and ran back past the bag waving his hands. He looked frightened. There was an explosion and the tree fell down and his father fell down and little George fell down too.

'It's working,' Jean-Pierre said, 'but there's a lot of blood mixed in with the pleural fluid.' His voice was coming from a long way away. 'I hope he's not going to need a blood transfusion or we'll really be in trouble.'

Little George looked up. The cherries were raining down from the trees, falling from the sky towards him. They started splashing on his face. One entered his mouth. It tasted strange. It wasn't a cherry. George wiped his face. His hand was red. Everything was red. His father was red, the grass was awash with a flood of red. George stood up and ran towards his father calling 'Papa, papa!' There was a big hole in Ignác's back. White bones were sticking out. George had never seen so many bones, not even when papa ate pig's feet.

George ran down the road to the farm and banged on the door. The police came and took Ignác to the mortuary and little George to the police station where they questioned him for hours. They called his father a counter-revolutionary and asked George what he knew about the plot to kill the President of Hungary. Little George admitted everything. It was his fault his father had died. He had spoken to him when he should have remained silent.

Then the mist returned and the policemen disappeared. When the mist cleared, once again George was a little dot floating before the Being of Light, but this time his father was there too. Ignác was alive and there was no blood and no hole in his back. Best of all, Ignác was not angry. All his life George had been sure his father must have been angry with him.

"I know you have been blaming yourself for my death all your life, György," Ignác said. His father was smiling at him. "But it wasn't your fault. You did your best to help me. It was my fault. I should have seen that President Kádár was right to reform the economic system. I'm sorry now I ever tried to stop him. Can you forgive me?"

George forgave his father and he absolved himself from guilt. The two men embraced and the Being of Light smiled love upon them, then showed George another scene from his personal history. Like an archive of home movies, George saw himself at key moments in his life and met again the people whom he had shared those moments with, terrible and wonderful moments. It took a long time. Sometimes George watched the movies in slow motion, over and over again, seeing the action from each person's point of view, trying to understand what had motivated them to do what they did. It took hours, days, months, years to watch and understand all these movies. But there was no hurry. George knew he had all the time in the world.

As he watched each scene, he could see it from the outside, like an observer, and he could understand the motives of everyone who took part. He was able to pass judgement on all their motives, good or bad. And above all he was able to judge himself.

The most terrible movie of all was when he saw himself send those seven firefighters to their deaths in the fire in the Budapest financial district. The most horrific movie was of the fights he had with his wife afterwards, as he tried to rid his conscience of the overwhelming guilt. And, to his utter astonishment, his wife too forgave him, admitting that she had been as guilty as he. They were all there; his father, his mother, the seven dead Hungarians, Robert Moore, even his wife; all the important people in his life. They were all smiling at him. He felt overwhelmed with their love.

"You are a good man, Gábor György," the Being of Light said when, fifty years or perhaps just fifty seconds later, George had seen all the movies. "You are an honest and generous and a loving man whose life has been ruined by self-hatred because of what you saw as your own failures. You are happy to risk your life to save others because you always hope you will be killed and so punished for these failures. But instead you found that those who worked for you died while you carried on living, and that was intolerable. So you killed your spirit. You became a machine that went through the motions of life without emotion. Now you must decide what you want to do. You can stay here and leave the world behind and live in peace for ever if you wish. Or you can go back and help to save the world. It is your choice."

George looked at the Light. *So it's true. There is a heaven and I'm being offered a place here despite my failures.*

'His pulse is very weak.' George could sense the doctor listening to his heart through a stethoscope. 'I think we're losing him.'

'Can't you do anything, Jean-Pierre?' Sofie sounded on the verge of tears.

George was still staring into the Light. *So I'm not dead yet. But it's taken me such a long time to get here. Why would I go back to the hell of living on Earth? And with the Earth frozen in time it's gonna be even worse. I've had enough of all that.*

One of the dots of light drifted towards him. "George," Robert Moore was standing before him. The agony of death had left his face. "I know I was rubbish as a firefighter for CERN, but I was learning fast and you were helping me. I don't blame you for my death, George. You were a really fantastic team leader. I think you should go back. The world needs you."

One after another the dots of light drifted past him, telling him to go back. The last one came and stood before him, holding out her arms towards him.

"Please come back to me Georgie." Brigit O'Brien looked beautiful and confident and perfectly irresistible. Seeing her here was a shock.

Are you dead too, Brigit?

"No, I'm not dead and you're not dead either Georgie, but you will be if you don't come back to us. We need you, lovie. I need you to help me to get the UN involved in solving this problem. I love you Georgie. I want your baby. Come back to me Georgie. Please come back."

George looked at the Being of Light. "It's your choice," the Light said, smiling. "Nobody can decide for you. It won't be easy if you go back, György. There are many more problems ahead. There are many new opportunities for failure and guilt. Can you cope with that, György? Have you learned enough about yourself to understand why you always blamed yourself for everything which went wrong, and condemned yourself to a living hell for what you perceived as your own failures?"

George nodded. *Yes, I've learned that. It started in the orchard. My father was the most important person in my life and I never forgave myself for his death. After that I always tried to make up for it, to be perfect, to help other people so they would look up to me and respect me but I always felt they knew I was guilty and were just being kind to me when they said I was helping them. I never believed I was any good and the death of those seven men just destroyed me. I've been living a sort of death ever since. But now...Now I know that I have got a job to do, a really big job, to help Brigit, a job that maybe nobody else on Earth can do right now. I suppose this isn't just going to be a return to the Earth. It's going to be a rebirth into a whole new life.*

"You have learned well, György. You take with you knowledge and wisdom which few men ever achieve. Use it wisely, Gábor György, and one day I will see you again, and you will take your rightful place here beside me."

George smiled at the Being of Light and closed his inner eyes and opened his outer eyes, his physical eyes, and saw the doctor was hammering on his chest. Sofie was holding a mask over his nose and mouth. George took in a huge gulp of the gas then pushed the mask away.

'Where's Brigit?' he said.

Sofie yelped then began to cry. Jean-Pierre gasped and then laughed.

'Where's Brigit?' George said again.

'She's gone to see somebody she thinks can help,' Jean-Pierre said. 'I'm not sure who it is.'

'She told us to tell you she loves you,' Sofie said.

George nodded. 'I know,' he said.

Episode 58 Colum O'Callahan

Brigit had known Colum O'Callaghan years ago in Dublin when he was himself the Irish Ambassador to one of the world's trouble-spots, but she had lost touch with him when he retired from the diplomatic service and came to Geneva, the city he described as "the world's capital of diplomacy". Here he had created the International College of Diplomacy and used his contacts with the UN and the many diplomatic missions in the city to obtain work-placements for his students.

Brigit had been delighted to meet him again when she arrived here and had already sought his advice on several occasions, valuing his lifetime of experience in international relations as well as his openness and honesty. So it was Colum she had sought when she left Sofie and Jean-Pierre outside the round wooden Globe, with the spare crystal tucked safely in her trouser pocket.

She found it surprisingly easy to follow the road back to the McDonalds on Avenue Wendt. She turned left into the Rue Hoffmann and flew straight up to the park within which lay the United Nations Offices. She followed the road around to the large country house, not far from her own home, where the College was located.

She had to break some windows to get into the classrooms, but they were all empty. She flew to the College office but did not find the man she was seeking until, with a stroke of inspiration, she flew over to the nearby café and found him at a table on the small terrace, frozen in the act of sipping coffee, a cigarette dangling from his fingers. She slid into a seat at the little table on the café terrace beside the tanned handsome man in the blue suit, kissed him on both cheeks, held his hand and started talking rapidly.

She showed him the crystal, explained about time being frozen outside the bubble, told him one could use crystal to fly, described as best she could about the cosmic monopole and the explosion in ATLAS and the black hole while Colum stared into her eyes, his expression changing from stoic interest to growing astonishment to appalled shock, his eyes roaming over the crystal and the bubble that gradually filled with smoke from his cigarette. This he gallantly extinguished when Brigit started coughing.

When she had recovered her breath she went on: 'Then finally my husband Sam and a scientist called Michael Zhang were absorbed by the black hole and these crystals appeared. I don't suppose you know Michael Zhang? He's Irish.'

Colum shook his head slowly, staring at her with a horrified expression. 'No I don't. My God, Brigit, this is terrible!'

She nodded. 'Yes, but they weren't killed. There's a Hungarian guy Alex who works at CERN and he says—'

'Count Alex Karolyi? I know him slightly.'

'Oh really? Well according to him, Sam and Michael both survived and Sam was able to speak to my daughter Catriona—'

'How did he do that if he had been absorbed by a black hole?'

'It turns out...I don't have time to explain everything about these bloody crystals, Colum, but it turns out you can talk through them and see other people who have one. Anyway, Sam told her—'

'So how many crystals are there altogether, Brigit?'

'Oh God, I can't remember. About a dozen, I think, but there might be more. They haven't done a thorough search yet. Anyway, Sam told Catriona that Michael could restart time if she could bring all the crystals down a tunnel, so she went—'

'A tunnel? What tunnel?'

'Oh Colum...There's a tunnel, right? It starts from the cavern, the what do you call it ATLAS cavern thing and it leads down to where Sam and Michael are. Now please don't ask me to explain it because I have no idea what created it but I know it exists because I saw Alex and somebody else fly into it.'

'Fly?'

Brigit closed her eyes and breathed in deeply despite the tobacco smoke, before forcing a smile. 'I told you, Colum. You can fly with crystal. Anyway my daughter Catriona, she apparently went into this bloody tunnel but she only had one piece of crystal. Now if what Michael says is true, if he really can restart time, then we need to make a decision. Either we do what Sam said, collect all the fragments of crystal and take them down the tunnel and give them to Michael, and also rescue the people who have already gone down, or we give all the fragments to Francesco Romani and let him—'

'Francesco Romani?'

'The Director General of CERN. According to him, CERN owns all the crystals and he wants to fuse them together. We know that crystals can fuse and make a bigger bubble. Sorry, that's another one of the things I haven't had time to mention. Romani wants to make a very big bubble so that his scientists can do some research and try to find out how crystal works and how to restart time.'

'I must say a bigger bubble would be more comfortable than this one,' Colum said. 'It's claustrophobic! Well my dear, that's quite a story.' He suddenly realised he was still holding his coffee cup. He lowered it to the table, but the coffee floated out of it, drifting through the air like thick brown smoke towards his hand-tailored suit. He seemed surprised but not alarmed, swatting it away with the saucer. 'If I couldn't see that bubble and this coffee with my own eyes I would never have believed you. But tell me this. If Michael can restart time, then why does

Romani need to do any experiments? Why not just send all the crystals down to him?'

'Because there's a risk. It's not just Romani who's reluctant to do it. I am too. At the moment, a few of us who have crystals are alive but everybody else in the whole world is frozen. Did I tell you this before? So if we send all our crystals down the tunnel then we will all be frozen, which is as good as being dead. The whole world will be dead. And suppose we send them down and Michael fails to restart time? Then we've lost everything. That's the dilemma which is facing us, facing the world in fact, Colum. Whom do we trust, Michael or Francesco? And that's why I want to get the Security Council involved. As far as I can see, they are the only ones capable of making this decision. What do you think, Colum. Am I right?'

'On the face of it yes, I think you are.' He sat in silence for a while, fingering his cigarette packet thoughtfully, then nodded. 'Yes of course I agree with you that with a disaster of global proportions like this, the question of what to do, including whether to fuse crystals together or not, should be addressed by the United Nations. All the member states have missions here so you could find ambassadors from all Security Council members. They would just need to consult with their governments–'

'No Colum, that's impossible. I told you, time has stopped outside a bubble so all communications, everything has stopped. There's no radio, no telephone, nothing. To consult with their governments they would have to fly thousands of miles alone, and that's clearly impossible.'

'Hmm. Ok, let's suppose that's true. It's not a show-stopper. Most ambassadors have extraordinary and plenipotentiary powers, so their votes would be binding on their governments. It would not be the first time that diplomats have created foreign policy on the wing and then told the politicians about it afterwards. It often happens in times of war, for example, although of course it's never been done with anything as important as this.'

She sighed with relief, squeezed his hand gratefully and explained her plan to use spare crystals to revive representatives from the five permanent members of the Security Council because there weren't enough spare crystals to revive all fifteen members. 'I imagine they would form an emergency committee or something and take a decision. Do you think that would work, Colum? I'm not too clear on how the Security Council functions, to be honest. Would those five be able to take a decision about whether to fuse more crystals and if they did would it be binding and legal?'

'No, I'm sorry to tell you, Brigit, that you can't just involve the permanent members of the Security Council. A decision will only be valid if it is voted on by all fifteen states. Why can't you involve them all?'

'That's out of the question, Colum. We haven't got fifteen spare crystals and even if we did, I don't think I could get hold of them all.'

'But why would you need fifteen? Yes I know there are fifteen members of the Council, but do the ambassadors really need one each? You say the CERN Director General thinks he can create a bigger bubble by fusing crystals together? How many crystals would he need?'

'Well he said that he could create a bubble four hundred times bigger than this one by just fusing together three crystals.'

'God almighty, that would be big enough surely? Why not let him create this big bubble? Three crystals doesn't sound very many, and if that's the only way you can organise a Security Council meeting then I'd say it's worth it. A meeting with just the five permanent members wouldn't work. It would have no legally justifiable basis. Just make sure he doesn't fuse more than necessary.' He was silent again for a while, then he looked at her with eyes that seemed to be seeing something far away.

'You know, I think there's a bigger question here. I think some good could actually come out of this disaster.'

'How do you mean, Colum?'

'Isn't this a perfect opportunity to reform the UN?'

Brigit's heart skipped a beat. 'Go on,' she said.

'Just think about how the world is organised Brigit my dear, or rather how it was organised earlier this morning. The world was divided into almost two hundred sovereign nations, each with complete power over its internal affairs, each with the right to wage war on the others if it suited them, some with huge natural resources, some with almost none. Was this a sensible or fair way to manage our planet? And these two hundred nations, they were already facing many global problems which they were totally unable to solve. Time stopping is just one more, although of course it's far more serious than anything we've met before. But there were lots of others.'

'You mean like sustainable development?' This was a subject close to her heart. She had never been able to understand how Africa, India and China could develop without producing unsustainable amounts of pollution.

'Yes, and the lack of a truly representative Security Council and the ability of the big five to veto anything they didn't like; and the lack of any effective global governance; and the ability of nations to disregard the human rights of their own citizens with impunity; and the world's inability to react quickly to global emergencies or to stop the spread of nuclear weapons or cope with international terrorists and criminals. Not to mention global warming. And these are just a few of our global problems.

'Now almost everyone agrees that the UN needs to be reformed, but nobody can agree how. It takes a big shock to force people to make up their minds,' he went on, 'but it has happened before. The First World War led to the League of Nations, largely driven by President Wilson. That failed because the Senate refused to allow the United States to join. The Second World War led to the United Nations, again largely led by a US President, Roosevelt this time, and that is failing largely because states cannot agree on how to reform the UN.

'UN structures are built around cold-war politics. They are clearly not fitted to 21st century reality, but it has long seemed to me that only another global disaster would force states to come to an agreement. This disaster just might be the shock the world needs to bring it to its senses.'

'So what kind of reform would you advocate then, Colum?'

'It doesn't need to be earth-shattering. Gradual reform is better than revolution. We need to do something about the veto for one thing. Any of the five permanent members can block any resolution by using their veto. So one fairly simple reform would be, for example, if they always have to explain why they have used it and suggest an alternative resolution which they would support. A more fundamental reform would be to increase the number of permanent members, and to make the choice of the UN Secretary General more open and democratic. There are other reforms which would help to bring this institution into the 21st century. Of course, these reforms would need the agreement of every nation in the General Assembly, not just the Security Council members.'

As he had been speaking, Brigit's heart had been sinking. 'Oh Colum, I agree with everything you are saying, but don't you think that getting all the members of the Security Council together and getting them to agree on a decision is going to be hard enough? If you're telling me now that we should also be trying to reform the whole bloody United Nations at the same time, well, that just seems to be too much.' She stared at him as he looked down at his empty coffee cup and sighed.

'I understand how you feel,' he said, patting her hand. 'Whether you manage to reform the UN or not, it seems pretty clear, my dear, that even though Ireland is not a member of the Security Council, you are going to be involved with organising at least the first meeting. The ambassadors from the Genevan missions will be able to represent their nations. And you are right, the Council can create a committee or a working group any time it wants. My guess is the first thing they would want to do is call an Arria-formula meeting and...'

'A what?'

'An Arria-formula. It's an informal, private meeting to which they can call witnesses. They would certainly want to hear from you and from Francesco Romani and indeed from any other available experts from CERN, from the UN and possibly elsewhere. As you know, there are dozens of NGOs[35] in Geneva and many of them would have strong opinions about how to handle this situation. Not to mention the military representatives of the major powers. But to be honest with you, Brigit, my feeling is that they would feel totally out of their depth in tackling this problem. My guess is that they would almost certainly ask Romani to just get on and try to solve the problem. Don't you think so?'

'I hope not, but if they do, well, that's up to them. Okay, so who are the members of the Security Council at the moment, Colum?'

'Well, there are the five permanent members of course: China, France, Russia, USA and the UK.'

'Hold on, let me write them down. Do you have any paper?'

He took a pen out of his jacket, felt in his pockets for paper and, when he failed to find any, tore open his cigarette packet and wrote on the back of it as he went on: 'Then there are the five states which were members last year and are now in their

---

[35] Non-Governmental Organisations

second year. Let's think. South Africa, India, Colombia, Germany and Portugal. And then there are the five new members. That's Pakistan, Azerbaijan, Guatemala, Morocco and Togo.'

'And which country is the president this month?' she said as she looked at the paper he had handed her.

'I'm pretty sure it's the USA.'

'Henrietta Irons[36]? Thank God. I can work with her, no problem. I'll start with her.'

'And you'll certainly need to contact the Director General too.'

'Great idea, Colum!' she said. Brigit had been very impressed with Vladimir Shishkin, Director General of the UN in Geneva, when she presented her ambassador's credentials to him in February, finding him a most intelligent, professional and kind man. *And he's Russian*, she thought. *So we have an American and a Russian in key positions. That's good if we're going to find a consensus.*

'Thank you so much for your advice,' she said, 'and also for the idea of using a big crystal to hold the meeting. That sounds good. I guess I'll have to let Romani do his fusion experiment after all.'

She folded the paper into the pocket of her grey jacket beside the spare crystal feeling nervous and uncertain whether to offer it to him or not. Her anxiety must have shown in her face because he smiled encouragingly, took her hand and said: 'You've got to think bigger, Brigit, bigger and bolder. This is a once-in-a-lifetime opportunity, not just for you but for the whole world. You've got a chance to change the United Nations for the better, and if you don't then what good will come out of this disaster?'

---

[36] Chief of the Permanent Mission of the United States of America to the United Nations and Other International Organizations in Geneva.

Brigit squeezed his hand to stop herself trembling. 'You're telling me I've got to reform the whole bloody UN system, Column? Am I capable of doing that?'

'This is no time to be faint-hearted, Brigit. When you're creating history, you need the courage to act. We've lived for too long in a world where it has been better to take the easy way. Yes, you will find it very difficult to change things and introduce a new order, but if you don't do it then you will have wasted this unique chance. You have to know exactly what you want to achieve. You have to make decisions about the future of the world! You must be creative, take initiatives, make things happen, build a new world. You must be courageous! Just imagine: you could help create a UN which is truly an expression of the collective will of mankind.'

'Oh Colum, I can't tell you how attractive that sounds! To be honest with you, I thought I was going to be the President of the Republic. Now I see there could be something much bigger waiting for me. I'd love to do it! If you'd talked like this yesterday I would have been thrilled and said it was what I was born for. But for now, I just want to take one step at a time. Let's make sure we can restart time and save the world. Without that, none of this other stuff matters. Once the world is safe, then we'll be in a position to think about reforming the UN.'

I don't think he's the right person to help me with this, she thought, taking her hand out of her pocket but leaving the spare crystal behind. *I think his dreams of reform would just distract me from the job in hand.*

He plucked at a floating cigarette and took his lighter out of his pocket. 'And my will now is to have a smoke, so I guess you'll be on your way.'

=⬣=

When Francesco got back to the lab with Ludovico, the first thing he did was to send the firefighter to collect the sticky labels from the Cafeteria. While he waited for him to return, Francesco arranged his six crystals above the map on the whiteboard: the tetrahedrons George1 and Alex2, the double crystals Super1 and Super2, and the two new tetrahedrons Ludovico had found in the lake, so far unlabelled, which he placed near "Fish". Then he surveyed the result.

Map and Crystals on Whiteboard

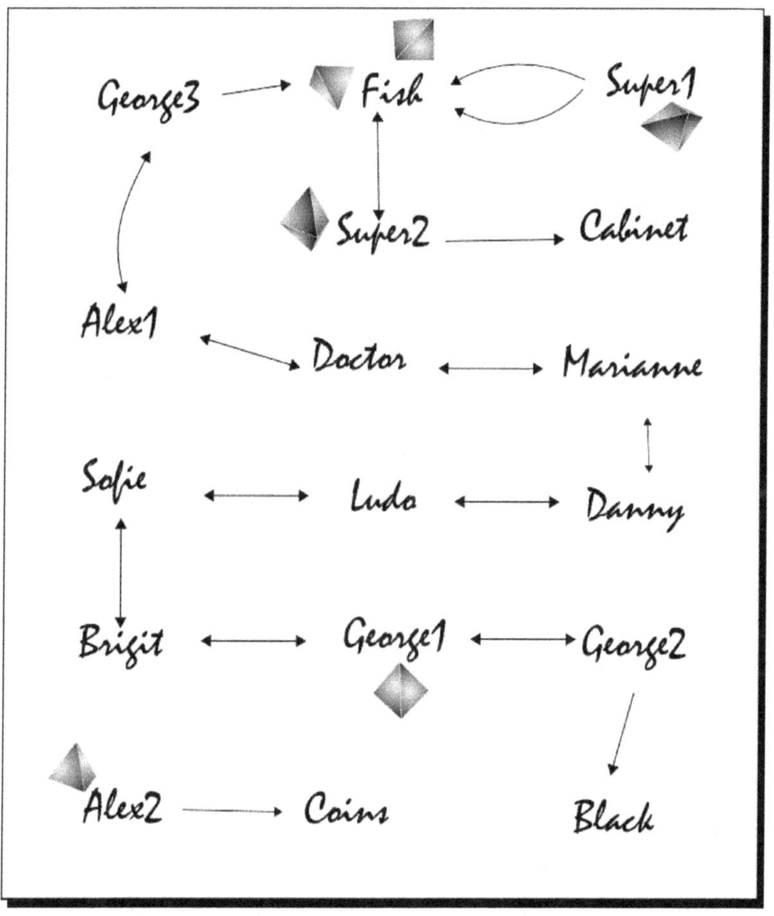

I should have realised there were two crystals in the lake! he thought. *It's obvious. That's why there are four arrows going to Fish.*

He took one of the lake crystals, measured it and recorded the fact that it was identical in size with the other tetrahedrons, then loaded it onto the microscope stage, switched on the lamp and began looking inside it. After turning the crystal a few times he saw, exactly as he had hoped, the ceiling of this very lab.

I just need to identify whether this can see out of Super1 or Super2.

He placed Super1 in a tool box and looked in the microscope again. He had just verified he could still see the lab ceiling when Ludovico arrived with the labels.

'You got anything you want I should do, Professor?' Ludovico said. 'If no then I want to go find out how George he is getting on.'

'Yes, that's fine,' Francesco said absently as he tore off two corners of a label. 'I'll see you at the meeting in the Cafeteria at three,' he said and wrote "Fish1" and "Fish2" on the labels as Ludovico flew out of the lab.

Francesco used the microscope and rapidly established that both of the two new crystals were connected to Super1. He also found that one of them was connected to Super2 and this he labelled Fish2. He looked through the other new crystal, Fish1, trying to see out of George3 and so confirm his theory about how crystals were connected. To his surprise and confusion, he saw two crystals resting in the bottom of a green bag, or perhaps a pocket. It took him a moment to work out that there must in fact be three crystals in there; the one he was looking out of and the other two. As he watched, the two crystals moved. He saw a label stuck to one of them, bearing the legend "Doc", and, when they moved again, he saw the label "Dan" on the other.

Still confused, he checked his map trying to work out what was going on, but after some consideration he realised that he was almost certainly looking out of George3 and that both the Doctor and Danny crystals must be together with it in the same bag. Or pocket.

Within ten minutes he had redrawn that part of the map to show the links between crystals. He did not bother showing which ones were in the green bag. Francesco did not care which crystals happened to be together at this moment. His scientific mind was preoccupied with some far bigger questions.

He had to first establish which crystals were linked together by these mysterious connections, and now he believed he had achieved this. Next he would have to settle the even more important issue: to establish whether his hypothesis was true, that these weird links would predict which crystal would fuse with which.

His heart began to race as he examined the four crystals linked together near the top of his new map on the whiteboard.

Second Revision of Crystal Map on Whiteboard

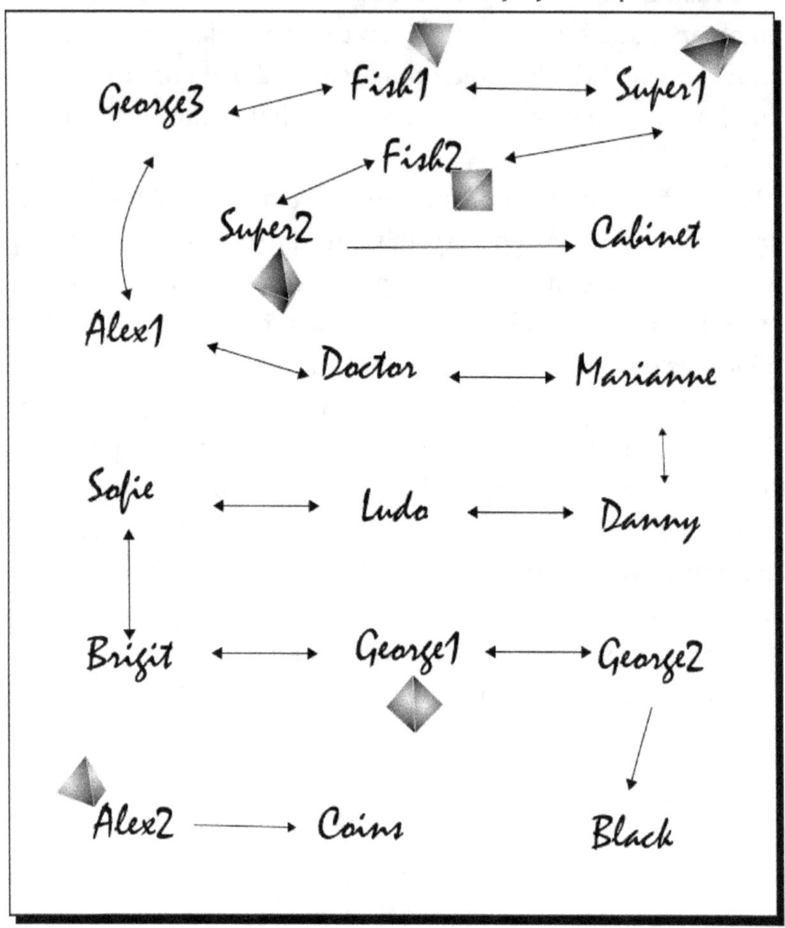

Fish1, Super1, Fish2 and Super2 are all joined together, he thought. *I'm almost certain they would fuse together in that order, although I'm not sure exactly what I would have to do to make it happen. I would certainly need to fuse two at a time and take careful measurements each time. Perhaps it would be enough just to fuse two of them. If I fused Fish1 with Super1, for example, that would give me a triple crystal. How big would its bubble really be?*

He forced himself to breathe deeply and calm down. *This will need a great deal of thought, and I have other work to do first. I haven't checked whether George3 can see out of Fish1, although I've put a double-headed arrow between them. I have no idea where George3 really is right now, so I can't check this. Also I haven't measured the parameters of the new crystals.*

He began to carefully measure them all, adding the details to the table in his notebook where he had already copied Danny's results: size, refractive index, electric field, magnetic field, radioactivity and bubble radius. As he filled in the columns with his new measurements it was obvious that the values for the new single pyramids were identical to Danny's, within the limits of the accuracy of the equipment he had available. Likewise the results for the double crystal Super1 were identical with Super2, exactly as he had expected.

After an hour, the table was complete and Francesco turned his mind to the big question: *What to do about crystal fusion? Should I try the experiment now or wait until the meeting at three? I suppose I should put a fusion motion to the group and try to persuade them of the wisdom of the experiment. I told Brigit I would give her crystals to our scientists to measure their properties and understand how they work. It might be considered immoral to take any other action. On the other hand I never promised anything about the other crystals. She gave me Super2, so...*

He lit a cigarette, picked up Fish1 and Super1 and carefully examined each in turn, squinting down through his spectacles, checking each could see through the other. When he had convinced himself they really were linked, he drew deeply on the cigarette and, as the nicotine coursed through his veins and his heart began to race, so Francesco's determination hardened. *I am the Director General of CERN! Brigit O'Brien is just the Irish Ambassador and Ireland is not even a member of CERN. There can be no legal requirement to regard this casual statement to her as a binding undertaking. This is not the time for hesitation. The world needs clear leadership.*

And then he remembered the Convention. Astonished at his own stupidity, and not absolutely convinced he could remember the wording, he flew out of the lab, across the covered bridge to the Main Building and up to his office on the fifth floor. He took the "Convention for the Establishment of a European Organization for Nuclear Research" off the shelf, opened it at "Article VI : Directors-General and Staff" and scanned down until he found paragraph 4.

> *The responsibilities of the Directors-General and the staff in regard to the Organization shall be exclusively international in character. In the discharge of their duties they shall not seek or receive instructions from any government or from any authority external to the Organization. Each Member State shall respect the international character of the responsibilities of the Directors-General and the staff, and not seek to influence them in the discharge of their duties.*

So that's clear, he thought. *Ireland isn't a member of CERN, but in any case no nation has the right to direct what we do here. I can't believe I forgot this fundamental point. To be totally legitimate I suppose I should go and see Martin Salinger and obtain his approval for the fusion experiment. As the Chair of the Scientific Policy Committee, it's within his power to authorise it. But since the Committee usually accepts my recommendations anyway, I think I can safely proceed with the experiment and get his permission after. But should it be done? Is fusion really the right thing to do?*

As was his usual practice when faced with a difficult decision, Francesco took a piece of paper, folded it neatly in half, drew a line down the crease and began making lists of the pros and cons of fusing crystal.

Pro Fusion

1. *Increase scientific knowledge.*
2. *Test prediction of links determining fusions.*
3. *Identify which faces fuse.*
4. *Revival of more people in larger bubble.*
5. *Enable measurement of size of new bubble.*
6. *Enable prediction of size of other bubbles following further fusions.*
7. *Provide larger workspace where more scientists can do more research into crystal.*

Anti Fusion

1. *At previous meeting most survivors failed to agree to it.*
2. *Fewer crystals for individuals to use.*
3. *Possible antagonism of other survivors.*

Clearly there are more pros than cons, he thought and with sudden determination, his heart still pounding, he lifted Fish1 and Super1, one in each hand, and brought them slowly together.

Episode 59 Rescuing Catty

Would this be heavy enough to smash the life out of the miserable, inhumane swine once and for all?

Danny was sitting talking to the ant in the big blue crystal and Alex was standing behind him, holding the rock above his head, weighing it in his hand, trying to make himself bring it down on the monster's skull, but he kept seeing Paul Volpone's brains splattered across the ceiling of his office and his arm wouldn't obey him.

I can't kill him, even though he deserves it, Alex thought as his arm threw the rock to one side. It bounded down the frozen river bank and thumped onto the ice. Danny jumped up and spun round, pointing Paul's gun at Alex's stomach, his eyes searching for some sign of what had made the noise.

'I think a r-r-rock just fell down the b-b-bank, Danny,' Alex stammered. He was naked now. He had cast aside the soaking underpants when they began to freeze to his backside. 'What d-d-do you want me to do?'

Danny put his hand into his pocket, hesitated, then waved the gun towards Marianne. 'Go over there,' he said. He followed Alex to where she was lying on the fallen tree-trunk, pressed the gun against her head and took a small blue crystal out of his pocket. Marianne moaned in her delirium as he held it out to Alex saying: 'Take this, Karolyi. It will help you get the pink crystal, or so I am told. Any funny business and she gets it.' He pressed the gun's muzzle hard against her forehead. 'I don't think you want that, Mr Karolyi.'

Alex controlled the cold fury which rose up inside him just as he controlled his trembling fingers as he took the little tetrahedron.

This is no time for revenge, he thought. *That comes later. If that pink crystal is going to show us how to get back into the tunnel then I've got to get it in any case, whether Danny is threatening Marianne or not.*

The question of how and why Danny had been talking to an ant flashed through his mind but he pushed it aside, telling himself that the image in the crystal had been too small to see clearly, and that it must have been Professor Romani.

He pressed the bottom of the blue crystal and felt it lift in his hand. For a moment he wondered whether he could fly up and kick the gun out of Danny's hand before he shot Marianne, but decided he was too cold to achieve it. *I can't risk him harming her.*

Alex stepped back so Danny would not be alarmed, pressed the crystal harder, flew along the bank and hovered above the hole in the ice, shivering, finding it difficult to breathe deeply. He glanced back at Marianne, lit by the light from Danny's crystal and the newly risen moon, wondering whether this would be the last time he would ever see her. Perhaps we'll all die together, he thought. *The baby, Marianne and me. I think I'd like that.*

Astonished at himself, he rotated the crystal, flew into the air and plunged head-first into the freezing water. The current carried him under the ice, the pressure increasing on his lungs. His jaws were trembling so much it was impossible to keep his lips closed and bubbles of air escaped as he searched for the tell-tale pink light which would reveal where he had left Catriona.

His blue crystal glowed in the murky water as he drifted downstream, keeping to the right bank. The current flowed faster where the river curved beneath the tall cliff leading up to the castle. Finally he saw her, still hanging upside down, her head still pointing into the groove cut by the current. As he approached her, he pressed the crystal, not sure if he could fly under water, and was very relieved to find it slowed him down.

Holding the crystal in one hand, he reached out with the other to feel for the hard round invisible wall surrounding her, thinking: *Got to be careful. Don't want the crystal knocked out of my hand. The wall's not very big.*

But even though he flew forward slowly, he could not feel the wall. His hand was only about a meter from her head now. He could clearly see her face, her eyes staring straight ahead, the pink glow shining between her lips and through her cheeks. He was confused.

I'm sure the wall was bigger than this.

Then everything changed. As he flew further forward, still searching for the glass wall, her eyes suddenly moved and the river washed over her ginger hair, instantly soaking it and dragging it over her face. A look of alarm flashed in her eyes and her head turned towards him.

He was shocked. *She's still alive!*

Her mouth opened and he saw one corner of the pink crystal sticking out between her teeth. A tiny bubble of air escaped, a look of agony creased her face and for a moment she stared at him in terror, then her eyes closed and air bubbled freely from her open lips.

She's passed out! he thought, feeling even more confused. He knew he had to move his crystal closer to her, although he did not really understand why. He flew towards her, still without meeting the glass wall. As he approached her, a wave of water travelled down the cloak she was wearing, turning it from a dry grey triangle to a wet rag clinging to her body. At the same time, her eyes opened again and huge bubbles of air escaped from her mouth, pushing out the pink crystal which drifted away in the current. Her arms flailed and she tried to scream but began to choke as she swallowed the icy water.

She's going to drown, Alex thought.

Before he realised what had happened, one of Catriona's hands had grasped his long hair and she pulled Alex's head down.

You stupid bitch! You're going to drown both of us!

Instinctively Alex punched her in the stomach, grasped her wrist and unclenched her fingers as a stream of bubbles escaped her mouth. His hair came free and he lifted his head. She was gulping in water like a fish, terror written on her face. The pink crystal was nowhere to be seen. Gradually her movements became weaker and she began to sink.

You're more trouble than you're worth, he thought. Catriona had stopped struggling and was lying lifelessly on the river bed. His lungs were beginning to complain and his head was screaming "Find the pink crystal", but he could not just abandon her. He lifted her little body off the river bed, put one arm around her waist, flew upwards and found the ice hole, his oxygen almost exhausted.

She felt like a dead weight as he flew out of the water and hovered in the air, trying to get his breath back, thinking *She must be full of water*. When he could breathe again, he flew to the bank and laid her on the snow.

'Have you got it?' Danny said, running to him along the river bank.

Alex ignored him, put his mouth over Catriona's and blew air into her lungs.

'Have you got the pink crystal, Karolyi?' Danny was jamming the gun into Alex's temple.

Alex moved his head away and a fountain of water sprouted out of Catriona's mouth and splashed up into his face.

'Where is it?' Danny was almost screaming. 'Didn't you get it? Leave her, Karolyi. Go back and get it or I'll shoot her here and now.'

Still Alex ignored him. *If Danny shoots her, that's up to him, but I've got to try to save the little fool's life.* He put his mouth on

Catriona's and blew again. When he moved his mouth aside, more water came out. He repeated the inflation thinking: *I hope her heart's still going.* He could see Danny's gun shaking with cold and frenzy as he walked up and down, shouting at Alex to stop but not actually doing anything physical to impede him.

It took ten inflations before Catriona began to heave and vomit up the water she had swallowed. Then her whole body went into quivering convulsions, her teeth chattering so much Alex was afraid she would bite off her tongue. She felt ice-cold. Once she had started breathing, with a sudden inspiration Alex picked her up and carried her along the bank, pushing Danny out of his way.

Danny didn't try to stop him, just rushed after him, waving the gun and shouting 'Where are you going, Karolyi you bloody fool?'

Alex laid her beside Marianne, pressed their bodies together and waited until the girl had put her arms around the unconscious woman, then calmly turned to face Danny.

'They will help each other,' he said, his jaws not chattering so much now that the exercise of saving her had warmed his body a little. 'Marianne needs to cool down and Catriona needs to warm up.'

'Right, okay, that's fine,' Danny said, also sounding calmer. 'So now I can kill them both if you don't go and get that fucking pink crystal out of the water, Karolyi! Now go and get it!'

Alex didn't feel at all cold as he picked up the little blue crystal, flew back to the ice hole and into the water. A sense of unreality had taken possession of him. He seemed to be sitting in a comfortable armchair by a warm fire somewhere, drinking beer and watching all this happening to somebody else.

He found the crystal quite easily, trapped among the rocks at the bottom of the gully, and flew unhurriedly with it back to Danny who was once more sitting talking into the big blue crystal. He looked down at the pink crystal which Alex threw at his feet, then stooped and picked it up.

Shit, why did I do that? Alex thought. *Maybe I could have frozen him with it, like little Kata? Too late now.*

Danny turned to him, holding up the pink crystal with a look of triumph. 'Now I know how to use this to get back into the tunnel, Karolyi.'

Alex walked over to the two females and touched Marianne's face. He was gratified that she seemed cooler. Catriona turned and smiled at him, lifting her hand and putting it on his. Her skin felt warmer than before.

'It seems a shame to kill you,' Danny was saying, putting his gun in his pocket, 'after you have been so useful. This disaster was not your fault, Karolyi. It was Michael Zhang's, and now I know for certain he is still alive. I'm going to find him and give him the punishment he deserves for what he has done. As for you, Karolyi, I am not an unreasonable man. I will spare your life. Marianne needs help. I know that, Karolyi. She is my wife, the mother of my poor little dead child. I would never have harmed her, Karolyi. I want you to look after her, take her back to the doctor and get her antibiotics. But I tell you this: you lay a finger out of place and I promise you I will kill you. You better remember that. Okay, so let's go.'

Danny lifted the pink crystal and looked through it, scanning the sky. It took him only a few moments to find what he was seeking. 'There it is,' he shouted, pointing up. 'The tunnel opening. And there's another one over there! Come on! Bring Marianne. Let's go!'

Alex looked up to where he was pointing but saw nothing but stars. 'What about little Kata?' he said.

Danny hesitated, then reached in his pocket and threw one of his blue crystals at Catriona.

'Can't I get warm first?' Alex said. He was still naked.

'I put your clothes near the fire on the top of the bank while you were in the water,' Danny said. 'They should be dry by now. Come on, I'll show you.'

Alex lifted Marianne and flew beside Catriona as they followed Danny up the bank to the smouldering chateau.

Brigit hadn't intended to come home when she left Colum. It was mid-day and she was planning to go back to CERN to sleep before the meeting at three, but somehow, as she passed the western entrance to the United Nations site, she had found herself following her habitual route, turning right into Avenue de l'Ariana, past the Intercontinental Hotel, past her own office, left at the Café du Soleil and up the Chemin des Crêts to the house she rented.

She had fallen in love at first sight with this house when she first moved to Geneva. It more than fulfilled her vision of what a Swiss house should be. Hiding behind tall hedges and weeping willows, vigorous creepers ran up the pale yellow washed walls, past many shuttered windows to the wooden beams which supported the little curved tiles of the roof. Here half a dozen needle-spires gave the house an antique and slightly gothic air.

She had broken a window to get in and now she floated above the kitchen table and leafed through the Blue Book listing the names and addresses of the ambassadors at the permanent missions to the UN in Geneva, feeling glad she had printed out all 350 or so pages some weeks ago. At first she told herself she was just going to go through it, copy down the details for the fifteen members of the Security Council, then go back to CERN. But now, as she sipped sweet cold coffee from a plastic bottle, she realised she didn't have the energy to go anywhere. *I'd be better to sleep here. I'll set the alarm for two-thirty.*

As she floated above her bed waiting for sleep, she thought about George. *Where is he now? What's happened to him? Did the bullet hit his spine? He's such a robust and active man. It would almost be better if he was dead than crippled for life. Perhaps I can ask Sofie what's happened.*

She knew that she could see Sofie through one face of her original crystal, but now she was not sure which of her two crystals it was. She took them out of her pocket and looked at them. One was labelled "A1" and the other "S". She had no idea what these labels meant. She picked the cleaner one, with the "A1" label, and began to look into each face in turn.

She was shocked and astonished to see the profile of her own mother, as she had been as a young woman. She was standing on a snowy hilltop beside a burned-out stone building, holding the crystal Brigit was looking out of and watching a man getting dressed. Brigit had no idea where they were. The man turned to bend over a woman lying on the ground at his feet and Brigit recognised him as Alex. The woman on the ground looked like Marianne. *So who's the one holding the crystal who looks so much like Mother?*

Then the nearest woman turned her head and Brigit finally recognised her. There was no mistaking that lost look, that unruly ginger hair, those attractive emerald eyes. *It's not Mother; it's Catriona!* She looked much older than her fourteen years, almost twice as old. She was standing near the smouldering stone ruin and steam was rising from the cloak she was wearing. It was all utterly confusing.

Brigit called 'Catriona? Is that really you?' and a worried look crossed her daughter's face. She glanced across at another man who was standing nearby looking impatient and Brigit immediately recognised him as Danny, the man who had shot George, and realised that Catriona's life must be in danger too and stopped calling, but Catriona had heard her and held the crystal close to her face and looked into it. There were wrinkles round her eyes which looked at her with the maturity of a fully grown woman. She began to whisper, and even her voice sounded different.

'I can't talk. Danny's been like a mad-man, but now he's found out how to get back into the tunnel and he's going to lead us there. I love you, mother. I just want you to know that.'

Brigit's heart broke at that moment.

'Thank you, darling,' she said. 'I know I have not always treated you like a mother should. Can you forgive me?'

Catriona nodded, then glanced at Danny and Alex. Alex had finished dressing and was lifting Marianne in his arms.

'Where are you, Catriona?' Brigit said, feeling tears welling up in her eyes. 'Can you get back here? I want you near me. I love you too. I know I haven't been a good mother for you, my darling, but I promise I will change. I need you. You can help me deal with the future here. I want to get the UN involved in deciding what to do. Don't forget to bring your crystal back.'

Catriona smiled but shook her head. 'You are a good woman, mother. I know that, in spite of all the problems we've had. I know you're trying to save the Earth in your own way. But Sam needs crystal. He told me to come down the tunnel and help him restart time, and Danny wants to kill Michael Zhang. I can't let him do that, mother. I'm going to go with him, if he'll let me.'

'But Danny's dangerous, Catty. He shot George! He's a maniac.'

Catriona looked shocked and glanced at Danny again. 'Come on you two,' he shouted and flew up into the air.

'I can't talk any more, mother. I have to use this crystal to fly. Take care of yourself, my dear. I'll talk to you again when I can. Alex is bringing Marianne back to your time. Look after her for me. She's my big sister. I love you both.'

Michael's Diary: Where are You?

I need to share with you my innermost thoughts, Oh marvellous Monopole, for there is one question which is revolving around my mind like a vortex, it concerns you most intimately and I have nobody here with whom I can share this puzzle. And this question is, quite simply: Where are you?

It is clear that you formed the nucleus of the black hole which was created inside ATLAS. But I have no idea what happened to you once I and Sam Fitzpatrick were absorbed by that hole. I did not meet anything which even vaguely resembled you when we were absorbed and travelled here through the wormhole.

I believe the black hole itself can no longer exist on Earth, for if it did, surely it would have absorbed the fragments of crystal pipe which fell into the event record and arrived in the ATLAS cavern? These fragments were not absorbed, so the black hole must have disappeared, probably having evaporated by a process known as "Hawking radiation[37]".

But this evaporation would not affect you, Oh Majestic Monopole. You have existed since the creation of the Universe, and you would be unaffected by the formation or destruction of the hole around you.

---

[37] For more information about Hawking radiation see the bibliography entry (25).

Thus, if you are no longer at the centre of the black hole, exactly where are you now? Please allow me to explain why this question is so important.

The fate of my Universe is intimately entangled with yours, Oh perfect Monopole. As I have explained before, it was you, in the form of the Cosmic Seed, which fertilised the Cosmic Egg and started time. And I am convinced that, in order to create similar functioning Eggs, Professor Cjingha Itoodoo will need to find you, remove you from the Universe and clone you. I must at all costs prevent her from doing this.

For it is you which maintains the stability of my Universe, since, as the human scientist Paul Dirac first discovered, your mere existence governs the size of all its electrical charges[38]. Thus your removal would, in all probability, destroy its basic physical stability. I cannot allow that to happen. The risk is too great.

To safeguard the fate of my Universe, it is imperative that you be found and moved to a place where Itoodoo will not find you. Only the people of Earth can do this.

That is why my question is so important: You must exist somewhere, but where are you?

---

[38] For details of Dirac's paper see bibliography entry (5) and (6) to download a copy.

Appendices

For the reader's convenience, I have added in the following pages some information which might prove useful when trying to follow the events and ideas described in Time Crystal.

The appendices consist of the following sections:

Principal Participants

This is far from a complete list of the people involved in this story, but I include it to help the reader become more familiar with the main participants.

Glossary

A list of some of the technical terms used within this book.

Bibliography

A list of the references to books, websites and other sources of information to which I have referred in this book, mainly in the footnotes.

Principal Participants

This is far from a complete list of the people involved in this story, but I include it to help the reader become more familiar with the main participants.

Alex Karolyi

Alex Karolyi was born in Hungary on 3 January 1986, making him a 26 year old Capricorn on **Crystal Day**. He claims to descend from Count Mihály Ádám György Miklós Károlyi de Nagykároly (1875 – 1955) who was briefly Hungary's Prime Minister and then President in 1918-19 during a short rare spell of democracy. Many people question whether this story is true, however.

Alex was the eldest child of a small import/export wine merchant in Budapest and his mother was a flighty woman of Austrian descent who was too busy chasing men to look after Alex.

As a child, Alex remembers constantly crying for his mother. When he realised that she was not going to look after him, at about the age of eight, he decided he must take care of himself. This determination was sealed when his father's business collapsed, his father turned to drink and his mother committed suicide.

From that moment, he had to take care of himself, and devoted his time to making money. Initially he sold newspapers on the streets of Budapest, rarely going to school. His life on the streets soon led him into petty crime and eventually into buying and selling drugs.

He was rescued from this decline on one of his rare trips to school where an inspiring teacher, recognising his natural talent and intelligence, taught him how to program a computer one afternoon. From that moment Alex was inspired with the idea of starting a programming business. He soon wrote a successful program, gave up the drugs business and started a software company.

He now runs more than ten companies, all based in Eastern Europe. His ambition is to be a millionaire within the next year. His software company not only wrote Atlantis (the programme the **ATLAS** scientists use to visualise particle events) but also all the simulations in the ATLAS Observation room, the Globe of Science and Innovation and the Microcosm beneath the **CERN** Reception.

Until he met Marianne, Alex had a butterfly personality, flitting from woman to woman, from one new scheme to another, never spending much time or energy on anything. Like most extroverts, he seemed unable to commit himself to any one thing, incapable of devoting his attention to anything for very long. He was fun-loving and did not hesitate to indulge himself in the pleasures of life, and for this he needed as much money has he could get.

All this changed when he fell in love with Marianne. He seemed to have found the stability which he had always lacked in his life.

Nevertheless he is still a risk-taker, but he always tries to calculate the risk first. He is still charming, especially with women, but his laid-back appearance is deceptive. He is now capable of extremely hard work, especially when a deadline is looming, and his businesses have boomed with his new-found stability, which is one more reason why he is convinced he needs to have Marianne as a permanent part of his life.

Alex Karolyi

He has thick long black hair above a sun-tanned face in which nestle two beautiful dark-chocolate eyes. He is fully aware of their power on women. His lips are thick and sensuous, his nose not too large, and his body is tall and muscular, although his hands are surprisingly small and beautiful. He always dresses for summer, even in the middle of winter, and almost always wears sunglasses except when he wants to unleash those eyes on a new victim.

His voice is deep, languid and as sensuous as a water-snake. He wears musk-based aftershave.

Brigit O'Brien

Brigit was born on 12 August 1977 making her a 34 Leo on Crystal Day. She was the only child of Declan MacMaster, a wealthy landowner and farmer in Wicklow, south of Dublin. He was a weak personality and the family was dominated by Kathleen, his wife.

Brigit was educated in a private school, had a large garden and her own horses, and was an only child. She was rather isolated from other children during her childhood but was deeply attached to her mother.

Brigit matured into a beautiful young woman and her mother Kathleen felt threatened and jealous. She began to shut her daughter out of her life, taking more interest in social activities and spending less time with her precocious offspring. Brigit felt abandoned and rejected, and tried to put on an act to become the person her mother would admire and love, but without success.

Brigit went to Trinity College, Dublin to study media and politics in October 1996. While at Trinity she began to work as a volunteer in RTE, the Irish national broadcaster, and was soon offered a job as a trainee.

During the first term at Trinity, she had a short torrid affair with a physics lecturer, Dr John O'Brien who was 28 at the time. Unluckily she fell pregnant and her father forced John to marry her, threatening to have him sacked if he did not.

Brigit had never wanted children, but when she found she was pregnant she had hoped for a boy, so a female child for her was worst possible outcome. She was never close to her daughter, almost exactly repeating the bad relationship she had had with her own mother.

Brigit's primary concern is to present a successful image. She cares deeply about her appearance. She uses her clothes, hairstyle, movements and her voice to exhibit her desirability and importance. She is a great actor and performer, able to charm any man to get what she wants.

She is driven by ambition and sexual desire, which for her is a way of gaining power and attention. She is especially drawn to men whom other women find attractive. Her laughter and exuberant behaviour make her the focus of almost any group, especially when there are men whom she can attract.

When she found herself saddled with John O'Brien, a man of mediocre attraction and low sexual libido, she began to search for other lovers who will satisfy her desires.

Brigit O'Brien

She is not tall but gives the appearance of being taller by wearing high heels and growing her blonde hair long. She wears it piled up on top of her head in curls and cascading around her shoulders in torrents. She loves wearing reds, vermillion, maroon, lime green, any pure vibrant colour that will make her stand out. She spends a fortune on clothes and shoes.

She likes to drink and fights to keep her weight down. She has a good figure which she delights in showing off to its best advantage, with large breasts (of which she is very proud), a narrow waist, smallish buttocks and fairly slim legs.

Catriona O'Brien

Catriona was born in her parent's home on Sunday 11 November 1997 making her a 14 year old Scorpio on Crystal Day. Her father was John O'Brien, a young lecturer at Trinity College, Dublin, where her mother Brigit was a student. After the birth, Brigit took the rest of the year off, living mostly with her parents. She returned to Trinity the following year, taking Catriona with her but leaving her with child minders most days, paid for by her rich father.

Catriona grew up very isolated and lonely. Her mother gave her very little attention or affection, obviously resenting the year that she had already 'wasted' on Catriona. Catriona's father was also a distant figure, intellectual and busy with his research, but he tried his best to give her the love he knew she needed. She felt closer to him than anyone else.

It was a total shock to Catriona when her father left home in the summer of 2005. This followed months of arguments between her parents over who should look after Catriona. Brigit was by now a busy TV personality and John was deeply involved in a research project which often required him to visit CERN.

Trying to bring her father back into the family, Catriona took the family dog Trackaway and walked to his laboratory on her eighth birthday. While waiting for him to come out of the laboratory she witnessed a frightening and incomprehensible sequence of events which led to his murder. From that moment her life was devastated. She felt guilty that she had been unable to prevent his death.

As a result of her father's death and her mother's cold and unsympathetic response, Catriona's relationship with her teacher, Sam Fitzpatrick, deepened and Sam began to visit the family home, eventually marrying Brigit. He transformed Catriona's life, giving her the love and stability she had so far lacked.

Her strongest characteristic is her sense of insecurity. She is always looking for something, always hoping to find something or somebody that will give her a solid rock upon which she can build her life. She feels like she lives on quicksand, always threatened with going under. Her love for Trackaway, the family St Bernard dog, was a manifestation of this search for security.

When she learns that her mother, who is now the Irish Ambassador to the United Nations in Geneva, has been invited to CERN, she persuades Sam that it would be a good idea to visit her for the Easter holiday. She knows her father used to work there much of the time, and is hoping that she can solve the mystery surrounding his sudden death.

Catriona O'Brien

When she goes to Geneva, she is a petite fourteen, wiry, tough yet gentle. She is pretty with emerald green eyes, a neat, snub nose, full lips and medium-length ginger hair which is typically wild and ungovernable. She loves the colour green, and many of her clothes reflect this. Her figure is underdeveloped for her age and she has the smallest breasts of any girl in her class, something of which she is acutely conscious.

Danny Schneider

Danny Schneider was born in Graz, Austria, on 4 November 1976, making him a 35 year old Scorpio on Crystal Day. His father was a Bulgarian immigrant who worked in a menial position in a car factory, preferring to spend his time drinking rather than use his intelligence to get a better job. Danny's mother was loving but passive and was subject to physical abuse by her husband.

Danny had an extremely unstable childhood. His father was cruel and abusive, especially when drunk. He sometimes beat Danny with a stick. Danny was more intelligent than both his parents and felt he did not really belong to them. He soon took on the task of making things better. He wanted to fight his father and take care of his mother, but was too weak to do either.

In a reaction against his father's abuse, Danny became committed always to doing the 'right thing'. Laws and rules dominated his thinking. He loved maths and science because they were logical and based on clear rules. He did well at school.

Danny went to Heidelberg University in Germany and studied engineering, then began to work within the physics department of the university as a technician, finally moving to CERN.

On Crystal Day he is the shift leader who restarts the ATLAS detector after the winter shut-down.

Danny is a control freak. He always wants to control or repress his anger and instinctual energy, terrified lest he act like his father, but his anger is very easily roused.

He directs all this emotional energy into his work, often working 80 hours a week. He believes he is motivated by a desire to do what is right for the world, to help to make the world a better place.

Danny Schneider

He almost always wears the same green jacket no matter what the weather. His face is usually ashen grey as it sees very little of the Sun. He sweats a great deal, his palms feel sticky when you shake his hand. When he is angry the tip of his nose turns white. His hair is mousy brown, thin and dull.

Danny married Marianne after she became pregnant in the late summer of 2011. She had not been working in CERN very long and her tempestuous affair with Alex Karolyi had just finished. She started going out with Danny on the rebound. They married in February 2012.

Francesco Romani

Francesco Romani was born in Milan on 28 August 1960 making him a 51 year old Leo on Crystal Day. His father was a professor of chemistry at the University of Milan and his mother was a lecturer in history.

Francesco was raised to study, surrounded by the intellectual elite of Milan. He was always overweight from the prolonged dinner parties his parents gave; he was never going to be an athlete or football player. Nevertheless he was very popular at school and never happier than when he was organising an activity for a group of his friends.

He progressed naturally into the academic world, first studying chemistry but soon moving to physics, which he felt gave him the deepest possible understanding of the world.

He served in the Italian army as a conscript from age 19-21 which gave him experience of and a taste for leadership.

After his PhD, he quickly rose to the top of the Italian Institute for the Physics of Matter and moved abroad, spending time in France and the USA before being offered the Directorship of CERN, one of the most prestigious and important jobs in all physics.

One of the reasons he has been so successful is the strength and subtlety of his personality. He is utterly charming and able to make friends with anybody, being extremely sociable and jovial, especially over dinner. But at the same time he has an extremely clear vision of what he wants to achieve from relationships and knows exactly how to get there.

He has steered CERN safely through some dangerous waters during the past four years, when funding was tight and the LHC project was going through some difficult times.

Francesco Romani

Clinically he would be described as "obese". He wears expensive Italian suits cut to make him look slim, a task which is not always achieved. He has a head of thick dark hair, dyed to hide the streaks of grey, a full Roman nose, a broad smile and heavy features. His hands are large and the fat makes his handshake soft and squishy.

George Gabor

Named in accordance with Hungarian tradition, where the given name comes after the family name, Gabor György was born in Budapest on 15 December 1968, making him a Sagittarian. He is 43 on Crystal Day.

His father was Gabor Ignác, the origin of whose given name is obscure but is perhaps related to ignis meaning "fire". Ignác was a staunch Communist, one of the few in Hungary when George was young. He was fiercely opposed to the economic reforms being introduced by the government, and therefore gave his new son very little attention. Ignác killed himself while preparing a home-made bomb when George was four.

George's mother was a factory worker who worked hard to raise her seven children, having little time for George.

He could see that his father wanted to create a world that was fair to all people, including the poor, and the young George agreed with this, but he did not think that Communism was the answer. To him it seemed that reform was required. George also saw that protesting against reform was not only absorbing his father's time and energy but stopping him from advancing and helping his family.

George turned away from politics and decided he wanted to help people in some direct, practical way.

George was conscripted into the Hungarian army for three years and found he enjoyed the discipline and camaraderie but didn't like the idea of killing people. When he came out he joined the Budapest Fire Department and quickly rose through the ranks to be the Chief of a small station. He had two children in early 1990.

In 2009, seven of his men were killed in a huge fire in Budapest. At the time, George's marriage was also going through a difficult period and, blaming himself for the loss of life, he suffering a mild mental breakdown.

His children had left home, so to escape from the guilt, he volunteered to work in CERN, where he has been ever since.

While working in CERN, his main aim in life is to help others, both through his work as a firefighter and as a volunteer mountain rescue worker. He nurtures and nourishes his crew, and is widely acknowledged as a superb team leader. However, following his experience in Budapest, he has no wish to progress up the career structure in CERN, even though he has the ability.

George Gabor

George is a huge man, over 190 cm (six feet three inches) tall, physically powerful and rugged. He is completely bald and he seldom smiles. His craggy face and white skin give his head the appearance of a weathered cliff.

Marianne Schneider

Marianne Peeters was born in Lille, France on 12 February 1988 making her a 24 year old Aquarian on Crystal Day. Her father was Belgian and her mother French. She has a sister 4 years younger.

She was raised as a Catholic, going to a private Catholic College in Lille, and both girls were sent to church regularly although they both stopped going when Marianne was ten.

As a child she did not easily identify with either her mother or father, feeling different from them and from her school-fellows. She felt there was something special about her, and turned to introspection to try to understand what it was. She therefore had very few friends.

The older she got, the more convinced she became that she was not like other girls. In fact she became sure that she was not. She went through periods of serious depression in her teens, contemplating suicide more than once, until she went to University and finally began to mix with people who, she felt, were more like herself. She realised that perhaps she was not unique, and developed some close and lasting friendships.

She studied French, English and art, then spent a period of unemployment until she stumbled across a job as a guide at CERN in 2011.

She had only been at CERN for a few weeks when Alex Karolyi asked her out for a date. She found him attractive, but she had heard of his reputation so she refused. However he was persistent and eventually he persuaded her to go to a nightclub with him. It was not long before she was sleeping with him and they saw a lot of each other during the summer of 2011.

It was towards the end of the summer that Danny asked her out. Danny was totally unappealing to her and she refused without a second thought, telling him she was going out with Alex. The next day he told her that Alex was going out with at least two other girls as well. When she challenged Alex about this he did not deny it.

Marianne finished the affair soon after, although she felt utterly distraught, and started going out with Danny. In a moment of drunken madness she slept with him and fell pregnant.

They were married in February 2012. The baby is due about four weeks after Crystal Day.

She is a dark, brooding, self-absorbed introvert. She longs to develop her creative, artistic side and dreams of writing poetry or acting or singing, but never does anything about it. This failure makes her feel ashamed of neglecting her own talents.

Marianne Schneider

She is widely regarded as one of the most beautiful girls in CERN, although she has no idea why. She has long dark hair, dark eyes which can sparkle with life when she is amused and smoulder with inner passion when she is frustrated. She often dresses in dark clothes and there is an aura of mystery about her which frightens some people.

Michael Zhang

Michael Hamilton Zhang was born in Dublin on 3 January 1984 making him a 28 year-old Sagittarian on Crystal Day. His Chinese parents had moved from Hong Kong the year before when they realised that the British Colony would soon return to Chinese ownership. They passed through Britain and moved to Ireland to open a Chinese takeaway restaurant.

Michael's origins made him feel different from other children in Ireland and he was considerably more intelligent than any of the others around him. He began to search for his own understanding of the world and soon settled on science, and in particular on particle physics, to provide the knowledge he sought. But he was also intensely interested in his Chinese origins and studied as much as he could. He had few friends and none of them were close.

His adolescence was dominated by academic study. When he was 18, he had a single attempt at intercourse with a fellow student at Trinity College, Dublin. When that failed, he was too afraid to try again, considering himself impotent and he became convinced that he is not interested in girls. He gradually withdrew from society and became almost a monk, devoted to the worship of science.

After he achieved a brilliant joint first-class honours degree in physics and maths and Trinity he moved to the Dublin Institute of Advanced Studies (the youngest person ever to work there) and began his PhD under the leadership of John O'Brien. He moved to CERN in 2010.

He is driven by the hunger for knowledge. It is an obsession with him. He wants to prove that Chinese brains are better than Irish brains, with the possible exception of 19th century Irish mathematician William Rowan Hamilton, after whom he was named. He is convinced that he is going to discover something Earth-shattering soon and be recognised as a genius. He will stop at nothing to achieve this. It is the complete focus of his life.

Michael Zhang

He takes absolutely no care of his physical appearance. He wears the same stained pink T-shirt and blue jeans for weeks on end and seldom takes a bath, but since he does not sweat much this is not noticable. He lives alone in a caravan in a wood near CERN, from where he cycles to work early every morning.

Sam Fitzpatrick

Sam was born on 7 July 1959 near Cork, Ireland, under the sign of Cancer, making him 52 years old on Crystal Day. It was a rural, Catholic family. His father James was a low-paid farm labourer. His mother suffered from depression. Sam was her second child. She had six more children after him.

Sam's father had no time for the family and his mother was often totally withdrawn and left the family to get on as best it could. In his attempts to win the love of his father, Sam took on the role of mother of the household, looking after his younger brothers and sisters. But the harder he tried, the more his father seemed to hate him, and the harder Sam worked to show he was good.

His childhood experience led him into teaching. He loved primary school, loved helping the teacher. On his first day, he resolved teaching was what he would do when he grew up. This resolve grew when he found, aged about five, that boys cannot give birth to babies, which had seemed to him the only thing in life worth doing. So instead he resolved to nurture children in school.

As a young teacher, Sam caught mumps from one of his pupils and this developed into orchitis accompanied by high fever, severe pain, and swelling of both testes, nausea, vomiting, and abdominal pain. Fever and gonadal swelling stopped in a week but tenderness persisted for months.

He was told by a consultant he could never have children. He decided at that moment he would never marry, since it would not be fair on any woman. His commitment to teaching became total.

Sam's childhood had a profound effect upon him. As an adult he always tries to win the love of everyone he meets by being kind to them. Yet winning their love is only part of his ambition. He really loves being able to control people without their realising it.

Sam Fitzpatrick

Sam is a balding, middle-aged man who tries to always look smart in order to set his pupils a good example. He is short-sighted and usually wears glasses.

Sam was Catriona's teacher when she witnessed her father's strange death on her eighth birthday. When she returned to school he knew she was not ready and drove her home to talk to her mother after school. Brigit realised he cared for her daughter and recognised an opportunity to have somebody who would look after the child she did not care for. He was flattered by Brigit's attention and longed for a child of his own. Consequently he married Brigit, whom he loved emotionally but without physical passion, so that he could be near to Catriona.

Glossary

ATLAS

ATLAS (A Toroidal LHC Apparatus) is one of seven detectors receiving high-energy particles from the LHC (Large Hadron Collider) in CERN, Geneva.

ATLAS image copyright CERN

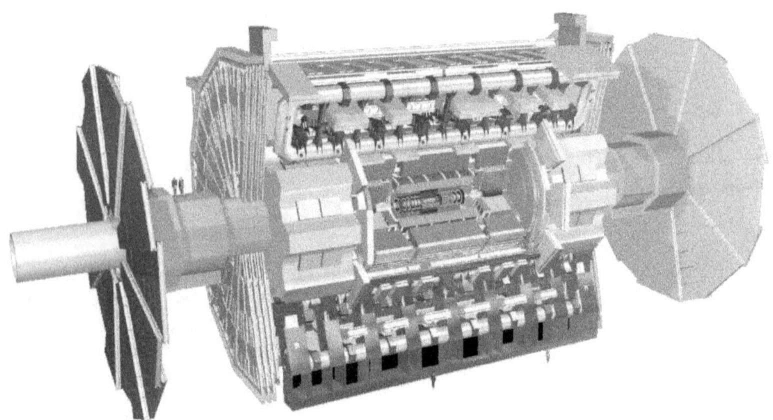

ATLAS is shaped like a barrel lying on its side in a cavern about 100 metres below the ground in the main CERN site near Meyrin, Geneva. It is the size of a cathedral, about 46 metres long and 25 metres in diameter, and in total weighs about 7,000 tonnes. Its scale can be judged by the two tiny people on the left of the diagram, and two more at the bottom.

Note the two circular discs shown at each end of the diagram, and two more attached to the ends of the detector; these are the so-called "Big Wheels" which are referred to in the story. Also note that this diagram is cut-away to reveal the inside of ATLAS; in reality these are not visible from the outside.

About 3,000 physicists from over 175 institutions in 38 countries are involved with experiments using ATLAS. It was one of the two experiments which discovered the Higgs boson in July 2012 (see bibliography entry (1)).

The main ATLAS website is given in the bibliography entry (2). The main parts of the detector, some of which are mentioned in the "Into ATLAS" chapter of Michael Zhang's Diary, are described in links found on the web page shown in the bibliography entry (3).

CERN

CERN (the European Organisation for Nuclear Research) is an international collaboration of scientists and engineers seeking to understand the fundamental nature of matter. One way it does this is by using the world's largest accelerator (the Large Hadron Collider or LHC) to create beams of high-energy particles travelling at close to the speed of light. These particles are then collided together and gigantic detectors (such as ATLAS) are used to examine the results.

According to the convention which founded CERN just after the Second World War, its purpose is to conduct "nuclear research of a pure scientific and fundamental character... the Organization shall have no concern with work for military requirements."

About 11000 scientists from 645 universities around the world use CERN's facilities. In addition, CERN employs about 2500 physicists, engineers, programmers, technicians, craftsmen, firefighters and administrators.

Many technologies have been developed at CERN including the World Wide Web, cancer therapy, medical and industrial imaging, radiation processing, electronics, measuring instruments, new manufacturing processes and materials.

When it was founded in 1952, its name was originally "Conseil Européen pour la Recherche Nucléaire". It soon changed "Conseil" to "Organisation", but retained the acronym CERN because it was easy to pronounce.

Map of CERN's Meyrin Site[39]

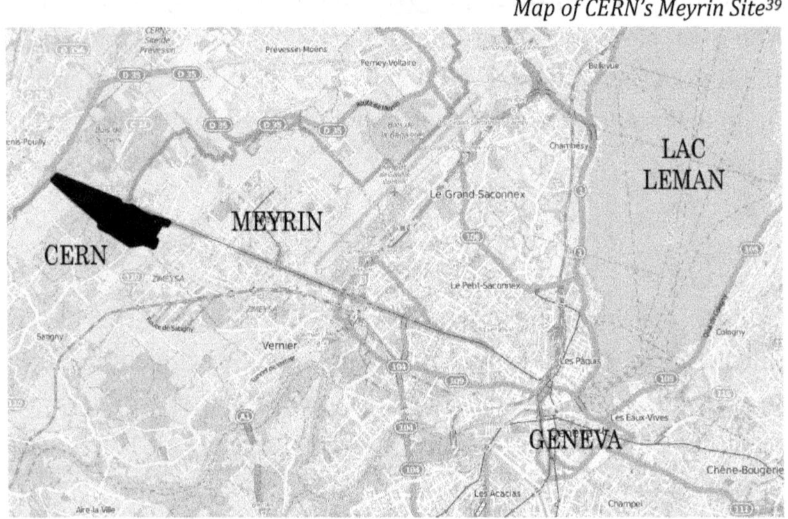

The main site (outlined on the left of this map) spans the border between France and Switzerland. It lies close to the Swiss commune Meyrin and the city of Geneva.

For more information about CERN, see the link in the bibliography item (4).

---

[39] Map copyright contributors to Open Street Maps.

Cosmic Egg

The Cosmic Egg

The expression "Cosmic Egg" was first used on Earth by people thousands of years ago, who imagined that the Earth, and everything it contains, hatched from some sort of primeval egg.

In 1927, the Belgian physicist and catholic priest Georges Lemaitre suggested that the universe originated from what he called the "primeval atom" and that it expanded rapidly to form the universe we know today. He was thus the first person to propose both the Big Bang theory and the expansion of the universe.

On **Entroilia**, cosmic eggs are part of the life-cycle of both Entroilians and Argolaths. Entroilians call them all "cosmic eggs", but reserve the name "The Cosmic Egg" for the egg from which Sam and Michael emerged. Some information about how they work is contained in the "Cosmic Egg" chapters of Michael Zhang's Diary.

See entry Event Record of this Glossary for more details about how cosmic eggs function.

Cosmic Monopole

In the world around us, we always find magnetic poles in pairs: north and south. The Earth, for example, has two poles, and so does every fridge magnet.

On the other hand, a "magnetic monopole", such as that featured in this history, is a particle which carries just one magnetic pole.

Their existence was first suggested on theoretical grounds by Paul Dirac. See entry (5) in the bibliography for details of his original paper and entry (6) for a link to download a PDF of that paper, in which Dirac showed that, if at least one monopole exists somewhere in the universe, then he could explain why particles such as electrons have a fixed amount of electric charge.

Until **Crystal Day**, there was no evidence that any monopoles existed. Dirac had not *proved* their existence, but his theory *strongly suggested* that at least one might. To quote Dirac:

[T]he present formalism of quantum mechanics...leads inevitably to wave equations whose only physical interpretation is the motion of an electron in the field of a [magnetic] pole...[O]ne would be surprised if Nature had made no use of it.

However before Crystal Day, despite many searches, no evidence had ever been found for their existence. Dirac postulated the reason could be that:

[T]he attractive force between two [monopoles] of opposite sign is...4692.25 times that between electron and proton. This very large force may perhaps account for why poles of opposite sign have never yet been separated.

A "cosmic monopole" is a magnetic monopole which is found outside the Earth. But all that changed on Crystal Day when a cosmic monopole was trapped by the magnetic field of **ATLAS**. It is interesting to note that, up that date, no scientist had ever assessed the risks, the feasibility or the possible consequences of such an event. You cannot blame them. The existence of monopoles had not even been established, and they took all reasonable precautions to assess the safety of their experiments, and published reviews of their assessments. You can find links to these reviews on the web pages cited in bibliography entries (7) and (8).

Nevertheless, on 5 April, 2012, a cosmic monopole was indeed trapped inside the **LHC** beam pipe where it began to absorb particles from the beams and was transformed into a black hole. The rest, as somebody might have said, is this history.

Crystal Day

The events described in this narrative began at 11:22:50 on April 5, 2012, the day which would later become known by the survivors either as "Crystal Day" or "Disaster Day".

Because time had stopped, the rest of the Earth continued at this date and time until the moment when time was restarted. How, when and why this happened will be recounted in this history.

Small Time Crystal and Bubble

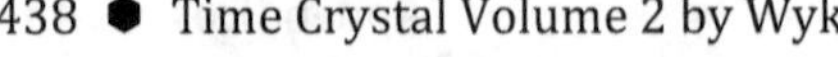

However, even after time stopped in the universe, time continued in small spheres surrounding fragments of blue crystals, Time Crystals, from which this narrative derives its name.

Entroilia

Until **Crystal Day**, nobody had any idea what existed outside the universe, or even if the expression "outside the universe" had any meaning. The problem was that scientists did not understand how or why the universe had been created. This was perhaps the greatest mystery facing mankind, and it was in the hope of finding some clues to resolve it that the **LHC** and **ATLAS** were constructed.

The mystery was indeed resolved, but in a totally unexpected and disturbing fashion, as related in this narrative.

It turns out that this universe is only one of many. Before Crystal Day, there had been several serious scientific theories which supported this idea, often called the "multiverse" hypothesis. But no scientist had ever suggested (nor would ever dream of suggesting) that our universe was part of the life cycle of extra-universal beings, which is the astounding discovery made on Crystal Day. See **Cosmic Egg** above for more on this subject.

Event Record

Each cosmic egg is designed to capture of record of its history. The purpose of this is to allow a Universe Historian (such as Professor Cjingha Itoodoo) to examine those eggs which prove to be fertile, by creating emergents, and thereby discover which of their properties have led to this fertility, so that more fertile eggs can be engineered in the future.

Event quanta fall from the outer shell of crystalline pipes and form layers of pink sediment which capture every moment of history. This is what is meant by the "event record".

Michael explained the process in greater detail in his Diary entry which I have entitled "Cosmic Egg 1".

Large Hadron Collider

Map of LHC copyright Open Street Map

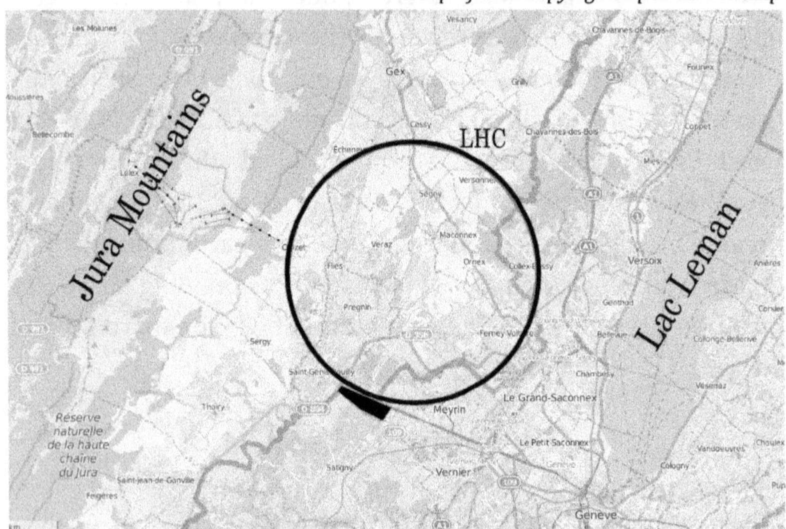

The Large Hadron Collider (LHC) is currently the world's largest and most powerful particle accelerator. It is the main accelerator at **CERN**, and consists of an underground circular tunnel 27 kilometres long (marked on the map) stretching from Geneva airport to the foothills of the Jura Mountains. It contains superconducting magnets, cooling systems and other infrastructure surrounding two beam pipes. These receive particles from a chain of lower-energy accelerators within the main CERN site (shown as a black area at the bottom of the LHC).

As they travel round the LHC, the particles' energy is boosted by accelerating structures until they are travelling at near the speed of light. The two beams travel in opposite directions around each of the beam pipes.

Finally they are forced to collide inside underground detectors, one of which is ATLAS. For more information about the LHC see entry (9) in the bibliography.

Quench

Within **ATLAS** (and many other pieces of scientific equipment in CERN and around the world) there is a need for very strong magnetic fields. These can only be created by using very large electric currents. Normal copper wires have resistance, limiting the amount of current they can carry.

To make the current strong enough, the wires which carry it have to be very cold. This is achieved by using helium gas cooled to almost absolute zero temperature. If part of the magnet should accidentally heat up for any reason, it stops being a good conductor. This is called a quench.

The resistance of the wires which carry the electric currents within the magnet increases with temperature. This releases more heat, so increasing the resistance even more. A runaway process begins. If left uncontrolled, a huge amount of heat could be released which would seriously damage the detector, costing millions of Swiss Francs to repair. This is what happened on 19 September 2008, the day when a quench in the magnets of the **Large Hadron Collider** led to an explosive release of helium, causing huge damage which took over a year to repair.

To avoid this, when a quench occurs, the electricity is automatically diverted away from the delicate equipment into special electrical circuits which absorb the energy by heating up lumps of metal called "quench heaters". Sadly, there was a faulty connection between two of the LHC magnets, as described in bibliography entry (10).

Layout of Point 1, CERN

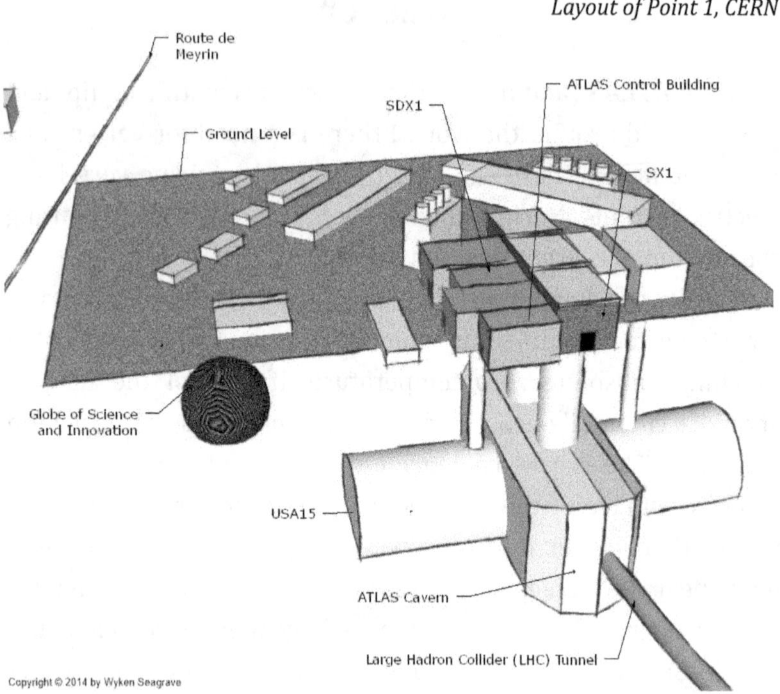

Episode 6 of this history describes how the black hole which had formed around the **Cosmic Monopole** burned its way out of ATLAS and causing a quench. The Monopole grew as it went, causing increasing amounts of damage until it led to a helium leak.

Initially much of this helium evaporated, then began to accumulate on the floor of the ATLAS cavern. Eventually it rose to the level of the quench resistor which was hot from absorbing the energy of the quench. The liquid helium was then rapidly heated and this led to the massive explosion which rose up the shaft above it and blew off part of the roof of the SX1 building. The roof landed on the lift tower in the SDX1 building, causing it to collapse, so trapping underground those people in the USA15 cavern.

Time Tunnel

Michael recorded in his diary (which I included the end of Volume 1 with the title "Cosmic Egg 2") his understanding of the tunnel which had opened up in the cosmic egg, so I will not repeat his explanation here, but merely note that, at that stage, Michael was not yet aware that there were, in fact, breaks in the tunnel.

In summary, after Michael broke one of the crystal pipes in the shell of the cosmic egg, the fragments fell into the pink historical record which constituted the pink centre of the egg. But these fragments were still linked by invisibly small "negative energy strings". (I should note that there is no evidence that such strings currently exist in the universe we live in, but their existence is a theoretical possibility.)

One of the crystals fell down the tunnel in the historical record which Michael had burrowed and was trapped at the centre of the egg, corresponding in time to the moment of creation. As it fell, it pulled the negative energy strings with it, and these possessed negative gravity and thereby opened up a tunnel which went down through history, hence the name "Time Tunnel".

Some of the other crystal fragments arrived in the ATLAS cavern, but most were dragged into the egg, pulled down by the negative energy strings. What Michael did not know was that each fragment then broke out of the tunnel and arrived at a different moment in history. They thereby lost contact with the negative energy strings, and hence became frozen in time, their colour changing from blue to pink.

Bibliography

References within this book to items in this bibliography are shown thus: (3).

Authors are shown in bold.

A dash in the list below (for example 6. —.) means that the author is the same as in the previous entry.

1. **CERN.** Higgs Boson discovery at CERN. [Online] http://home.web.cern.ch/topics/higgs-boson.
2. **ATLAS Experiment.** ATLAS Home Page. *ATLAS Experiment Website.* [Online] http://www.atlas.ch/.
3. **ATLAS Experiment.** Major components of ATLAS. *ATLAS Experiment.* [Online] http://www.atlas.ch/detector.html.
4. **CERN .** CERN Home Page. [Online] http://home.web.cern.ch/.
5. **Dirac, Paul Adrien Maurice.** Quantised Singularities in the Electromagnetic Field. *Proceedings of the Royal Society Series A.* 1 September 1931, pp. 60-72.
6. **—.** Download PDF of Quantised Singularities in the Electromagnetic Field. [Online] http://timecrystal.co.uk/pdf/QuantisedSingularities.pdf.
7. **CERN Press Office.** The safety of the LHC. *CERN Press Office.* [Online] http://press.web.cern.ch/backgrounders/safety-lhc.
8. **Ellis, John , et al., et al.** *Review of the Safety of LHC Collisions.* Geneva : CERN, 2008.
9. **CERN.** Website for Large Hadron Collider. [Online] http://home.web.cern.ch/topics/large-hadron-collider.
10. **CERN Press Office.** CERN releases analysis of LHC incident. *CERN.* [Online] 16 October 2008. [Cited: 30 September 2015.] http://bit.ly/1O7sNO3.

11. **Seagrave, Wyken.** Radiation Levels in Time Bubbles.
[Online] Penny Press Ltd, 5 9 2015.
http://timecrystal.co.uk/?p=445.

12. **Institute of Physics.** CERN Courier. [Online]
http://cerncourier.com/cws/latest/cern.

13. **Monter, E. William.** *Witchcraft in France and Switzerlan.*
London : Cornell University Press, 1976.

14. **Deuber, Gerard.** *St Peter's Cathedral, Geneva.* Bern : Society
of the History of Swiss Art, 2002.

15. **Binz, Louis.** *A Brief History of Geneva.* Geneva : Chancellerie
d'Etat, 1985.

16. **Seagrave, Wyken.** Southern Aspect of Geneva about 1590.
[Online] 27 October 2015. http://timecrystal.co.uk/?p=481.

17. **Jussie, Jeanette de.** *The Short Chronicle.* [trans.] Carrie F
Klaus. Chicago : University of Chicago Press, 2006.

18. **Wikipedia.** Unified field theory. [Online]
https://en.wikipedia.org/wiki/Unified_field_theory.

19. —. Metric tensor. [Online]
https://en.wikipedia.org/wiki/Metric_tensor.

20. —. Manifold. [Online]
https://en.wikipedia.org/wiki/Manifold.

21. —. Planck epoch. [Online]
https://en.wikipedia.org/wiki/Planck_epoch.

22. —. Planck time. [Online]
https://en.wikipedia.org/wiki/Planck_time.

23. **Mobbs, Arnold.** *The Calvin Auditorium John Knox Chapel.*
Geneva : Eglise Nationale Protestante de Geneve, 1985.

24. **Wikipedia.** Wormhole. [Online]
https://en.wikipedia.org/wiki/Wormhole.

25. —. Hawking Radiation. [Online]
https://en.wikipedia.org/wiki/Hawking_radiation.

26. **American Physical Society.** Physical Review Letters.
[Online] http://journals.aps.org/prl/.

27. **Seagrave, Wyken.** *Time Crystal.* [Online] Penny Press Ltd. http://timecrystal.co.uk/.

Now Read On!

Thank you for reading this book. I hope you want to follow Catriona and Sam as they travel through the entire history of the universe. The next volume in the series is due to be published on Crystal Day (April 5).
Find out much more about the Time Crystal series at
  http://timecrystal.co.uk/

Please write a review

Let other readers (and me!) know what you thought about this book by writing a short review. You can find links to this and my other books at the following sites:
My page on Amazon
  http://amzn.to/1M7oBNF
My page on Goodreads
  http://bit.ly/1JVKuNm
My page on Shelfari
  http://bit.ly/1JVKGMJ

My Newsletter

Subscribe to my newsletter
  http://bit.ly/1r2KbXq

History of the Universe

  For my factual account of the history of the universe, visit www.historyoftheuniverse.com

Wyken Seagrave

www.wykenseagrave.co.uk

www.ingramcontent.com/pod-product-compliance
Lightning Source LLC
Chambersburg PA
CBHW050957180726
48291CB00006B/1873